Severance
The Elifer Chronicles Book Three

Julie Boglisch

ISBN: 978-1-62420-636-8

Editor: Sherry Derr-Wille

Published in The United States

Dedication

To my parents, of course, who have dealt with me and my crazy antics for so many, many, many years. My editor who has seen my highs and lows with these books. My publisher who constantly had my back and of course... My dogs, Jasmine and Paisley. Oh, and the fans, love you guys too!

Chapter One

Arik gazed over the burning landscape. The devastation of the gated community, thought to be impregnable, was something he never believed he would be able to witness. It was burning to ashes. Was it worth staying away from Emma? He paused, remembering her cheerful smile, the twin braids that bounced with her movements. The way her voice, so soft and earnest, could become so strong and resolute. He felt a clawing at his throat, worry overcoming him. Was she okay? Would she come back alright? He knew the dangers, but he also knew she could take care of herself. Still, he wasn't sure if he could handle it. Handle being separated from her in something like this. He'd promised her he would stay out of any Resistance-related endeavors...he was seriously regretting the promise as he waited and waited and waited—

"What a sight," Mitchell breathed.

Arik jumped, spotting Mitchell out of the corner of his gaze. He noted the boy's expression, alight in relief and vindication. The sight caused Arik to place a wide grin on his own face that felt faker than usual. An unsettling feeling sat in the pit of his stomach. Strange. He thought he would be elated to watch those Richies burning to a crisp for all the crap they put his father and the rest of the citizens through. What they put Emma through. He figured he would be in jubilation, just like the crowd his father was working to control.

He wasn't.

"I'm heading back with Andrew. Are you going to wait for Emma and the others?" Mitchell turned to Arik with a curious gaze. Andrew watched stoically from behind.

Arik nodded, part of him wondering, once again, how the kind-hearted Mitchell and sweet Emma could be part of such an organization that would cause this massacre.

Mitchell waved, smiling, before hurrying after Andrew, shouting for him to wait up. Arik shook his head and turned back to the screams and explosions resonating from the Richies section. He wasn't sure how long he stood there, waiting, but eventually, he noticed a group of people coming through the side alleyway. He quickly noted that Emma wasn't among them, but to be honest, he wasn't surprised. She would probably be catching up shortly. After all, she did have a lot on her plate and the rest weren't members of the resistance. They hadn't noticed him, which gave him a moment to identify everyone.

First and foremost was the middle-aged woman who was sickly thin, pale and in a hospital gown. That must be the twins' mother Emma was talking about, the one they originally went in to retrieve. Guess the infiltration was a success all around. To think they would actually manage to rescue one of the kidnapped victims. He turned his gaze to the person supporting the woman and frowned. There was Lex, their informant and the person he knew the least about. The older boy held himself strangely, a mix of upright and concerned.

The last two he spotted, trailing a little behind, were the set of fraternal twins he'd gotten to know recently who appeared surprisingly alike. He wasn't sure which one was older, even after speaking and working with them over the last few months. Maxwell seemed it with his patience and calm appraisal of things, but from what he heard from Emma, Karina was the more protective and caring. She was more hot-headed, sure, but right now, they both appeared disturbed and dazed.

He shouldn't be surprised. They basically just escaped from a mini war zone.

Still, they were as strange as usual. While they were soot-covered and obviously a little battered, they didn't seem harmed overall and, more importantly, they didn't appear sick.

A surge of pain shot up his leg from the open wound he procured from the stupid as heck epidemic. He grimaced and glared down at his leg, wishing it wasn't like this. He was so sick of this disease, this constant presence that hung over all of them like a malevolent cloud of gunk. His mind flickered to a few months prior, when both Karina and Maxwell outright admitted that they were still clean. He hadn't thought too much on it, but now, months later, he couldn't help but wonder.

Even as he examined them as indiscreetly as he could, he began to think that if they were clean, how was it possible? Even if they were clean months ago, there was no way they could still be clean now. Yet, he spotted no open wounds, shallow skin or pockmarks, almost no injury at all, actually. They didn't even appear to realize how healthy they looked. The lightly tanned skin, bright eyes, light muscle-tone in Maxwell's case and pretty, curvy figure in Karina's case, were all signs that they were still unaffected. Yes, they were bandaged and that made it a bit more speculative, but how did they avoid it? Even after all these months, did they? He'd been denying the idea for the longest time. He wondered if the others noticed after that initial conversation.

He paused in his thought process as they spotted him. Throwing on his fake grin, he hurried up to them. "There you all are," he spoke, gaining the rest of the group's attention. "Andrew and Mitchell came out earlier..." he trailed off, turning toward the community.

Again, he knew he should feel elated. His father no longer had to worry about whose side he was on, or about not being able to arrest someone whom he knew was bad due to the influence of the gated community. He should be like everyone else here, cheering and delighted... "Why did it have to happen this way though? Why do such violence?" He let out a heavy breath. "Come, this way. I'll lead you to their safe house."

He turned after receiving a nod from the four of them.

He waited, hoping one of them would say something, but after a few turns, he had enough of the silence and worry. He finally turned to Karina. "So, where's Emma? She had to stay behind to do something, right?" He noticed Karina stiffen and that unsettled feeling intensified. "She was with you, right?" He could almost feel the shift in the air, the way none of them would meet his gaze.

He found his feet slowing to a halt as the mother spoke up. Her voice was hoarse and soft, but clear, so clear, it pierced him. "She didn't make it."

The mother's words froze him to the core. Everything else fell on deaf ears, or so it felt as he tried to grasp at his shattered heart. The prickling ice only hurt even worse with her last words. "I'm sorry."

"What... what happened?" he barely managed to choke out, his brain not quite meeting his mouth. "How— How did she-"

"She was shot," Lex spoke. "She was protecting Karina."

Karina? Emma...Emma died because of Karina? A memory, so clear even now flickered through his mind.

"Can I ask for a favor?"

"Favor?" Karina turned, her attention, like his own, cast toward Emma as she retreated past the tree line.

"Can you watch out for them?" Arik spoke up hesitantly. He didn't want to ask, if anything, he wanted to help, but... "I can't do much from out here, not with my father's position, so...can you watch them in my place?"

Karina seemed surprised for a moment before her features softened in hesitancy. "I can't make any promises, but sure, I can try." She grinned. "After all, I'm going to be watching out for Maxwell. What are a few extra people?"

A few extra people... Those words rang around his head, making it so, he wasn't sure what happened next, not really. He moved without thought, grabbing Karina's shirt in fists so tight, he almost thought he heard tearing. Karina's eyes were watery, her gaze uncertain and filled with anguish. Some part of him, deep-down, noticed. He pushed that notice to the side, grasping at the pain in his chest and the vehement words that seeped out of his voice. "You promised! You promised to keep them safe! Didn't you say what was one more?"

"I tried!" Karina's voice startled him, but he didn't really show it, even as she reached her hands up. They were trembling.

When she grasped his hands, they were firm and strong. She threw them aside. There were traces of tears, barely seen through his own blurred gaze. "And I said I WOULDN'T promise. I said I would try and I did!"

"Obviously, you didn't try hard enough. How could you let her die?"

There, he said it. The emotions poured out and he couldn't stop the tears, the dam broken. He tried to rub at his cheeks, tried to ignore the stabbing feeling piercing his chest. He shouldn't have trusted her.

The fake sick.

He knew it. A clean person, someone unaffected, wouldn't care about someone like them. Wouldn't care about someone sick or dying like them.

After all, she had nothing to fear. Why would she or her damn brother? Why would any of them care if Arik or Mitchell or someone died? After all...

They weren't the ones slated to die.

Chapter Two

The room was quiet as the sun slowly rose over the city's horizon, golds and reds shining through the lone window, changing steadily to a gentle blue, illuminating two sleeping teens and a young man seeming way older than his age, or so Veronica could assume as she gently slid her fingers through her children's hair in a calming gesture. The food given to her earlier finally settled into her stomach. "Leonard-"

"My name is Lex." The man spoke up, his voice soft.

He was a younger fellow with long black hair under a woolen-like hat. He was tall and dressed in a vest, long pants that were stuffed into a pair of sturdy combat boots. A deep frown crossed his face, worry lines already starting to appear on his forehead.

Veronica gave a weak smile. "Ah, my apologies. I only ever heard your name through my work."

"So, you did work under my father." Lex leaned back, arms behind his head and seemingly tracing the ceiling in silent thought. "So, what happened to you down there?"

Veronica winced, fingers stilling over her children's heads. She saw them shift, but they didn't wake. "First, I want to know why Karina and Maxwell are both here. I thought I told them to run. Not to look for me..."

She might have said that, but she was proud as she gently held her kids. Proud and sad to find her little twins growing up so quickly.

"They did run, that's honestly how I met up with them." Lex chuckled. "Though they had no idea of how this world worked when they first arrived, that's for sure." His expression softened. "They are quick learners though."

"You're right on that."

She stopped as sirens screeched by and she glanced out the window. Was the fighting over?

Lex pushed himself up, trailing his legs over the edge of the bed. "Well, you know who my father is...was..." The moment of silence that followed felt strange to Veronica, not heavy, just strange. "You met my brother Caym earlier, so I don't have much to say in that regard. As for those two..." He winced. "I'm sorry, I did the best I could, but..."

"You have it hard enough, being the son of such a high-level corporation, to think you survived this long outside the gated communities and helped my children. I thank you deeply." Veronica bowed her head, startling the young man.

He appeared vaguely uncomfortable. "Yes, well. They shouldn't have to worry about any black-market kidnapping or anything."

"Wait, what?"

"Uh, don't worry about it."

Veronica glared at Lex.

He sent her a quick shrug. "Seriously, the police captured most everyone involved."

"That tells me absolutely nothing. What the heck happened to them while I was captured?"

"That's a bit of a story, actually. Those two are the better ones to tell you." Lex shrugged again.

She was getting a bit sick of him doing that. Veronica frowned but didn't argue, hearing a low grumble. She glanced down as Maxwell blinked, eyelashes fluttering as green irises, glassy with sleep, peered up at her. Brown hair trailed around his face. He was thin, but not necessarily frail, which she was happy to see. "Ma?" he muttered, as if not believing what he was seeing.

Veronica smiled gently. His eyes widened before she almost fell over from a strong tackle.

"MA. So, I wasn't dreaming."

His arms wrapped tightly around her as she felt wetness cling to her shirt. It only took her a moment to get out of her shock as she put one hand behind his back, rubbing circles into it. She spotted a little brown clip and chuckled. She wondered if Karina got that for him, it was the only reason he would wear something like that. Part of her wanted to reach over and pull it out, but she decided against it. If Maxwell was okay with it, she would let him keep it; it was the least she could do.

Speaking of her daughter. She glanced worriedly down at Karina. Karina's long black hair trailed around her shoulders and down her back. It was strange for it to be out of its traditional ponytail, only emphasized with the scared words she was muttering under breath.

"Kari?" Maxwell blinked, pulling away and glancing around Veronica.

"I'm sorry. I tried. Please..." Karina said quietly, curling inward.

Before Veronica could even do anything, Maxwell was on the other side of her, kneeling on one knee and shaking his sibling carefully. "Come on, Kari, wake up. It's just a dream."

After a moment, her mumbled cries quieted. She shifted, attention drifting toward Maxwell. She reached forward, touching Maxwell's face hesitantly before dropping her arms in relief. "Thank gosh," she murmured before facing Veronica. She stared for a moment before sitting up and hugging Veronica tightly. "It's so good to see you, Mom."

Maxwell chuckled as he stood. "Yeah." He glanced toward the window. "It's morning already?"

"Actually, it's closer to noon."

Maxwell and Karina jumped as Veronica peered toward Lex, who gave a subtle mischievous grin. "You two looked quite cute, sleeping there."

Maxwell blushed and Karina snapped, "Hey. Can you blame us?"

"I was going to argue about the cute comment," Maxwell mumbled soft enough that even Veronica, sitting right next to him, barely heard. Karina did though, since she shot him a look that included rolling her eyes.

"No. I can't." Lex dropped his grin before turning the expression into a small genuine smile. "But, it's good to know you are feeling a little better."

Karina paused while Maxwell's blush disappeared as he glanced down at his trembling hands.

Veronica examined her son as she said, "Maxwell, dear, what's wrong?"

Karina turned away, squeezing one arm tightly as Maxwell gave a weak expression that screamed false. "It's nothing."

"Maxwell." Veronica's voice was stern and both her children winced.

"I...I..." Maxwell clenched his fists before he turned to Lex with such a troubled expression, it actually hurt. "How do you deal with it?"

Lex gazed at him quietly. "Deal with what?"

"Deal with...life...taking someone's life."

Veronica stilled, stunned. Lex inhaled slowly, as if he expected something like that. His gaze flicked to Karina as his fingers drifted to his waist where Veronica could just barely make out the bulge of a gun. That didn't keep her attention much once she noticed Karina crumple in on herself. Maxwell himself was exuding such an uncomfortable and depressed air, it worried her deeply. "Maxwell, honey, what are you talking about?"

Maxwell hesitated, his gaze meeting with Veronica's before glancing away once more. "When we were trying to rescue you, Karina and I split off from Lex and..." he gritted his teeth before continuing. "A guard caught us." He stopped; jaw slamming shut.

"Maxwell ended up killing him to protect me." Karina's voice startled Veronica and she jumped, not expecting it. Karina tilted her head up, face set and impassive. "He was protecting me."

"I still took a life."

"You did it for the right reasons," Lex interrupted, seemingly resigned, if his slumped posture was any indication. "Not that killing another person is ever correct, but think of it this way. Would you have done anything differently? That man was probably aiming to kill you, right?"

Both Karina and Maxwell remained silent, telling Veronica and Lex all they needed to know. Veronica reached forward, pulling her son close. He sat down and leaned over as she put a hand to his head, not saying a word and just letting Lex speak. "You asked me earlier how I deal with taking a life. I'll be honest. I don't."

That seemed to startle both of them.

"What?" Karina cut in.

Lex seemed uncomfortable, shifting to stare out the window. "It's never going to get any easier to take a life. You just get numb to it." Lex shook his head. "However, one thing you need to do is remember." Lex glanced back at Maxwell, catching his gaze. "Remember why you did it. Remember what would have happened if you didn't. Heck, remember his face if you have to. Just let yourself remember and move forward. This probably won't be the last time, after all..." He gave a weak chuckle and a small smirk. "With you two being the cure for a country-wide epidemic, I highly doubt you'll manage to save everyone or get the cure out there before someone dies."

Veronica glared but didn't say anything, after all. As much as she hated it, Lex was right. Just because her children had the cure didn't really mean anything if they couldn't find a way to spread it without killing her precious children.

Karina shifted from foot to foot, her expression downcast. Maxwell buried his head in Veronica's side, not crying, but just kind of lost. A moment of heavy silence invaded the room. Veronica saw Karina fidget, her gaze drifting around the room, as if trying to distract herself, before landing on the backpacks, set up in the corner. Her lips twitched upward, a vague hint of amusement before she paused. "Maxwell?"

Maxwell tilted his head up, face toward her, but not moving away. "Yeah?"

"It's in my bag, right?"

Veronica noticed the momentary confusion on Maxwell's face before it dissipated into understanding. "It is."

Veronica blinked, exchanging befuddled looks with Lex as Karina walked over, squatting in front of her bag. Karina rummaged through it for a moment before she stood, keeping something out of Veronica's line of sight. Her daughter's gaze stayed on the object for a moment, hesitant before she turned and walked right up to Veronica. Maxwell sat up but stayed close to her side, a faint smile on his lips.

Veronica heard a hum that sounded of recognition before Lex chuckled. Veronica barely spared him a glance as she finally took notice of the black leather of a familiar book.

Her heart pounded in her chest, her tongue blocking up her throat as Karina held it close to her own chest for a moment before holding it out to her, cover up. "We found it back home, when you were taken. I figured I would return it to you, now that we've found you."

Veronica stared, hands shaking as she reached forward, fingers clasping on the rough and oh so familiar pages. Warm memories fluttered through her mind of quiet afternoons and cheery chatter, gentle rainy days and laughter. She pushed the pad of her thumb into the cover, tracing over the familiar worn damage, and some of the new.

"I can't believe you found it," she choked out, feeling tears gathering. Her precious heirloom was back in her possession, by her own just as precious, if not more so, children. She was happy, unbelievably happy and yet...

She spotted Karina staring at the bible before glancing at her. Maxwell was chewing on his bottom lip, gaze on the floor, deep in thought. Her fingers danced over the cover before she placed the book into her lap, catching Karina's gaze. "Thank you for taking care of it for me. But I think it's yours now."

Her son started, head snapping up as Karina almost stumbled. Their gazes locked for a moment before both turned to her with such similar expressions, something she'd kind of missed. She chuckled faintly before picking up the book and putting it into Karina's grasp, startling her more. "I'm not sure if you were aware, but that book actually belonged to my grandmother, who received it when she was a little girl. It is precious to me, but I think you two need it more."

"Ma—" Maxwell's voice came out choked and pitched.

Veronica felt a smile trail over her lips. "How about this, if you think it would be best for me to have it, give it back when we are all safe, all of us."

At that her gaze flickered to Lex, causing the boy to promptly look away. Karina didn't seem to notice, her gaze firmly on the black cover.

Her ever observant son blinked, examining them both quietly, confusion clear on his face as he mouthed out her words before understanding dawned. He bit his lip. "Alright."

"Maxwell?" Karina's head snapped up, seeming aghast.

Maxwell sent Karina a weak glance before turning back to Veronica. "Ma, can you promise that you will stay safe so we can give it back to you? Please?"

Veronica noticed Karina stiffen, but she nodded anyway, pulling her son close before holding her other arm out for her daughter. Karina hesitated before she sighed and, holding the book once more close to her chest, let herself be enveloped in Veronica's hug.

Veronica hummed softly, pulling the two close. She could feel Maxwell shaking, still not recovered from his earlier conversation, while Karina, her dear daughter, was quiet. Very quiet. She knew she'd made the right decision to let them keep her book, but a heavy sadness filled her at the same time. She turned her attention to Lex who just sighed.

He pushed himself to his feet, brushing his clothes down in more of a thoughtless manner than an actual need. "I feel like I'm intruding, so I'm going to check to make sure everything is going alright." He hesitated. "If..."

"If they do anything to you, I will make sure these two aren't caught up in it. Just be careful."

"If they were in connection with Emma, then they will know soon enough. I can't hide my heritage forever. You know that as well as I do."

"I know." Veronica said, her voice faint. "All too well."

"Lex?" Maxwell spoke up, pulling away from Veronica once more. "Thank you for telling me that."

"Idiot." His voice was soft-spoken, but gentle as he trailed to the doorway. He glanced toward Karina before he slipped out the door.

~ * ~

Lex let out a long breath as he peered back at the closed door. The tension between those two was palpable and he knew his words, while truthful, hadn't helped. He was glad Karina and Maxwell were able to talk with their mother though; they needed it. Though he was a bit surprised Karina remembered to pull out the bible in the first place. It made him wonder what she was thinking when she did, or was she just trying to think of something else?

His thoughts flickered to Caym and he leaned his head back against the door. What happened to Caym? Why did he try to capture them, even after Lex said he would come back? Why did he resort to hurting them, getting Emma killed? Lex stared up at the ceiling. His brother changed since he last saw him. While before he'd been cold, now something was just wrong. Like part of Caym was gone. He tried to explain that he would be back, but if he left now, would he be able to find him? Did he survive the attack? Probably, but what was Lex supposed to do now? Part of him wanted to stay with the twins and watch them, while part of him wanted to go home and try to dissuade Caym. If he managed to convince his brother not to go after them, then maybe they would have a better chance. As it is now, they would be hunted down with him and he knew Caym would pull out all the stops. That was one thing that hadn't changed, that stubborn strength to get what he wanted done. In this case, though, Lex had a bad feeling it would do a lot more harm than good.

He pulled away from the door and shook his head. He couldn't think of this, it was too dangerous. While he wanted to find out what happened to Caym, he was scared. He would admit it.

He descended the stairs. It didn't take long to get back to the living room. He noticed Leon and a couple other people, adults now, were working vigorously on a couple computers. Wilma stood over them. She glanced up upon his entrance and nodded. "How is everyone doing?"

"As well as they can be when trying to sleep in a safe house."

He huffed. Safe house wasn't the word he would use normally, but he didn't feel like arguing with the people who were using the small two-story home as a transference point. The fact that it was far away from the apartments was another thing entirely. "What are your plans now? You're going to leave this city, right?"

"That is what I said, yes." Wilma peered over the group. "Unfortunately, a good portion of our side died in the raid, though we did achieve our objective."

It wasn't hard to guess what their objective was. "So, the gated community?"

"It's all in ashes." She smiled. "The outer community is digging through it now to scavenge what they can for goods and such. We'll let the citizens have that."

"So, the Resistance isn't taking anything?"

"No need. We did our duty. If anything, we need to retreat as quickly as possible, as to not draw a bigger target on our back. We will be leaving in about twenty minutes. My crew is just wrapping up the last-minute adjustments."

"What are they doing?" Lex asked as he leaned against the doorframe, arms crossed.

Wilma shrugged. "Gathering all the data. We'll parse through it when we get to our headquarters. You and your comrades will be joining us." She spoke as if it wasn't a question.

Lex hissed, but did nothing else. As much as he hated the idea, there weren't many other options. Maxwell and Karina weren't exactly in the right state of mind at the moment, even with Karina's stout resolution to seem okay. Veronica wasn't applicable at the moment, considering she looked like she could be brought down by a breeze, and Lex had nowhere to go. He wished he did, he wished he knew where Caym was, but... He was pulled from his thoughts when Wilma shot him an even expression and continued, "When we arrive, we'll finish what we started."

"And that is?"

"We're keeping track of who died in the raid and cataloguing it for their families. We're also making sure to obtain any information from that laboratory where that woman with you was held. It seemed to be a disease research lab." She tapped one of the computers, a strange expression on her face. "It doesn't matter, though, they had no means of destroying this stupid epidemic."

She winced as she leaned too heavily on one foot and quickly switched. Lex barely gave it a glance, well aware of the pain she was probably in. So she, like everyone else, was in the third stage. He should have guessed.

"How? The gated community, as well as the city, will be swarming with Enthrope and other lower organizations soon, if not in less than an hour."

Wilma observed him quietly, scanning him in such a way that

unnerved him. "You seem to understand better than most..." She turned away. "We will be leaving by vehicle, just like the other escapees. In the chaos, we'll be able to slip out. We've made contact with all of our remaining members and they have already begun the evacuation. The only ones left are here."

Lex watched as some of the adults finished up on their computers and started packing them. The efficiency was astounding as the large appliances were disassembled as much as physically possible before being packed in rolling carts. The speed was astounding, but he could tell it would still take a bit longer for everything to be packed up and cleaned out. He wasn't sure whether he was happy about that or not. Lex watched them go, spotting Leon still typing away at his laptop. So, was that Leon's own? It was one of the more advanced. He would have to ask the boy later. He turned back to Wilma. "I'll let them know."

"Please do. I'll have one of the boys escort you all when we are ready to leave." Wilma gave him a nod as she helped in the disassembly.

Lex walked outside, not wanting to get in the way. He stepped to one side as people hurried back and forth, loading a car which he could barely see through the swinging door at the end of the hall. He heard footsteps and turned as Arik and Mitchell walked up to him. Well, to be more precise, it was Arik stomping up to him with Mitchell trying to drag him back, digging his heels in the floor. Arik stared at him, anger roiling under his skin, just barely visible, but present nonetheless. "I want you to tell me the details of what happened to Emma."

"Are you sure?"

Arik nodded, glaring at him. "Karina promised she would keep her safe and instead, I'm hearing it was the opposite, so please, tell me exactly what happened."

Lex stared at Arik quietly before he let out a tired sigh and traced a hand through his hair. "There isn't much to tell. We were running from the attack when someone turned a gun on us—"

"Why? They should have known she was with the Resistance."

"Do you think the Resistance was the only ones with guns? Don't be an idiot," Lex shot right back, glaring, stopping Arik in his tracks. "In that mayhem, no one knew what was going on. We were trying to run for our lives. Yes, maybe we shouldn't have stopped, but we all needed a quick rest and Veronica was in no condition to continue on."

Arik pursed his lips before glancing away. There was the soft sound of footsteps and all three turned as Leon slipped out, laptop under his arm and attention on Arik. "Don't worry, we will collect the video." Leon spoke up, voice quiet.

Lex was very glad he could keep up a damn good poker face, because he slammed it over his expression faster than they could blink. "Video?"

"Yes, we attached a camera to each of our operatives in the attack. Emma, Mitchell and Andrew all received one. I kept a line on them, but it got damaged during the attack. We're trying to extract that data now. Arik, we will find out what happened, alright? I've already managed to recover a little of it as we speak. There is no sound, but..."

Arik, not exactly sated, just nodded, looking away.

Lex knew he needed to get out of here, before they finished analyzing that video. Unfortunately, the twins were by no means capable or willing to leave now.

He couldn't just leave them, not now, not after what just happened. As much as he wanted to see his brother and fix this whole misunderstanding, he knew it would do no good. Maxwell and Karina would still be in danger and he wasn't sure where Caym actually stood.

A small part of him, one he didn't want to recognize, was scared. Scared that Caym was no longer who he remembered. When they caught fireflies late at night or - he reached a hand up, gripping the pendant—the only gift he ever really received that was his and his alone.

There was a beep and all of them glanced toward the laptop.

"That's it, isn't it?" Arik spoke up, hurrying up to Leon. "Get to the last thing recorded, please."

Leon glanced at him and nodded before he stepped to the side, pulling his laptop up and placing it lightly on his hand. The lid opened and, after typing away for a minute with one hand, he turned it toward Arik. "As I said earlier, I'm not going to be able to get audio, but video should be alright."

Lex didn't want to watch. He held no illusions to what would be shown. He caught a glimpse anyway as he pulled away.

The camera was shaky at best, not that high quality. "If you will excuse me," he muttered, slipping past and up the stairs, reaching into his vest pocket.

His fingers curled around the packet of cigarettes, but he stilled his hand. He just had one not too long ago. Just because he had a high tolerance didn't mean he couldn't eventually get addicted. He pulled his hand out and stuffed it into his pants pocket, leaning back against the wall as he thought.

He would have to talk to Maxwell and Karina then... Then what? Disappear? He was dead, no matter what he did. If he stayed here and they finished parsing through that data, they would realize he was the brother of Enthrope's head, their main enemy and, more importantly, a denizen of the gated community. Considering they just burned one to the ground in an all-out aggressive attack without any warning, it was safe to say he would not be accepted.

His thoughts flickered to Emma, the young girl who led them into the community and who died protecting Karina when his brother demanded their capture and death. Emma had been ready to kill him herself and all he'd done was show them the way, help them.

Help them destroy his own people. He let a hand run through his hair, thoughts dipping into despondency.

Well, he would just have to wait and see. Leaving now would only raise more questions.

Chapter Three

Karina blankly watched out the window, lost in thought. The past few hours were something else. Her grip tightened on the bible, causing her to recall her mother's words, that they would need it. She was kind of grateful she could still keep it, but it felt strange, thinking it was now theirs. She sighed and walked over to the backpack, slipping it back inside. Her brother was talking animatedly with their mom. He seemed a bit more chipper after Lex's talk, though the crinkled brow and slightly too wide smile indicated otherwise.

She wasn't in the mood to pretend. Instead, she slipped out of the room and downstairs after Lex. She wanted to talk with him. As much as she hated the idea, he still had the gun these people gave her to protect herself. She knew it was foolish, trying to get it back when she'd been unable to do anything with it, but that was the point. Her own folly led to her brother having to kill a person and for Emma to die. She couldn't let it happen again. She spotted Lex in the hallway, hands twitching, gaze locked on the far wall, lost in thought.

"Lex?"

Lex glanced at her, not jumping at her call, though he'd clearly been out of it. He hummed, curious, but didn't say a word.

"You still have my gun, right?"

Lex raised an eyebrow. "I do."

Karina could practically hear the question in his voice. She gulped and, steadying herself, she extended her arm outward. "Can I have it back?"

"You sure?"

"Yes." She spoke firmly, causing Lex to widen his eyes, surprise flitting across his face for a split second before it was schooled once more.

"Just don't be an idiot." He shrugged and pulled it out of the waistband of his pants.

The safety was on and, though Karina hesitated, she eventually took it from his hands, feeling the cold metal on her skin. This was her only means to defend herself and Maxwell. "Thanks."

"Don't thank me. Just learn how to use it properly. We don't want a repeat of what happened."

Karina found her shoulders hunching as she remembered what Lex mentioned. "So, we are probably going to end up with more lives on our hands."

"More than you can count," he whispered, his voice weary. "I wish that wasn't the case, but..."

Karina stared down at the gun, hands trembling as her thoughts raced. After a moment, she reached down and carefully slid it into the holster still on her waistband.

She heard the sharp sound of pounding footsteps as the stairs creaked and moaned at the abuse. She straightened as Lex glanced over his shoulder. Coming up the stairs, anger brimming in waves off his figure, was Arik. Mitchell was behind him, desperately trying to calm him down.

"Come on, Arik! You didn't even watch the whole video. Let it go. It wasn't like Karina forced her to do that, she did it willingly. You should feel proud—"

"Proud? I lo—" Arik stopped, growling as he glared at Mitchell, who didn't back down, his own stark expression quite different from his usually laid-back air.

"Yes, we all know you loved her, you two were dorks like that." Mitchell didn't hide the pain that flashed on his face. The brief moment of hesitation was enough for Arik to whip around and stomp right up to Karina. Before Karina or Lex could react, he pulled a hand back and punched her. She stumbled back, hand clutching her jaw in shock.

"Arik," Mitchell cried, glancing up from having turned away. He grabbed the other arm that seemed to want to do a follow-up swing, surprised and worried. "Calm down. Come on, man, this isn't you." He grunted, trying to restrain Arik as Arik's attention, glued on Karina, screamed murder.

"You. How could you let her die like that? I know you said she was killed, but like that? How could you?"

His voice echoed down the hall, completely ignoring Mitchell as Karina recoiled, unable to comprehend what he was saying. Lex went to move forward, only to stop when Mitchell, struggling to maintain his grip on the struggling Arik, began to cough.

The hallway suddenly chilled as Karina froze, all attention snapped to Mitchell. Even Arik stopped his movements, slowly turning his head. Mitchell's hands shook before he stumbled back. One hand clutched his chest as the other raced to his mouth, his coughs coming out raggedly, that is, until Karina spotted the blood slowly dripping through the gaps in his fingers.

Arik whipped around, grabbing his shoulders. "Mitchell. Come on, what's wrong? Please tell me this is another false alarm."

Before Mitchell could respond, he crumbled, falling onto his knees as more violent coughs ripped from his throat, starting to sound more like gargles. Tears gathered, trailing down his cheeks as he tried and failed to speak. Karina hesitantly took a step forward, fingers twitching. She needed to find something sharp, anything. Maybe her blood could save him? Like Maxwell's blood helped Lex? She had to try, she had to—

"Don't touch him." Arik snapped, glaring at her as he helped Mitchell to his feet.

Karina took a step back while Lex glared.

"Don't be stupid, he's clearly suffering from the epidemic, what could she do to him at this point?"

"She's a monster," Arik retorted, arm firmly around Mitchell. "She's been clean for months, along with her brother. Yet the rest of us are on death's door and why? She doesn't do anything."

Karina's heart clenched, her throat closing up at the words being practically shouted at her.

"She and that twin of hers probably don't care. They don't have to worry about this stupid epidemic, do they?"

"Arik." Mitchell tugged, gasping as blood trickled down his lips.

"Please, stop." Mitchell's voice, while shaky, was filled with worry and pain. Faint footsteps, distant to her ear, yet clear in resonance, were coming up the stairs.

Arik snapped his mouth shut. Even so, his words still rang in Karina's ears. *Don't care?* Of course, we care. Part of her wanted to step forward to help, but another part of her was too stunned to do anything.

Arik's face twisted for a moment and her gaze flitted back to him as he inhaled sharply. Arik opened his mouth as if to shout, only to balk. Karina wasn't sure what happened. One moment, he seemed fine, though a little winded from all the yelling, then he was on the floor, trapped under Mitchell's weight as he started gagging.

"Arik." Karina squatted down, only to stop as he sent her a glare that froze her to the soul.

"Don't call me that. I don't know why I believed you. After all, you're the same person who let her brother be beaten, who let Emma get captured and now got her killed. I should have—" He coughed, a rattling breath sounding from his lips as his words trailed off.

Mitchell's coughs increased into full body convulsions as Arik scrabbled at the ground, voice a mere gargle as blood trailed from his lips. A wound on his neck, one she'd never really paid attention to, split open, red pouring down his throat like he was sliced. She stumbled back, falling onto her butt. No, he was lying. He was lying! She tried, she tried, she tried. Karina's hands had no idea what to do, just like her brain, which screeched to a complete halt.

"That's enough, there is no reason to blame her for this."

Lex slipped forward, stepping in front of Karina.

"Ha. That's rich. Still, this is over. I didn't think it would end this way." Arik spoke, voice cold as his eyes slid closed and he slumped under Mitchell's weight.

Karina felt herself on the verge of collapsing. Arik was already dead. How was that possible? How could he die so suddenly? Mitchell, laying above him and having succumbed first, was still struggling, gasping for breath. Those ringing footsteps, she could hear them, rounding the corner, but her full attention was on the boy in front of her. How? It was all in an instant. He was standing there, yelling at her, and the next moment...his twisted face lay slumped under Mitchell as the boy weakly tilted his head, a sadness adorned his features. The words, "I'm sorry," slipped from his lips before his body fell, blood flowing freely, but his gaze nothing more than empty glazed sockets. Why? Why did Arik die so quickly and Mitchell had to suffer?

She hadn't...she hadn't meant for this to happen. She couldn't convince her trembling body to move. She could have helped them, could have done something... Right? His words froze her to the core and she still couldn't find it in herself to go over there, to reach a hand out to them. She found her gaze trailing toward Lex. Lex returned her attention with a pain-filled gaze.

Lex already saw his best friend practically die before him, even if he hadn't actually seen his death, she knew he knew the pain. To see it on someone else, someone they came to see as friends? She felt a strange hopelessness fill her. What was the point? What was the point of all this? She hadn't been able to protect her brother, or her friends. She made the situation worse by involving them and stopping Caym from taking Lex. Now she was unable to save Arik or Mitchell. Yes, they didn't want her help, but she'd also been too scared. She couldn't convince herself to try. She wasn't like Maxwell. Her selfless, thoughtful younger brother. Maybe they were wrong. Arik's words rang in her head like bludgeons.

"Your mother is here, alive and well. Just focus on her."

Lex's voice caught hers and she turned to him.

He glanced briefly at the two before he squatted down in front of Karina. For a brief moment, she thought she saw Leon before he disappeared down the stairs. It wasn't long before footsteps and heavy grunts sounded out, but she ignored it. She was at least grateful that Maxwell didn't have to see this.

Then again, he'd grown, maybe he would be able to handle it. She faced away from Lex, pushing herself to her feet. "I'm fine," she murmured, her voice cracking.

Lex didn't respond for the longest time. She could hear rustling and grunts, followed by the sound of a zipper. She didn't want to watch Arik's and Mitchell's twisted frames being dragged away.

The memories of what just happened trailed through her mind

over and over and over again.

"Of course, you're not." Lex finally sighed, laying a hand on her back. "Let's just go back upstairs. They're going to need some time to take care of the bo...of them."

"You were about to call them bodies, weren't you," Karina spoke, voice monotone, almost dead. She found herself unable to put much energy into it. "Why? Why did they die like that?" She forced the words out as her hands clenched tightly at her side.

What was the point? Whether by this stupid epidemic or her own inability, people were dying. There was nothing she could do.

Lex hesitated before gently placing a hand on her shoulder. "It happens. The death throes, we can't predict how it will affect someone. What you just saw is not unusual."

"That's—" she cut herself off, fingers digging into her other arm. "Lex, what if you can't handle it?"

"What do you mean?"

Karina closed her mouth, finding she didn't have an answer, as they walked back into the room. The sound must have caught Maxwell's attention, for he was watching them curiously, worry shining on his face.

Barely a split second later, he seemed to stiffen, body tensing as if he noticed something. Karina quickly plastered a grin on her face and waved it off. "Sorry, that took longer than I thought it would. I'm back now though."

"What happened down there?" Mom asked, sending her a curious gaze.

Karina held in the wince, but not well enough, considering Maxwell's eyes narrowed and his brow furrowed just slightly in contemplation.

"The epidemic struck again," Lex cut in, walking back to his seat on the bed, attention warily on her.

Maxwell examined Karina for all of two seconds before those words seemed to sink in. "Wha... Why...?" He cut off before grabbing her upper arms, startling her. "Why are you trying to SMILE?" he yelled, worry clear in his voice as her expression dropped.

"I..."

"There is no reason to be smiling. You saw it, didn't you?" Maxwell's voice failed near the end as Karina shifted away, shoulders hunching.

His grip tightened and she winced. He seemed to notice, pulling back, but not moving away. "What the hell, Karina?"

"It was all I could think to do. Why should I worry you anyway? Plus, I am fine."

"Like hell—"

"Who was it?" Veronica spoke, interrupting Maxwell who seemed to be on the verge of blowing up at her.

Lex stayed silent and Karina found her voice didn't want to work, no matter what she did. After some time, Lex seemed to slump as he pulled one leg up to his chest, other laying limply over the edge. "It was Arik and Mitchell."

"Wait, what?" Maxwell's voice shot up, strangling slightly. "That can't be, both of them?"

His gaze flitted between Karina's and Lex's face, confusion foremost, along with pain.

"The death throes," Mom murmured with a shiver. "We don't know enough about it at this stage or how it even gets to that stage, but I'm guessing both of them were under stress of some sort?"

Her gaze flitted to Karina and she found herself not wanting to meet her mother's worried gaze.

"You're not wrong."

"Karina, what happened?" Maxwell spoke, words firm and low as he tried to get into her line of sight.

She promptly made a point of turning away.

"It was nothing, alright? They saw a video of what happened to Emma and—"

"They saw it?" Maxwell froze.

His gaze finally fell onto the cheek that she'd turned away from him at the get go. His hand reached up, barely brushing against it.

"Yeah." She chuckled weakly. "I was careless and Arik kind of got upset and well..."

"Kind of?" Maxwell's voice was low and, if Karina didn't know

24

better, dangerous.

Maybe she didn't know. She allowed herself to search his face, and spotted a sharp anger that was quickly buried under concern.

That face, it brought her so close to just breaking down then and there. He already spotted the fake smile she'd already given up and called her out on it, what was one more? Yet, she couldn't. She wasn't sure why, what was stopping her. A flippant pride that she was barely holding onto? The need to stay strong so that she didn't crumble under the weight of everything and be buried? Either way, she found she couldn't allow herself to cry, so, unable to cry and not wanting to pretend to give that awkward and downright awful smile, she kept up an impassive expression. She wasn't sure, but it seemed to worry her brother even more.

Still, he seemed to get that she needed time, since he pulled back and turned to the rest of the room, half his attention on her.

"So, what now?" Maxwell spoke up quietly, scanning Karina with that worried, analyzing gaze.

She would usually call it stupid twin recognition, but she highly doubted she was doing that well with hiding it. "I don't know," she murmured, a phrase she'd come to hate over the past few months and one she found herself saying just a bit too often for her taste. Maxwell closed his mouth, silent.

Mom sat back, watching them with a sad expression before she stood and walked over to Karina.

To Karina's surprise, she felt warm arms wrap around her, a hand pulled her head to her mother's chest as another gently trailed up and down her back. "It's okay, Karina, I'm proud of you."

Karina bit her lip hard, tears threatening to trail down her cheeks. She didn't want to cry, not yet, not now. The warmth of her mother, something she longed for so long, was right there.

She knew, she could feel it in her gut like all those other times. That she couldn't break, not now. She pulled away. "I'm alright, Mom. I think we need to decide what to do. Where are we going to go now?"

The room was once more filled with silence, everyone deep in thought before Maxwell quietly piped up. "I know this might seem like a bad idea, but what if we go with them? Right now, we have no place to go."

His gaze shifted to Lex before he continued, "If we try to leave, Lex would have to go separate from us and considering the chaos of the city right now with part of it burned. I don't think just the two of us will be able to take care of Ma, especially since we don't have any provisions or any means to leave this city." He shook his head. "I don't like it, but I think our only option IS to go with them. Ma needs to rest and this city is probably not a place to do it. Caym is probably still around and this city is most likely going to be shut down, searching for the people who..." He trailed off, turning to Lex. "I know you're probably not fond of the idea." Maxwell hesitated before taking a deep, steadying breath. "Can you come with us?"

Lex's brow furrowed, deep in thought, before he eventually let out a long, tired sigh. "I am not fond as you say, but I can deal. Plus, I don't trust them enough to leave you two alone."

His attention drifted to Veronica before he continued, "I figured, earlier, that it might be the only option, so I'm not surprised."

"So, we're going with them?" Karina spoke up, feeling a little relieved they at least had a direction. Though it didn't seem to be the best.

Maxwell examined her for a long moment, making her almost want to shift in discomfort before he nodded.

Karina genuinely grinned, ruffling his hair, causing him to squawk and glare. "Good, then let's get ready to go, alright?"

He hesitated, examining her once more before a smile blossomed on his face. "Yeah."

They heard a knock on the door. She glanced over as Lex stood up and walked over to the door, peering out. His expression turned sour as he opened the door fully. Outside stood the woman they met earlier. Karina couldn't quite remember her name off the top of her head, only having really met her for the short time they were downstairs, but Madeline stood next to her, so it was probably her mother. Madeline's expression was morose, and she couldn't blame her.

"Are you all ready to go?" the woman asked.

Karina glanced sidelong at Maxwell then over to her mother and

Lex.

"Yeah." She nodded, shrugging as she stepped forward.

Maxwell scurried after her with Lex and Mom behind, exchanging a short conversation in seconds.

"Good, we are the last to leave, so it's going to be close. Keep quiet and hurry."

She turned and descended the stairwell. Karina found the place fairly quiet, matching with what the woman said. She stepped outside into the beating sun. It was bright, definitely closer to noon, her stomach attested as it rumbled softly. Madeline glanced over before turning her attention to her mother, talking in hushed voices.

"We'll stop to get something to eat of substance after we leave the city. Will that suffice?"

The woman peered over her shoulder toward Karina. Karina wasn't sure how to respond and Maxwell simply shrugged. Lex appeared indifferent and Mom just seemed tired. Sitting on the pavement was a large van with tinted windows and a deep green coat. The trunk was full to the brim and Leon was already sitting in one of the seats. Madeline opened the door and Karina stepped inside, ducking her head so she didn't hit against the top. She slipped to the backseat, grabbing the window.

Maxwell huffed, but sat next to her with Mom next to him. Lex took the seat in front of them, which left one open seat, even with Leon, which meant it had been for Mitchell.

Karina's fingers dug into her chin as she leaned her elbow on the sill, gaze focused on the gray buildings outside. The car pulled forward as they moved away from their temporary rest stop. People meandered through the streets, shouts in the air and alcohol sloshing. She knew there was a reason everyone seemed so joyous, but it made her feel so sick. People died and they were happy. People Lex knew, people she knew, everyday people struck down with ease and it was because of them.

She could spot the disease, though, notice as someone else collapsed out of the corners of her eyes, only to get lost underfoot in the loud chatter of the crowd. It made her so sick she wanted to retch. She pulled her gaze away, appraising the upholstered seats and the dirty carpet underfoot.

"Hey, Kari?"

"Hm?" she hummed softly, allowing her brother to speak.

"Do you think they realize how many lives were lost?" His voice was soft, only for her ears.

She glanced toward him. His attention was focused on the outside, lips trembling. She leaned her head forward, catching his gaze so he would stop looking.

"Does it matter?" she spoke firmly, catching her sibling's attention. She was saying these words, both for Maxwell and herself. Somehow, they felt right. "Lex said it earlier, we can't save everyone, but we can do what we can. Father's letter was right, this country is messed up, but that's why we're going to help fix it, right?"

His gaze drifted back to her and she grinned, pulling away. "Come on, little bro, we're leaving this behind. No point on worrying about it now."

Thoughts flashed across his face, along with worry and a hint of fear before he nodded, a small smile gracing his lips. "You're right. Sorry."

"What are you apologizing for?" she huffed, arms over her chest. "You wouldn't be you if you weren't such a worrywart."

"Kari." He rolled his eyes, but the word was said with such fondness, Karina chuckled. Her sibling glanced forward before peering back at her. "So where are we going?"

She shrugged and swiveled so it was easier to pay attention to the front. Madeline and her mother were talking in quiet tones and Leon was on his computer. Lex was staring out the window and Mom was asleep. Considering she'd probably stayed up to watch them, Karina didn't mind. Her mom seemed so tired that Karina was glad she was getting some sleep. She cleared her throat and spoke up. "Hey, Leon, Madeline, where exactly are we going?"

Leon glanced back for a moment before exchanging looks with Madeline. Madeline waved and he nodded, continuing with what he was doing as Madeline turned in her seat. "We're heading to our base to the west a ways. We'll be passing a few quarantine cities, but other than that it shouldn't be a problem."

"Right," Maxwell muttered.

Karina frowned, her thoughts flickering back to the map she saw so long ago. What had Collern City been? Yellow? Blue? She couldn't remember. She glanced out the window as they left the outskirts of the city and drove through quiet suburbs. Abruptly, it ended as they passed over a bridge and got into large flat lands. The sun reflected off the crops which swayed in the breeze as they continued down the main road. She felt her sibling press into her side as they both peered out the window and over the landscape. It was pretty, Karina conceded, a nice change of pace. The smells that assailed her were dispersing as hints of the farmland wafted through open windows. When they'd been opened, she wasn't sure, but it felt good. In the distance, she could see gates, piercing into the sky. It was a good couple miles away, but they were visible from here.

"One of the quarantine cities." Madeline must have noticed her expression because she spoke up, gaze out into the distance. "Though the gates only finished being put up recently."

"How do they keep them quarantined?" Maxwell leaned forward, peering toward Madeline, who glanced at him before turning away awkwardly.

"Through force." Leon spoke.

He pushed his glasses up, groaning as he closed his laptop. "The tactics are pretty simple, really. Military grade equipment is put around the areas of escape; mines, tanks; they're all there until those fences can go up. Once the fences are up, they are electrified. I don't know why they don't do it in areas besides quarantined zones, but it's no surprise. The Richies don't want to be shocked every time they get close to their own walls, right? Then, well..." he shrugged.

Karina peered into the distance, staring at the fence that glowed in the sunlight. So that was electrified. She shuddered at the thought. That's what must have happened to New London City.

She pulled away, too awake to sleep, but too bored to do anything else. She wasn't in the mood to talk and neither was Maxwell, it seemed. Lex never was one for talking.

Finally, Mom awoke and Maxwell, ever the worrywart, asked if she was okay. Their conversation afterward was basically just a general gist of what happened to them up till this point. Karina noted how careful Maxwell was being with his information with the letters and completely forgoing their time in the gated community after Caym first found them months ago.

Karina kept her attention on the road as they passed the city in the distance. Was this the right choice? Going with the Resistance? What Maxwell said made sense. Still, a part of her wanted to run, run far away and not look back. After all, she was riding in a van with people who were willing and HAPPY to slaughter an entire community for their own personal reasons. However, could they have really run? Mom was in no condition to be traveling by foot. She knew she was way too out of it to be of much help and Lex, while probably able to do it, would also be distracted by worry of meeting up with Caym once more. It fit with what Maxwell said, she supposed. While she was out of it, Maxwell would have to bear the burden of both herself and her mother. She couldn't do that to him. She let out a breath. As much as she hated it, Maxwell was right, this was really their only option.

They stopped to grab lunch at a gas station that seemed like it had seen better days. The gas pumps were grungy, along with the windows, and the bored teller was fervently talking with them as if he hadn't talked with anyone in ages.

Considering how few people were traveling this way, though many were probably fleeing the city, she wasn't surprised.

A little while later, they started spotting homes that appeared to be falling apart. Leon tensed as Madeline glanced at her mother.

"I know, but we have to, we need to get as far from the city as possible and they won't expect us to drive through here," Madeline's mother said soothingly, glancing sidelong at her daughter.

"But..." Madeline bit her lip, glancing back at Maxwell with worry and fear.

Karina narrowed her lips and leaned forward. "What are you talking about? What's wrong with this place? Sure, there are a few—"

"Kari, you should take another look." Maxwell's choked voice caught her off guard and she glanced outside once more.

The entire town was silent as the dead. No one walked to and fro, shattered doorways swung in a weak breeze and animals scurried, unbidden, over the devastated homes and, Karina choked, graves.

Graves lined the entire side, warning off travelers.

"My god," Mom muttered, hands to her mouth as Lex grimaced.

"What?" Karina barely managed to get the word out.

A long-drawn-out sigh sounded from the front and she ripped her gaze away to face Madeline. "This town was known as Fellsment, a quaint town that mostly dealt with farming and trade. They were ravaged by the epidemic a year ago, everyone succumbed to the fourth stage within a week from each other. I think only recently had those outside the town gotten around to burying the dead, though by that point..."

Karina's fingers pressed firmly over her mouth as bile rose in her throat. Maxwell appeared just as sick, head turned away, as trembling fingers covered his mouth.

She dropped her hand, which still shook as she spoke up once more. "Why are we..."

"Why are we driving through?" Madeline's mother spoke, voice solemn. "It's because we don't have time to take alternate routes, and, if anyone followed us, they would stop at the boundaries. Those that went in to bury the dead knew the risks. They had a few extra bodies to bury while they worked, or so I've heard."

"So, why isn't this place quarantined?" Maxwell spoke up, voice hoarse.

"Because there is no one left here to quarantine, not a single survivor." Leon spoke, tone quiet and stilling all other arguments in the car.

The windows, Karina noted, were shut tight and now she knew why they rolled them up after the station, though it was so hot in the car.

They continued through the town, Karina's attention glued to the damaged buildings and the rows of graves. It was so painful to witness. She dug into her bicep; a reminder that it wasn't a dream or nightmare, it was reality.

Finally, they left the town and continued on their way. She wasn't sure why, but her heart was pounding, that uncomfortable feeling making her shift and glance over to Maxwell who seemed to be bent forward.

Mom turned her focus to Karina as she rubbed soothing circles into Maxwell's back. "You alright?" she asked, words soft.

Karina could only nod. Her voice failed her.

Mom smiled and, carefully pulling her hand away, reached over to Karina's face, moving a piece of hair behind her ear. "It'll be okay."

Karina swallowed roughly and Mom nodded before turning her focus back onto Maxwell as he glanced over. Karina turned away, deciding not to meet her brother's gaze. The drive was awfully quiet after that. The sun was just starting to set when Madeline's mother pulled to a stop. Karina, blurry from tiredness and endless painful thoughts plaguing her, blinked and peered out the window. It seemed they were in another small town, almost reminiscent of home, just without the trees. Houses lined the quiet street, one or two stories, with gardens out front. They were surprisingly well maintained. There were lights on in the houses, and the faint sound of music playing from a car that passed them.

"This is our stop."

"Where are we?" Maxwell asked, yawning.

"We're in Alcert, northwest of Collern City. Our base is nearby, come on." Madeline gestured as the door opened, Leon slipping out first.

Huh, so they were finally here.

Chapter Four

Maxwell was enamored by the small town they now resided in as he hefted his bag over his shoulder. It was nostalgic, in some ways, yet new. It was also a huge step up from the town they'd passed through a few hours prior which he and Karina were trying hard not to think about.

Speaking of his sister. He glanced sidelong to Karina as she stared over the homes, her expression guarded, just as it was most of the ride. Usually, he could so easily read his sibling, tell how she was feeling, but all morning, ever since he called her out on that fake, almost scary smile, she was quiet and to say he was worried was putting it way too mildly for his taste. He bit his lip at the thought. So, Karina ended up seeing their deaths, didn't she? From the sounds of it, she wasn't able to do anything, or at least, he didn't think she would be able to do anything. He wanted to ask her, but she didn't seem to want to talk and he couldn't bring it up with everyone else still around. He would have to wait until they could talk alone.

He wrenched himself away from that thought, helping guide Ma as they entered the one-story home they'd parked in front of. He wasn't sure why they were going in here, but he didn't worry too much about it. They stepped inside to find a plain entranceway with a quaint dining room off to one side. Down a short hallway, he could spot a couple other doorways to what were probably other rooms and a kitchen, wide open to both them and the sunlight that gleamed off tile and marble. In the dining room, resting on a comfortable couch, was a single person sitting next to a small fire. The person perked up before scrambling to his feet. It was a scrawny boy with barely any meat on him. He was fidgeting as he hurried up to them.

"Darrell, what are you doing up here?"

"Guard duty, ma'am," he choked out, wringing his fingers in worry.

Madeline's mother, Wilma, wasn't it? Yeah, he remembered overhearing it on the way over, spoke up. "Well then, have the others already arrived?"

"Yes, ma'am, everyone is already here."

"Good."

Maxwell watched the exchange in silence. He wasn't sure what to feel, a sense of trust muddled with a sense of uncertainty. His attention flickered from his sister, who was staring distantly down the barren hallway, backpack firmly in her grasp, to Ma who was leaning on the wall, probably tired. Finally, his gaze landed on Lex. His friend seemed fearful, though his expression remained stoic. His lazily crossed arms and bag slung over only one shoulder belayed the rest of the tension and Maxwell didn't have to wonder why. He wasn't sure if Karina realized what kind of danger Lex was in, coming with them, but he was deeply worried, and his mother's words only reinforced that worry.

He saw Emma's anger before she was...he heard the rough words and didn't miss the joy at the destruction of the gated community, the vehemence at the idea of a Richie helping them. He got a glimpse of what Leon was working on in the van and he knew Lex was watching it with just as much attention. From the glimpses, Maxwell could tell he was extracting the video information from an encrypted file. It was both impressive, and made him curious. Where did he get such a high-end laptop? Whenever Maxwell went out, he never saw those, only the larger, more cumbersome computers.

His thoughts were interrupted when the sound of a door swinging open caught his attention. He turned as, down the hall, a doorway stood open with a set of steps leading downwards into the basement. He glanced over toward Kari who eyed it cautiously before stepping forward, taking the lead, well, the lead behind the ones who knew this place, such as Leon, Madeline and her mother. The boy who they met stepped out of their way, returning to the couch as a semblance of normality. There were pictures set over floral wall paper and a side table set up near the dressing room as they passed. In all honesty, it appeared like a cozy home.

Maxwell shook his head, following them down with Lex behind him and Ma on his left. Hesitantly, he grasped his ma's hand. Why? He wasn't particularly sure, probably because it was a reminder that she was still here. They descended below, the wooden stairs creaking at their weight as a single pale lightbulb without a cover shone, swinging gently above their heads. The basement itself wasn't anything grand, dusty and cobwebbed. A single boiler, that hardly seemed used in the past decade, sat to one side of the room, with a bookshelf along the far side. Other than that, the place was spartan, with very few items and even fewer marks of livability.

Karina was barely in front of him at this point, warily scanning the room with a tense posture. Madeline, Leon and Wilma seemed relaxed as Wilma stepped over to the boiler. He wasn't sure what she did, but it seemed like she pressed a switch of some kind. There was a faint rumbling, then the boiler itself shifted, revealing another stairwell that had been placed distinctly underneath the now moved boiler.

"Creepy," Karina muttered and Maxwell chuckled nervously.

He couldn't argue with that. They descended down the stairs. Maxwell spotted Wilma press something, like a switch, near the wall and he heard a rumbling from above. He glanced back, along with the others, as the stairwell slowly descended into shadow. The boiler moved back into place, or at least, the slab the boiler was on. He shook his head and decided to ignore the claustrophobic feeling he held in the pit of his stomach. It wasn't exactly going to do him any good right now. They descended the rest of the stairwell, their feet clacking against the stone, reverberating off the walls that were slowly going from rock and dirt to metal. Just pieces here and there until they finally reached a corner and turned to the right into a surprisingly well-lit corridor.

The first thing Maxwell noticed was how bright and warm it was. A long metal hallway with different branches leading to the left and right at consistent intervals with strings of lights that adorned the ceiling running along the edge. He could feel something faintly move over his skin, a ventilation system? Made sense. Karina let out a quiet gasp as Lex raised an eyebrow, a mix between amused and stunned. Ma just shook her head, as if having expected something like this.

He'd have to ask her about that later.

"Well, we're here," Madeline proposed, turning to face them as Leon nodded to them and hurried down one of the hallways. It seemed the only one that wasn't metal-plated was the one that led back to the house. "Pretty cool, right?" Her gaze met his before turning somber. It was as if she had to rip her attention away toward the others.

"Madeline, show them their rooms. You recall where I told you, correct?" After receiving a nod, she continued, "Afterward, we'll meet in the communications center." Wilma's voice was curt.

"Of course, Mother," Madeline said, though her expression indicated she probably wasn't much of a fan of the idea, at least for a moment before a poker face quickly slid into place.

Wilma nodded to her before walking off, leaving just the travelers and Madeline. Madeline groaned, rubbing a palm down her face.

Maxwell was honestly surprised by all this. Wasn't she still upset about the deaths? About Mitchell and Arik? Emma? As he stared at her, he didn't notice any of that dourness or pain, just vindication, certainty. "Well, guess I'll be showing you to the residential wing. I'll give a brief description, but that's probably all the time we'll have." She waved. "Anyway, notice how there are eight different halls, yet only one door?" She gestured behind her. "That door leads to another section of this place, a security measure in case someone tries to infiltrate. There are a couple other doors around as you'll see, but that is the main one." She turned, walking down the hall before taking a right at the second branching path. "The first two halls lead to defensive areas, both sides hold weapons and even a few riot shields. This, the hall across from us, and the two just past are all residential corridors. This one is specifically for guests or, well, the injured." She gestured toward Ma before she continued on with her explanation.

Maxwell tried to listen closely as he examined the walls. There wasn't really anything spectacular about the place, but it was clean, warm. There were occasional doorways, either open to a room with someone inside, or closed tightly. Karina seemed annoyed, but quiet as they continued on. Maxwell could feel a hint of sympathy for his sister. This wasn't her thing and he knew full well that being in this underground area, surrounded like this, was probably very much testing her nerves.

He could handle it somewhat because of being more of a stay-at-home person, but Karina? Walking like this through labyrinthine tunnels of just metal. He shook his head. She was actually handling it better than he expected.

Lex, as usual, seemed uninterested. Lex examined the surroundings, more out of wariness than curiosity, but he didn't seem nervous or twitchy like Karina.

Ma, however... "Ma?" he called, keeping his voice low, yet catching her attention.

She jumped before letting out a long breath. She reached over, pulling him into a close side hug before placing her chin on his head. He would have moved away, if it wasn't for the slight trembling in his mother's body. She was pushing herself and part of him wondered why she wasn't going to get checked. They had yet to look her over. It didn't make him feel good about this place. Wouldn't they want to check if Ma was fine? Did they not care, or were they too busy with something else? He was grateful to have his mother still with him, but...

"I'm fine, sweetie, but thank you."

Her voice was soft as the trembling died down a little, not completely, but enough to make Maxwell feel a bit better. He nodded, causing her to pull her chin off his head but keep her hand around his. He decided just to leave it where it was. He wasn't in the mood to try to pull away from his mother right now.

He returned to Madeline's explanation of where they were, annoyed that he missed parts of it. "...cafeteria. I'll show it to you later. Ah, here are your rooms."

Maxwell glanced over to a set of rooms that seemed to be near the end of the hall. At the end was another doorway like in the first area. Madeline must have seen where his attention was because she chuckled.

"Yep, as you can probably guess, that is another defensive one. Though in this case, it's locked from this side, where the other is from the other side. I'm not sure if you noticed, but we curved as we walked, so you can think of this place as a giant circle, each path connecting to its corresponding one. In halls like this, the lock is on our side. In the main path, it's from the other. I know, confusing, but you'll understand as you get used to it here."

Maxwell was a little overwhelmed at the size of the place and the different means of security. He wasn't sure what he'd been expecting, but it wasn't this. He heard Karina's soft curse and furrowed his brow. Speaking of, the way Madeline spoke...how long would they be stuck here? Had he made a wrong choice? Though he'd laid out the problems of leaving alone, he was beginning to wonder if that would have been better. He peered toward his sister, who was already a bit twitchy, then to Lex, who seemed a little disconcerted. Madeline, however, didn't seem to notice, almost expectant of his response.

He turned back and blinked. "Uh..."

She sighed and huffed. "You didn't hear me, did you?"

"Sorry." He felt his face heat up as he stuttered out a response.

She blushed a bright red before turning away, muttering so soft he wouldn't have been able to hear her even if he was right next to her. She shook her head and placed her hands on her hips, facing him. "So, your rooms are these four. They aren't set up or anything, since it was such late notice, but Mother was able to get a few things together from what I could tell her. The ones on the right are Maxwell's and Karina's, while the ones on the left are yours." She glanced toward Lex and Ma before turning back to Maxwell. "You saw how we got here, so hopefully, you can get back. Speaking of..." She cut herself off, turning fully to face Veronica. "Mother never said anything, but I have to ask. Are you okay to keep going or should I bring you to the infirmary? I'm aware you want to be with Maxwell and Karina, but..."

"I'll be fine for a little longer, but I would appreciate it," Ma spoke up, a faint smile on her lips.

Madeline nodded and Maxwell smiled, feeling appreciative. Madeline must have noticed because she promptly looked away, face brighter red than before. He faintly heard Karina chuckle.

"Anyway, do you want to check out your rooms or continue on?" Madeline turned to Karina, still shifted away slightly from Maxwell.

"I would rather we just get this over and done with," Karina said.

"I'm worried about Mom."

"Yeah, we can check them out later." Maxwell spoke up before he grinned, glad his sister had said something. "So, communication center?"

Madeline nodded, turning to the doorway before pulling out a key. She clicked it open and gestured them through. Maxwell blinked, surprised they would be going through one of the locked doors already. Well, that was beneficial. Though, he frowned as they moved through and she slipped the key back into her pocket. That didn't give him, or any of them, many options for moving around. Kind of worrying now that he thought about it. His analysis was jerked away by Madeline's next words. "This side is the more protected. It holds our communication center, as you can guess, as well as various supply areas and military training. It also leads to our jails and an atrium for public announcements that are to be given to the entire place face to face."

"Why would you need a jail?" Karina muttered uneasily, a slight quiver in her voice.

Maxwell pulled away from Ma to step up to Karina. She sent him a look and he stopped reaching toward her as they continued down the hall.

Madeline turned, walking backward with her hands behind her back. "Just in case. They're used more as correction centers then anything. Like if someone tries to steal from another and things like that. You need to have some form of control in a place like this."

"Understandable," Lex muttered.

Maxwell turned toward Lex. Maybe it was because he knew him at this point, but he didn't miss the momentary spark of fear in his eyes that showed nowhere on his face, the way his attention seemed to flit to the endless metal and firmly closed doorways, searching for something that he couldn't find. Madeline nodded, as if not noticing as she turned back to face where she was going.

"Anyway, the communication center is right up ahead. This way." Within no time, they found themselves stepping into a wide-open space, reminiscent of the room Maxwell saw when he entered the gated community underground area. It was a wide circular room with desks in the middle and doorways leading off to different directions. The only major differences were that it was packed full with people working on different computers with screens occasionally splayed out on the walls and cameras shifting as people talked over each other.

So that was the sound he heard earlier. The walls were relatively sound-proofed, though, considering he heard some conversation faintly through the door, it wasn't the case all around. "Here is the communication center." Madeline spread her arms as a phone rang and someone picked up.

Maxwell spotted the occasional landline, the snaking wires plugging into the floor or walls. Papers littered the tables as much as pens and the humming of computers sounded loud in his ears. A few people glanced up at their entrance, waved toward Madeline, then returned their focus back to their work.

"Right now, we just had a major influx of information from the attack on the gated community. They're parsing through the data now, contacting other bases and setting up information that can be spread to the people, such as through newspapers or radio. It's a lot of work, but we have good people to do it." Madeline grinned before her smile slipped slightly. "Mitchell was very good at that...at making sure everyone felt comfortable." She shook her head and the grin returned. "Anyway, my mother should be somewhere through here. Just..."

A door opened and Wilma stepped inside with a bundle of papers. She placed them down and walked over. "Welcome. I'm guessing Madeline's all set. Come with me, if you will."

She gestured to another doorway. They exchanged nervous glances before stepping after the matriarch. The room was warm, definitely set up as a conference room with its oval table, comfortable chairs and... was that a water cooler at one end?

Karina darted over, getting herself a cup of water before downing it. Right after, she grabbed a few more cups, filled them, then came back, passing one to Maxwell, Lex and Ma.

He took his gratefully before taking a seat, his sister to his right, Ma on his left and Lex next to Karina.

Madeline, who seemed uncertain, was gestured to sit next to Wilma, who was across from them. The room, he noted uncomfortably, only had one exit. "Well, now that we have a moment to not worry about Enthrope breathing down our necks, welcome." She smiled pleasantly, leaning forward with her hands lightly clasped on the table. "Now for proper introductions, my name is Wilma Tutor, this is my daughter Madeline, as you know." She gestured to Madeline, who seemed disconcerted. "I am head of this branch of the Resistance."

"Branch?" Maxwell murmured quietly. He wanted to know, but part of him really didn't.

Wilma nodded. "I know quite a bit about you two from Madeline. I am eager to learn about the rest of you at a later time, but for now, I should explain the situation."

"That would be helpful." Ma spoke up, for the first time, sounding almost stern.

Wilma barely gave her a glance before she continued, "Now, I'm not sure what you know about the Resistance, so I'll start from the beginning." She stood and walked toward one side.

Maxwell spotted a projector on the table and blinked. How had he missed that? Wilma finagled with it for a moment before it flickered on, shining onto the wall with a prerecorded message seemingly already embedded into it. So, they gave this speech a lot. He wasn't too surprised, but...

"Welcome, new recruits, to the Resistance, or America Liberation, as some call us. As many of you might know, America has been in isolationism since the end of the Eternal War Era, following the Vietnam War."

The woman on the projection wasn't that much younger than the current Wilma, standing before a picture board with a map of the United States stretched across. It was easy to compare the woman on the projector and the one sitting across from him. The woman before him, in reality, was probably five or six years older than the one in the projector. So, why were they using such an outdated version? He examined the woman in the projector mutely. She could barely be in early thirties. Maybe because she seemed to exude more of an accepting air? He wasn't sure. She held a long thin pole that she was using to point at places on the map as she continued, "We are a group that started around that time, wishing to argue for globalization. Our country already tried isolationism during the World Wars and many of you know how that ended." She paused as she stepped forward. "Each of the places I pointed to earlier are bases of operation that were developed during that time, when the country was still debating its options. The government was doing something similar, but as of now, we still do not know what those were."

Maxwell stiffened, wondering if that pertained to his hometown.

"Our objective has been the same over the years. To free the country from the constraints of isolationism and, as of recently, to protect the citizens from the latest strain of an epidemic known as the SS level phenomenon."

Maxwell found himself shifting, trying and failing not to show his discomfort. He could hear the enthusiasm and determination in her voice, the strong vindication of what she was saying was right.

After all, what she was saying made sense. The way she spoke made it all seem black and white. They were the good guys, freeing a constrained country and helping the people. He shook his head and turned back to the projector once more, having missed a bit of her dialogue. He expressly ignored the narrow-eyed gaze he could feel drilling into him a bit too strongly.

"What you are about to endeavor into is a time of renewal. We will demolish the old system of repression, take down the gated communities, and lead this country's people to a better future, one without worry. One where they can explore this whole world as they see fit. America is big, yes, but the world, the planet we live on? It is massive in scale. A virtual paradise for us to explore."

Maxwell could almost feel Karina perk up beside him; this was right up her alley, after all.

"Yes, we will have to go through terrible times, probably lose loved ones and friends, but for a goal this grand? This powerful? Why shouldn't we sacrifice everything we have to be able to gain that freedom? America was the land of the free, and we will bring that back, bring our chance of that back for us and the generations to come."

With that final proclamation, the projector cut off, startling Maxwell into turning toward Wilma, who held a slim finger to the button.

She had a faint smile on her face. "So? What do you think? Think you can help us make this country better?"

Maxwell hesitated. Karina appeared pleased with what she heard. Ma was silent, but interested. As usual, Lex was hard to read. His eyes glowed with a look of uncertainty, maybe knowing something they didn't? It wouldn't be far-fetched. He would have to ask Lex later. After all, he did grow up in the gated community with a father at the head of a huge governmental branch.

He heard movement and noticed as Madeline stood. She walked around the table, all attention on her before she hesitantly touched his shoulder. She swallowed heavily. "Would... could..." she didn't seem to be able to speak.

"Madeline?" Karina called, curious, and Madeline seemed to blush deeply before she pulled in a sharp breath.

"I know it isn't my place, but I want you here. I want you to stay here, so please... could...would you be willing to stay here and work...?" she trailed off, the bravery from before vanished, but Maxwell could get the gist of what she was saying.

He opened and closed his mouth, unsure how to respond.

"Madeline, this isn't like you. Just speak with him properly." Wilma's voice cut through the atmosphere and Madeline practically spasmed, eyes snapping to behind Maxwell.

"Yes, Mother." She spoke curtly before turning back to him, no longer meeting his eyes, but over his shoulder. "I would like you to work with me. I am a side branch that works in reconnaissance and acquisition. We search for new recruits and convince them to join in our noble cause. I feel you and your sister would be good, especially after the loss of some of our agents in the field."

The way she said that, so straight-faced and cold, made Maxwell shiver. He scrutinized her face, seeing the impassiveness, yet...

Pain. It lingered and clung to her. She was trying hard not to cry, not to stammer and say something else as he sat there. He wanted to just let it go. To agree, but... "What about Ma or Lex?"

"I already have a position for them once your mother recovers, if they are willing. Plus, it seems Madeline is set on having you join her.

I'm not fond of it, since I also had plans. However, I will allow it," Wilma spoke up, leaning back as one leg crossed over the other.

"Where are Lex and Mom going to work?" Karina spoke up, voice curious and a little wary.

"Your mother will be working the telephones so that she doesn't have to do any strenuous work. Of course, that is after we have her checked out. We can't have her working while still in recovery. Lex here will be working alongside me."

Maxwell could almost hear the snap as his head whipped to face Lex. Unaware or more likely unperturbed by the motion, Wilma continued, "He seems like a smart lad and I can use the help."

"Are you serious?" Karina jerked, startled. "But..."

"Karina." Maxwell cut in, grabbing his sister and forcing her back into the seat she almost vacated.

"What?" Karina frowned. "It's not fair to Lex. He doesn't know about this place and..."

Her mouth shut, but, to Maxwell's consternation, Wilma seemed to notice.

"Is there a problem with your friend working with me?" Her voice was low.

"I see no qualms in it." Lex spoke up, shooting the briefest of looks their way, filled with both annoyance and a hint of gratitude, though Maxwell was sure it was a bit misplaced. "I do agree that I do not have experience working in a field such as yours. Working with you directly seems to be a bit of a leap."

"There is no need to worry." Wilma waved, pulling back in her seat.

"If you insist, plus you are allowing us to stay so I have no means of argument."

If Maxwell knew him any less, he would have definitely missed the fear quaking in his voice, or the way his shoulders tensed for the briefest of moments. His sister still appeared upset, but thankfully he stopped her from saying anything that might put Lex in a difficult position. He wasn't sure if she realized it or not, but Lex was on thin ice. Well, all of them were in some way, it seemed.

"Mother, what were your intentions with Maxwell and Karina?" Madeline spoke up hesitantly.

"It is of no concern, as long as he is willing to work with you, as seems to be the case since he has yet to argue."

Maxwell let out the faintest of breaths before smiling toward Madeline. "Right, so I guess Karina and I will be working with you for now. Thanks."

Lex could take care of himself. He would have to stop worrying about him for now.

Her shoulders seemed to lift and her taut fist seemed to unclench. He almost wished he wasn't so astute on these things, maybe then he wouldn't have to watch the struggle everyone felt when they were forced to lie, or be someone else that they weren't. Then again, it helped them over the past year or so. Could he really complain?

"Thank you." Her voice was incredibly soft, her lips barely moving, but she must have realized and he grinned, waving it off as Karina would usually do. She straightened and nodded. "Alright, Karina, Maxwell, come with me. Lex and..." she turned to Ma.

"Veronica." Ma spoke up and Madeline nodded.

"You two may rest up, explore the place a bit until Mother needs you. That is alright, correct, Mother?"

Wilma gave a sharp wave. "Yes, I do not need either of them right at this moment and I believe our doctors would like to have a check-up for Veronica. If you could go there first, it would be most beneficial."

Ma stood, sending a smile over to Maxwell before turning to Lex. "Well then, Lex, dear, would you like to help me find the infirmary?"

Lex only nodded, following after Ma as they departed the stuffy room.

Wilma stepped out after them and, through the still open doorway, Maxwell heard her call for one of the workers to escort Lex and Ma. Well, at least that was being taken care of.

Madeline put a hand on Maxwell's shoulder, gently pulling, catching his attention. Maxwell sighed, but stood up with Karina at his side. Madeline led them out of the room, past Wilma who watched silently as they rounded some of the desks to the opposite side of the room.

He was glad to get those scrutinizing eyes away from him, at least for a moment.

"Sorry about that," Madeline said softly, seeming upset.

"No problem." Karina waved it off before stepping forward, back to her normal perky self. "Want to tell us what's wrong? That formal stuffy language didn't suit you."

"That 'formal stuffy language', as you so call it, is practically my modus operandi, at this point, at least to new recruits." She pursed her lips while Maxwell found himself befuddled and a hint amused at the terminology she used. "Mother convinced me, long ago, to memorize it." She shook her head, as if getting rid of certain thoughts before she turned to Maxwell, this time in more excitement. "Still, I'm glad you're willing to join me. We can always use the help of people our age." She brightened as she hurried to one side of the large room, easily dodging the desks before she stopped in front of a desk at the end, where Leon was seated. Andrew stood beside him, one hand on the desk as the other stayed glued to the top of the computer. They seemed to notice their approach as Andrew sent them a glare.

Maxwell blinked, before noting Andrew was scrutinizing where Madeline was holding onto him as she pulled him along. She hadn't let go yet. He carefully extracted his arm and she glanced at him, a flash of emotion crossing her face before she turned back toward Leon. "So, what have you got?"

"Not much." Leon shook his head. "Most of it transferred properly, but the damage she took and the fact that we weren't able to physically extract it messed with the encryption and coding. I've managed to pull out bits and pieces, but it'll probably take a while to get everything. I think the others are having better luck than me, but not by much." He gestured to the rest of the room. So that's what everyone was doing.

"Madeline, what are those two doing here?"

Madeline perked up, glancing over to Andrew. "I asked them to join our team. We won't be going on a mission anytime soon, but I figured it would be best to get them used to this place first and you know Mother." She sighed. "If I hadn't convinced her to have them work with me, they would be flitting between all the different locales in this base and, well..."

Madeline waved and then whispered conspiratorially. "I kind of don't want anyone getting any ideas. I wasn't able to do much for Lex or their mother. Hopefully, they'll be alright."

"You really think someone here will do anything to those two?" Leon raised an eyebrow as Andrew sent them a deadpan expression.

Maxwell decided it was best not to feel offended by the way he was talking about them instead of to them. For now, at least.

"Though, regarding Lex, I don't think you need to worry about him. He was able to deceive a gated community for months, so a few weeks or months here wouldn't be an issue."

Months. That thought sent a trill of fear up Maxwell's spine. He wasn't sure why, but he didn't like the sound of that at all.

Madeline huffed. "I'm just saying, plus, these two at least are terrible at acting," She grimaced, shooting both of them a hesitant expression. "No offense."

"None taken." Karina waved, grinning, "I can't exactly argue, right, Maxwell?"

Well, we could, he thought, but now would probably not be a good time. Maxwell nodded, mentally shaking his head as Madeline continued, "Anyway, you saw it during the kidnapping. It's only thanks to the fact that those black-market creeps were in a rush that we were able to nab them then. The cleanliness..."

All conversation trailed off as Maxwell grimaced and Karina shifted, their fingers darting to the pretend bandages around their wrist and neck respectively. Leon shook his head and sighed, returning to his computer as Andrew muttered something under his breath.

"What was that?" Madeline glared and Andrew rolled his eyes.

"I was just saying, it is weird that they were clean for so long, but are you sure they are still?" His voice was low, eyes darting to Maxwell for a moment, as if hoping he wouldn't hear. Though, to his annoyance, Maxwell could very clearly hear anyway.

"Did you ever notice them hit the first or second stage? Of course, they are. Though I would like to know how they avoided that too, but..."

"Did you tell—?"

"No." Madeline cut in, gaze firmly on Leon, a small frown flitting onto her face. "Speaking of, they're right here..."

"Shouldn't you tell them though?" Leon asked quietly as he pushed his glasses up.

Maxwell bit his lip harshly. Karina stood beside him, shoulder to shoulder and tense as the metal surrounding them.

Madeline shook her head with a sigh and a wave. "Mother wouldn't like it, she would call it suspicious and you saw the state their mother was in, do you want them on that?" She trailed off before jerking and turning toward Maxwell. "I didn't mean... I'm sorry, I meant to include you in the conversation, but..."

"It's fine." Maxwell spoke up tersely.

"But it IS suspicious. I know Arik, Emma and Mitchell were thinking the same thing. You can't deny it—"

"I can. There are other people, even here, that don't have the disease." Madeline turned, whispering harshly, "Would you keep it down?"

"They were born here. They didn't live outside in the outer community and we are careful with who they interact with so they don't catch it."

"We can't know how to avoid that completely. We don't even know what causes it, or how it spreads. Nothing."

"Well...?" Everyone turned to Leon, who slowed in his typing, palms lightly resting on the keyboard. "Actually, we might." His narrowed eyes gleamed behind his rimmed spectacles. "Your mother. She was pulled from a part of the gated community that was looking into the cause of the disease. If we can finish procuring and translating the information salvaged from the lab, then maybe we can find the reason behind it. Obviously, it won't allow us to create a cure, considering there was no wide-spread announcement about them developing one, but it will tell us what to try to avoid."

"That... That's brilliant." Madeline perked up, clasping her hands in delight before she winced. She shook her head and beamed. "It would be a huge help." She paused, seemingly noticing something on his face, smile falling. "You okay?"

"Yeah, we're fine." Karina spoke, a little harshly. "We did just get here and this is a lot to take in."

"Oh, right. Right..." Madeline grimaced and turned to Leon and Andrew.

Boy, once again Maxwell was glad Karina was with him. He was probably the only one who noticed the nervous tremor in a voice that was intentionally filled with annoyance. He didn't miss, however, how scared she seemed to be as well, carefully hidden behind a veneer of relaxation that he was starting to dislike.

The trio's conversation hit way too close to home to feel comfortable. What if they questioned them? What would happen if they realized the reason behind why they were clean? He wanted to meet these other people who managed to avoid the epidemic, but...

He heard a cough and the room froze. All eyes darted to a figure at one side of the room. He didn't have a wound on him, other than a powerful coughing fit. He actually seemed surprisingly healthy with tanned skin and strong features. Yet that coughing fit...the man sniffled, then shook his head, grinning. "Sorry," he called. "Allergies."

Maxwell wasn't sure if anyone believed him or if he believed it, but he turned away anyway.

"Andrew..."

"On it." Andrew hurried away and Madeline turned to them.

"Andrew is grabbing one of our doctors. It may just be a case of allergies, but it's hard to tell when it's an allergic reaction, an actual cold, or whether it is the first stage of the sickness. So, better safe than sorry."

"Why?" Karina pointed out, as they walked away from Leon's desk, toward one of the hallways, passing through the doorway and away from the slowly increasing noise level.

"Hm?" Madeline paused before turning to face them. "Don't you know? If it is the Epidemic, it's actually better not to give them cold medicine. It lengthens the first stage, yes, but it also shortens all the following stages. Give him penicillin and the like? He'll be dead anywhere between a week and a month, tops."

Maxwell stiffened. "How...?"

"Well, that's not the case with everyone, but most people are that way. We're not dumb, like the gated community believes. We have good doctors here, as well, who have been working on the disease. It keeps mutating, so they can't create a strain of vaccine for it. They can track it and keep track of what contemporary drugs do. Everyone who has the disease knows not to do it unless they want to die quickly." The last part, she spoke softly.

"If I may," Maxwell hesitantly started, garnering her attention, as well as Karina's. He gulped and pushed on. "When did you first get sick?"

Madeline stared at him for a long time before she turned away. "A year ago. Why?"

"Just wondering," he trailed off, catching his sister's attention.

She barely reacted besides a small nod, but stayed silent as they walked through the halls, the sound from the center already being cut off as they rounded another bend. Madeline examined them in silence, her brow furrowed before her shoulders slumped.

Why did she seem discouraged?

"Hey, Karina?"

Karina blinked, startled as Madeline spoke up, leading them back to their rooms. She leaned forward, trying to meet Madeline's eyes. "Huh? Did you want to ask something?"

Madeline hesitated, fingers flexing as if she wasn't sure whether to grip them into fists or leave them laying against her sides. "Can I speak with you? Alone?"

Maxwell and Karina exchanged looks before Karina shrugged. "Sure, whatever."

Madeline was definitely startled by Karina's straightforwardness, but that wasn't a new thing. Maxwell found himself relieved when a warm smile slowly formed on Madeline's lips. He turned, noting as they reached the doorway, which was propped open. Maxwell could not deny his confusion as he scrutinized the open door. What's the point of keeping them open if they were a safety measure?

Madeline must have noticed because she let out a faint chuckle. "We only locked it because new people were coming in. We have motion sensors outside as well as cameras. Anyone we don't recognize gets close? The doors close, simple as that."

"Ah." Maxwell found himself saying, before shaking his head. This place would definitely take some getting used to.

Chapter Five

"So, what did you want to talk about?" Karina took a seat on her bed as Madeline closed the door behind her, fidgeting uncomfortably. Maxwell said good-bye, saying he would like to find Lex first and rest up. Madeline let him, and Karina figured it was because Madeline thought Maxwell was giving them space to talk, which wasn't completely far off, but still.

"I was wondering. What did Emma tell you about my feelings?" Madeline kept her head down and Karina raised an eyebrow, trying hard to keep her emotions in check as her memory flashed to Emma's bloody corpse.

She shook her head sharply and crossed her arms over her chest, examining the room instead of focusing on her. It wasn't anything spectacular, but it would do. "Sorry, but you'll have to clarify. The only thing I know is that you like my brother, which wasn't hard to miss by the way, and I was okay with you being interested in him because I heard from Emma you were a good person. It took a while, but I couldn't deny what Emma said, regarding, well, actually caring."

Madeline seemed startled by her words, straightening slightly. Karina huffed, waving in her direction. "Geez, I'm not oblivious. Maxwell might be better able to spot people's intentions, but I'm not blind. I can tell you truly do care for him, though I'm not positive on your reasoning, so I let it slide."

"I— Then— Thank you, Karina." Madeline stood up. A firm resolve locked on Karina. "You're right. I do care for your brother. More than I ever thought I could care for someone."

Karina blinked, surprised at the sudden explanation, not having expected Madeline to flat out say it.

Madeline sighed and hesitantly took a seat besides Karina. When Karina didn't push her away, she relaxed and shifted all her attention to her lap. "I'll be honest. When I first saw your brother, I was conflicted. One part of me thought he was absolutely ado— cute, cute, yeah." She blushed deeply and Karina chuckled. Her chuckles faded as she sobered.

"But wasn't the first time you met my brother—"

"No."

Karina stiffened as Madeline messed with her clothes, picking at the seam of her blouse. "The first time I met him, we didn't interact at all." She took in a breath before facing Karina. "We, Emma and the others as well as myself, were returning from a meeting with Mother after Arik found out about Emma and the rest of us being part of the Resistance. We were able to convince her from talking with him by mentioning how his father was part of the Police Brigade. She was suspicious, but she allowed it." She shook her head. "The main point is that when we were returning, we happened to pass the hostel around the same time when you two were leaving, or maybe you just arrived? I wasn't sure. Maxwell was talking to you and you kept glaring back at the hostel. None of the others noticed, too engrossed in conversation, but I did." She paused, fingers curling around her knees, causing the cloth to scrunch up under her tight grip. "It was a couple months ago. Probably three days before you joined us at the apartment complex. Your brother, Maxwell, he seemed so worried about you. He barely gave us a glance before turning his attention back onto you." She frowned. "Though it probably didn't help that there were two people making out right in public. From what I gather, he's not exactly a fan of that sort of thing."

Karina chuckled, unable to deny the statement, getting a returning weak grin from Madeline.

"I'm not sure if your brother remembers that moment, it was so brief it would have been easy to miss, but I couldn't." Madeline continued, fidgeting in her seat. "When I found him again, I felt anxious, stuttering and just being a mess. For a while I couldn't understand why I kept acting like that, after all, he was just another cute boy." She trailed off before turning her attention fully onto Karina. "It took a while for me to realize that I might like him as something more."

Karina watched her for a moment, thinking over what she just said. A lot happened when they were at the hostel, she barely remembered stuff like that, only just that her brother was incredibly worried about her and, thus, distracted.

Dammit, she made her brother worry way too much.

"Well..." Madeline's voice pulled Karina back as she pushed her fingers together, head once more leaning down. "As you can guess, I was surprised when you two joined us at the apartment complex in the states you were in. I wanted to tell mother but I couldn't. You two were so hurt and I wasn't about to do something right after. I was annoyed. That was it and then..." she trailed off. "I got a chance to watch you two, watch how you interacted with Emma and Arik. Your brother, he has such a kind smile. It was something I never saw before."

Karina let her posture soften as her mind flitted to the people Madeline knew. Of everyone, Mitchell and Emma had been honestly the only two who were warm to them. Everyone involved with the Resistance from Wilma to Andrew seemed almost cold and distant.

"Whenever I tried to talk to him, he always had this guarded expression on his face. Though sometimes it was one of worry, confusion and I— I wanted to be able to bring up those smiles he always sent your and Emma's way. I wanted to know more about him as you probably realized when I tried to set up a date and, well, failed spectacularly."

"You're able to talk to me just fine now, right? My brother's not that different from me," Karina pointed out and Madeline slumped.

"I know, you're both thoughtful and kind. I understand that. I— I usually talk to Emma about this, but..."

At that, Madeline stifled a small sound. Karina stiffened, finally spotting the tears staining Madeline's clothes, the tightly clenched fists almost ripping her pants as she trembled. "But Emma's not here. You are the only other girl I know my age and..."

She choked slightly and Karina panicked on what to do. She wasn't the comforter, well, excluding her brother. "I'm sorry."

"What? Why are you apologizing?" Karina demanded. Huffing as Madeline jumped, turning to her, tears streaking down her cheeks. "Last time I checked? Crying because you lost someone you deeply cared for is not a bad thing. Hell, I would be worried if you didn't." Karina waved. "If anything, I'm glad you came to me, you know?" She leaned forward and grinned at Madeline's startled expression. "Now I know for certain I don't have to worry about you going for Maxwell. If you can say all of this to an overprotective numbskull like me, then you're fine in my book."

A smothered laugh came from Madeline's throat as Karina shifted her attention toward the ceiling. "Anyway, I'll just continue staring at the ceiling, do whatever you want."

A choked sob came out before the bed trembled and Madeline outright cried.

The sobs reached her ears as Karina reached for the girl's head, pushing a hand through her hair like she would her brother. Madeline didn't move into it, but she didn't pull away either, just continuing to cry.

Finally, the crying slowed to sniffles and Karina leaned forward enough to peer up at the girl. "Feel better?"

Madeline's face was streaked with tears, her cheeks blotchy and stained as she used her arm to wipe away the last of the tears. "You're terrible at comforting," she choked out, but smiled softly.

Karina huffed and pulled back. "Hey, what do you expect? You suddenly started crying on me. I wasn't going to punt you out of the room like that. Didn't give me very many choices."

"Thanks." Madeline's voice was soft, but a hint of a smile shone through as Karina turned toward her.

"Thanks for what?"

"For listening to me. For allowing me to..." Madeline gestured, blush returning to her face. She shook her head, determination shining through her straightened posture. "I'm glad you are giving me a chance to date your brother."

"Whoa." Karina muttered and Madeline's grin widened.

"You've heard my comrades talk about what I'm like away from him. I'll just have to pull more from that when talking with him so I'm not a blabbering idiot."

"You have a lot of work to do," Karina pointed out and Madeline stiffened. She turned away, sheepishly pushing two fingers together.

"He already thinks I'm strange, doesn't he?"

"Well, I'll just say he doesn't know what to think about with you, how about that?"

Madeline slumped and groaned. "Oh." She sighed. "Well, I did want to get to know him better, and so I guess it's a good opportunity to get him to know about me as well. I guess." The last part, she muttered and Karina rolled her eyes, standing up.

"Well, first off, why not just talk to him like a NORMAL person? You're either stuttering, or using that formal crap. It gives me whiplash."

Madeline bit her lip as she stood up straight. Her blonde hair was frizzy as she used her nails, as if hoping to fix it and failing. "Well, yeah," she muttered. "I'll try. Since Emma's no longer with us. Will you help me?"

"Oh, no." Karina crossed her arms. "I was okay with allowing you to attempt to set up a date with Maxwell. However, I'm NOT going to try to get him hitched up. He's still my brother, after all."

Madeline chuckled. "I guess I shouldn't be too surprised." She turned fully to face Karina, extending her hand forward. "We can promise to both watch out for him, deal?"

Karina stared down at the proffered deal, hesitant. The last time she made a deal, it backfired horribly. She was leery about the promise they made to Mom about the bible, but it was Maxwell's decision. She wasn't going to argue. She shook her head. "Maxwell is my brother. I'll take care of him, no matter what."

Madeline hesitated before she nodded, pulling back. "I'm not sure if I love him, not yet. I do care for him and as such, I will do what I can for him as well. Not as a sister, but..."

"That's good enough for me, now why don't we make sure you're cleaned up? We can get going after." Karina loosely crossed her arms over her chest as Madeline blinked. Noticing her confusion, Karina groaned. "Lunch? Dinner? Food? Take your pick?"

Madeline sheepishly turned away as a loud growl sounded in the room. "Er, right on that." She paused before she wiped her cheeks once more. "Seriously though, thank you. When I found out Emma died, I..."

"She was a good friend," Karina said, keeping her voice soft. "She helped us when we needed it and I can tell she was a support for you."

"More than you can know." Madeline's voice was warm and weary. "I've known her for so long. We shared a lot of secrets with each other." She smiled faintly. "Did you know? She told me that, after the mission, she was going to ask Arik to go out on a date? She was so excited about it."

Karina winced, glancing down as the memories of Arik's anguish, despair and outrage passed through her mind, intermingled with the death gurgles.

"To have lost them both in such short succession. I thought I would be used to it by now."

"How would someone get used to something like that?" Karina's attention snapped back to Madeline, who was cleaning up her face with a handkerchief she must have kept in her pocket.

Madeline paused, face somewhat obscured by her hair. "We're supposed to." Her voice was tired as she spoke. "If we don't, we could be the next to die."

Karina didn't say anything. She wasn't sure what she could say as Madeline pulled away, the tears and redness from before practically gone. All that was left was a despondent expression which promptly disappeared into a faint smile. "Still, I guess I have to thank you once again for listening." She shook her head. "Anyway, we should probably get ourselves something to eat. Now that I've calmed down a bit, I'm quite hungry."

Karina chuckled as Madeline turned toward the doorway. Karina followed a bit slower behind her. Madeline definitely was an interesting character. She wasn't Maxwell, but it was hard to miss the pain Madeline seemed to be carrying. She rubbed her arms at the thought. How could anyone get used to death? Especially considering how painful it was. Though, did she have the right to think that? All of the people she loves are immune to the disease and can take care of themselves in a fight. She was... She cut off her spiraling train of thoughts and shook her head. Right, time for a change in subject, she thought. She decided to focus on the next topic as Madeline led her to the kitchen. Karina wasn't fully sure what attracted Madeline to her brother, but she could tell that it wasn't just because Maxwell was good-looking. Something she, even as his sister, could readily admit. He almost took after their dad, or what she could remember of him.

She quickly pulled away from that thought before she could start descending into misery. It didn't take long to reach the cafeteria. The different smells almost overpowered her after the sterile smell that seemed to invade this place. She could smell broiling meat and cooked vegetables, a medley of different breads and spice. After a little searching, she spotted Maxwell talking with Lex. *Mom must still be in the infirmary,* she thought as she walked over. They were sitting to one side of the place. Lex's plate was clean, but Maxwell's was layered in different foods, including, to none of her surprise, an orange. She grinned and walked over as Madeline stiffened. Karina followed Madeline's gaze, spotting the laughter on her brother's face and the amusement on Lex's. She held back as Madeline cautiously stepped forward. Lex spotted her, but Maxwell hadn't yet.

Though, he noticed pretty quickly when Lex went quiet and turned. Karina hung back as Madeline stood there, biting her lip as her leg bent backward, toe almost drilling a hole in the ground with her fidgeting. Karina was close enough that she could hear their conversation, but far enough where she wasn't intruding.

"Would— Maxwell—" She took a deep breath and then, almost shouting, said, "Would you go out with me?"

The room froze and Karina almost slammed her palm into her face, but resisted, more curious about her sibling's reaction. Lex seemed amused. Maxwell's face, however, almost sent Karina into a fit of giggles. His mouth was floundering and he was staring wide-eyed at Madeline, whose face was clenched tightly, everything in her seemed withdrawn, waiting.

Maxwell opened and closed his mouth as Madeline slumped, as if making her own conclusions.

Come on, Maxwell, say something.

Maybe he heard her thoughts, or maybe his brain just finally snapped into what was going on, but he quickly spoke. "Uh, Madeline, what?"

"I want to go out with you. I want to know more about you and maybe..." She stopped before blurting out, "Would you be my boyfriend?"

Karina almost choked. That was farther than she expected, but it seemed Maxwell already deduced that was where it was going because he was hesitant, unsure how to respond. Lex must have prodded him, because he looked back toward him before he cleared his throat, opened his mouth and stopped. He let out a sigh and nodded.

Madeline practically jumped forward, hugging him tightly. "Thank you."

Maxwell's face turned so red Karina would have thought he'd lain in the sun for hours. She finally decided to step forward, coming into his line of sight. The we'll-talk-later flashing through his expression was telling, but she ignored it as he huffed. Madeline pulled off, practically beaming.

This was definitely going to be interesting. Too bad Karina didn't have a camera on her.

~ * ~

He said yes. He actually said yes. Madeline's pounding heart decided it wanted to pause for the briefest of minutes before accelerating once more. This beautiful boy agreed to go out with her. Her, of all people. She withheld the want to hum and just smiled, taking a seat next to him, arm around his. Karina joined her on Maxwell's other side, chuckling all the way.

She would have to thank her again later.

"Um, so why do you want to be my, well..." Maxwell's soft voice caught her attention. She peered up at him, pulling back a bit so he could move his arm. He shifted it, but didn't fully pull away.

She could already feel her smile slipping into something more genuine as she observed the boy before her. He was fidgeting slightly, but already calming down.

"I like your smile," she said, noting as his nerves seemed to return.

Did what she said fluster him? From Karina's outburst of laughter

59

and the way he turned a glare onto her, Madeline would probably have to say yes. She shook her head and continued, letting her tongue go for once. "Well, you're also sweet, and, from what I've seen, very caring. Emma liked talking about you and, well, I wanted to know more about you."

As Madeline talked, she seemed to go from her blunt admission to a stuttering mess. Why did she always do that? Why couldn't she just talk with him like Karina, Leon or Andrew? As frustrating as it was, it drew Maxwell's attention. Stunning green eyes examined hers in a way that felt thoughtful.

She heard shifting and glanced over to the man the twins were always with, Lex. She was honestly not sure what to make of the man before her. At moments, he exuded a sort of strength that she recognized in her mother and some of the upper echelon. Right after, it seemed he noticed and he would crumble slightly, making himself less noticeable. It was subtle, a shift of a brow here, a slump of a shoulder there. She could tell he deeply cared for her new b— bo...gosh darn it. Her new boyfriend. Mentally huffing now that she got through that exercise in futility, she returned to her thought process as she spotted Maxwell grabbing Lex's sleeve.

"Don't."

His words were soft and, if she wasn't paying attention, she would have missed the hint of pleading. She bit her lip. Well, it made sense. In a lot of ways, she was a stranger to him and it frustrated her. She wanted so badly to know more about him, for him to know more about her. But what could she do?

"Maxwell, you are an idiot." The wince was evidence enough. "You have your sister right there. You don't need me."

Maxwell slumped and muttered a quiet curse under his breath before giving Lex a weak smile. "Alright, have a good night."

A weak smile that still spoke of caring more than she'd ever gotten.

Her mind, slipping into turmoil, only returned after she noticed that Lex was gone and she was with Maxwell, alone.

"Huh?" she muttered. "Where's Karina?"

"Grabbing some food. She asked if you wanted anything, but you didn't respond."

"Ah, I was zoned out."

The scrutinizing and semi-worried look he gave her made her feel uncomfortable. She was not giving him a good impression. She didn't mean to zone out.

"I'm going to go get myself something to eat."

She promptly stood up and hurried toward the food area, noting where Karina was. She could tell the girl was taking her time choosing, which was both encouraging and not. She quickly grabbed up her food, catching an amused expression from Karina before she hurried back to the table.

When she returned, she noticed he was examining the ceiling, noting the way the metal glowed with the constant lights and sounds. He didn't say anything for a while, seemingly lost in thought as she took a seat beside him with her full tray. He was slowly munching on his and turned when the metal of her platter hit the plastic of the table.

She took a deep breath before quickly speaking up, afraid she would lose her nerve. "Maxwell. Is there anything in particular you would like to do or know?"

Maxwell tilted his head just enough where he could watch her before letting out a sigh, slumping. "I'll be honest. Not really. This place is a bit overwhelming and, well..." he flung his hands outward. "You did just up and decide to ask me to be your...in front of everyone."

She mentally slumped when he didn't say boyfriend, picking up a bit of cheese to chew on before rallying herself. "Yes, I'm aware."

She was acutely aware of her bluntness. The whispering words, the somewhat loud conversations. However, she was also used to it at this point. It came with her position and parentage.

She was never able to escape it.

"Is that all your eating?" he asked, glancing down to her plate.

"Huh?" She blinked, following his line of sight. She hadn't gotten a lot, just basics like cheese, and some salami. "Oh, I don't eat much." She glanced down at herself. "I have an image to uphold, that's all."

Maxwell's brow furrowed in worry. He glanced down at his own plate which, earlier, had been filled with stuff. Considering it was already half-gone he must have been hungry. "Here." He picked up one of two oranges he set to the side and gently passed it over.

She blinked, startled as he returned his attention back to his food. "At least eat some fruit." A faint warm smile crossed his face as he picked up the other, peeling into it. "Oranges are good for you after all." He seemed to pause for a moment in thought before he continued, popping a segment into his mouth. "I prefer oranges in general. If you were curious."

"Really?"

She glanced down at the fruit in her palm. They weren't her favorite, but she didn't hate them.

"Yeah, If I could eat just oranges, I probably would, but that's not exactly healthy either."

He chuckled, placing a few slices to the side to go back to his other food.

She stared, unable to pull her attention away from his warm expression before her attention drifted to the fruit in her hands. Fruit like this was expensive. They only had a few down here and for Maxwell to give her one when they seemed to be his favorite was telling.

Her mind was running a mile a minute trying to make calculations. Could she convince her mother to get more? Maybe she could talk the chef into making more orange dishes, or she could try to make her own.

Forcefully returning to her senses, she focused back on her food, relishing in the sweetness of the orange along with what little else was on her plate. Just as she thought, he was a sweetheart and in a way that she couldn't understand. She stilled in peeling the fruit as thoughts echoed in her mind, making her feel sad.

After all, she was the reason he was there. Both him and Karina. She wasn't blind, she could tell how nervous both of them were. The way they fidgeted and shifted. The way they glanced around the building, similar to when she was searching for avenues to escape during a mission. The tension in their bodies, while well hidden, was still visible.

In some ways, it broke her...knowing she was part of the cause of that tension, that even now, he was coiled up, only showing her bits and pieces of a personality. She knew it wasn't fair to berate him like that, especially since she wasn't much better. She wasn't able to completely relax either, no matter how much she wished to.

Then again, when had she ever gotten a chance to truly relax?

Chapter Six

Lex let out a long breath as he headed toward his room. That display was quite entertaining. It should help the twins, at least a little in this underground bunker. Though jail felt more fitting. He grimaced. What was his luck like to be tied up to work with Wilma, of all people? He managed to avoid outright cursing, but... He was almost to his room when an uncomfortably familiar voice stopped him.

"Lex?

Lex turned around, noting Wilma's expression. "Yes?"

She stepped forward, leaning on one foot heavily as that hand went to her hip. She waved as she spoke. "I talked with Andrew and Leon. They confirmed with me that you were their informant. The one that infiltrated the gated community. It means I picked correctly in having you work with me, but beside that, I wish to talk with you."

"About?" Lex knew, but he hesitated, curious on what she would say.

The woman examined him with a tilt of her head. "We've been trying to infiltrate those communities for ages, to get someone on the inside. Then you, someone we've never heard of, infiltrate the very same community without a problem. Mind explaining how you managed it?"

Lex scanned her silently, the gears in his head turning rapidly as he kept himself steady. "Not much to tell. I grew up in Reinmark, close to the gated community. So, I grew up watching them. One day, I happened to acquire some clothes that were thrown out and used those to slip inside. I was only really a servant, but..." Lex shrugged. "I'm more surprised you haven't gotten anyone in, what with the supposed reports of slavery and such going between the gated community and the outer one."

The woman leaned forward, face expressionless. "Since you infiltrated the community, you must know what they think of outsiders like us. Why would they want us?"

Lex expression narrowed into sharp thin lines. "Are you saying that the slavery is a lie?"

The woman leaned back. "No, there definitely is slavery." She passed it off by shifting onto her other foot and continuing, "If you were just a servant, how did you get into the highest security location in that gated community?"

"Are we really speaking of all this here? In the middle of the hallway?" Lex countered and the woman shrugged, as if unconcerned.

"There is no problem, after all, it's information I'll be sharing with the rest of my people later. So, there are no worries of rumors or problems."

Lex's arms slowly crossed over his chest in a relaxed posture, though he felt stiff. "To answer your question? I'll be honest, I don't know."

She blinked, surprise flitting on her face before she gestured for him to continue.

He shrugged. "Not much to tell you. The head took a liking to how I worked and got me a position. As you said, they don't particularly like people from the outside, so they're a bit limited on what they have on the inside."

"Very true." She gave him an uneasy look. "Still, to go months without..."

"Them realizing? Why would they? Once I'm in, I'm in."

Wilma stayed silent after that, in deep thought, before she turned away. "I see. Well, I best check on the progress of our data analysis. Thanks to your help, we were able to extract a good amount of data about our enemies." She grinned and tossed her hair over her shoulder. "I have to congratulate you on a job well done, you and those twins." With that, she walked away.

Lex grunted quietly, thinking a very strong, good-riddance which was only marred by the fact that he would be working with her tomorrow.

His luck was on par as usual.

If he was being honest, he really didn't like this place. The words from the projector rang in his ears. They were said so sweetly, such lies. Yes, he wasn't fond of isolationism, but from what he heard from his father, what little pieces he could gather, he wasn't sure completely eradicating the government, as the Resistance planned to do, would be a good idea.

Oh, he hated the format that existed now, he wouldn't deny that. Yet, other than the epidemic, there wasn't much to fear. Yes, the outer communities were falling apart, but even then, there weren't many people hungry or without a place to sleep. Yes, there were beggars, as he recalled from rescuing the twins who'd been idiotic enough to walk down the ONE lane where every scavenger rested, but they usually had someplace to go back to. Isolationism wasn't good, but it wasn't terrible either. There was more communication between people, and the discrimination was only really between who had money and who didn't.

He sighed. It was a fanciful ideology. Maybe globalization, like Wilma talked about, would be better, but he wasn't so sure, and anyway, who would take over if the government did collapse like that? He wasn't sure he wanted anyone that he'd met so far taking over.

Wilma held a brutal coldness to her, which he sensed both from their recent conversation and the way Madeline cowered in her mother's presence, though the girl tried to keep a confident air about her. He shook his head as he returned to his room. Maybe he was thinking too much into this. He would have to get some rest and hope things worked out. If they would. At least he would be entertained.

~ * ~

Maxwell could readily admit, he had no idea what the HELL to feel and yes, he was completely prepared to swear this time. He glanced toward Karina as they returned to their rooms. Lex's was already locked and Ma was still in the infirmary being checked. Madeline said she would check on Veronica for them, so Maxwell let her, wanting to talk with Karina anyway.

Karina glanced at him with a raised eyebrow and he gestured to his room. She groaned. "Max, I've literally been talking to EVERYONE today. Can we do something besides talking?"

"Kari, what else can we do?" He deadpanned, gesturing around him. "Explore this place? I'm not exactly keen on the idea, especially without a guide like Madeline and I know you're getting fidgety just from being down here."

"I've been trying hard to ignore that," Karina muttered, crossing her arms over her chest. "Alright, then..."

"Plus, we don't have anything else. We need to figure out what we're doing next and I don't think either of us wants to stay here longer than we have to," he pointed out, causing Karina to sigh and slump.

He sent her a weak smile before turning and stepping into his room. She hesitated before following after him and taking a seat. He closed the door and walked over, sitting beside her. "By the way, are you alright?"

Karina blinked. "Yeah? Why do you ask?"

Maxwell shot her a stern expression, noticing her shift uncomfortably before she groaned. "I'll be fine, now what do you want to do? We have Mom so..."

Maxwell sighed and leaned back. He stared at the ceiling, lost in thought. What did he want to do? His thoughts flickered to Madeline, how ecstatic she was when he said yes. The way she beamed when he mentioned about the orange, before digging into the food. Her mood seemed to shift so easily. In some ways, she was hard to read, but others, she was like an open book. Was that just for him or...

Still, she wasn't pushy, which he was thankful for and she was willing to help Ma and talk with Karina. His gaze flitted to Karina. He could probably guess at the reason for Madeline's sudden declaration, if his sister's expression earlier was anything to go by. He shook his head. Other than that, though? There wasn't any real reason to be here. Was it safe? Maybe for him and Karina, but maybe not, considering how Madeline, Andrew and Leon were talking earlier. If one of them said something, or if someone else noticed, what would happen to them? A roiling mass of emotions settled into his stomach, not helped by the fact that Karina's own face twisted into a faint hint of misery. She quickly hid it.

He wanted to ask, but knowing his stubborn sister, she would just brush it off and talk about something else. So, he held his tongue. "Do you think Ma will be alright?"

Karina pulled her legs up, crossing them on the bed, her fingers trailing over her leg for a second in thought before she shrugged. "I don't know. She was still Mom, but..."

Maxwell grimaced. He noticed how jumpy their mother was, how she flinched at a touch unless she was the one who did it. How she grew nervous in that hallway which very much resembled the hallways in the gated community. How sickly and pale she appeared. "Do you think she's sick too?"

Karina went to respond before snapping her mouth shut. That was answer enough. Maxwell could feel his fingers curling into the quilt, catching on the fabric. He tilted his head down.

Karina let out a long breath, shifting to catch his attention. "I think she might be, after all, according to Father's letter both of them should only have partial immunity."

"So why do we..." Maxwell pursed his lips. "If it is something stupid like gene splicing, then..."

"Yikes, let's not get into that." Karina grimaced, waving it off and Maxwell felt his lips curl upward in amusement. "All we know is that we have the full immunity. If we didn't, we would be sick by now, right?"

Maxwell wasn't sure how to respond, or if he could. So, deciding to change topics a little, he turned away from Karina. "Either way, Ma is sick and I don't think there's a way we can cure her without making a scene."

"No, you're right." Karina pulled her legs up, chin leaning on the knees. "I don't want to just up and leave either."

"So, I guess our next course of action would be to create a serum."

"Serum?"

Maxwell glanced sidelong to Karina. "We can't just use our own blood. We don't know how much it took to help Lex, since he needed a pint for his wound anyway. Maybe it needs to be concentrated. If so, we don't have that much blood to spare." He spoke quietly, unsure at the quality of the walls around here.

Karina stayed silent in thought for the longest time. Long enough that Maxwell was starting to wonder if she would respond.

"That makes sense. Do we ask one of the doctors here? Maybe they can make one?"

Karina's frown spoke of what she thought of that, her lips twisting downward more with each word. Karina seemed incredibly uncertain of her own words and he wasn't sure either.

He thought for a bit, watching the way the light curled over the ceiling, glinting faintly off the rigid metal. It would be so easy to just walk over there and say, hey, we have the cure. The thing was, he wasn't sure he trusted them. He knew he didn't trust them with Lex, especially now that Lex was working alongside Wilma. He shuddered for a moment, thinking of how that could have ended much worse if he hadn't stopped Karina. "I honestly don't know. I know we have to get the cure out. I don't think either of us want any more incidents like what happened with Arik and Mitchell." Maxwell spotted the telltale cringe that he was expecting from Karina. He didn't like bringing it up, but he knew he needed to. "So, should we just talk with the people here? Figure out what they have to say?"

"No." Karina shook her head, determination flashing across her face. "They didn't even check up on Mom. It was Madeline who did that, not anyone else. Even that Wilma person, Madeline's mother, just kind of ignored it, passing it off only at the end as an, oh right. If they are doing that with Mom, a victim of the gated community they seem to hate, then what would they do with us?"

Maxwell blinked, surprised before he felt a faint relieved smile cross his face. "We agree then." His words seemed to catch Karina off guard as he placed his hands onto the bed, back stretching as he examined the ceiling. "I've been thinking of the 'what-if's' since we arrived." He peered sidelong toward her, noting the way she shifted, one leg stretching out over the covers. "What if we told them? What if we tried to explain, not only about our situation, but about Lex's? Maybe if we talk to them calmly, they will not hate him, but..." Maxwell shook his head. "The more

I've seen of this place, the more I find myself unable to believe in those what-ifs..."

"Plus, we're not that fortunate," Karina cut in, a faint smirk on her lips.

Maxwell rolled his eyes, but agreed. "That too."

"Maxwell, I know what you mean." Maxwell turned to face his sister as she placed her palms on her lap, fingers curling over her knees. "I'm worried, that they will find out and there'll be nothing we can do. They don't seem the type of group to care about two no-name teens such as us. Plus, everyone is so desperate, what, with this disease, do you think we can make it out with our blood still in our bodies?"

Maxwell winced at the mental image. He hated to say it, but he understood what Karina was saying. The people here were blood-thirsty, in a different way than she was describing, but still. If their methods were extreme enough to destroy an entire community, who's to say what they would do to the two of them? He didn't want his sister and him to be separated, because they were careless, because they trusted when they shouldn't have.

"Karina, if they are like this, and the gated community is too, then is there a point?" He wasn't usually one to be so pessimistic, but he couldn't help it. The thought churned in his head.

Karina stared at him for the longest time. "Well," she sighed and gave him a faint smile. He couldn't tell if it was fake or not. "How about this. We save who we can. Martha, Agatha, Mom. It might not stop or create peace between the two communities, but it won't hurt, right? I guess that is another reason against telling them. After all, we both know the Resistance will only treat those from the outer community, and would it be so far-fetched to believe that the gated community would then be destroyed?"

Maxwell winced, realizing the truth to the words. Yeah, now that he thought about it, they couldn't just give the cure over to the Resistance. Not if what he saw was true. If the whole Resistance was like this, then... No, it would be better to speak with someone more neutral, who was willing to help either side. Where would they find someone like that?

He took a deep breath, counting in his head to calm himself before letting it out and turning to Karina. "We'll wait." Maxwell finally spoke up. "Once they go through all the data, we'll make a decision. While I agree with you. I'm not doing anything before we know Lex will be okay staying here or won't, as we both probably suspect."

Karina opened her mouth then closed it with a snap, probably realizing what he was trying to say. "That could take a while, we don't know how long..."

"Madeline's been sick for a year, Lex was probably sick for two. Ma's only maybe been sick for a few months. Yes, she was probably experimented on, and quite a bit." Those words tasted rancid in his mouth and he quickly spat them out, disgusted as much as Karina seemed to be before he continued. "That's just it, though. This Epidemic is long-lasting, it's almost like torture."

"Why are you equating it with that?" Karina whispered and Maxwell opened his mouth, only to pause.

Why was he equating the two? He grimaced. He knew why. "It's because it's slow, painful, and there's no means that anyone except us knows of to stop it."

Karina stayed silent, thinking over his words. Maxwell sighed and stood. "However, I don't want to just be pessimistic. If we do stay here, fine, we can just let them know and hope that what we were discussing doesn't actually happen. Have them take care of spreading it for us, and just head home with Ma, but if not..." he trailed off.

Karina glared. "You know, now that you've said it..."

Maxwell groaned. "Well, the idea was a pleasant thought, but yeah, coming from my mouth, that sounded WAY too easy."

"So, plan A?"

"Not plan B?"

Karina raised an amused eyebrow and Maxwell just huffed. "Okay, fine, plan A." He shook his head. "So, if it doesn't work out, we'll have to find another doctor."

Karina paused, fingers to her lips before she pointed at him. "Wasn't there another letter we received? Before Mom and Dad's?"

Maxwell frowned before his thoughts bolted to the unopened letter he got from Doctor Girshwin. The young doctor who helped them all the way back in New London City after they were caught in a riot. It was only thanks to him that Lex was still alive and that Karina no longer carried a bullet wound in her shoulder. He smacked his head, feeling stupid that he'd forgotten the man, or the letter he'd asked them to send to his mother. "Of course. We still have to deliver that letter."

"Doctor Girshwin was kind. Maybe whoever receives the letter is the same." Karina waved, before crossing her arms over her chest. "Though it is a bit far. California, right?"

"What's left of it." Maxwell hummed as he headed toward his bag that he'd dropped off earlier. He dug into it, retrieving the letter and looking it over. It definitely saw better days, but the envelope was still mostly white and the letters were strewn in a gentle, neat cursive.

He slipped it back into his backpack, noting as his sister leaned over his shoulder. "So?"

"I guess that works, but what about Ma?"

Karina gnawed at her bottom lip, pulling away from Maxwell. "Well, maybe she can stay here?"

Maxwell slowly blinked and turned his head as if in a horror movie. "Are you saying, that if it doesn't work out and something happens to Lex, we leave our mother, whom we've been looking for, for months, with the very same people who would have no qualms doing something as horrific as burning an ENTIRE gated community to the ground?"

Karina bit her lip even harder, almost making it bleed.

Maxwell sighed, shaking his head. "Sorry, that came out..."

"No, you're right."

Maxwell jerked, surprised. "Huh?"

Karina sent him a glare as she returned to the bed, flopping back on it. "What else can we do? Where else can she go? I don't want to try to go home with her, and anyway, if she managed to get home, she would still be sick in an area that they've already captured her in once before. Who knows if we can get back there anyway? Plus, it's in the complete opposite direction from where we SHOULD go."

Maxwell licked his suddenly dry lips as he realized the truth to Karina's words. Then, it hit him with the force of a collapsing building. It wasn't so much that they shouldn't go home. It was that they outright

COULDN'T. His mind shut down as he rationalized the implications, part of him noted the way Karina seemed to stiffen, teeth crashing shut as she also realized what she said, but that part was quickly shushed. "We can't go back home, can we?" The words came out in a stiff whisper, tremulous at best.

His thoughts flickered to his home, were the windows still broken? The carpet pulled up and sink stained, yet upstairs still clean and precise, the way they left it? Was the church bell still ringing, echoing across the plaza, as people he knew, kids his own age, raced to school? He could feel a pressure around his head, mind twisting, but he wasn't seeing a thing.

"No."

Karina's voice shocked him out of his thoughts. That one word held so many different emotions, very few of which he equated to his strong older sister. His head whipped up as his fingers dropped from gripping his hair. Karina had her arms up, fingers trembling as she stared at them. Right after, she hugged herself tightly, curling inward. "We can't. Not until, when?" She turned to him, pleading. "When can we go home? We can go home eventually, right? Please, Maxwell. Tell me we can go home."

Maxwell wasn't sure what convinced him to do it, but he pulled his sister close as she trembled in his grasp, or was that him trembling? He buried his head in her shoulder as everything slammed into him. The pain and fear of the last few days, the changes and emotions, the joy, the despair. He gripped his sister tightly.

He could tell, without looking, that his sister was just sitting there, hugging herself.

He was the only one crying.

Chapter Seven

It was sometime later when he finally managed to get his wits back in order and Karina seemed to calm down as well. He was unnerved to know his sister hadn't broken down, but when she gave him a weak but sincere smile, he knew it would be alright. He pulled back, letting her uncurl from her position. "Sorry."

"What are you apologizing for, doofus?" Karina chided. "Still, thanks."

"Huh?"

Karina seemed to blush as she turned away, mumbling under her breath too faint for him to hear. He leaned forward on all fours, tilting his head enough to catch her expression. "What was that?"

She jerked back and he chuckled, pulling back to sit cross-legged. She glared at him before letting out another breath. "Just for being there, I guess. I didn't think it would hit us so hard, the idea of not going home."

"I know what you mean," Maxwell said, gathering his thoughts. "I think it wasn't just that realization. It was everything that happened lately, I guess it was too much."

"True." She grinned, flicking her finger.

"Ouch." Maxwell yelped as his hands darted to his forehead. "Karina."

She let out a laugh before letting herself fall backward.

Maxwell relaxed as he thought over what propagated the conversation and break down to begin with. As much as he wished it, there was no possible way for them to go back to Claremore. It didn't matter if it was with their mother or not. With Ma still being sick, it made it less likely, plus the government was still after them, along with the whole cure thing. It was impossible.

He sighed, standing up and walking over to Karina before flopping over, his head landing on her stomach. She let out a sharp breath of air and lightly smacked him on the head but didn't push him off. His feet dangled over the side of the bed as his arms crossed over his stomach. "So, maybe, do you think Madeline would be willing to take care of her? Even if I leave?"

Karina's body tensed under him before she sighed. "Stupid." Her voice was faint. "You're only going to hurt her if this happens. You know that, right?"

"Then why did...?"

"I convince her to talk to you? Because I was getting sick of the dance she was doing and I... Emma wanted for Madeline to be happy, and I knew you needed someone else."

Her unspoken words hit Maxwell like a hammer and he shot up, elbows on the bed as his head snapped in Karina's direction, noting how her attention was firmly away from him. "Karina, are you...?"

She sat up and yawned, stretching toward the ceiling. "So, to recap. It would be suicide to stay here, but since we don't have any other options, we will wait until we can't anymore. We'll speak with Madeline to have her watch out for our mother and hope that nothing happens to Lex, though we both know that the likelihood of that is the same as us being able to go home in one piece as soon as we leave. Along with the whole fact we can't go home any time soon, even if we wanted to. Did I cover everything?"

"Kari!"

Karina, seemingly ignoring him, nodded to herself. "Well then, since we're probably entering a shit-storm..."

"Karina!"

"We might as well get some rest." She shot a look toward Maxwell, causing him to clamp his jaw shut, though he still wanted to argue. "We'll be no good if we're tired and panicking. You know this as well as I do. There is also the fact that..." she trailed off and sighed, palm pressing against his cheeks, causing him to yelp. "You never did get a chance to dry your eyes. Now, let's get some rest, got it?"

He didn't get a chance to say a word as she stood and walked straight out the door, jamming it shut as she left.

"Dammit, Kari," he muttered, plopping back on the bed as he stared up at the ceiling, spotting the fluorescent lights that sent an eerily pale glow around the room.

He knew his sister was right. He was well aware. Still, the way she pushed off his concern, how she ignored him, didn't try to let herself cry and just left it at that. It bothered him more than he knew it should. Plus, their conversation only worsened his mood. If he felt trapped, he couldn't imagine how Lex and Karina were feeling. Lex was fearful about when, not if, they found out about his heritage and Karina, well, he knew his sister. She hated being confined. This underground place away from the sunshine and fresh air was probably eating at her nerves. As Karina pointed out, however, what were their options? They couldn't just leave Ma, but... He groaned, letting his jacket sleeve drape over his eyes, allowing them to rest from the harsher light. He hated this, the uneasy feeling that was only ratcheting its way upward with each passing moment. Karina's unspoken words pierced him, knowing full well what Karina meant to say there, and it only made the whole situation worse.

He could almost hear them, the somber tone so out of tune to Karina's usual demeanor, yet no less painful. *"I knew you needed someone else. Someone besides me."*

~ * ~

The week passed and Maxwell was frustrated beyond belief with Karina. Ma was in the infirmary for a good portion of the week, due to complications. He often found either himself or Karina at her bedside, checking on her. She was fine. At the same time, it was worrying and solidified the notion that she wouldn't be traveling with them any time soon. Karina avoided him in a way that seemed natural, but he knew his sister. There was no way she wouldn't meet up with him at least once while they were trying to get a grasp of the place. Even Madeline had trouble finding time to get the two of them together.

Well, at least with them going their separate ways, they would get a better layout of this underground bunker, especially since his own mental map of the place was starting to look like a drawing done by a baby with way too many crayons and paint.

Lex was usually held up in his room or scanning over the information they collected from the gated community so far. As for Madeline...

Maxwell glanced sidelong toward the girl next to him, who was holding his hand lightly. He had to admit, she was very pretty. Yeah, he told his sister a while ago that he wasn't interested, but that was because he didn't know her. Heck, right now, Karina probably knew more about her than he did, but...

She glanced at him and smiled softly, a hint of worry shining on her face. "You okay?"

Maxwell shook his head before nodding. She blinked, probably confused by his actions and he chuckled weakly. "Yeah, sorry."

She huffed, but didn't let go, seeming unsure what to say. It was all so awkward. Neither of them knew what to say or do. Yes, they were 'going out', but there wasn't exactly anything to DO down here. Madeline already showed him the few shops that were down here and that didn't mean much. They were reminiscent of the stands from home without the warmth and liveliness.

"Hey, I heard Leon managed to take everything off the camera, including audio. Do you want to watch? I know it may be hard, but..."

Maxwell stiffened and glanced toward Madeline, who was biting her lips. "You want to go, don't you?"

She bit her lip harder, one sharp tooth glinting in the uneasy light of the underground. "Yes," she whispered, seemingly forcing herself to relax, fists slowly unclenching. "It feels like... It feels like an invasion of privacy. I usually..."

"Don't feel that way?" Maxwell asked and watched as she slowly nodded, trembling. Maxwell sighed. "I think that's a good thing."

Her head snapped his direction. He noticed the shock, her attention firmly on his with an expression of wonder and worry. He shifted, slightly uncomfortable, though he did note how beautiful her gaze was before he turned away. "I'm just saying, that means you cared. No, that you do care. Something I've noticed while here this week. Not many people here CARE." He emphasized the word and glanced sidelong at her. "They imitate concern, but there is a detachment in this place. Everyone is here for a different reason, though they have the same primary goal."

His words seemed to jog something in Madeline as she turned away, her hair falling softly over her slender shoulders. He sighed. "You've been watching out for Karina and me since we arrived. I mean, before, you could have left us alone."

"NO!" Madeline's voice echoed down the hall, startling him as she turned to him, grabbing his wrists as she leaned forward. Her face was close to his, very close, though she was a bit shorter, which he noted with surprise. "I couldn't." She bit her lip, glancing askance. "After you did so much, you and your sister, to help Emma, how you apologized, even though I'd hurt you by lying to you and pushing off your requests, how you trusted me enough to tell me what's going on, to save your mother. How you trust me now, though we used you to attack the community. Don't lie and say you weren't affected by that." She tilted her head back up at him with a piercing, pained expression. "I could see it, when you got back. It wasn't just Emma's death that damaged you two. The whole situation hurt you and your sister, your friend." She shook her head. "I didn't want you witnessing this part of me, the part where I can so easily kill and send people to kill. The worst thing is I'm so HAPPY. Happy that we destroyed that community."

Maxwell stiffened and Madeline seemed to realize, stopping in her tracks. "I..."

Maxwell shifted, finding himself pulling away from her, more than a little uncomfortable. "Madeline—"

She quickly grasped his hand. "I'm sorry." The words fell out of her mouth as she grabbed his attention, cutting off whatever he was going to say. "I know I shouldn't feel happy, you've already told me your thoughts on the matter. I know I hurt you every time I bring it up, but I can't help it."

She turned away as Maxwell examined her quietly. "After all, because of all of that, you are here and, well, I'm happy to have you here, though I lied to you like that. I'm happy that you said yes, though I can tell you don't like it here. How you and your sister don't like it here."

Maxwell relaxed, a gentle smile forming against his will on his lips as she stood, shaking in front of him with faint tears. Her words were sincere. She must have spotted his smile because a watery one crossed hers. He chuckled and gently reached forward, before deciding, heck with it, he took her hands, startling her. "You're aware, right? So, there's nothing wrong with that." He spoke up, pulling her forward to continue their walk down the hall, her stumbling after him in surprise. "We all have our own things we don't want others seeing, emotions are..." He huffed. "I think I'll use Lex's term here, utterly stupid. They make us feel things that make no sense to us. Happiness? Joy? They are still just the same as sadness and grief. It's human, and last time I checked, we weren't robots." He shrugged, earning a snort from Madeline.

"So, you do take from your sister in some cases."

"Hey, we are twins, and anyway," Maxwell grinned, "as annoying as Karina is sometimes, I wouldn't have it any other way."

"You look up to her."

Maxwell glanced sidelong toward Madeline, who was watching him in curiosity. He hummed, swinging their clasped hands gently as he responded, "Well, yeah. She's strong, stubborn to a fault at times, but she's kind. She has a stupidly adventurous personality that always makes me worry about her. She's also reliable and always there when I need her. We're practically inseparable anyway." He shrugged, earning a giggle from Madeline who glanced forward.

"Yeah, she's something else."

"Considering you were talking to her before asking to go out with me? I'm guessing she helped you with that?" he teased.

Madeline blushed deeply and turned away. "Well, I figured. I mean, she was great to talk with, though her...she could work on her socialization skills."

Maxwell burst out laughing. That was his sister for you. Though he wasn't much better in that regard, but still.

He heard a soft laugh beside him and glanced over. Madeline laughed behind her palm, body practically shaking to suppress the giggles. Her face shone.

He quickly turned away. He had to admit that she was fun to talk to.

"Madeline."

The voice pulled both of them out of their thoughts and Madeline quickly sobered as she spotted Andrew at the end of the hall, arms crossed over his chest and gaze flicking to their clasped fingers, a disgruntled expression on his face.

Maxwell could hardly miss the way she shifted into military mode as he decided to call it. Her shoulders moved back, her head straightened and her hand, which squeezed his for the briefest of moments, twitched to let go. For some reason, he held on, startling her enough to momentarily break her from that strange stance. A warmth shone for a moment before she nodded and returned to her formal posture, this time without letting go. "It seems that they are all set, do you want to come?"

Maxwell hesitated before he sighed. He didn't want to watch, but he also wanted to know what their reaction would be. He checked his phone, glancing at the already made text message he had ready to send to Lex if it all went downhill, but he wasn't sure if it would be enough. He knew something like this was coming, but... He shook his head and walked over with Madeline beside him. Andrew turned and headed into the main room. Most people were still working on their projects, but a few stood around Leon and his computer. Sound was already playing from the speakers, soft enough not to disrupt the others, but loud enough to still be heard. Maxwell took in a breath and walked over in time to note that they were in the underground tunnel that connected the outer community to the gated community. Leon glanced toward them. "I fast-forwarded to when the two teams split up." Madeline nodded, professionalism showing once more, though she didn't let go of his hand.

Maxwell peered over, watching the choppy, yet still clear camera as it bounced with Emma's steps, the words sounding almost whiny over the speakers as they split up. Lex and Emma went one way, heading toward the right. Out of the corner of the camera, it was easy to spot himself and his sister heading the other direction.

"Why did you want to join me?"

Emma's voice caught Maxwell off guard, almost painful to his ears, especially knowing that this was the last time he heard her and, as Madeline mentioned, it was supposed to be private. He saw them walk through the barren halls, curious. Was this why Lex decided to go with Emma?

"I could ask the same to you. Why did you have your comrades break off when it was clear that I, your informant, was leading you to where your objective is?" Lex seemed to want to say something else, his voice deepening slightly at the informant part before continuing.

The camera rustled, moving up and down in a shrugging motion. "Contingency plan. Just in case..."

"Just in case what? I threw you all to the wolves?" Lex's voice was so unamused, Maxwell had to suppress a chuckle. "I could have done that any number of times, including at the end when you idiots decided to just bang on the door like it was nothing." There was a moment of pause as the camera swiveled enough to show Lex peering up at a set of flashing red lights, embedded into the ceiling. "Let me guess, those sirens are your doing as well?"

Madeline clenched and he winced at the same time that Emma said, "How...?"

"It's the same reason you had your friends split off earlier. You have another reason to be here, one that, while I'm not particularly thrilled about it, the twins would outright have your heads over." Those words seemed to catch some attention from the surrounding people.

"Smart boy." Wilma's voice caused Maxwell to jump, noting as a few more people wandered over. The sound of keys clacking and conversation quieted slightly as she stopped behind Maxwell and Madeline, briefly giving their tangled hands a cold glance before focusing back onto the camera.

"...what is that?" Emma's voice was cold, filled with such ice as to drop the temperature in the entire room.

Lex seemed to ignore it, just like he usually did, continuing on with an unbroken step just a bit ahead of Emma. "The fact that you used our invading of the underground as a means of entrance into the gated community...for not just the five of you."

"And what's wrong with that? You're from outside the community as much as us. Don't you want to get out of their shadow too? Or is it that you've grown so used to living here that..."

"You have no idea." Lex glared back at Emma. Everyone watching the video clip jerked back slightly at the venom in his voice and the shadow cast over Lex's face. "Why do you think my earlier statement stands? I don't care in particular what you do, but Maxwell and Karina do. The last thing I want on their minds during all this is that it's their fault if something happens to this community..."

Maxwell felt a hint of fondness as he listened to Lex's words, a weak, but gentle smile falling onto his face. Madeline glanced at him and he felt a squeeze that seemed almost reassuring before she loosened up. She was sweet in that way.

"But it won't be! They'll be heroes for—"

"For what? For helping to..." Lex shook his head. Maxwell was grateful his friend hadn't continued that train of thought. "Come, let's hurry, we don't have time to waste here, arguing."

Maxwell watched them run through the halls, meeting back up with Karina and himself. He winced as he spotted Karina's almost dead expression and his own panicked one. He felt Madeline shift, her shoulder pressing into his and he glanced over, noting that she was still watching the camera avidly. Did she do this on purpose? Unconsciously? Either way, he appreciated it. He turned his attention back to the clip, seeing them finding Ma and fleeing from the place.

He bit his lip, almost hard enough to bleed, Emma's words about the 'monsters' of the gated community still rung in his ears, not helped by the actual recording reminding him. There stood Caym in all his cold measured glory. Blonde hair hung around sharp features, accentuating the gray cold irises. He held a semi-off smile on his face and his words were as biting as Maxwell remembered. "Lex, were you about to renege on our deal?"

He could feel everyone around him stiffen, all attention jerked to him, but Maxwell ignored it as he continued to watch the recording, seeing himself speaking in shock. "Deal?" His voice sounded so hesitant and uncertain through the recording.

"The deal was reneged when Father died. I have..."

Father? A few people mouthed, uncertainty shining on their faces as Madeline's grip slowly tightened to the point where he was starting to lose feeling, but at the moment, he didn't care, his sole focus on the computer. He briefly noted that there was no longer any clacking or conversation. It was as if all attention had been pulled from other work to the video in front of him. He watched as the scene unfolded that would decide what their next course of action would be.

"Nothing to do with it? Well then, what about this?" Caym's gaze flitted to the camera and Maxwell realized, with shock, that Caym actually noticed the camera attached to Emma. How? He wasn't sure, but the way Caym spoke was directed more to the camera than to any of them. How hadn't he noticed at the time? Oh, right, he had been preoccupied with Ma, his sister and the burning community. "It seems like you've teamed up with the Resistance. I wonder what they will do to you if you go with them."

"He'll be fine. He isn't..." Maxwell heard his voice crack and felt as Madeline's other arm curled around his bicep.

He wanted to run, to do something else. His free hand flipped his phone open carefully, knowing the screen was already on the text function and waited, hovering above the button as Caym's ultimatum cut him off.

"So, they won't do a thing if they find out he's the son. No, brother of Enthrope's head chief?"

Maxwell wasn't sure if he ever heard such a deafening silence. All movement froze.

The scene continued to play, but Maxwell doubted anyone was listening anymore.

"Leon."

Wilma's voice startled Maxwell so badly, he almost pressed the button. He knew she was behind him, but the word seemed to resonate through the room. He glanced back, only to flinch. Wilma's intimidating presence startled him much more than he would like to admit. Why did she seem like a predator all of a sudden? "Replay that last scene. Now." The steel in her voice caused him to stiffen as her attention trailed from him to Madeline. "Madeline, unhand the boy, we don't..."

"He's not involved." Madeline spoke sternly, shifting so she was slightly in front of him. "Him, nor his sister. I know that."

"They obviously knew."

"Here." Leon's voice was quiet, as he hit the replay, and those same, death-clanging words rang out. Leon made sure to pause this time, frozen on everyone's scared and shocked faces seen in the camera.

Wilma stared at the screen before sharply turning on her heels to the rest of the people. Maxwell almost shrunk into Madeline's embrace, suddenly grateful she'd defied her mother and hadn't let go. For the room was suddenly burning and freezing at the same time. A rage whipped up, practically vibrating in the air. His finger went to slam on the button when Wilma grabbed his wrist and tugged it out of his pocket, pulling him forward away from Madeline in the same movement. He yelped as he stumbled forward, only stopping when Madeline dug in her heels and pulled back. "Boy, what were you about to do?"

Maxwell winced at the grip, feeling like he was going to snap between the two women.

"Let my brother go." Karina's voice rang out around the room.

She had her phone out and she appeared out of breath. She stuffed it away and hurried over, almost shoving Wilma away and standing in front of him as Madeline pulled him back, checking over his wrist. He was surprised. While anger burned in Madeline's gaze, she was gentle.

"You're not angry?" he whispered, soft enough for only her to hear as Karina snapped at Wilma behind him.

Madeline's eyes darted up to him, fire burning. "Oh, I'm plenty pissed, at you, at this situation, at that friend of yours." She spat the last bit out before returning her focus to his wrist, conflicted. "But you.... I heard from Leon how Emma died. Though they didn't have audio at the time, video worked and, well, she'd been willing to protect you two and..." She bit her lips. "I don't know about that 'friend' of yours."

Again, the word was spat out, causing Maxwell to wince, but she ignored it as her fingers gently rubbed circles into his wrist, soothing the pain. "You're not from the gated community. I know that. Just like we all suspected." She shook her head and tilted her head up to him. "I want to believe that you two are good. That you aren't with those monsters."

"Lex is still our friend." Maxwell spoke softly, matching Karina's words with ease as she said the same much louder.

Wilma's response, however, cut off all farther conversation and caused Maxwell to feel anger thrum through his veins, along with fear.

He heard a sharp thwack followed by a loud thud and clang. He whipped around. Karina cradled her cheek, pushing herself up with her other trembling hand. Her legs were tangled and her elbow was bleeding slightly from slamming into the cement flooring. Thankfully, she managed to cradle her head in time, from what he could tell, but... He wrenched away from Madeline, who let him go. He squatted beside Karina, checking her over before glaring up at Wilma, who only peered down her nose at them. All the words he wanted to say, all of them, ended up stuck in his mouth, slipping out only in a low growl.

"Mother—"

"Enough, Madeline, you're lucky you're my daughter, or I would have you whipped for your insolence. These two are just as much at fault for this treason as that scum."

"No, they aren't." Madeline hurried in front of Maxwell and Karina. Maxwell could almost feel her shaking, pale and taut. "They are just like their mother, victims."

"Madeline," Karina voiced quietly, wincing slightly as she sat up, leaning heavily into Maxwell.

She was cradling her head, a bruise already starting to form on her cheek from what was probably a hard slap. He could feel his anger sear upward. What was the reason for attacking his sister? She did nothing. How could that woman hurt her like this?

Karina must have sensed what he was feeling, because she quickly sent him a look that caused him to pause. She was pissed, he could tell, but she was also holding back and practically demanding him to do the same. He hated it, but he knew she was right. If he put himself out there now, it would only end badly. He would have to leave it to Madeline and hope for the best. He tuned back into the argument, spotting as Madeline slashed her arm to the side, other hand in a tight fist.

It was Wilma who spoke. "Yes, their mother is a victim, and I agree she is not a part of this, but these two were willingly working with that thing. I don't care if they are friends or related. Anything and anyone from those disgusting places has no place here. You know that. Now..."

Wilma sent the two of them one last glower before turning to the rest of the group, who were either sending them disgusted looks, or were clambering amongst themselves for a chance to get at the 'damn Richie.'

Wilma's arms spread wide as she spoke, tone clear. "What should we do with this liar and imposter?"

Murmurs filled the room, words more sinister than the next: torture, maim, murder. They revolved around Maxwell's head, making him feel sick. He pulled Karina close. She didn't protest, shaking badly as the pressure and hatred filled the air. Though, then again, that could have been him shaking as well. It was hard to tell.

One particular voice spoke. "He's a fraud. So, treat him as one."

Maxwell couldn't convince himself to acknowledge the voice, to turn his head as the person continued to speak with venom and disgust, "He'll have information, being related to the head of Enthrope. We can use that to avenge Emma." For the voice that spoke those words, that caused a cheer to ring through the room and for Wilma to demand Lex's capture.

It was Leon.

Chapter Eight

Karina felt her heart stop as the people flooded out of the room, snakes after a mouse. She wanted to get up and run. Though she wasn't sure if that was toward where Lex was or away from this place. She never thought she would think of Lex as a mouse. Her hand tightened around her phone as her cheek and body throbbed. She'd been able to send a message, but...

Wilma turned to her, her features twisted into one of contempt, and she felt a surge of hatred. "You and that boy behind you are lucky." Her voice was soft, probably would have been pleasant, if it weren't for the ice in her words and the stiffness in her frame. That and the fact that Karina was still on the floor from that person hitting her, that too. "I, and everyone else here, cannot stand traitors, especially people from the gated community. You will do well to remember that. To remember the mercy, I and my people are giving you now."

"What about our mother?" Karina glared, as she felt the need to tremble under Wilma's upended glare.

Her brother helped her to her feet, keeping her steady and she didn't resist, only sending him a quick nod of gratitude before turning back toward the cold woman.

"Your mother has no involvement with the situation, a victim of unfortunate circumstances. She will be fine." With that, Wilma turned, walking briskly away.

Maxwell seemed to hesitate. It wasn't hard for Karina to guess what he was thinking with the way his fingers twitched while holding her as he stared at the retreating mob.

"Don't." She whispered quietly, catching him off-guard.

"But..."

"We can't do anything if we get caught up in that mob as well." Noting his anger and frustration, she continued. "I hate it too, but you noticed as well as I did what Madeline did for us."

Maxwell's fingers tightened on her arm enough to cause her to wince. He promptly loosened his grip, a little pained and apologetic. "Right, sorry." He let out a breath before turning to Leon. "Why?"

Leon slowly pushed his glasses up, one arm dangling over the chair. "Why what?"

"Why did you suggest such a thing? Lex helped you guys."

His voice trembled, but Karina was slightly surprised to note it wasn't in fear. It was in a barely subdued fierce anger. Madeline stepped up onto Maxwell's other side as he let go of Karina.

Andrew stood behind Leon, staring at the boy in a mixture of curiosity and, shock?

Leon examined Maxwell and Karina, the disgust plain on his face. "You know why Arik hated you? Went after you?" Leon hissed.

Karina curled inwards, surprised, and Maxwell took a step back. Karina grabbed his sleeve, pulling him close and he didn't resist. "He saw the same thing I did. Emma's anger and sacrifice. Emma was one of the cornerstones of our group and you just...you three ripped her away."

A rage Karina never noticed before seemed to linger in his words and posture. "I feel terrible that I was part of the reason for Arik and Mitchell's untimely end, but I know both of them would have preferred dying like that than like she did."

Karina's breath hitched. Wait, did he know?

"What do you mean?" Maxwell leaned forward as Leon turned toward his computer, before speaking once more.

"Maxwell and Karina Elifer, do you know how I got your names? Your first and last names?"

Maxwell stiffened, as Karina felt her heart drop. Had they told them? She couldn't remember for the life of her.

"Leon, what are you saying?" Madeline's voice came out in a whisper.

"I got curious, just like you two, why these two weren't sick like us." His voice was cold, calculating. "I did some research, dug into the archives. I knew what to search for, so I dug into the information on their mother. Do you know what the Richies were researching on her?"

Karina wasn't sure if her heart was beating or not. Her breath caught in her throat and her head spun.

"Leon, this isn't like you." Andrew's voice was gruff, yet worried.

"Of course, it is." He spoke softly, pushing his glasses up. "The quiet one, the one you don't notice, the geek without a personality. It's not that hard to stay in the background with such strong personalities like Madeline's, Emma's or Mitchell's, but now two of them are gone and it's Maxwell's and Karina's fault."

"No, it isn't. No one here is to blame for what happened," Madeline spoke sharply.

Leon was silent for the longest time before he returned to his typing. "From what I managed to scavenge from the records, Veronica Elifer was confirmed to have a partial, if degrading, immunity."

"Wait, immunity?" Andrew asked, hesitation ringing in his voice.

Karina took a step back, her movement in sync with Maxwell's.

"Correct. Which means those two can very well have partial immunity as well." Leon's piercing gaze met their own. "And they know it."

Madeline and Andrew whipped around to face them, shock clear on their faces.

"You said yourself Mom's immunity was degraded," Maxwell bit out, voice stammering for good reason, in Karina's opinion. After all, it wasn't normal for her brother to have to lie so strongly. "We didn't know she had immunity. How were we supposed to?"

"This is a shock to us too," Karina managed to choke out and it wasn't necessarily a lie. She only really 'knew' because Maxwell found a paper talking about it, that's it. Did that count?

"That's right." Madeline turned to face Leon, hands on her hips. "Even if they did have a partial immunity, that doesn't mean anything, partial is partial. It just means—"

"That they are somewhat protected against the epidemic," Leon cut in, glaring. "An epidemic which has killed some of our friends just recently. Did you forget that?"

"I didn't."

"Leon, what are you suggesting?" Andrew crossed his arms over his chest, stoic expression back in place.

Leon paused before he sighed and turned back to the screen. "I'll be honest. I don't know. I was just so angry that..."

"That's their FRIEND, not them. They have nothing to do with the gated community. They're victims just like us, just like their mother."

"I know that," Leon shouted, pushing away from the computer and turning to Madeline, shaking for the first time. "I know that full well, but it still hurts. Knowing we trusted someone, only to be lied to."

"We all have secrets we want to keep," Madeline responded, causing Leon to slump.

Andrew sighed and turned away. "I'm not dealing with this," he mumbled before walking away.

Leon watched him leave before turning to Madeline.

"Madeline, I hope for your sake that you know what you're doing." With that, he left, head bowed down.

Madeline watched them go, before almost crumbling in on herself.

Karina could feel Maxwell hesitate. She pulled from her panic, finally catching her breath before gently nudging her brother forward. Maxwell glanced back at her before turning and gently laying a hand on Madeline's shoulder. She didn't start, but she did shift her attention to him with worry. He sent her a gentle smile. "Thank you for standing up for us."

Madeline stiffened, only for her shoulders to sag a moment later. "You're welcome." Her voice cracked, and it didn't take much for Karina to realize why.

She turned to Maxwell, catching his gaze. He hesitated, unsure.

"Madeline, where are they going to go?"

Madeline spared her only a moment before turning downward. "I..." She grew silent, all the determination from earlier gone. Karina couldn't blame her, Wilma wasn't someone she would want to mess with if she could help it, contrary to how she argued with her earlier.

Maxwell's attention drifted toward Karina, as he pulled Madeline into a hug, whether unconsciously or not. "Kari, I think we should wait," he said softly as Madeline shook in his embrace.

Karina peered toward the tunnels. Once again, she hated this feeling of inadequacy. She wasn't able to do anything. She was scared, for herself, Maxwell and Lex. Unfortunately, her options were limited. Trying to quell a mob like that was near impossible, and she didn't want Maxwell to get hurt.

Lex was smart and should have received her message. If not...hopefully, they would have time to find a way to help him before... To be honest, she didn't want to think about it. She hated this feeling. Couldn't she go back to a time when she didn't have to fear for Lex or Maxwell's life?

~ * ~

Why was this happening? What was going on? Did they lie to me? No. No, they never... Madeline's mind raced as she shook, pushing into Maxwell's warmth, briefly noting as he glanced her way, somewhat surprised. She didn't cry, she wasn't supposed to cry. She could still feel her heart pounding, her breath sounding louder and louder in her ears. They were friends with a RICHIE. A damn, traitorous Richie. What was she supposed to feel?

It was overwhelming, something her brain couldn't quite handle at the moment. Why? Why were they friends with the very people she was trying to fight? Not only that, but what about what Leon said? What was she supposed to think of that? That they might be partially immune? Part of her was jealous, achingly so, but another part felt such a weight of relief lift from her shoulders at the thought, the prospect that the one she'd become infatuated with, the one that meant so much to her wasn't going to have to deal with this...this thing. That, surprisingly enough, was what finally allowed her to calm down. She took a deep steadying breath, trying to get her thoughts back in order. There was too much that needed to be done for her to be in panic mode.

Though whether that work was to help Maxwell and Karina or her mother, she wasn't sure.

Actually, who should she help? Fear still trailed up her spine from her mother's expression and words, a phantom pain slashing down her back caused her to shiver, pulling away from Maxwell, startling him. She already disobeyed Mother a lot. She was on very thin ice.

"Madeline," Maxwell's voice jerked her out of her thoughts. "I don't...I don't mean to make this difficult for you. Just point us in the right direction and..."

Madeline shook her head, stopping him in his tracks. Karina watched, fingers twitching but staying silent. "No." She straightened her back. "We should probably check on your mother first and make her aware of the situation. That's as far as I will help. Alright?"

A relieved and warm smile bloomed on Maxwell's face as Karina huffed, but nodded. "Alright, then. Can we go?"

"Kari." Maxwell turned. "Well, I guess I can't fully argue for once. Still... Thanks, Madeline."

Madeline, if she were being absolutely cliche, felt her heart skip a beat as Maxwell turned his warm green eyes back onto hers and gestured, calling her forward. She took one step, then another.

She was disobeying her mother, but was it wrong?

~ * ~

Lex coughed, bending forward as metal clanged, snapping around his wrists tighter than necessary. Curses and spit shot his way with equal momentum as he was dragged through the metal halls. He was grateful for Karina's warning, but it hadn't been able to buy him much time. He'd been with their mother, and, as a result, farthest from the outside doors. Resigned to his fate, he told her what to tell the twins. He expected this anyway, so he contacted Antonio a few days prior, seeing if he was willing to set up a ride to at least get them out of the area. He managed to send a quick message after Karina's text, but it was still too early. He wasn't sure if the ride would be here in time.

He figured the twins would be okay, what with Madeline's support and the fact that they weren't actually related to him. However, he couldn't be too careful. He gave Veronica the phone number to contact

Antonio, as well as an apology to give to the kids. Right after that, the doors were slammed shut, stopping anyone from escaping. At that point, he just simply waited, unable to do anything else in the limited time that he had. He heard the pounding of footsteps, and the sharp shouts, crying for vengeance and pain.

Their attention shifted toward the doorway.

"Leonard."

"It's Lex." Lex sent a weak smile over to Veronica. "Just tell the twins what I told you, okay? I'll..." Lex trailed off and sighed. "No point in saying that phrase." He pushed himself to his feet. "I've gotten soft. I guess I can't keep calling them idiots if I'm doing the same thing as them." He chuckled.

Veronica turned, uncomfortable and apologetic. "I'm..."

"Don't apologize. You're still recovering and the twins did warn me." He briefly noticed that he was somewhat trembling. He chuckled morosely as he clenched his fists. He hadn't felt this terrified in a long time. Not since Allen...even when home, he wasn't terrified, he was more worried, scared and nervous. This? His thoughts shifted to the burning bodies of the gated community. The remaining ringing of the hoots and hollers of the Resistance members as they poured through the busted gates, killing everyone in sight. He thought he was used to death. He'd taken more than enough lives in the past, but those flames, the way the people here rejoiced at the slaughter was another thing entirely.

He tilted his head up just as the door slammed open. It was the last thing he could follow. The mini mob, for there was really no other word for it, came in, surrounding him in no time. Veronica let out a yelp of surprise, but the group ignored her. They grabbed Lex and threw him forward. He stumbled, trying to catch himself, only to find a foot sticking out. He twisted, but was unable to stop himself from sliding across the floor, wincing as pain shot up his side. He was only grateful he was no longer sick, or that would have hurt a lot worse.

He rolled, twisting and turning to try to get out of the people's grasps, thoughts flying faster than he could follow, but it was useless in the tightly filled corridor and, in no time, he could feel fingers, digging at his skin, as someone kicked out his legs. He was pulled down the hall.

When he tried to kick out, one of the mob stomped onto his leg. They stopped dragging him long enough for the man who'd stomped his leg to put all his weight on it. He suppressed a sharp howl as something cut into his skin, digging deep.

Lex mentally cursed, unable to hold back the grimace as he was tugged forward once more, feeling the blood coating his pant leg. At least it wasn't to the bone, though he couldn't say how far off it was. He wasn't sure how long he was pulled roughly down the halls. He would occasionally struggle, only for them to stop dragging and for one of the mob to kick him or spit on him. At one point, one of them pulled out a knife and slashed at his cheek. He could feel throbs of terror pulse in his veins, his sight narrowing in barely hidden panic that he was desperately trying to keep at bay. Soon enough, he could tell they were close to the jails that Madeline spoke of, the walls turning more grayish then metallic. What were they going to do with him? Part of him thought they would have killed him on the spot, but it seemed that wasn't the case. It almost made the feeling worse. The faces all seemed to blend together, all glares, curses and the occasional moments of vindication. His ribs, arms and legs smarted. His clothes were ripped and tattered from being dragged unceremoniously across the floor for so long.

There was no way he would have been able to run, not in a place he knew almost nothing about. He didn't know where he was, not having figured this place out within the one week span. One week did not give him enough time to get a full layout, especially with Wilma at his side at almost all times. He heard a clang and tilted his head slightly to see a metal door swing open. The fear went up a notch, but he quickly schooled his expression, hoping desperately they hadn't noticed.

A cursory glance of the room was enough for his mind to partially shut down. To one side was a rack of items he had no wish to experience and a little off from the middle was a table with straps. It seemed that wasn't where they were heading though. Once they were to about the middle of the dull colored room, still a few feet away from the table, the duo who'd mainly been dragging him there let go. He collapsed, quickly catching himself, only to wince as a hand grasped his hair. He bit his tongue as he was jerked roughly upward. He came face to face with one of the people he saw working in the communications center and occasionally interacting with Wilma. A bleeding line stretched down the man's cheek, a wound of the third stage, as a wicked grin crossed his face. He smelled strongly of cologne and smoke. His breath caused Lex to curl up his nose against his will. The man must have seen because, as Lex felt metal clamp onto his wrists, pulling them behind his back, the man before him slapped Lex hard across the cheek. Unable to turn with the tight grasp on his hair, Lex couldn't help but hiss, pain singing from the stinging wound.

"You should have stayed in the gated community and burned with the rest of them."

Lex briefly wondered if the twins were able to mention that he was the one who helped, but he doubted that would do anything to pacify the angry crowd that swooped down on him. He felt something cold touch his neck and he caught his breath. Were they serious? Handcuffs, he could understand, but... He ended up holding his breath as metal, cold and hard, snapped around his neck. He felt a sharp kick to the side as the man holding his hair let go. Unable to catch himself, and pained from the suddenness of the kick, he slammed into the floor. He managed to twist his head so it wasn't completely face first, but that didn't mean much. He bit his lip harshly, tasting a trickle of metallic ichor as it trailed past, wondering what they were doing. He blinked. It was all he could do not to curl inward as his attention was caught by the crowd standing around him. One or two sneered down at him, others seeming encouraged and pacified. He spotted someone squatting down next to him, arms draped between her legs as she smiled sweetly. The same way Mother would during a party at home. Light fingers tilted his head up, holding his chin firmly as he stared straight at the woman with a sharp glare.

"Such a handsome boy." Her smile turned into a scowl. "Wasted on you putrid Richies. If it wasn't for the information you have, we would kill you now. A slow painful death just like your kind has caused to our people. We would leave you to rot just like you did to us and have been doing." She gripped Lex's jaw tight before letting go and standing up, peering down at him. "I hope you rest up. We," she gestured to the surrounding crowd who glowered and leered down at Lex, "we all have a lot to talk with you about. You damn Richie."

With those words, Lex felt the same hands from before grab his arms and wrench him up. He couldn't stop the yelp as he was tugged at an angle he highly doubted he was supposed to be in, shoulders twisted almost backward and above him. He tried to tilt his head back as he automatically leaned forward to compensate for the angle. Unfortunately, someone noticed and grabbed the chain that seemed to be attached to his neck shackles. He felt something tug, and coughed as the shackle tightened on his neck, forcing him to look up anyway. He spotted a hook overhead, embedded into the ceiling, and could see the chains draping over them, keeping him angled. He licked his suddenly dry lips, tasting the hints of metal from when he bit down too hard. He was already trembling with the weight of his own body as he tried desperately to keep himself up at an angle that wouldn't snap his shoulders out of their sockets. If he let go, dropping even a little bit, he knew he would dislocate his shoulders. That would be all he needed.

He tilted his head down just enough to see the departing crowd. He heard the door clang open and watched as most of the people filed out except for two, the man and woman from earlier. Fingers tapped on the woman's thigh as she examined him, gaze piercing. "Don't worry, hon, we'll be back after the meeting. Wilma is our leader, after all. She'll decide your fate."

"Wilma will probably just say have at it." The man shrugged and the woman followed his movements, turning.

"That's probably true. Still, I know I wasn't the only one who wanted to stay here and have a little...chat."

"He's not spoken a word since we found him. Wouldn't even scream when they slammed that dull-bladed boot into his shin."

"How DID he get that, by the way? Too bad it didn't cut all the way through, but still, I could have sworn..." The discussion faded as the door clanged shut, allowing him to let out a heavy breath. He could hear the faint drip of blood trailing down his leg, even as the sticky feeling coated his left cheek. Speaking of, how much did he lose just on the way here? It wasn't an encouraging thought. Though, he wasn't in an encouraging mood. The room was quiet, only a faint humming from the overhead florescent breaking the silence. Lex forced a breath through his nose, and slowly out of his mouth, focusing on his pounding heart. His fingers clenched and unclenched above him as he put his thoughts in order.

They hadn't killed him right away. So, was what that woman said right? Did they want him for information? The thought sent a trill of panic down his spine. He swallowed harshly. He knew what was in store for him. He could easily tell from the glares sent his way, and even the pain that was pounded into him on the way down those long corridors. Being stretched like this wasn't helping his injuries. His body wanted him to curl inward, to hold his ribs to reduce the pain. His mind screamed what a bad idea that would be. He briefly wondered, once again, what happened to the twins, only to let out a weak chuckle. Blood slipped into his mouth and he spat to the side, coughing. He was being an idiot. An utter and complete idiot.

It was fully his choice. He knew this would happen. He expected it. He could have left any time. He could have gone to his brother, but he didn't. A part of him knew he couldn't have, even if he actually wanted to, fearful for both his brother and his brother's sanity. He closed his eyes, a faint red glow from the florescent shining through his closed eyelids. He would have to hope for the best...and expect the worst.

~ * ~

Maxwell followed as Madeline slowly led them down the corridors, her thoughts seemingly distant. It was quiet, much quieter than he was used to. He shook his head and stepped next to her. "Madeline, are they going to bring Lex to the jails?"

Anger flashed through her posture before she began to slow, semi-ashamed. "I guess I should tell you." She took a deep breath before continuing, "You are right. They probably already dragged him there. We have one just for traitors or spies. Anyone captured from the gated community, really. It's rarely used, but..."

"What's in there?" Karina demanded, her voice hitching up in pitch.

Madeline turned to her with a haunted gaze. "You're better off not knowing."

"Are you saying...?"

"They're going to torture him?" Karina finished off his choked words with a slight shriek of panic.

Madeline winced, confirming their words. Maxwell exchanged a scared expression with Karina.

"We need to hurry to Mother," Karina spoke, the fact that she didn't say Mom indicated just how frightened she was. "We have to make sure what Wilma said was true, that she's alright."

Maxwell nodded before turning to Madeline. Madeline hesitated before turning. "Well then, let's go, the infirmary isn't much farther..." she trailed off, as she returned to her original pace. For a few metallic steps, she was silent until she let out a sigh. "I know I already said this, but I'll not do a thing in regards to that friend of yours. I'm like-minded to everyone else here when it comes to the fate of a Richie."

Maxwell gritted his teeth. Yes, she said that and he still wanted to yell at her that Lex had NOTHING to do with it. That he was a victim just like them. That he tried to RUN from there. It didn't matter though, he knew his words would fall on deaf ears. He convinced himself he was grateful she'd already done as much as she did for them. He wasn't so close-minded as to miss the way she was practically fighting with herself not to stop right there and turn on them. "Lead the way," he pushed out grudgingly.

Madeline must have noticed his brimming anger, and Karina's barely put together expression.

"Right," she whispered.

Her whole posture seemed to slump, a despondent cloud dwelling around her. They continued through the halls, their footsteps and breaths ringing off the walls.

"Speaking of... Where is everyone?" Karina spoke. "Well, despite the obvious."

"Probably meeting in the atrium. They'll stay there until a consensus will be made on who will take care of your friend."

Maxwell hated the way she said those last words, but he pushed it away as they found themselves promptly in front of the infirmary.

"Maxwell? Karina? You're okay," their ma choked out as the two stepped inside. She was sitting up, fingers clenched in her lap and whole body trembling.

"Mom, we're fine, but Lex..."

Ma shook her head and gestured them forward, her gaze flitted to Madeline before turning back to them. "Lex knew they were coming. He got your message."

Maxwell heard a faint gasp from Madeline but ignored it. However, Ma noticed and paused, turning to the still open doorway. She stared at Madeline, causing the girl to shift, looking left and right before muttering a, "I'll just be waiting outside, let me know if you need me."

She stepped back, reaching up to close the door.

Maxwell caught her gaze, completely conflicted. Her gaze was the same; hurt, angered, sad and...lonely. That was it, that was what he'd been seeing since he met her. Though there were so many people down here, she was lonely and now, the people she decided to help were pushing her away.

He sighed and caught Karina's attention. She noticed and huffed, quickly glancing between the now closed doorway and Maxwell. "You want to say something to her, don't you?"

He grimaced, but didn't argue.

"Maxwell, dear..."

Maxwell turned to Ma, unsure what to do.

She seemed to notice and smiled softly. "You know, it's okay. The only reason I didn't say anything in front of her was for your sake. If you trust her, then by all means, let her know. I think she needs to hear it."

"Mom's right." Karina sighed, arms crossed. "She did help us, and we both know that wasn't easy."

"You don't have to tell me that." Maxwell grudgingly agreed, getting a sharp look from both his sister and mother. Yet, it made him feel a little better as he turned and hurried up to the doorway. He opened it, causing Madeline to start, turning to him, eyes wide and brimming with tears, only confirming his earlier realization.

"Maxwell..." she stuttered out, seeming a mix of shocked and unsure. Her fingers were tightly curled into her clothes and she was fidgeting from foot to foot.

"Sorry." He spoke softly. "We didn't mean to push you away like that. You were already helping us, there is no point in stopping you now, right?"

Madeline huffed, turning away. Her fist tightened into her clothes. "I am well aware of what meetings I should and should not intrude on. As I stated, I will not be helping you any further than this." She spoke, that same monotone. "Plus, it is not my place to interfere in such—"

"Would you stop that?" Karina called, startling both of them.

Karina popped up behind him, chin over his shoulder, causing Madeline to jump. "I think Maxwell here has probably already told you, you don't need that stuffy language around us. Now will you two get in here so we can figure out what the hell we're doing already?"

"Karina," Maxwell groaned, yet paused when he heard a weak chuckle.

He turned as Madeline tried and failed to stifle a faint laugh. "Right, sorry."

"You don't need to apologize," Maxwell spoke before heading back inside, dragging his sister with him. Karina rolled her eyes, but let herself be pulled along. Madeline hesitantly followed, closing the door as she did.

Karina pulled away. "So, back to what we were saying. What was Lex telling you?"

Ma held a fond smile on her face before she turned to Karina, the expression dimming. "He knew he didn't have much time. He gave me this and told me to tell you..." Ma trailed off before leaning up to them, placing a gentle kiss to both of their cheeks. "Get out of here."

Karina stiffened and Maxwell felt like he was slapped. "What?" Karina's voice was more a shriek than words. "No way."

Ma shook her head solemnly. "He said you would say that, and to give you this." She held out a crumbled piece of paper. "It has his informant's number on there. He said to call him as soon as you get out of here."

Maxwell took the paper, scanning the contents. He heard faint footsteps as Madeline stepped up to him. She seemed indecisive, stopping a few feet in front of him. He closed the paper, placing it in his pocket as he peered toward her, curious. She seemed to take note of the action but didn't say anything for a bit before focusing back on his face. "He's serious. He really does care for you two."

"Of course. He's our best friend," Karina snapped, stumbling only slightly on the description. Not that Maxwell could blame her, he wasn't sure how to qualify Lex sometimes. He was a good friend...but in some ways, he was almost like a strange family member. He wanted so badly to help Lex. Part of him wished Karina hadn't stopped him from chasing after the mob. The other part rationalized that she was right, it would have been stupid. He shook his head and glanced once more at the number. He knew who the informant was. Antonio...

Ma gave him a gentle smile. She folded her hands across her lap, over the pale sheets and spoke. "That's not what you're doing, is it?"

Karina scoffed. "Hell to the no. The idiot needs a good whack to think we would leave him to be tortured. It's our fault he's here in the first place."

"What Karina said." Maxwell stood, now more determined to get to their friend. "Madeline."

Madeline stiffened before she faced him. "I already told you, I won't help your friend, but..." She bit her lip, shifting from one foot to the other. "You did allow me to stay and you..."

"Madeline, dear. You've already helped enough. Thank you for taking care of my children. They obviously trust you, so that is enough." Veronica stood up, startling Maxwell. Her legs trembled as she took a tentative step or two toward Madeline.

"Ma?"

"Not now, Maxwell."

She shot him a stern expression before walking the rest of the way over to Madeline. She turned the girl to face her, away from Maxwell. She lowered herself a little, catching Madeline's full attention. Her hair shone in the dim lighting as her figure, suddenly seeming frail, trembled. "You've done a lot already. It's not easy, going against a parental figure, going against everything you've known." Her palm gently caressed

Madeline's face, resting on her cheek. "You know as well as I do that they can't stay here, no matter how much they might trust you. It wouldn't matter, whether it was this, or something else, they would have left soon anyway."

"But..."

Madeline gnawed at her lip and Maxwell felt like he was slapped in the face as he realized the other reason why Madeline didn't want to help them. It wasn't just because of Lex.

"You don't want us to leave," Karina voiced out his thoughts and Madeline tilted her head away, confirming their theory.

"I finally found someone who MEANS something to me, who trusts me and wants to be there and..."

Maxwell felt uncomfortable, but it was Ma who spoke, cooing softly. "Just because they're leaving doesn't mean they won't come back. You saw what they did for me and I don't doubt that my son cares for you. He wouldn't have said yes or brought you back in here if he didn't."

Madeline tilted her chin up just a little. Maxwell felt sheepish and uncomfortable as those beautiful, vibrant eyes—her strong gaze met his, mainly because he couldn't deny Ma's words. He wasn't in love with her, far from it, but he did care for her as a friend and, if they had more time to actually talk, maybe...

He nodded, Karina besides him. Ma smiled and turned Madeline's face gently back to her. "See? Don't be afraid. My children won't just keel over or disappear. You've seen how stubborn they are." The words were spoken in a light joking fashion that caused Maxwell's overbearing panic to quell a little, something he only really noticed now as it receded. "And don't forget, I may not be much, but I'll be here as well. Alright?"

Madeline stared at her for the longest time until she leaned into ma. Her fingers clasped her wrist as she trembled. Karina grabbed his wrist and turned him away, pointedly facing away from their beleaguered friend, as quiet sobs echoed in the room.

Maxwell felt anger surge over the panic. Just what had Madeline gone through that would make small acts of kindness seem so overwhelming? All Ma said was that she would be a friend, someone for Madeline to speak to who would listen.

All they did was accept her, though they could have easily ignored her and left her out there.

The fact she broke down because of something like that...

It made him worry more for Ma. Though, he knew there was nothing he could do about it. They couldn't save both Lex and Ma. He would just have to hope Madeline would watch out for her and that Wilma wouldn't do anything...

He shook his head and peered toward his sister. "Karina."

"Don't worry, Maxwell, I know." She spoke firmly, glancing sidelong to him. "We have to work fast though, don't we?"

Maxwell nodded, face set into a grim line. "More than you probably realize."

Karina scoffed, jabbing her elbow into his side, causing his breath to whoosh out in surprise. "Being so dramatic doesn't suit you."

Maxwell glared before crossing his arms. He glanced briefly back toward Madeline before focusing back on his sister. "I'm not wrong," he pointed out, causing her expression to fall.

"No, you are not." She let out a groan before kicking her foot out, deep in thought. "So, what are we going to do?"

Maxwell tilted his head down, chin into his chest. The metal flooring glowed under his feet as he thought. They really needed to know what was going on, but they also needed to make sure Lex was okay. It was also true that they really didn't have much time at all to accomplish either task. "We might have to split up."

"What?" Karina whipped around to face him, hand on her hips. "Last time we did that, it did NOT end well."

"What other choice do we have? Ma can't move from here. Madeline is already sticking her neck out as it is and no one else here will help us." He listed everything off, watching as realization and then annoyance shone from his sister. "Yet we don't have much time before they make a decision dealing with both us and Lex. Just because Wilma said she wouldn't touch us doesn't mean the others will follow suit."

Karina grimaced.

"I can help lead you."

Madeline's voice startled Maxwell and Karina out of their

thoughts, causing both to turn toward the girl. She was wiping her eyes, red-rimmed from crying, yet determination was clear in the way her shoulders were back and her stance rigid. "I agree with Maxwell in that you two will need to split up." She turned toward Maxwell, expression hesitant. "I'll give directions, but..."

Maxwell felt warmth surge through him. "Thank you, that would help us a lot."

Karina seemed to pause before letting out a long breath. "I guess I don't have much room to stand here so, okay, we'll split up."

Maxwell breathed a sigh of relief before gathering his wits for the next battle. He knew Karina wasn't going to be fond of his next statement, but he felt it was best. "Alright than, I'll go to Lex to get him out while Karina checks on what is going on with the others."

Karina nodded along for all of a minute before slashing her arm out, fist clenched. "What? That's dangerous."

In all honesty, Maxwell didn't agree, hating that he had to do this to his sister. Technically, Karina was in more danger, but he knew she could take care of herself and she was much faster than he was. "Either one is dangerous." He kept his voice quiet, calm. "I don't like it any more than you do, but..."

Karina stared at him for the longest time before reaching toward her waist and retrieving her gun. "Here."

He jerked back. The cold metal gleamed in her palm. "What?"

"Take it, you'll..."

"No," he cut in, part out of fear, but mostly out of anger.

He was sending HER into the more dangerous situation, she needed it more than him. He placed his hands under his sister's and pushed the gun back toward her chest. "Keep it. You're going into an area with an angry mob, we've already seen how bad those can get." He shook his head, taking a step back as she stayed frozen. "Please, Karina, I'll be fine."

He would, he knew he would because he wasn't about to leave either his sister or friend here. He peered toward Madeline who was watching in a mix of awe and sad understanding. Turning back to Karina, he noted her lost expression and massaged the bridge of his nose. "Why don't we keep our phones out and connected so we can hear what's going on with the other? Like a bastardized form of a walkie-talkie. That way, we'll be able to tell if something goes wrong, okay?"

Karina hesitated before she slipped the gun back into place and pulled out her phone. Maxwell felt a smile form on his face, glad Karina was willing to work with this ham-handed rescue attempt. As he called Karina's phone, his attention drifted to his mother, who was watching patiently, fondness and pride foremost in her gaze. She happened to notice and smiled.

He hated that he needed to leave Ma so soon after finding her, but they didn't have many options. "Madeline."

Madeline must have seen where his attention was because she grasped his free hand and squeezed. "Don't worry, I'll do my best to watch her for you two, alright?" She faced Karina who chuckled.

"Alright then, let's get to rescuing that idiot."

"Lex?"

Maxwell grinned, amused at her naming decision. She waved it away as Madeline blinked.

"Anyway...so, Maxwell, it shouldn't be too hard, but you'll be taking quite a few turns, so listen carefully." Madeline spoke up, drawing Maxwell back to the girl as she explained the way to the jail.

He could only hope that he would actually REMEMBER all the directions. It would not be a good idea to get lost at this point.

Chapter Nine

Karina felt bad for leaving Madeline here, especially after she helped them with this. Karina might be oblivious a lot of the time, but the fact that her gut was twisted in knots since she arrived told her enough to know to worry about the place. She found she was unfortunately right to worry. The shadowed corners of the underground spoke darkly of the anger and fury brimming under the surface of everyone there, the coldness and ruthlessness she saw during the attack. She hurried to the atrium. After Madeline gave them directions to their locations, Maxwell left in a hurry, having farther to go than she did. She went to follow right after, only to be stopped by Madeline. The girl grabbed a slip of paper and quickly wrote something, shoving it into her palm.

"I promise. I won't let Mother do anything to your mother. At least she acknowledges that your mother is a victim, that will protect her."

Karina gauged Madeline for a moment before a wide grin fall onto her face. "Thanks, Madeline, that means a lot, to both of us." Karina spotted the numbers, before she shoved the paper into her pocket. She would take a better look at it later. She smiled. "Thanks. Oh, and don't worry. We aren't just charging in to help Lex blindly." She waved, leaning on one foot. "We've already got a pseudo plan, Kinda. That means..." She shook her head. "Thanks, Madeline, you've been a big help, and..." she hesitated before turning. "Thank you for being my and my brother's friend."

She heard a faint gasp behind her but ignored it as she hurried out the door, saying one more quick see you soon to Mom as she left. She heard the faint laughter and felt a warmth run through her veins. Yeah, Mom would be alright. She had no doubts that Madeline would keep to her words.

Now, she could focus just on Lex. Helpful, considering that was what demanded her attention right now. Her phone sat heavy in her pocket. She felt annoyed that both she and her brother failed to warn Lex in time. That they were resorting to this ham-handed rescue attempt, as her brother might call it. She heard faint noises and footsteps over the phone, indicating her brother was still connected. It really was a bastardized form of a walkie-talkie, but hey, it worked. She wasn't going to complain.

She turned the last corner, before she quickly stepped back behind the wall. She reached around the corner and carefully peered around, trying to stay out of sight as she examined the atrium. She would have preferred rescuing Lex, but Maxwell was insistent. She knew he would probably be safer as the person to help Lex than to be here, where one of the angered mob might spot him, as he pointed out. Speaking of, boy, were they angry, Karina noted as she peeked around the corner, staying low.

Wilma did a good job riling the people up. They were talking avidly back and forth, words cruel and impersonal. The group of people was much bigger than the mob that left the control room earlier. Karina had no doubt that this was the rest of the base gathered here. They talked of Lex as if he was a piece of garbage to be used as a thing, to humiliate and throw away. She was disgusted. These are the people fighting for freedom? Yet, she knew a mob mentality when she saw it. She saw it enough over the past few months, after all. She wondered what she would think, if she had never met Lex. If she had been subject to the same things as those in that room while living a life in the outer community. She lived a rather safe life, in retrospect, and she knew nothing of what it was probably like for everyone in there.

Still, she didn't think she would be willing to torture a man, especially one who helped them, just because he was from the gated community. She glanced toward Wilma, wondering why the woman wasn't mentioning anything about Lex's help. On either side of Wilma, she spotted two people. A man and woman, respectively. They were dressed a little nicer than some of the others there. Were they higher up on the chain or something? It would make sense that Wilma would have some people working under her. Yet, those two were just as vindictive as the rest of the crowd. The woman was swaying forward and backward on her high heels, humming, a leer on her face. The man had his hands behind his back in an almost militaristic pose, a strange grin on his face. Had Wilma not bothered to mention to those two that Lex was the REASON they got into the gated community in the first place? She supposed not. After all, nothing showed except a grin that twisted her face just the wrong way. Wilma was just like Leon, like Arik and Emma.

All of them held such hatred for the gated community, it messed with their thoughts.

Her thoughts shifted to Martha and she remembered the woman's sudden and brutal outburst at the radio announcement, all those months ago. Karina shivered before turning her gaze back on the group. She almost cursed as Wilma caught her trying to hide, her face turning into an even and unassuming expression. How stupid could she get? She let herself lean out for too long instead of pulling back to think. Heck, she hadn't been fully paying attention because of her thoughts. *Stupid, stupid, stupid.*

"Why, child, what brings you here? I thought you would be with your friend." Wilma's words were spoken in such a way as to silence the crowd, but not to be a shout. It was unnerving, to put it lightly.

Karina gritted her teeth, mentally cursing, but stepped out of the shadows, feeling the attention of the crowd on her. "I would, but I wanted to see what was going on here. I was wondering why you never mentioned the fact that Lex was the reason you were able to GET into the gated community in the first place. That he wanted to be away from it as much as you all despise it." Karina forced the words out, as she felt tendrils of fear crawl up her spine.

She pulled away from her cheek, having felt it twitch in wanting to cradle the already forming bruise.

"Impossible." Someone spoke up from the group.

Another person took over, scoffing. "Turn down a cushy life inside those pearly gates? That's like saying a starved dog would turn down warm food. It doesn't happen."

"They're right." Wilma spoke, as if speaking to only a child, trying to convince her otherwise. "There is no possible reason someone from that scum-driven area would produce a decent human being."

"They're human though." Karina pointed out, stabbing her finger downwards. "I saw them, spoke with them. They fear and they cry and they experience joy just like you or any of us."

"Lies," a person shouted, being caught up by a few more people.

Her anger spiked at the way they seemed to be ignoring her words. She growled. "How the heck did you all manage to get into the gated community? Through Madeline or Emma? Through Leon's technology? No. You saw the video. Lex was willing to HELP you all burn down that community! So why...?"

"So, he's a traitor to his own community as well." Wilma spoke, stepping down from the podium, the crowd split as she walked through. "In some ways, doesn't that make him worse?"

Karina took a step back, or at least attempted to before changing her mind and instead stepping forward, fist up to her face. "If you want to be technical, aren't you all traitors too? To a system that says to remain outside? You all are trapped like rats down here and have the gall to complain when someone who is just as trapped actually manages to escape. This place is no better than a gated community." She slashed outward, anger overriding her thoughts. "You want to be free. I get that. So does he and others from the gated community. You don't need to torture him."

She could hear talking and chatter faintly over her pounding heart. Even so, her gaze was firmly locked on the impassive one of Wilma's.

"There are different types of freedom..." Wilma spoke, voice firm. "We are fighting for everyone's freedom. That Richie you are fond of? He fought for his own alone. What reason is there to treat him with kindness? He would as soon turn on us as he would his own community for that freedom you speak of."

Karina gnawed at her lip as the chatter quieted. Wilma walked forward, moving beside her, head tilted down enough so that her next words were only for her ears. "Considering your own words, you and that twin of yours are no better than that scum of a human."

Karina stiffened as Wilma turned, hand grasping her shoulder tightly, a vice grip if she ever felt one. "Poor child, you have been deluded by one of those vile creatures. They have oppressed us since the closing of the borders. They are the opposite of the freedom we all crave. Don't you want the freedom we offer? A freedom for everyone so that they no longer need to fear for their lives or being?"

"Of course, I do, but this isn't freedom," she said through gritted teeth. "We're all stuck in a hole, quite literally, with no place to go. Just like those from the gated community, just like the people in the outer community, every, single, person is the same." She punctuated the last few words as she glowered at the crowd.

She knew she'd lost, Wilma's earlier words solidified the people's hatred toward Lex, but she couldn't help but dig in one more time, as the grip on her shoulder tightened to almost painful levels.

Wilma shook her head as a few people exchanged looks. "Don't worry, child, we'll help you realize your error."

That was all the warning she got before Wilma pushed her toward the crowd. Thankfully, it was enough. She crouched down, out of the way of someone who tried to grab her before twisting and bolting past Wilma, grasping at her gun before tugging it out. She heard footsteps and spun, letting a bullet rip down the hallway before she continued her spin and returned to running.

Well, this went poorly. She could only hope her brother was doing a bit better.

~ * ~

Maxwell cursed quietly as he slipped past the last guard and up to the door. He hadn't found the keys, and wouldn't be surprised if someone at the atrium actually had them. He peered through the glass window in the door and actually grimaced as he spotted Lex, hanging in the middle of the room. Disturbed greatly by the way Lex was hung, he scrutinized the latch. He bit his lip, partially wondering how Karina was spotted as he listened to his sister argue faintly with the people in the atrium. He was grateful he found a set of headphones, though they were Madeline's, and they worked with his phone. It allowed him to listen quietly. He kept one ear on the argument as he searched for a key. Nothing.

His fear crept up as the words of the argument continued on punctuated by cries or shouts from the rest of the mob. It sent a shiver down his spine. He was glad he convinced Karina to keep her gun, but he was definitely not liking his sister's chances right now. He shook his head, returning his focus onto the lock before him. What could he do to open it?

He stiffened as words met his ears that made his heart skip a beat.

"Don't worry, child." The words were said softly, but in a tone that left nothing to the imagination. "We'll help you realize your error." A sound of rustling, followed by running footsteps and a gunshot was all he needed to hear.

"Shit." The word slipped from his mouth as his fingers trembled, wrenching at the lock.

He needed to help his sister, pronto. He glanced at the guard, spotting the already forming bruise. He stopped the wince, reminding himself that he didn't have the time to worry about knocking people out. He was just grateful he didn't kill him this time. He turned as he reached up to fix the headphones, only to pause.

Of course. He reached up, tugging the hair clip out of his hair and slipping it into the lock. It wasn't a key, and he wasn't a lock-picker, but by gosh, was he going to figure this out. He felt around carefully, feeling resistance and movement. The metal was warm against his skin as he held one hand on the lock, gripping tightly, as the other pushed and prodded.

This is taking too long, his mind supplied, but he quickly shushed it. Finally, after what felt like ages, he heard a click. He pulled the clip out, wincing at its bent and twisted state before slipping it back into his hair. He felt it slip and sighed, tugging it back out and thrusting it into his pocket. He would have to apologize to his sister. He hurried inside, racing up to Lex. He saw a lever off to one side and slowly pulled it. When he noticed the chains loosen, he tugged it sharply down. A wheel screeched, dropping Lex to the floor, where he crumbled, drawing in deep breaths as he choked out a cough. Maxwell hurried over, spotting a table nearby with a key to the chains. *That's cruel in its own way*, he thought. He picked it up and unlocked the bands, seeing the redness and lacerations already on Lex's arms and legs, along with cuts and bruises coating his leg and cheek. He winced, realizing blood was dripping down one leg, a nasty cut near the shin.

Lex groaned and pushed himself up, holding his stomach. "You idiot," he coughed out.

Maxwell rolled his eyes, getting one of Lex's arms over his shoulder as he carefully tugged him up.

"Tell us that after we get out of here." Maxwell grunted, lugging him forward.

Inwardly, he was panicking, both at Lex's state as well as Karina's situation, but there was only so much he could do at the moment.

Any farther thoughts were cut off as a set of shots rang out in his ear, causing him to stiffen. Lex caught his expression before pushing away, swaying for a moment. "I'm going to guess your sister is somewhere else?"

"She..."

"Well then, let's hurry." Lex spoke up, grunting in exertion as he hobbled to keep up with Maxwell's quickening pace.

Maxwell unplugged the headphones from his phone. At least that way Lex could hear as well. He stuffed them in his other pocket though he had no doubt he would probably forget about them. Lex sent him an expression of gratitude.

That was wiped clean a moment later when one more bang, followed by a click, sounded out from the phone.

"She's out of ammo." Lex gritted his teeth, trying and failing to take the lead.

Though, with every step, Maxwell didn't miss the way his features twisted in agony as his feet stumbled. His wounded leg dragged behind him. Still, Lex's words only heightened Maxwell's panic. He could faintly hear pounding footsteps, scrambling. He rounded a corner just as a figure slammed into the wall next to him, held by a young man with a feverish expression. Lex stumbled to a stop as Maxwell slid. He heard a sharp groan and hiss.

"Let go!"

Maxwell didn't have to turn to know who was speaking. He whipped around, sweeping his leg low to catch the man off guard. The man stumbled and Karina wrenched herself free, scrambling back. Her gun was back around her waist, her loose blouse bunched up at its side as if she'd rammed it in. She seemed to be in slight shock and Maxwell didn't have to question why. He grabbed her wrist and turned, racing in the opposite direction. He heard Lex behind him and someone must have seen, because suddenly cries sounded farther back, of outrage and contempt. He took turn after turn, trusting as Karina shouted out directions and Lex backed them up. Finally, they reached the tunnel that turned into dirt and bolted forward. Where was it, where was...there. His palm slammed down on a switch and he heard a rumble as the boiler shifted, yet he didn't stop, darting up the rest of the stairs with the others in tow. To his surprise, when Lex got through, he heard movement and jerked back, the boiler closing behind them.

His gaze darted up to meet Madeline's stern but soft expression. She tossed three bags over, causing him to stumble as he caught two of them and Karina caught the other. "Madeline, what...?"

"I'm not going to let you leave without saying good-bye, and I definitely was not going to let you leave with seeing me crying." She spoke sternly before a faint smile crossed her lips. "I'll see you soon."

Maxwell felt his chest tighten. "Yeah..." He felt warmth flood his veins. "We'll see you again." With that, he turned and raced up the stairs, Lex and Karina in tow. He could only hope nothing happened to Madeline because of them.

~ * ~

Karina followed Maxwell up the stairs, quickly mentioning her conversation with Madeline right after they separated. A relieved smile flashed on his face and Lex appeared amused, if a little weary. That only lasted a short time, quickly fading into silence as they stepped into the main hallway of the home they had walked through only a week before, her thoughts swimming over what just happened. She grimaced, anger flowing through her veins. Both at what they said in regard to Lex and her

113

own ineptitude to DO anything about it. She'd come to terms with the idea of just being the distraction, but...to think her brother needed to save her AGAIN. It hit harder than it really should have.

She couldn't stand it. Stand the feeling of being so...

She heard movement and shifted just in time. Something rang out as a sheen of metal flashed before her. She felt something sharp slam into her. It took a moment, only a moment, before the pain registered and she cried out, almost falling into Maxwell as she clutched onto something, anything. Her leg crumbled under itself. She could feel blood trail down her thigh as she gritted her teeth.

"Nobody else move, or I'll shoot again." The voice that rang in her ears caused her to blink through the pain, shooting a blurred glare toward someone standing at the end of the hall. The boy, or at least, she supposed it was one, was shaking, the gun wavering in his grip. It must have been that kid, the one they saw a week ago. All was silent for a moment, only to be followed by pounding footsteps.

"Max..." the voice cut off. Karina grimaced, recognizing it as Madeline's, before anger filled her voice. "What are you doing? You were trained to give WARNING shots. Not to shoot them."

"They were going to escape..."

Karina only had a moment to note the sharp clack of footsteps before Madeline slammed by, anger rippling from her. "Your training was specific, was it not?" Her voice barely wavered an inch, but it sent a chill up Karina's spine.

"Come on, let's go," Maxwell murmured out of the corner of his mouth, trying slowly to move around the arguing duo.

Madeline shot them a quick solemn look before returning to her berating. The guy tried to raise the gun again, but Madeline promptly took it, shaking a finger into his face, causing the boy to curl inward. Lex was behind them, watching in silence, a tired, yet even expression. Karina limped along with them until they were out the door. The backpacks hung heavy, but she ignored it as they continued, walking down the street, or, well, Maxwell walking while Lex and Karina limped along.

Maxwell constantly peered behind, gently trying to coax both of them forward just that little bit faster. She didn't blame him, she felt herself want to jump at every little noise as they eventually hit a small stand of trees.

At last, getting out of sight of the road and finding a pseudo hiding spot, the trio took a seat with Karina murmuring plenty of curses under her breath, though she already forgot most of them in her anger. She heard movement and turned as Maxwell began examining her leg.

"I'm fine," she muttered, getting a glare for her troubles and a sigh from Lex.

"Idiot..." Lex spoke up before turning to Maxwell.

He winced as Maxwell sent him an unimpressed expression, gesturing to his leg.

"What do you call that?"

"A wound that appears worse than it is. No need to worry over it. Now, do you—?"

"I have the number, yes, but you have him practically on speed-dial." Maxwell returned his attention to examining Karina's leg. "He's your informant."

Lex observed him, then let out a faint chuckle before nodding and stepping away. He snagged a roll of bandages, then moved behind one of the trees, digging into his bag for a moment before swiping the phone and bringing it up just as he slipped out of sight.

Karina snarled as a sharp pain flared up her leg. She shot a look to her brother who grimaced before letting out a hiss. He squatted down, gingerly touching the area. "I'm getting way too much practice with bullet wounds."

Karina huffed. "It's not my fault."

"Of course not."

Karina felt her mouth go dry at her brother's words. They were nonchalant, sure, said in the same tone as talking about the weather, indicating he was distracted. But...

No, that WAS the point. He was distracted because she hadn't noticed the scout who had been standing RIGHT THERE. She'd been oblivious, unobservant, whatever the hell the word was and got shot for it. Just like the past few months and every time. Every god damn time. It put them in danger.

They couldn't move fast because she needed to be bandaged. Sure, Lex was injured, but he was pushing through it. Madeline was putting her neck out there because Karina didn't think of the scout they would have. Lex was captured because she wasn't fast enough, wasn't aware of the situation enough.

Not just now. Her thoughts flashed through the past few weeks, hell, the last few months.

There wasn't a single damn thing she could do. There never was. If she hadn't forced her brother to come out with her, to show him her base camp all those months ago, they would have been home, helping Mom escape.

If she was more aware, Lex and she never would have gotten shot during that riot in New London City.

If she'd listened to her brother, listened to Maxwell when he warned her about that Lydia woman, they never would have been forced into the gated community.

The list just kept going on and on, spiraling through her head without reprieve.

"KARINA."

Karina jerked as Maxwell's voice snapped at her and she yelped, turning to her brother who was huffing furiously, panic practically rolling off of him. "Huh? What...?"

"What were you thinking? I couldn't get your attention at all." Worry was forefront, followed promptly by concern. "It doesn't hurt that much, does it?"

Karina opened and closed her mouth before forcing a grin onto her lips, her cheeks hurting from the effort. "What? Are you kidding?"

She pushed herself to her feet, tentatively testing the bandage. Damn, Maxwell worked fast. She wasn't sure what had happened, but she could put pressure on her leg. She didn't think it over too much. She crossed her arms over her chest, shooting her brother a cheeky smirk. "Something like that isn't going to keep me down. Now, are we going?"

Maxwell looked up to her, mouth open in surprise and still heavy concern. She could feel his searching gaze and made sure she didn't budge an inch, exuding as much positivity as she could. She couldn't suppress the roaring thoughts, but she could at least pretend enough that her brother would ignore it.

He hesitated, as if to ask her a question, only to be cut off by Lex's return, his leg bandaged. "Now that you two are all better, let's get a move on. We need to meet with our ride a bit from here."

He examined Karina, who sighed and waved it off. "I'll be fine, let's just get a move on."

Both males exchanged equally worried expressions before Lex shook his head and turned, heading back toward the road, keeping as much to the shadows as possible.

Chapter Ten

Madeline watched the twins leave, sadness and frustration welling up in her as the scout, Darrel, returned to his seat in a foul mood, gun in his lap and head lolled back. Madeline stared at the closed door before turning just as she heard a faint rumbling from down the hall. She winced, heading to the kitchen to splash some water on her face in preparation for the next bit. Either way, it wasn't going to be good.

The rumbling stopped as she turned the faucet on, letting water splash into the metal sink. She cupped her hands, splashing some on her face and allowing her hair to hang down, obscuring her gaze. The coldness was both refreshing and worrying...no, that wasn't the term she would use as footsteps rang out around the house, along with Darrel's confused comments.

She braced herself before grabbing a towel, wiping her face and turning toward the door as it opened. Her mother's proud and angry figure stepped through. "Madeline, what are you doing up here?"

Madeline turned to her, back ramrod straight. "I was pursuing the twins. I was tracking them after you all left. However, they escaped my notice. I decided to wait here."

"Somehow they still slipped by you?"

"I heard a gunshot and came out to berate Darrel since it might give us away." Madeline spoke, the lie coming out as easily as if she was telling the truth, though it wasn't necessarily wrong. "I saw the door close, but that was it."

Wilma examined her with a practiced eye before turning to the people who were just entering. Madeline withheld a wince as she spotted her mother's head executives, Priscel and Huxley. Priscel walked

118

forward, arms draping around Madeline. "Oh Madeline. I haven't seen you in ages."

"Hello, Priscel, when did you return?" She kept her voice even.

Priscel leaned her chin on Madeline's shoulder, shrugging.

"Not that long ago, maybe a few days after Hux here. Guess my timing was quite good, wouldn't you say?"

"Priscel, how many times need I tell you the name is Huxley." Huxley spoke up without turning from his examination of the room. "Speaking of, do you want us chasing those kids?"

Wilma tilted her head before turning. "You may do so, but I suspect they've already fled the area. Notify the other bases about a potential problem and gather any information you can on those three and their mother." She turned toward the doorway before pausing. "Speaking of, Madeline, if I could have a word with you later about your conduct. It was not necessarily wrong to keep an eye on them, but your actions were a bit more...counter to what you say. I'll want a full report from you later." She turned fingers to her lips. "Speaking of, I heard something interesting from Leon as we were heading to our meeting regarding that Richie." She peered back, brow pinched. "I heard their mother has a partial immunity to this disease of ours, If we should find out that those twins have something similar..." She peered down her nose at Madeline before she disappeared out the door.

Priscel's and Huxley's expression were unreadable for a moment or two before Priscel hummed. "Oh, ho? Immunity? Well then, that's something." She pouted, pulling away from Madeline. "Well, at least now I can tell why those kids have piqued your mother's interest." Priscel turned her head toward Madeline, sharp-toothed grin spreading over her face. "That female twin has quite a mouth on her, gave Wilma a bit of a run for her money for a moment there."

"She was certainly vocal at least." Huxley stepped away from the door, taking in Madeline. "It seems you are alright, even with staying close to them. Though you need to be more careful siding with a stranger over your mother. We can't have the leader's daughter getting injured in something petty such as this."

"Oh," Priscel sighed, "I wanted to play with that boy a bit, the

Richie? He gave me the impression that he was quite the stubborn one."

"You'd break him before he could talk," Huxley commented monotonously.

"Oh, hush now. I wouldn't do that, maybe." She sniffed before turning to Madeline, who had to agree with Huxley's assessment. From what she knew of Lex he would sooner break than talk, much like the twins, actually. "Mads, I haven't seen you in ages. Didn't get much news besides the obvious where we were. Anything interesting to note?"

Madeline shook her head, stepping away from Priscel and heading toward the door. "You can read the activity reports for that, either way. It has been a long day..."

"What about that boy you were with, the one you stopped your mother from hurting?"

Madeline stiffened for the briefest of moments as Huxley stepped in her way, looking down at her as a sharp grin started across his lips. "He was one of the ones to escape, correct? You didn't..."

"If what you are insinuating is that I let them go, stop there," Madeline spoke harshly.

Huxley watched with a careful expression before letting out a sigh.

Priscel stepped over, tapping Madeline's shoulder as she passed. "It's not far-fetched to ask, you're still young." Priscel's smile disappeared into a worried frown. "We're concerned that you might have been a bit swayed by feelings. After all, I did hear that you asked him to go out with you and he accepted. News travels fast, my dear."

Madeline was grateful for her years of training, if it wasn't for that, she would have definitely flinched at Priscel's accurate commentary. To her credit, all she did was continue forward past Huxley. "That may be true, but as soon as he betrayed the Resistance, he was of no concern to me. After all, there is no such thing. My mind is set on helping the Resistance like my mother, nothing more, nothing less. Now, Priscel, Huxley, aren't you supposed to be doing something for Mother?"

The two exchanged looks before Priscel shrugged. "Can't fault a girl for trying to avoid paperwork. Don't worry, we'll get to it, right, Hux dear?"

"Huxley." Huxley let out a groan.

Madeline watched them leave, withholding a shiver at Priscel's words. As usual, Priscel thought chasing after people, hunting them down, was paperwork. Well, Priscel was quite experienced at it, if anyone could find the twins, it was her and Huxley... and that's what made Madeline nervous. She let out a long breath before staring out the window. She didn't allow herself to relax, she couldn't, but she did allow herself to feel a bit of pride regarding fooling her mother and those two. At least, for now.

Gathering her thoughts, she walked after them, spotting Darrel talking with another of the Resistance. Darrel caught her gaze before looking away, annoyed. She couldn't blame him. Technically, he had been doing his job. Still, remembering Karina's cry and her pained expression cut off any farther guilt as she turned away from Priscel and Huxley to head back down stairs.

She had a mother she needed to talk with and it sure as hell wasn't her own.

~ * ~

Veronica quietly listened to the chaos of her children's escape as she prayed a quiet prayer, asking for mercy on both her children and the poor girl helping them. Veronica wasn't sure how long she sat there, head bowed in prayer, but eventually, the faint sounds of footsteps reached her ears. The door swished open quietly and, in the doorway, stood Madeline. She appeared roughed up and tired.

"Come here," Veronica said, gesturing to the bedside chair.

Madeline hesitated before slowly stepping forward. Veronica pulled her into a one-armed hug, not saying a word.

Silence enveloped the place until finally Madeline spoke. "They're gone."

"I know, thank you." Veronica kept her voice soft and it seemed to do the trick as Madeline relaxed into her embrace.

"Leon. He...he and Mother know about you."

"Hm?" Veronica hummed, curious.

"They know about your partial immunity, we all do. Well, we all will." Madeline curled inward, as if debating with herself.

Veronica couldn't get the energy to react, she could only sigh. Madeline must have noticed, because she continued hesitant, as though finally realizing her own words. "Does that mean? Maxwell...?"

"He will tell you when he's ready." Veronica turned to Madeline as her brow furrowed at the thought.

For the longest time, a peaceful quietness filled the space before Madeline broke it up, all her attention on the floor. "Alright, I'll wait."

"Are you sure, dear?" Veronica leaned forward enough to examine her around the falling curtain of hair.

Madeline didn't turn away, her scrutiny remained fixed in place. "Yeah. He looked at me as me, not as my mother's daughter like everyone else does. Plus, Karina was there for me after Emma and Mitchell..."

"Are you sure you won't regret it, even if...?" Veronica wasn't able to finish the sentence before Madeline snapped upright, brimming with determination and defiance.

"After what I saw, hearing the way Karina was treated by my mother and her people. How they were willing to trust me though I could have just as easily turned on them when I found out about everything you told them. I wouldn't care if they were the cure itself, as impossible as that is. I still care deeply for them, for Maxwell after all." She grinned, bright and warm. "Everyone has secrets they want to keep, isn't that right?"

"You are strong." Veronica spoke softly.

"No." Madeline shook her head, smile dimming. "If I was, I could keep that cold façade Mother demanded I learn. Then, maybe I wouldn't feel this way." Her words trailed off into a faint whisper.

Veronica said nothing, only continuing to rub circles into the other girl's...no, woman's back. What could she say, to a statement like that?

She continued to pray.

~ * ~

Lex winced, rubbing his wrists gently so as not to mess with the lacerations decorating them from his earlier struggle. He remained alert, listening for a sound or movement. He hadn't noticed anyone following them, but he continued to stay observant, just in case. His leg still ached, but it was minimal, compared to Karina's injury. Now that they were far enough away and close to their arrival location, he'd allowed himself to grimace, his mind admittedly quite dizzy. Still, even through the dizziness, he wasn't remiss enough to notice the way Karina was holding herself...or the lack thereof. He didn't miss the way Maxwell was hesitantly following behind as if she would suddenly just drop dead. He definitely didn't miss the blood coating the grass, or Maxwell's pants that got messy as he desperately plugged up the wounds before it bled out.

To his relief, it appeared like it avoided any major arteries, but Maxwell did end up using one of his knives to help dig out the bullet. He quietly cleaned off the knife, out of sight, and slipped it into its proper place at his waist. Good thing he thought to hide it in his bag, he supposed.

Still, he was grateful that there was no lasting damage for either himself or Karina. From what he gathered, the wound only grazed the muscle. What worried him, however, was that he knew full well how painful such a wound would be. The fact that Karina wasn't panicking but Maxwell was on the verge of throwing a fit, made it obvious that somehow, the girl hadn't noticed anything.

Not a pleasant thought, but one Lex couldn't quite shake. He saw it enough times, after all, it wasn't as far-fetched as he would like to believe. He let out a soft breath but was startled to note Maxwell slowing to keep pace with him, hands wringing themselves white. "She's pushing herself. She didn't notice. I sat there, talking with her and trying to get her attention, as..." He glanced at his hands, still shaking and still covered in blood even after trying to use a handkerchief to clean it up before continuing, "She never noticed. Never saw me take it out, never saw it on the ground, almost didn't seem to care. That's not like her. I know something's wrong, I can tell, but..." The words were light, vacant. Lex caught them all the same.

"But?"

Maxwell tilted his chin up toward him, unease in his frame and on his tired and weary features. "I don't know what to do. I don't know what's wrong with her. I should know, we've always been close and yet..."

"I think we all are just stressed by the entire situation. Give her some time and be grateful she didn't notice the pain of getting the bullet removed," Lex muttered.

"I'm just glad it didn't hit anything vital. I think..." Maxwell gnawed at his lips, almost biting clean through. "The thing is, it was still bad. Even with the bandage, she's still bleeding quite a bit because of, well, I did have to dig with your knife. It was shallow but... I'm not a doctor, I don't know anything about repairing those types of wounds."

Lex spared a glance toward Karina before returning his attention to Maxwell. "At least on that regard, you are fine. It's understandable for you not to know how to treat such wounds. Still, your sister should be fine. She can take care of herself."

Maxwell hesitated before nodding. Lex sighed and tilted his head back, covering his eyes from the piercing sunlight. It would be a lie to say he wasn't worried about the twins. They already went through a lot to get to this point. He was honestly surprised by their strength, but everyone needed to break down sometimes. He just hoped it wouldn't be too bad.

"Would you two stop dilly-dallying and hurry up?" Karina groused, throwing a glare over her shoulder.

Lex didn't miss the way her voice dipped, nor the slightly reduced energy in her tone. From someone who always held too much energy? It was nerve-wracking, to say the least, and only verified Maxwell's concern.

It vaguely reminded him of when the twins first found out about the epidemic itself. He wasn't sure why he felt that way, but he did.

He didn't like the feeling.

Thankfully, it didn't take long until they arrived at the location. A very familiar truck arrived, parking to one side as a just as familiar driver stepped out, smiling.

"I didn't expect to find you here. Who knew you drove in the western regions?" Lex felt a grin cross his face as he gave Garrett a quick handshake. He hadn't seen the man since Reinmark, when Garret had been willing to transport the twins and himself to the next city in his truck.

He never did get to thank his uncle for that. He would have to get in contact with him soon.

The man chuckled, his beard just as full as ever and eyes sparkling in that way that spoke of too much. "Well, it's not like it's going to hurt me." Garrett shrugged, looking over at the twins. "Hello, it's been a while. How is everything going for you two?"

Maxwell and Karina exchanged glances, appearing confused for a moment before recognition dawned on both of their face. Maxwell grinned, the smile just a little bit too wide to be sincere. "Good." He hurried forward. "I didn't expect you to be our driver. You are, right?"

Garrett gestured. "Well, get in and we'll see."

Maxwell let out a quiet laugh before stepping into the truck, hopping into the back seat. Karina followed a moment after, glancing toward the back before taking a seat in the front, seat belt clicking into place.

Lex furrowed his brow at the action, surprised, but shook it off as her not wanting to climb between the seats because of her injury. He could understand that at least. He shook his head and turned back to Garrett, who was watching them with quiet respect. "You've taken good care of those two, haven't you?"

Lex hesitated before he sighed. "Not as good as I wished."

Garret's amusement was light, yet filled with understanding. "It's not easy, taking care of teenagers. They're still alive after all this time. I think that's something to be proud of." Garrett nodded toward the truck. "Now, why don't we get going? I hear you have a couple unruly people on your back again."

Lex couldn't help the smile from flitting on his face. "Sounds good to me." With that, he pulled himself into the truck through the driver's side door, briefly noting Karina wasn't paying any attention. Garret hopped into the driver's seat and settled in for the long haul.

~ * ~

Maxwell kept a sharp eye on Karina, as she drifted off into a fitful sleep. Why did she sit in the front? Sure, she did that before but this time it felt different. Was she ignoring him? Why? His thoughts were running faster than he could handle, and they weren't just about his sister, though she was his main concern. He could still remember how dazed she was, staring at the sky as he carefully cleaned up and bandaged the side of her leg, speaking, but not really saying anything important. He'd been wondering if Karina was in shock. He remembered that he was kind of glad, actually, at first. Because then she wasn't in pain. As it continued, as he dug in with the knife he had grabbed from Lex's bag to get to the bullet, as he forced himself to breathe, wrapping his fingers around the bullet to pull it out, as he bandaged her leg securely, nothing changed and it sent his already frazzled mind into a panic. It wasn't exactly a small wound. Yet, now, Karina seemed fine. Smiling and joking and everything she normally did. It unnerved him, because he knew, KNEW something was wrong. He could feel it, and yet... He tried to shift his thoughts, but only ended up instead thinking of his mother, Madeline, even Martha.

His grip tightened on the backpack in his lap.

His thought veered toward Karina once more, who was seated in the front seat, fast asleep in the cushioned air seat. Maybe it was his imagination, maybe she was being her normal self. In his panic, he could have missed her trying to stay strong like usual. He let out a yawn but didn't let himself slip into a nap. Lex was awake, but only just. His gaze was on the bit of sky that they could see from the back of the truck.

Maxwell's attention drifted back down to the semi-stained rug covering the floor as the truck rattled under him. They needed to get the cure out. They had to find some way to do it. He hoped and prayed that Dr. Girshwin's mother would have something, but he knew, without a doubt, that it would be a longshot, and it was only the beginning. Once they manufactured a cure, they would have to spread it and how could they when all sides were vying for it? It felt like such impossible odds. The government on their heels, the Resistance dogging them for Lex's head and, eventually, because he held no doubts that they wouldn't find out about his and Karina's status, vying for the cure, for them. Something Karina and he tried to avoid when they decided not to say anything.

It was overwhelming, to say the least. The last time he felt this way was when he saw that damn map back in New London City. He shook his head. No. He felt this way for a while, he was just able to ignore it except for the momentary blip when he was talking with Karina over a week ago. After all, it was relatively peaceful the past few months and his full focus was on Ma. Now, he didn't have that focus, that direction. Their ma was safe, relatively speaking. He trusted Madeline to take care of her, but he still wasn't sure how to feel.

His head found itself buried into his shaking palms.

Then there was Karina, his strong, courageous and injured sister. He couldn't pinpoint what it was, but he had a bad feeling.

Chapter Eleven

They arrived in a small town a few hours later, almost the same size and design as the one they just left. If not a little smaller. Maxwell blinked, somewhat surprised he actually fell asleep with his mind racing the way it was. He shook his head and groggily stood up from the back seat almost forgetting it wasn't just a bumpy couch, grateful that there was enough room in the large sleeper. He'd forgotten how big Garret's truck was. Reasonable, considering it took him a while to remember when he met the man before. Lex was already up, heading toward the front of the truck. He pushed the curtains out of the way as Karina blearily sat up. Garrett was glancing their way with an uneasy smile.

"Sorry, but this is as far as I can take you. I need to get back to my routes before anyone notices anything amiss."

"You've already done enough for now, thank you." Lex spoke, a faint smile on his lips.

Maxwell nodded as he helped Karina wake up and slip out of the truck, making sure not to look toward the ground. He heard Lex's voice dip as he continued, "By the way, say hi to my uncle for me. I haven't been able to get in contact with him."

"It's no surprise." Garrett shook his head. "That man has a lot on his plate after Caym's visit. Speaking of, do be careful. It seems he's already in full control of Enthrope, though it has barely been two weeks."

"I'm aware, but still, thank you for the warning."

Garrett chuckled and waved them out. "Then I guess I don't need to say anything else. Take care of yourselves. If you need anything, don't hesitate to call. That informant of yours is quite helpful in that regard." He nodded.

"Of course. Though, I have to ask, where are you heading off to now?"

"Have to head back east, I don't have the jurisdiction to run in the next state, I had a drop-off nearby, but any further, I would be crossing over borders I can't travel to right now."

Lex winced. "Alright, thanks for all your help. Stay safe heading back east." Lex smiled back before stepping away from the truck that roared back into life.

The door shut and, after a moment, the truck slowly reversed. After a complex series of turns, it disappeared back the way they came, no one the wiser.

Maxwell watched it go before turning back to Karina, who was leaning against him. Whether she really noticed or not, he wasn't sure.

"Well, let's get a place to rest for tonight. I know some of us slept in the truck, but that wasn't anywhere near restful."

Maxwell nodded before grimacing as his stomach twisted and he realized with a pained jolt, that he hadn't eaten all day. "First, food?"

All attention turned to him before Lex let out a fond sigh. "That's fair."

~ * ~

The walk around town wasn't really anything thrilling, Karina noted, purposefully focusing on the town proper. It almost reminded her a bit of Claremore, if only with the aesthetics. Though the houses were much farther apart, it did take a while before they found a small diner, nestled between a couple old shacks that were falling apart at the seams.

She hesitated before following Maxwell and Lex inside. The place wasn't anything spectacular, but it was clean. There were wooden benches and a small area to the side filled with barstools, some occupied, but most empty. A waitress spotted them and walked over, scrutinizing them warily. Karina took note of the mask and sighed.

Couldn't escape it out here, not that she was surprised. The simple fact was probably what made it worse, that she didn't FEEL anything in regards to it. Speaking of, her leg felt numb. She knew, mentally, that it should be screaming in pain, aching badly. She didn't feel anything besides a pressure, pins and needles more than anything. She figured it was because of Maxwell's quick work, but she wasn't sure if it was that or that her mind was too preoccupied to really care.

They quickly took a seat at one of the benches, the waitress bringing over three glasses of water before hurrying away. Karina stared at the menu absentmindedly. Shouldn't they be doing something? It just felt so...

She couldn't find a word, nothing popped into her head. It bothered her to no end.

"After this, we should get a place to rest, like Lex said, and head out in the morning. Maybe see if we can find a vehicle or something to use. I doubt we can walk it with both of you injured," Maxwell muttered into the menu as he closed it and looked up. "Lex, any ideas on travel? Obviously, Garrett is out of the question, what with his inability to go any farther west."

"I can't really say." Lex shrugged, placing his own menu down. "At this point, the best bet would be to pick up a car, but..." he hesitated, glancing toward the waitress. "With our lack of funds, that's going to be difficult. I haven't been able to contact my uncle lately, and the funds he's been sending have stopped because of what Caym has done." Lex shook his head. "We're completely on our own."

Maxwell shifted in his seat, appearing more than a little worried and uncomfortable at the thought, not that she could blame him. At least in Collern they had jobs for money, now they had nothing.

"So then, what do we do?" Karina tried to keep the helplessness from her voice, she really did, but some slipped through anyway, causing the others to still. It seemed she was voicing everyone's thoughts, because Maxwell ended up focusing on the table as Lex faced out the window toward the setting sun, already mostly gone. No one said a word.

When the waitress came up, they each ordered, with all the energy of a fourth level victim. A morbid thought, but one Karina couldn't erase as she handed back the menu. She was too tired to force herself to pretend, but thankfully, with Maxwell and Lex seemingly in similar states, she could allow herself that.

To everyone's seeming relief, it didn't take long for the food to hit the table, or for them to scarf it down.

It took even less time, to her surprise, to actually find a place to rest. The little motel room was being shared amongst the three of them and, while she would usually go against that, Lex's earlier comment about their lack of funds drew her up short. She stepped inside, noting there were two twin-sized beds and a large chair. The beds were big enough for one person and that was it. She took a seat on the chair, curling her good leg up close to her. Maxwell paused. "Really, Karina?"

"What? You two need the sleep and this is perfectly fine..."

"No, it isn't." Maxwell cut in before a yawn slipped from his lips. He quickly smothered it and shook his head. "With your leg the way it is, you won't be able to sleep. Come on, sis, I'll take the chair tonight. You take the bed."

She just stared at Maxwell, noting vaguely that Lex was leaning against the wall, just watching the exchange. She noticed him wince, shifting his stance so most of the pressure was on his uninjured leg. "Come on, Maxwell, you're the only healthy one among us. We need one person to be awake and, well, working properly." She shrugged, snuggling into the chair. "Knowing you, you wouldn't get any sleep, then what? All three of us will be out of it or injured. No, get some sleep in the bed."

"That's..." Maxwell trailed off, staring at her with pursed lips. "But..."

"You're not changing my mind." Karina spoke up, shooting a sharp glare toward Maxwell. "I'm comfortable." A lie. "Anyway, Lex is about to fall over."

Maxwell jerked, peering back at the man as he crumbled onto the bed. Maxwell yelped and rushed over, before letting out a breath.

"Sorry, I tried to sit down and my leg collapsed underneath me." Lex grimaced, pushing himself up slightly. "I don't think I'll be standing up again, well, not right now until I give it some rest."

Karina let herself rest against the side, vision blurring. She listened as Maxwell said, "Do you need me to get something?"

"No, I'm fine. I just need some sleep."

That, Karina couldn't deny. She needed sleep as well, but she wasn't tired. At least, not in the way she was used to. Physically, she was exhausted, but her mind kept running, racing around and around in circles.

She heard shuffling and movement before there was a quiet breath of relief. A moment later, she heard footsteps and felt a hand press gently against her shoulder. "Karina, what are you thinking?"

She didn't respond, pretending to slip into sleep. She didn't want to deal with Maxwell right now. She heard another heavy sigh and more shuffling. A moment later, something soft draped over her and she felt Maxwell tuck whatever it was around her. "Why are you so stubborn, Kari? Can't you let me protect you too?"

She withheld a wince as he stilled.

"I can't tell if you're pretending or not. What happened? I don't understand you anymore, Karina." There was a heavy pause. "If you are still awake, just, please, talk to me. I'm worried about you."

Worried? Why? Maxwell, you shouldn't worry about me.

There was another long pause before Maxwell let out a sigh. "You're so stupid sometimes, Karina."

The clacking of footsteps and the sound of mattress springs proved he finally took the bed. However, she only briefly noticed it, as her entire thought process froze at his words. He thought she was stupid. A part of her, a small part of her mind argued that's not what he meant, but it was quickly drowned out by everything else that suddenly bombarded her thoughts, her mind racing, twisting.

Yes, she was. She was so idiotically pathetic. She only had gotten worse. She was the one who needed protecting. She was the one worrying Maxwell when he shouldn't have to be worried. She wasn't sure how long her mind spun, but she eventually opened her eyes, noting the way Maxwell was curled up on the bed, only a thin sheet around him. The quilt was draped over her, pulled tight over her shoulders. She held onto it as she stared at her sibling, noting he already slipped into a deep sleep. Of course, he had. Maxwell was probably exhausted and yet, he stayed up because of her.

Her head was pounding, the words, both her own and his slamming around in her head. She pulled her legs into her chest, against her better judgement. She grasped the pain, holding onto it tightly in fear she would break down, but it was no good. The memories and emotions bombarded her and Maxwell's whispered words caused her heart and mind to ache. She could feel the tears forming. She buried her head in her legs, tears staining her pants as she tried desperately to keep the sobs quiet, the shaking to a minimum. She knew it. She'd known it for a while now, but this just...

She was a hindrance. She'd been a hindrance from the get-go. Maxwell had to care for her, not the other way around. He was worried about her. They couldn't understand each other anymore. Even before all of this she knew she messed up. She knew she stressed her mom with her constant disappearing act and with dragging Maxwell everywhere, sometimes without his consent, but she never thought anything of it. She never considered how it was hurting them. She wasn't a bookworm like Maxwell and didn't know the first thing about cleaning or caring for someone's wounds like he did. She held no delusions that she could protect herself like Lex, or talk someone down like the both of them.

Hell, she wasn't even positive if she was the cure. If that was the case...if that was truly the case, then what was the point? Would anyone care? Half the country wanted them; the other half wouldn't give a crap if one of them was dead. After all, she was able to understand enough in science to know that one can still have a use in death.

Her hands felt numb with how tight she was gripping herself and the quilt. She could feel the shaking through the chair, desperation keeping her sobs as soft as possible so as to not wake her brother or her friend.

To not wake the people she cared most about, but was unable to do anything for.

She was useless. She finally let herself acknowledge it. She was completely and utterly useless baggage. Injured and, even after trying to learn defense, unable to protect a thing.

"She's a monster." Arik's words rang unbidden in her head. "She's been clean for months. The rest of us are on death's door and why?"

Karina's heart clenched, her throat so dry and swollen she

couldn't breathe. The memories were more than enough to stop her tears, but in a way, that only made her feel WORSE.

"She and that brother of hers probably don't even care... Don't call me that... I don't know why I believed you. After all, you're the same person who let her brother be beaten, who let Emma get captured and now got her killed."

"I'm sorry," she whispered, unable to stop it. "I'm sorry. I've been trying." She slowly turned, spotting the two beds where the two were sleeping, unbidden to her plight. "I tried. I've been trying, I'm just— I'm so—" she gasped and tried to push away the tears, her lips trembling under her teeth, which were so close to just biting clean through, to just end this.

It hurt.

She couldn't get those thoughts out of her head. The thought that she was a burden and yet, she couldn't go home. She wasn't needed here, nor there. She forced herself to stare at Maxwell and Lex for so long she was surprised her head wasn't glued into that position. Finally, she stood, the quilt falling over the ground, one thought running through her head. "I'm sorry," she choked out. "I've just been a burden. I've been a complete idiot. You've grown so much and I..."

She slowly picked up her backpack, staring at it in silence before reaching in and pulling out her mom's bible. She stared at it for what felt like hours before gently laying it on her seat. After all, Maxwell was the one who promised, who would return it to Mom. She didn't have a say, never did. She stared down at the quilt, her gaze locked on it for a while. She gripped the backpack tightly. She bent down, picking up the quilt before carefully placing it over Maxwell. Noticing him stir slightly before settling. "I'm sorry, Maxwell. I'm such a pathetic older sister. I'll be back."

She turned away from the two beds and walked toward the doorway. She slipped outside, walking down the moonlit street, backpack on her back, giving her a sense of nostalgia and almost peace. It was something familiar in all the unfamiliarity, even the wound which was beginning to throb, as if demanding her to think about it. She'd gotten injured so much at home, it wasn't anything new. She chuckled at the memory of Maxwell berating her as he dressed a wound she received when she accidentally fell from the vines she used as a swing. She always did crazy idiotic shit like that. Her moment of reprieve faded as her chuckling fell away into silence. She gripped her backpack tightly, only to freeze as she noticed the car.

She slipped into a side alley as a car sped by, taillights bumping over the paved roads. Her blood slowed in her veins, her thoughts flipping to just a week ago. It was the same car, the very same that brought the three of them and Mom to the Resistance base. Part of her tried to get her mind's attention, noting that it was dark, hard to see, how could she be certain? Another part of her squashed that thought down. Of course, it was that car. That was their luck. The Resistance would find them because they weren't fast enough, because she'd gotten herself injured.

She scrutinized the road before glancing back the way she came. She could go back to the hotel room, but... No. It would be safer for her to just leave. Get the car's attention and make a break for it. She briefly thought of warning Lex and Maxwell, of sending a text or call, but the thought was just as quickly pushed to the side as she figured the car wouldn't still be here in the morning anyway. Not if she caught its attention. Plus, Maxwell and Lex would be fine. They didn't need her there, not like this.

So, with those thoughts firmly in her head, she set out. It wouldn't be hard to get the car's attention. If there was one, there were bound to be more. She would walk around the streets for a while, then hurry into the forest, by then at least one would have noticed her.

She started down the street and pulled out the phone, looking at the time. It was ten o'clock. Not exactly late, but late enough, confirming her earlier thoughts that Maxwell and Lex would be safe until morning. By then, she and the car would be gone. She stared over the screen, seeing the numbers blinking up at her. That reminded her, what would she do once she got away from the cars?

She would decide where to go later. That wasn't important now.

She grasped the phone tightly, fingers pale and arms trembling. As she continued down the street, part of her prayed that the screen would light up. That her brother would call, asking where she was. That one of them would stop her, tell her that she was about to do was dumb and inconsiderate. The thing was, Maxwell already called her that. She chuckled morosely. Of course they wouldn't call. He already thought that.

A small part of her was unsurprised, but she still felt dismayed as the screen never lit up and the phone never rang its cheery song. So, as she padded back into the street, she felt the last of her hope disperse and fall away. She needed to be away from him. After all, she couldn't protect him. She was only slowing him down.

So why not cut the last piece loose? She knew he would be able to handle it. She wiped at her eyes viciously before deciding just to leave her arm up there as she stole into the night.

Chapter Twelve

Maxwell awoke, feeling off. He blinked blearily, pushing himself up as he rubbed his face tiredly. No, he'd actually slept pretty well once his head hit the pillow, though his mind still whirled with worry, so that wasn't it. He yawned, pulling himself out of bed, briefly noting that the quilt he put around Karina was now over him. He paused at that, staring down at the sheets with a slight frown cutting through the fatigue. Speaking of, where was Karina? He didn't see her bag, though she did have a habit of bringing it with her after what happened in the hostel all those months ago.

He hummed, looking left and right before he sighed. She went off again by herself. He thought she'd gotten over that while they were in Collern, but it seemed that wasn't the case. He just hoped she was okay; while the wound was manageable, it was still a wound. As evidenced by last night, his sister was stubborn so it wasn't really surprising. He stood, stretching toward the ceiling. Lex was awake and getting changed.

"Morning." He smiled, earning a blink and sigh from Lex.

"What has you so enthusiastic this morning?" Lex muttered as he finished up, leaning against the wall with his good leg, attention drifting briefly to the chair.

Maxwell shrugged. "Don't know. I guess it was finally getting a good night sleep?"

Lex chuckled. "That's probably the case. Anyway, let's go get something to eat. Your sister's probably already down there since I didn't see her in the bathroom earlier."

"Yeah. Though I wonder why she didn't wake either of us?" Maxwell muttered. Lex watched him carefully with a raised eyebrow.

"Idiot. Last time I checked, she wasn't one to do that."

Maxwell opened his mouth to argue, but snapped it shut as he realized he didn't have anything to say. He grimaced, a small smile forcing itself on his lips. "Well, that's true."

He shook his head and quickly got changed. Lex politely looked away, before both of them hurried outside and down the stairs, remembering to bring his key at the last minute.

They hurried into the little dining area for patrons. There were a few people dotted here and there, but it was fairly quiet. Whether the silence was because it was later in the morning, or because there just weren't that many travelers, Maxwell wasn't sure.

Lex's gaze sharpened as a frown slowly began to form. "She's not here."

Maxwell followed his line of sight and paused, surprised. He didn't see his sister's cheerful smile, or her signature black-haired ponytail anywhere. He frowned. Maybe they just missed her? That didn't seem right.

"Let's just grab something and head back to the room," he muttered as he hurried up to the table, grabbing one of the paper plates and stacking food on it. He snatched a pitcher of orange juice, pouring himself a small glass before finding himself racing upstairs instead of walking. Juggling the food and drink, he somehow managed to get the door open and stepped back inside. He examined the room once more, that wrong feeling was stronger than before. He gently placed the food and drink on one of the tables, hesitant. "Karina?" he called, feeling nervous for some reason he couldn't fathom. He stepped into the bathroom, examining it before walking outside once more to be met with Lex. "Have you seen her?" he choked out.

Lex glanced back over his shoulder, a Danish in one hand and a cup of coffee in the other. He shook his head. "She's probably fine. Give her some time and she'll be back. If not," Lex gestured with his head to the phone, idling and charging on the same table as Maxwell's food, "give her a call."

Maxwell hesitated for a moment, unsure, but nodded. He sighed and stepped back inside.

"I'm heading back downstairs. I saw some computers down there."

Maxwell thought it over before he nodded. "Alright, sounds good. Call me if you find her."

Lex nodded before heading off down the hall. Maxwell watched him go before slowly closing the door. He ate in silence, staring at the wall. His gaze flitted to the black chair, but there was no one there. Maybe she slept somewhere else? He shook his head. She was stubborn last night, almost overly so. He had wanted to drag her out of the chair, but he didn't want to injure her, and Lex wasn't going to be able to help. Plus, well, part of him didn't want to wake her if she really was asleep. To be honest, he couldn't tell last night, which unnerved him more than he would like to admit. He groaned, pinching the bridge of his nose. Where was she? She couldn't have gotten that far, right? Obviously, Lex didn't see her, so she must have left while they were still sleeping. He paused at that thought, feeling his brow furrow.

Wait...

Maxwell stiffened, gaze firmly on the sheets. Karina wasn't one to up and leave like that. She was exhausted last night. There should have been no reason she would leave without notifying them, especially with everything going on. She wasn't dumb, she knew the risks of going outside alone.

He tried to think over what happened last night. If she was awake... He froze as the words echoed in his mind. Did she hear him calling her stupid? No, it couldn't be that, he said that all the time lately to both her and Lex. He knew well enough she wasn't an idiot, but he had gotten frustrated with her stubbornness.

"Sis, did you misunderstand me?"

He brought his hand up in thought, his mind whirling before it froze. Karina's demeanor, her dazed state, the way she was distancing herself from him, the way she fell asleep as if ignoring him. What was his sister thinking? Did she honestly think he meant it? If she thought he meant it, then...

Panic surged through his mind as he shot to his feet and more viciously tore the room apart. He hurried over to the chair, only to stiffen as something caught his attention, snuggled against the arm and barely distinct from the black leather of the chair. His hands shook as his mind tried to understand just what it was, he was looking at, as the last piece fell into place.

He picked up Ma's bible with trembling fingers as his mind ground to a halt. Karina always carried this with her, just like Ma. They decided, months ago, that Karina would carry that while he carried the letters, so it wasn't all in one place and that was reinforced when Ma gave it back to them. So...

"Karina," he shouted, grip tight on the book as he whipped around and ran to the doorway, slamming it open as he searched up and down the hallway. "Karina. Sister. Where are you?" he yelled, garnering some attention from the other residents, but completely ignoring it as he raced down the hall, scanning everywhere, as his grasp grew tighter and tighter on the precious item in his hands.

Finally, he found the room Lex was in, startling his friend. He didn't care, now having a full out panic attack. He sucked in hasty breaths, trying to stop his spinning thoughts. "Lex, please tell me you've seen Karina."

Lex blinked in confusion before spotting the book. It barely took two seconds for recognition to flash across his face, followed by a grim understanding. Lex pulled away from the computer, showing a search on means of travel, before turning to him. "Where did you find that?"

Maxwell tried to calm his jackhammering heart, but it was difficult. "On the chair. Her bag is gone and it's the only thing there."

"Have you tried calling her?"

Maxwell hesitated, suddenly feeling very dumb. Why hadn't he thought of that?

Recognizing Maxwell's expression for what it was, Lex shook his head with a fond sigh and reached into his pocket. He flipped the phone open, pressing the speed dial number and waited. The ringing was deafening, achingly loud in Maxwell's ears and, as it kept ringing, a frown formed on Lex's face.

He furrowed his brow as he redialed, and once again, no answer.

It was the third time, when it went straight to voicemail, that he showed the fear that Maxwell was trying desperately to suppress. He quickly left a message on the last try before promptly snapping his phone shut, stuffing it into his pocket. "Let's go. Grab your things. We're going to need to start searching."

Maxwell opened and closed his mouth before finally nodding as he raced upstairs.

Karina, where did you go? Why did you just up and leave? Was it because of what I said? Did I cause you to leave? His thoughts got him nowhere, as he shoved his clothes and other things into his bag, along with the bible. *Why leave this here? What are you trying to tell me? Are you alright?*

He couldn't stop the rampaging thoughts as he swung the bag onto his shoulders, ignoring the ache as it slammed into his back. Lex was already done, on his way out. Maxwell took one last look around the room before rushing after him, determination sweeping through him. *Wait for me, Karina, I'm going to find you. I'm not going to let it stay like this.*

Chapter Thirteen

Karina winced, lifting her leg a little higher as she shifted past the wooden fence and slipped out of town. The image of the car sat firmly in her mind as she trundled down her own path. She'd spotted it again and made a beeline out of town. Did it see her?

Her woozy and tired mind was saying this was dumb, but what else was new? Another part, a paranoid part was saying no, it wasn't. She needed to do it. She needed to find some way to help Maxwell. She limped, avoiding putting as much pressure as possible on her leg. She had not anticipated how much pain it would bring her as she scooted through the farmland. The wheat grew to her waist on either side of her. She hoped no one saw her. She wasn't in the mood to worry about the problems with trespassing. Finally, after a while, she found the other edge of the fence and slipped into what seemed to be a prairie. Tall grass grew on either side of the dirt road. The road had deep grooves in the dank muck that indicated traffic. Her shoes sunk into the muck as she continued forward.

She wasn't sure where she was going to go. Just away from Maxwell, away from Lex... Was she running away? No. She shook her head. Finally, she found a small copse of trees and sighed, slipping against one and slowly letting herself slump against the harsh bark. Her leg throbbed and her eyes were droopy with tiredness. The sun was now fully up in the sky with a partial cloud here and there drifting by. It was surprisingly quiet. The few trees, as stunted as they were, sang softly in a faint breeze. It reminded her so much of home. A home she couldn't go back to.

She curled up. She had made no plan, had no map or idea of where to go. It wasn't like her. She knew that. Unfortunately, she couldn't convince herself to care. The image of a town, decorated in graves, flashed through her mind. Emma's shattered body, Arik's twisted face as he cursed her in anger...and Mitchell's sadness. Maxwell's heartfelt and heartbroken expression at never going home and leaving Mom behind, Lex's fear, yet strength as he followed them through all this crap. She yelped as the pain finally registered and she pulled her fingers away from her leg, having accidentally dug into the wound from before. Right, the wound. What bullshit. She couldn't avoid getting hurt like some damsel.

That's what she was right now, wasn't it? Some damn fairy tale damsel. She wasn't someone to be protected. It was her job to protect, to make sure everything was alright.

Who was she kidding? Maxwell was the one being optimistic lately. Were her fake smiles fooling him? Helping him? She doubted it. She let out a long breath, realizing her mind was whirling and, no matter how drained and tired she felt, she couldn't sleep.

She dug into her bag and pulled out another bag with snacks. She'd come to always packing them after all their sudden moves and change of place. She bit into the bar, pushing herself to her feet as she continued on. She was going to have to find some means of transportation. Now that she was away from him, her mind calmed. He would be safe, away from her. Lex would take care of him.

That left the next question. Where was she going to find transportation out here? She sighed and decided to just continue walking. She would figure it out when she arrived in the next town or city...whatever came first.

To her relief, and to her leg's relief, she found what seemed to be an old train station. The wooden platform was rickety with age and wear. A small ticket booth was set off to one side, not even manned, with a map of rail-lines placed beside it. The tracks were studded with weeds that somehow survived. She took a look at the map, her fingers gliding over the plastic covering. There was to be a train stopping to drop some things off and heading west. Would that work? She didn't have the money.

She groaned and slumped over to take a seat under the overhang of the platform, the bench creaking with her weight. She wasn't sure what else she could do. As athletic as she was, she was not keen on the idea to walk all the way west. No thank you. She pulled the backpack off, placing it on her lap as she blinked tiredly. She needed some sleep. She could feel it, heavy on her eyelids. Yet, she knew she couldn't sleep, she had no place safe to sleep.

She wasn't sure what happened. A cool breeze was blowing over her cheeks and there was a faint pitter-patter of rain. She blearily awoke from what seemed to be sleep. Her bag was still in her lap, her fingers cramped from their position as clamps. She carefully stretched and looked around. The air held a humidity that weighed down on her, the rain not doing anything to lighten it. It was faint, causing a haze, but not much else. For a brief moment, she wondered what woke her, before she heard the sound of a whistle. She started, scrambling to her feet and whipping the backpack back onto her back. She looked left and right before spotting something in the distance. It was black and held a metallic sheen in the dimming light.

Seemed that she'd slept for a good couple hours, she must have been tired. Good thing nothing happened. She stepped closer to the edge, seeing if she could tell exactly what was coming. She felt a drop of rain on her nose and quickly pulled back into the safety of the overhang. Another whistle sounded and she could finally make out the details of the approaching train. The cab itself was black and almost ragged. Behind it, she could see a good set of boxes and what was it called, a caboose? A freight train? Possibly. She noticed it was slowing and perked up. Was it possible that this was the train she saw on the map heading west? She reached into her pocket and stilled. Right, she didn't have any money.

She cursed, clicking her tongue. Of course, she would forget about that. She spotted the train and pulled back, shifting behind one of the poles to try to stay out of sight of the engine car. To her relief, it pulled to a stop. She glanced sidelong, down the path. Quite a ways down, she could see someone hopping off the train and disentangling one of the flat beds. So, they'd been transporting something here.

Now was her chance. She snuck up to the train, out of sight of the workers, and quickly perused her options, mentally cursing as she tried to tug at one of the locked box car side doors. She heard movement and, without missing a beat, she grabbed the metal of one of them, noting the ladder nearby and clambered up, flopping onto the top. Her leg stung, but it only slightly hindered her climb. Still, it was just in time as she heard shouts. She peered carefully over the edge, noting the flatbed was already taken care of. She saw the workers walking up and down the rail, as if searching for someone like her, before heading to the engine compartment. She gulped. She wasn't exactly in the best place, on top of the train like this. It was terrifying, actually.

She scanned her surroundings. The compartment in front of her was a sheer metal top with no means of crawling down on the slick metal. She didn't dare get back off as the rain suddenly picked up, making the metal ladder much slicker. Plus, she did have to head west and this train looked like it was probably heading that way. She glanced behind her. The car behind her was another flat bed with boxes strapped down by rope similar to a pyramid. She didn't like her odds with that.

She didn't have much more time to think as she felt the train shift under her. She yelped and quickly scrambled to the back, hands and feet slipping on the wet steel. She would take the ropes over being on the top of a wet and moving train. She slid down and, using the momentum, hopped onto the boxes just as the train started to pick up speed. She took a seat on a box near the middle of the pyramid, slightly surrounded by a few other taller ones and wrapped her arm around one of the ropes, holding on tightly.

She shifted back into the little enclosure when she noticed there was a door to the cab in front of her. For a moment, she was too nervous to reach forward to check if it was unlocked. As the train shifted once more, she figured to heck with it and, holding on with one arm to the rope, leaned forward, stretching toward the handle. She tugged sharply and, surprisingly, felt the door shift. She glanced down, the only gap between her and the door was a few boxes and a connected chain that was already soaked in rain. She took a deep breath and swung herself forward. She landed on one of the boxes and, using her grip on the handle, swung the door open and pulled herself inside, feeling her feet skid on the metal briefly before she slipped inside. It was then she heard a whistle as the train fully picked up speed. She quickly closed the door behind her and let out a breath.

She peered around, noting it seemed she was in another storage cab, boxes were stacked all around with a thin hallway between them. She searched around before finding a little alcove she could curl into. Hopefully, it would be enough. As the train moved and swayed, she began to relax a little, though she could still feel trills of adrenaline pounding through her veins and she was soaked to the bone.

As the train picked up speed, she caught her breath, her leg throbbing almost in sync with her pounding heart. Thankfully, she had somewhere warm and dry to stay in, but she needed to keep watch for anyone coming in and find a way out quickly and quietly. She couldn't deny, however, the thrill of what she just did. It was a fun thrill, not the previous anxiety-inducing moments like when she was trying to find Mom or when she and Maxwell were attacked. Plus, she didn't have to worry about Maxwell. The nap from earlier did wonders as well to boost her energy. She leaned against the metal siding and let out a breath as her body slowly uncurled to get more comfortable, a faint smile pulling her lips. It was like a breath of fresh air, even with the smoke of the engine tickling at her nose, smothered by the metal of the train car.

The boxes practically surrounded her from the sight of anyone coming into this train car. Her bag pushed against her back awkwardly, but she didn't want to take it off for fear of leaving it behind. She wasn't sure where she was going. She could suspect and make grand guesses, but either way, as long as it was away, that was all she wanted.

She would just have to track how far she could get this way before she had to bolt.

A thought passed through her mind and she reached into her pocket, pulling out her phone. She flipped it open, staring at the screen littered with phone calls and left messages. A pang of uncertainty thrummed through her before she quickly pushed it away. She knew she should call them, let them know she was alright, but...

She pulled up the text function and quickly wrote to Lex, unable to convince herself to even look at Maxwell's number. Lex would understand, he would know what to do. She didn't want to scare them, that was the last thing she wanted to do, but she knew there was no way to avoid it with the decision she made. Maxwell would understand, he was smart...unlike her.

That caused her to pause before she sharply shook her head and sent the text to Lex. She flipped the phone closed and slipped it back into her pocket. That would have to do. Now, just to wait and find out where she was going. She would figure out what to do from there.

If there was anything she could do.

Chapter Fourteen

Caym stared out the window, lost in thought. The car's motor hummed, a slight whine in the silence of the area. The community was dead, he could tell, and he barely made it out himself after his encounter with Little Leo. A slight burn, just starting to heal, decorated one arm, fingers slightly charred from attempting to block out some of the blaze. The devastation around him wasn't surprising. A little over a week had passed and yet the community was still in shambles, only a few survivors remaining, having hidden in the mayhem of the subsequent looting and pillaging. The Enthrope workers were parsing through what was left in the rubble after they managed to extract all those involved from the outer community, with the help of the police brigade. It wasn't much, to his chagrin. If anything, the Resistance, as he figured out by those who died, did a number on the community and destroyed all research upon extraction.

He would have been more upset, but he didn't particularly care. The only reason he was here right now was due to the fact that he needed to make a public appearance to the community and the survivors who were already being moved to other locations. He had no long speech, he didn't need one, but his mind was very much preoccupied with other things. This was trivial, he would have completely forgone this whole thing, but he didn't want to be his father. He would let the people know, would point out the cruelty of the outer communities and bring Leo home. He stepped out of the car, spotting the TV station he asked for. A station that mostly operated within gated communities. Off to one side, he could spot the shattered gates and a crowd of outsiders throwing things in their direction. Enthrope employees in riot gear stood in a line to protect those within the community.

He heard someone clear their throat and turned to the announcer, a woman he couldn't remember the name of. She stepped up to him with a bow, the camera-man behind her. "We are glad that you could make it, Mr. Askren. Let us know when you are ready to begin."

"Of course, Make sure to note what happened here after I am done, understood?"

"We can do that." She glanced toward the cameraman, who was finishing setting up.

"Good, just give me a moment." Caym spoke, adjusting his clothes, swiping one hand through his hair before pausing. Huh, that was something little Leo did, not himself. He shook the thought away and focused back on the woman, nodding.

"We're ready to roll, get the camera up," she called, earning a nod in response as the cameraman did a thumbs up.

"We're rolling."

"Hello, America, this is Ellen Fox, your trusted news reporter from Collern City. Today, with much sadness, we bring you news of the destruction of the gated community within this fair city. With me, I have the new head of Enthrope Corp, Caym Askren, here to make a report on what transpired in this community and what plans Enthrope has to combat this destruction. Mr. Askren, what are your thoughts on the matter?"

"Thank you, Ellen." Caym bowed his head, putting a polite smile on his face. "This has been, as you all might know, a tough time for my family. With the suicide of my father, the control of this company has come down on me. For this to happen only a few days after brings me much heartache." He let his hand drop from his chest, focusing on the camera. "Please, know I am not my father. I wish to tell you of the devastation that afflicted this great city and these gentle people. The outer community has attacked, without hesitation, those within who did nothing wrong. They burned and pillaged, raped and murdered willingly. This will not be tolerated by Enthrope or the government as a whole. I will strive to bring justice down on the people who would do such heinous crimes in our homes."

He paused, his thoughts shifting briefly. "There is only one thing

I ask of those of you who still support this great nation. There is a man who I search for. My younger brother, Leonard Askren, was taken from me during the attack on the community by a set of twins." He spoke carefully, letting his smile drop. "I arrived in the community in order to check on my brother when the attack occurred. He was ripped from me, right in front of me and, as evidenced by my injuries, I tried and failed to retrieve him. I am only one man, after all." He brought his wounds to bare, earning a slight flinch from the reporter. "I want Leonard back and for those twins who took him from me to be brought to me to face the justice of Enthrope. More details will come in later reports, but, unfortunately, that is all the time I have for now."

"What a terrible turn of events." The reporter's expression shifted to imitate concern as she turned back to the camera. "A family split apart at the seams because of ruffians and traitors. As you can see, Mr. Askren here did not escape unscathed from the attack and yet, he has been willing to return to speak with us." The camera swooped, turning to show the burnt remains and scorched, pock-marked earth. "More information about the attack and the search for Mr. Askren's relative will be brought to you with the ten o'clock news. Now, back to you."

As the camera clicked off, the reporter let out a sigh, her mic dropping to her side as she turned back to Caym. "I am sorry for your loss." She bowed her head. "Thank you for joining us today. It was short, but appreciated."

Caym nodded. "Thank you as well." He reached into his pocket, pulling out a sheet of paper. The woman blinked, surprised. "Give this to your supervisor, he will know what to do with it."

The woman cautiously took the paper. She glanced at Caym, who waved, letting her know she could open it. She slid it open, quickly scanning through the words. "This is..."

"Pertinent information regarding the capture of the twins, the specifics on the attack and the information regarding the retrieval of Leonard Askren...as well as information important for rooting out the America Liberation."

"Why didn't you share all of this when I was speaking with you?" The woman actually seemed a little upset.

"As I said, I don't have the time. I need to return to work so that we might capture those who did this."

The woman pursed her lips. "I will give this note to my supervisor."

"That is appreciated." Caym turned away, heading back to his car. "If we want to end the scum of the outer community, it is important that we start now. Isn't that right?" He glanced over his shoulder at the woman whose attention was firmly on the letter.

She jerked and nodded, anger simmering that wasn't directed toward him in her gaze. "Of course."

Caym allowed his smile to become more sinister as he turned away and slipped back into the car. With the gated communities now more aware of the danger and Enthrope preparing to face the wrath of the outer communities, he could move forward with his plans. Now that he had the sympathy of the inner communities and those of the outer communities who might not be fully aware of the truth of the situation, he could focus on Leonard, or, well, his little Leo. Those twins would face his wrath for taking Leo away from him again. He would capture them, take their blood for all they were worth and watch them suffer. Just as his wife, Ariel, and his young daughter, Kiera, had to suffer at the hands of the outer community. His fists clenched as the car kicked into gear. Machael sat in front, wheel in his grasp.

"Sir, is everything all set for us to depart?"

"Yes, let's get going."

Machael nodded as Caym's attention drifted to outside the window once more. What a dangerous game he was playing. However, it would all be worth it in the end, once little Leo was safe and beside him once more.

Chapter Fifteen

Lex stared down at the message beaming up at him from the screen of his phone. Part of him was honestly surprised. Another part was furious. It was almost two days since Karina disappeared. Both he and Maxwell were worried sick. Now she had the audacity to send a quick text? That was it?

"Lex? Did you get something?"

What little hope still remained colored Maxwell's voice as he turned to him. It was obvious the boy was exhausted, unable to sleep with the fear of what might have happened.

He quickly pulled up the text, reading through and grimacing as he went. He almost didn't want to read it to Maxwell, it would hurt the boy more, but he knew that he had too. Right now, Maxwell at least deserved some confirmation that his sister was alright.

Lex handed the phone over to Maxwell, who greedily grabbed at it, reading the words with a vehement fervor that turned into heartache. "You...you stupid idiot..." he choked out, fingers clenching tightly around the phone. "What even is this?" He turned the phone back to Lex, who didn't need to read again. He basically had it memorized.

Hey, Lex. I'm sorry I just up and left. I wanted to make sure the Resistance didn't find you two. My phone's about to die and I left my charger with Maxwell. Anyway, let him know I'll be fine. I'll see you eventually. Take care. Karina. P.S. Maxwell has the cure. He NEEDS to go west. I know he's stubborn, so make sure you get him to do that. Thanks, Lex. Maxwell shook his head. "This is such bullshit. Who the hell is the stubborn one?"

Lex quickly grabbed the phone out of Maxwell's hand as he

noticed Maxwell shifting. "Throwing my phone won't do either of us any good." He pocketed it. "Your sister is alive and relatively safe. At least now we know she hasn't contacted us because her phone is dying. That's—"

"Lex, I get it," Maxwell cut in, voice choked as he tilted his head down, fists clenched at his side. "I should have noticed. I shouldn't have been so stupid. She was basically crying out for help and I didn't even notice." Lex didn't miss the way Maxwell shook, tears dripping down his face, having been held in for so long. "Was I the reason?" He tilted his head up toward Lex anger and pain twisting his features. "Is it my fault?"

"No." He quickly cut off that train of thought, both hands placed firmly on Maxwell's shoulders. "This is no one's fault. If you want to lay blame, I can take some of it as well. I'm older than both of you, I should have noticed as well." He shook his head. "Don't blame yourself for this. Karina's smart, she knows what to do and where to go and so do you."

He cautiously pulled back as Maxwell pulled up his sleeve, desperately wiping at his face. "West...she's going to head west. We'll...we'll meet her out there."

Lex winced. Sure, he said she knew where to go, but he never said that's WHERE she would go. The desperate hope in Maxwell's voice at those words hurt more than he would like to admit.

"We'll meet her there, right Lex?" Maxwell grasped onto the sleeve of his shirt tightly, his words on the verge of begging.

Lex forced a weak smile to curl over his lips. Maxwell wasn't in the best state of mind right now. "That's the only place she could possibly go." His words seemed to calm Maxwell slightly, though Lex didn't believe it. If she wanted to, she could go anywhere, but... He needed to make sure Maxwell would be able to continue forward. "For now, we'll head west. If we find your sister in the process, you can tell her your feelings then."

"When." Maxwell cut in with determination suddenly flaring through him as the weakest of smiles flitted over his lips. "When we meet her out west." He took a deep breath, reaching an arm up to wipe away the tears that already stained the sleeve. Lex let him, his thoughts flickering to what they needed to do next. They needed to find some way to travel besides walking. With both the Resistance after them as well as the government, the faster they moved, the better.

They didn't need to do much to get going. Maxwell and Lex were carrying their stuff with them while searching. The only difference was that Maxwell held the bible close to his chest almost all the time, though Lex knew it would have made the boy's arms tired and sore.

Lex glanced toward Maxwell as he took a deep breath, trying to center himself. "Alright, we have to find Dr. Girshwin. Karina will be heading there. I just know it. So, do we know where she lives?"

Maxwell nodded, only to freeze, gaze locked on the pavement in sudden horror before his attention snapped up toward Lex. "I don't think I do. He just said California." He paused for a moment, deep in thought. "I... I think he mentioned something about...Lynn? Maybe? I don't remember and if I don't, I don't think Karina will either. If she doesn't know where to go and her phone is dead, then..."

Lex cut in, stopping the panic before it got too bad. "We will figure things out. We'll keep track of news, information, whatever we need. We will find her, both her and the good doctor, you understand me?"

"That's... How?" Maxwell's voice was weak as he spoke, enthusiasm and hope disappearing quickly.

"Just like we always have. I have mentioned this before, and I will mention it again. You two are close, even now, and you both have the strangest luck. I have no doubt that once your sister gets her head back on straight, she will come and find you. She is also searching for Girshwin and I highly doubt there are that many doctors in California with that name. Sure, there may be a lot of PEOPLE with that name, but well-known doctors? I don't think so. Plus, I'm guessing the letter doesn't have her address on it?"

Maxwell shook his head, hands digging into his bag as he pulled out the clean white enveloped letter. Well, that was a bit discouraging. Lex took a deep breath and nodded. "We'll just have to work with what we can. Understood?"

Maxwell did calm slightly as he put the letter back in. "Alright..."

"There we go." Lex pulled back, holding in the sigh of relief as he turned away. "Let's get a car and get moving. The sooner, the better." He patted his pocket, making sure he still had money in there. He pulled a big chunk of bills out earlier, basically wiping out his bank account. However, he figured it was necessary to have on hand instead of in an account that Caym would have no problem finding and blocking.

He glanced down the street, spotting a rental shop. He stared at it for a while before letting out a grunt of annoyance. This was going to be expensive, wasn't it? He walked purposefully over to the shop, Maxwell only a few steps behind him. He had a feeling the boy was going to be quiet for a while.

The owner, a graying man with more holes than teeth, looked up. "What can I do for ya?"

"I am aware this is a rental location, but I would like to buy a car, the cheapest you have."

"Ah," the man grunted, looking him over before nodding. "I got an old clunker out back. Though even that ain't cheap with this here Epidemic and all."

"Don't worry, I have the means to pay," Lex spoke, following after the man out the back door.

Maxwell followed behind silently. They stepped into a small car park which held a variety of vehicles in various conditions. At the end was an old dual-seat pick-up with faded seats, a damaged bed and cracked side mirror.

"A little damaged, but this old girl still runs perfectly fine. Since you wish to buy her, it is ah twenty-five thousand upfront payment."

"Twenty-five thousand?" Lex raised an eyebrow and the man grinned.

"This here is the only car rental shop in this here area."

"I can understand that, however, as you said yourself, she is damaged. Plus, you mentioned upfront costs..."

"Ah, a down payment, if you will, I expect another twenty thousand at a later date."

"Now, see, we have an issue here then." Lex leaned on one foot as Maxwell glanced at him, obviously concerned about the expense. "There is no means for me to wire money to you at a later date and, from what I can tell," he gave a quick perusal of the vehicle, "I would warrant this vehicle wouldn't make the trip that I intend to purchase it for. Forty-five thousand is a bit much for this clunker."

"Then we have no deal."

Lex seemed to debate for a moment before turning to him. "I am a man with some means." Lex tilted his head just so. "To make sure this business gets what is rightfully deserved." He kept his voice neutral.

The old man's expression sparked in interest as he scrutinized him a second time.

"I may be able to make some adjustments."

"No, I can pay eight thousand. That is all."

"That's rubbish." The man's slight smirk twisted into a snarl. "I can't make a penny with that."

"Really? You said yourself that this is the only rental in town and considering the latest attack on a nearby gated community..."

The man ground his teeth before glaring. "I won't lower it below twenty-four thousand."

"Ah, I understand. So, you wish to make no money at all then?" Lex smiled, attempting to make his expression a little more sinister. "After all, I can simply walk out of here. I highly doubt you'll have many people traveling through, desperate to rent, nonetheless BUY a vehicle from you."

"Are you threatening me?"

"Of course not. I am simply stating facts. Call it an even ten thousand and we can both go on our merry way, you ten thousand dollars richer."

The man stared at Lex, scrutinizing him sharply. Lex kept his expression calm and serene. He had other means if this didn't work, but he would prefer if he could just pay money and get going.

"Fine, ten thousand. I need the payment now."

"Of course." Lex smiled, reaching into his pocket. "Give me one moment." He turned, pulling a small wad of bills out of his pocket before quickly counting it up. It was a bit pricier than he would have liked for that junker, but he couldn't complain too much. Once counted, he stuffed the remaining back in his pocket, Maxwell watching his movements with a furrowed brow as he turned back to the salesman. "Here, ten thousand in cash."

The man stared, shock coloring his expression as he took the money. "Oh, well, it seems we have a deal." He reached into his pocket, pulling a key off a jangling ring before practically tossing it toward Lex. "Now get out of here. I don't want to see your face around these parts again." With that, he turned and stepped away, hurrying back into his shop.

Lex snorted. He headed toward the truck, unlocking the door and pulling himself in. Maxwell, after waiting for Lex to unlock the other door, followed, examining the truck with a mix of interest and melancholy.

Lex turned the key, hearing the hum then roar as the engine came to life, rattling the seats just slightly. He lightly hit on the gas and pulled out of the rental place with a squeal of tires. He would have a few bruises where the seatbelt dug in, but not too bad.

"What was that back there?"

"A ham-handed try at negotiation," Lex admitted as they got on the main road out of town. "Caym was always much better at it than me, but I can at least somewhat do it."

"If you say so," Maxwell muttered and Lex chuckled.

"I'll just leave it as, it worked."

Lex was glad that the boy was talking again, even if it was to make fun of Lex's horrid negotiating skills.

Maxwell huffed but didn't respond. Lex shook his head and turned his focus back on the task at hand. First, figure out how the darn thing drove, then find their way out west.

For a brief moment, he wondered how Karina would get to the west, or if she would. He pushed the thought away. He would debate about that another time.

Chapter Sixteen

Veronica was surprised. Madeline came to check on her on a regular basis as the days passed, either to just talk, or for Madeline to just have a moment to relax, going so far as letting Veronica pull her into a side hug. Veronica was not against it, not after...she quickly cut off that train of thought, pushing away the terrifying memories.

Yet, it wasn't long after her precious children left, only a little less than a week, that Madeline came to her with steel in her eyes, yet sadness on her entire expression. "Leon managed to decipher the rest of the audio. We... He made a connection between your medical capture and the information we have acquired up until this point. They really are the cure. Aren't they?"

Veronica leaned her head back against the headboard, resting. "What if that is the case?"

"Why did they run? We could have helped them." Madeline spoke up, and Veronica wouldn't be surprised to spot the tears threatening to fall over her cheeks.

"So, you say they should have just left their friend to your mother's and the rest of the group's mercies? To be experimented on and abandoned? No, they made the right choice."

"Mother," Madeline choked and Veronica turned her head down, catching as the girl shifted in her seat, hands tightly clenched.

"Let me guess, something happened besides just the reveal about my children."

Madeline nodded, lips pursed. "The Richie, the one who is now head of Enthrope, he told the people we were the bad guys, that the inner communities did nothing wrong and were destroyed anyway. He said Lex was taken from him, ripped away from him. Just like my father was..."

Veronica sighed, not missing the poor girl's confusion. "It's difficult, isn't it?" Madeline glanced up, confused. "It's difficult when you start seeing bits and pieces of both sides. You maybe can't agree with them, but you can also notice the pain that is being caused. It hurts to watch. You start to question what the truth is. Am I wrong?"

"That's...no, you aren't." Madeline's voice was soft, shaken.

Veronica leaned forward, gently ruffling Madeline's hair. "I just want to point out, you called him Lex, not Richie." She smiled softly as she spoke.

Madeline stiffened and then looked away. "I don't know what you're talking about. This...Lex you speak of is a Richie just as much as the other I've been talking about. I'll be honest, I doubt we would have figured it out. If we didn't already have knowledge of how they are related to you and why you were a captive down there. Plus, I heard from others in the community that there was a broadcast just yesterday. They are still trying to obtain it, since it's supposed to be announced to the outside community later today. Still, there are too many coincidences and yet... I know I said that even if they were the cure, I wouldn't... I don't know how to feel."

"Keep with your instinct." Veronica spoke quietly. "What does it tell you?"

Madeline let out a faint snort, yet a weak smile flickered on her lips. "That I'm now even more interested in meeting up with Maxwell and having a good long talk with him and..." She slumped in her seat. "I guess I'm starting to feel that it was a good thing they escaped, because knowing them and knowing Mother, they truly would use the cure to save everyone, not just those who agreed with them, like..."

"Like the Resistance or the Richies would?" Veronica made sure to keep her tone gentle and her voice mellow.

Madeline hesitated before she nodded, just once. It was enough. It showed growth that the girl acknowledged the situation and maybe, it would turn out to be a good thing. Though, in the short term...

"What is your mother planning on doing?"

"Mother...she's getting together a task force to reclaim them as well as their friend. Huxley and Priscel are on their trail. They were following Karina for a bit, but lost her when she headed northwest by train. When they went back to track Maxwell and Lex, the two were already gone."

Karina and Maxwell were separated? How? What happened in the short time since they left? Veronica let out a long, tired breath. "Unfortunately, neither of us can help them. Still, my little ones aren't so little anymore, they've grown and not even I can predict what they are going to do now." As evidenced by those words. Why was it just Karina? Were her children alright?

She heard silence for the longest time, followed by a faint chuckle. "I suppose that is probably the case."

The moment delved into a silence that was surprisingly pleasant and calm. It didn't last long, but Veronica appreciated those moments when they lasted.

"Well, I need to get going. Mom wants me to be part of the investigative team. At least this time, I can remain here for that, but..."

"What of this Priscel and Huxley?"

Madeline stayed silent, a nervousness seeming to settle into her posture. "Right now, they are heading it. If either one of them catches Karina, Maxwell or Lex, then..."

Veronica didn't point out the use of Lex's name, just nodded. "So, we just have to hope that my son and daughter stay out of their sight."

"Yes."

"Thank you, Madeline."

Madeline opened her mouth to respond, before jamming her jaw shut. "You shouldn't thank me," she whispered hoarsely. "I'm part of the reason that this is happening in the first place."

Veronica shook her head. "It would have happened anyway. Karina and Maxwell, while smart, aren't always the quietest." Madeline chuckled at that as Veronica smiled before she continued, "Just, watch them for me, will you? If you can..."

"I'll try to pull Huxley and Priscel off their trail when I can, but I don't think either trust me completely after the twins fled."

"Every little bit helps." She paused, her thoughts flitting to her daughter once more. Veronica felt her heart stutter, just for a moment. "Karina, what are you doing?" she muttered, fearing the worst. Her children were so close, so what could have happened to convince her daughter to up and leave? To go on her own. Yes, she was the more adventurous type, but that wouldn't explain her separation from Maxwell after all this. It didn't make sense to her.

"I wish I knew." Madeline seemed to respond without much thought, her gaze sad, but determined. "Is it because of..."

Veronica stared at the young girl. She wasn't sure if that determination would still remain, but she was grateful for it nonetheless. She closed her eyes and leaned back as Madeline said her good-bye and departed. "Oh, Father, hear my prayer," she whispered, breath slowly flowing in and out of her lungs. "Be with my dear little ones and take care of them. Guide them so that they might know the way. Keep them safe in their hour of need and heal them of any plight." She opened her eyes, gaze on the ceiling as she muttered. "Amen," fell from her lips and faded into the white of the medical wing.

Chapter Seventeen

Karina stumbled, hurrying away from the shouts echoing behind her, or was it in front of her? It was so hard to tell. She spent a day on the train before she was almost caught by one of the operators. Thankfully, the train was stopped so she was able to leap off without much injury, but she was chased out of the area.

She wasn't sure what happened, day after day blended together. Part of her thought only about three or four days transpired between her leaving and her stumbling forward under a cloud-covered sky, but another part of her felt like it was months. She glanced over her shoulder, bangs falling into her face and trailing around her shoulders from the ponytail that was more loose hair than ponytail. She didn't notice anyone, but that didn't mean anything. She took another step and almost tumbled, her leg collapsing under her weight. She yelped and grabbed onto a nearby tree, holding on tightly as she put all her weight onto the other leg. She caught her breath, listening carefully. While her gut was still twisted in fear, the adrenaline from before had long since faded. She let out a long breath and gingerly pulled herself back to her feet. She carefully put some pressure on her other leg, only to wince, spotting a bit of blood leaking through the dirty bandage. She reached down, checking the bandage, briefly noting how warm the skin was on the edges, almost burning to her touch. She would need to get that changed, and soon.

She reached into her bag, digging around for something to eat. Her fingers finally curled around what was probably the last bar in there. Had she already eaten all of the others?

She shook her head, pushing herself forward. She could feel pain shooting up her leg with each step, but she didn't want to stop. She was still too close to the nearby town. She could have sworn she saw someone she recognized, but she wasn't sure. Her mind felt fuzzy, so it was difficult to tell.

Karina wiped her brow, feeling sweat drip down her face as she let out a shuddering breath, finishing the last of the bar and crumbling up the wrapper, stuffing it in her already filled pockets. Dammit, she was careless. Her leg throbbed and her head was beginning to swim, the damp heat of summer bore down at her. Insects droned around her as she passed over a road into another stand of trees, hoping to get out of the glaring sun as another shiver passed up and down her spine. She wondered how far she was from the next city.

She glanced out at the road, noticing another car pass lazily by on the dusty trail. The pavement simmered in the heat. Her phone was completely dead, so she couldn't check the time, and her water was running dangerously low again. She took another step and stumbled as pain flared up her leg once more. Dammit, it had gotten infected, hadn't it? She mentally cursed. Though, she wasn't surprised. She hadn't been fully paying attention, too preoccupied with staying safe on the train and getting away. There was also the travel afterward. It was hard to keep track, was the earlier shouting from the guards or from someone from one of the towns she saw when running? Either way, the wound was now infected.

It made her stomach turn and her thoughts falter. Maxwell...he mentioned about not getting infection, didn't he? That was because the cure ran through his veins. Did she only have a partial one? Like Mom and Dad? Was that it? Was she actually going to get sick? After all, they weren't identical twins, they didn't have the same complete genetic make-up or whatever it was. She shoved the thought away, stubbornly taking another step and pushing away the pain that throbbed with each movement. She wasn't going to think about it.

She walked down the side, trying to stay out of sight of the street, which seemed awfully busy with traffic. In the distance, she could spot something shimmering and, upon closer inspection, noticed golden gates. She couldn't stop the hiss as she realized where she was. A gated community, without a city in sight. Was that possible? She'd never heard of it. It seemed strange, then again, this whole damn country was strange. She took another step and stumbled, unable to catch herself as she tripped over some branches and crashed to the ground.

"Ow..." she moaned out, trying to push herself up. Her leg felt numb, and she glanced down, spotting the bandage, which was more stained than earlier.

Well, at least now she could pretend she had the sickness. She heard the sound of tires and stiffened as she spotted another car that she thought would simply pass on by coming to a stop. Had someone seen her?

She hoped not, remaining still and pushing herself down farther. Someone stepped out, looking around in confusion. It was a young woman with auburn hair, cut short. She was thin and dressed in pretty nice clothes.

"Ms. Fiona?" A male spoke up from the car, causing the woman to turn.

"Sorry, brother, I thought I saw someone."

"All the way out here? No one's come out this way for years."

"I know, that's why it startled me..." She turned, staring in Karina's direction. Karina forced herself not to move, pressing into the dirt. "Give me a minute."

To Karina's surprise, the girl lifted the front of her skirt and hurried up the slope. Karina's eyes widened as she almost instinctively tried to hide, scrambling away.

Pain throbbed up her leg as she felt a hint of fear course through her veins. She pushed herself behind a tree, but even then, she knew she was screwed. Her gut twisted painfully, and her mind screamed she'd moved too slow, been too late.

A figure moved around the tree, stopping right in front of her. Karina pushed herself back, feeling a hint of a growl rumbling up from her throat. The woman in front of her froze as she stared at Karina, before her gaze softened, flitting to her leg. "You're hurt."

"I'm fine." Karina cut in, using the tree as leverage to get up as she kept half an eye on the girl. Her stomach roiled and twisted. The pain in her leg was not helping.

The girl, Fiona, her mind reminded her, examined her before nodding. "Wait right here."

Karina blinked as the woman hurried away. She shook her head, scoffing at that idea before quickly racing back into the woods surrounding the community. Just like home, she suspected, a hidden-away location. She didn't recognize anything, but she was used to traversing through the thick undergrowth, so it wasn't much of a problem. She spotted a small hollow and slipped inside, almost snagging her bag in the process. She quickly grabbed some underbrush and covered the hole. She peeked through as she heard harried footsteps.

The girl from before was back and scanning the area, worry clear on her face. A young man with brown features and thin eyes surveyed the area and then, in a tired, if concerned tone, spoke. "Ma'am...Fiona," it was the same voice from before, Karina noted, slightly confused on why he called her ma'am. Weren't they brother and sister? She was pulled from that thought as he continued, "Are you sure you saw someone?"

"Of course, I did." Fiona turned, glaring at the man before turning back around, panic on her face. "She was hurt and tired. Maybe even hungry."

"Wouldn't that mean she's from the outer community?"

"What the hell does that matter? When have we followed those rules anyway?" Fiona snapped without looking at him and the man just shook his head with a sigh before pausing. He glanced at the ground.

Karina stiffened. Did he spot her tracks?

"Ma'am. What would you do if we find this girl you speak of?"

"Well, heal her, of course. We can bring her home and make sure she's treated right. You didn't see how young she looked or you would be saying the same thing."

Karina felt her stomach twist and she realized, as he clocked where she was that he had noticed her tracks after all, and knew she was there. There was nothing she could do as he squatted down, pushing away the undergrowth, earning a faint gasp from Fiona. Karina had her gun, but it was out of bullets.

That didn't stop her from pulling it out, arms shaking as she aimed it forward, panicked thoughts swarming her tired and frazzled mind.

"Don't move."

Her breath hitched, but she ignored it, trembling. She wanted to flee, or to tell them to leave, but her throat closed up after the words, her tongue dry and feeling like lead.

The guy raised his eyebrow as the woman's expression softened, examining her. "We're not going to hurt you. Though I'm going to slap Eren here for not mentioning something sooner."

She sent the man a sharp look. He simply shrugged, eyes on Karina, who slowly moved the gun back and forth between the two of them. Fiona shook her head before turning back to her, getting on one knee, but not moving any closer. "We're not going to do anything. I'm actually a medical student, I just want to help you, is that alright?"

A medical student? Karina narrowed her eyes. She didn't know there was anyone like that, but again, she only knew a little about the gated communities and, from their conversation, it seemed these two were probably from the one up ahead. She hesitated before pain flared up her side and she gritted her teeth.

Dammit, Maxwell would be able to figure out where they stood, whether they were trustworthy or not. He had that knack to him that she didn't remotely have. In her distraction, her gun dropped enough so it was facing the ground instead of the two before her, and she didn't notice until she heard dual relieved sighs and started, spotting the faint smile crossing Fiona's face. "There. Can you come out?"

"I'm not a child." Karina voiced softly, but, after a moment of debate, she slowly pulled herself out of the hollow and stood up, keeping half a pace away from the two in front of her.

She held her gun tightly, keeping it downward, not wanting to put it away, but not willing to pretend either.

Eren shook his head and turned, heading the way they came. Fiona glared at him before turning back to her. "Come on, we'll bring you to my place and get you fixed up. You appear to need a good bath and someplace to sleep."

"Thank you." Karina forced out, finally slipping the gun into her holster.

Fiona straightened, smile brightening as she nodded and gestured.

166

Karina hesitantly walked forward, surprised to find Fiona walking beside her instead of behind like she expected.

"So, are you from the outer community? I don't recognize you from around here."

Karina nodded and Fiona hummed, hands behind her back. "Really? That's actually pretty interesting. I've always wanted to have a good talk with those from the outer community, but it's honestly a bit difficult. Eren won't let me leave the car when we go through town, though I don't blame him with the epidemic going around. You appear to be pretty healthy in that regard, so I'm not too worried. Oh. I'm sorry, I never did introduce myself. My name is Fiona Everett. Eren is my brother. I've been staying with him for a while."

"Brother?"

"Yep. My parents died a long time ago, in a fire down south." Fiona's smile weakened. "You might not have known, but the gated community in Collern City that was destroyed the other day wasn't the first. Of course, now that I think about it, did you know of that community?" When Karina nodded, she smiled faintly and continued. "Well, needless to say, it was the first publicized."

Karina grimaced. That reminded her of what Madeline said about Martha's husband. Could it be? "So, what happened?"

Fiona stared ahead, lost in thought as they entered the main street and headed toward the car. Now that Karina had a better look, it was a nice car, sleek and shiny. She had no doubts that it was also quite expensive. Fiona's voice drew her attention back to the woman as she spoke. "I only really remember bits and pieces. Eren was away, so he avoided it, but I remember hearing screams and seeing smoke everywhere. Mother covered me in a wet blanket and told me to hide in the basement and keep my head down. He and I were some of the few survivors. It...it was a massacre and the one who did it committed suicide by the very flames he used to burn down my home."

Karina grasped her fingers tightly. So, it was the very same. "The Suicide Arsonist," she uttered, grimacing.

Fiona stilled, reaching for the car handle, face suddenly blank. She slowly turned to Karina, who took a step back, hand darting to her waist as she realized what she said. "How?" Fiona whispered, pleading. "How do you know that name? No one ever HEARD his name besides..."

"I heard about it, when I was in Collern..."

"You were there?" Fiona whipped forward, Karina almost jumping back in surprise. "What happened? Who did it? Did you see the twins who instigated it? Was it really the Resistance just like..." Fiona's grip was so tight, Karina could have sworn she heard the faint sound of tearing fabric.

Karina paused, confused and more than a little nervous. "Twins?"

Fiona stared at her, gaze firm, searching. Karina could do nothing but wait, trying and failing to calm her racing heart. Finally, Fiona shook her head and pulled back slightly. The vitriolic hatred that spewed up for a brief moment faded back to a quiet sympathy. "If you don't know, don't worry about it, but can you tell me? The rest of the things?"

Karina pursed her lips, but decided to leave it alone. "We...my little bro, Maxwell and I, we were caught up in it, along with our friend. That's how I knew." Karina didn't mention her part with the Resistance. She wasn't even going to dare that one.

Fiona scrutinized her for the longest time before turning. "Come on, we'll talk when we get home, but you need some rest." She opened the door and gestured.

Karina didn't want to get in. Unfortunately, she felt dizzy from the heat and pain along with feeling quite dazed. She didn't know what time it was, how long she'd been moving or where she was. She knew she wasn't thinking straight, plus she could feel cool air wafting from the inside of the car, caressing her face as she leaned down. Finally relinquishing, she slipped inside and took a seat. Fiona closed the door and joined her brother up front. Karina examined the interior, noting how clean the car was, the leather soft to the touch and the windows slightly tinted a deep black. She heard the engine start up again, a faint purr, before they moved forward. She could feel her heart pounding in her chest with anxiety. She tried to take a calming breath, focusing on what needed to be done as her eyelids drooped. She was tired, so tired. But...

What was it anyway? She paused in her thought process. What was she doing? She left Maxwell behind, trying to protect him and knowing he didn't need her. Now she was just wandering, lost. She didn't even know where to go. West? That was about it. Did she want to do that? Was there any reason for her to do any of this? Was there a reason that she...?

She looked down, spotting the bandage on her leg in the process. Her fingers curled inward as she realized the implications. No, there wasn't any reason. Arik was right in that regard. All she was was a monster, a proud, self-absorbed monster.

No. That's not right. She had a reason. Maxwell...

Her younger sibling, who could take care of himself. Who was probably already heading west to save the country when she obviously couldn't.

Her mother...

Whom she left behind and was unable to get to, even after everything they did to rescue her.

Lex...

Lex never NEEDED her. He was their guardian and friend, the caretaker. She was never able to do anything for him. Nothing.

She curled inward. Words raged through her head.

"It's your fault, you know. If you hadn't started this, then no one would have gotten hurt."

"You let her die. You promised."

"Emma was one of the cornerstones of our group and you just...you three ripped her away."

"Don't worry, child, we'll help you realize your error."

Shut up. shut up, Shut UP! Karina wanted to scream at the top of her lungs as the different memories plagued her. Now that she was no longer moving, no longer forcing herself forward, her brain was having time to think. While she was taking the train, she could push it aside, focus on a task, still distraught and distracted with her decision to leave. Now as she sat in a car that was already slipping through familiar gates so reminiscent of Lex's home, she found she couldn't keep ignoring it, couldn't keep pushing it off. She didn't notice until they stopped that her hands were on either side of her head as her knees practically met her chest. Tears flowed down her cheeks, unbidden. Dammit. She was a mess.

A complete and utter wreck.

She felt something tentatively land on her shoulder and, more instinct than anything, she slapped it away, shifting to the other end of the car. She was like some sort of wounded animal, and it had nothing to do with the wound on her leg, that was for sure.

She spotted Fiona squatting down near the entrance of the car, peering in at her. "Come on, we're home."

Karina stared before slowly finding herself crawling out. She knew she needed to get cleaned up. Maybe, maybe then she might be able to calm down a little. She still kept a wary gaze on the surroundings, but found that there were no officers, no people in black, either tuxes or uniforms and no one toting guns. She hesitantly followed after Fiona as she headed inside. Eren was already gone.

Fiona held open the door to a sprawling two-story estate, while not as grand as Lex's home, from what she could recall, it was still nice and comfortable. She slipped inside. The entranceway was cool, the gentle hum of the air-conditioner reaching her ears as she examined the place. She didn't notice any servants and made a mental note to ask if she ever got the chance.

"Come, this way." Fiona gestured up the stairs and hurried up. Karina followed only a moment later. It wasn't long until she was led to a large bathroom. Eren stood there, towels and clothes draped over his arm. He must have gone straight here earlier. Karina could still feel the nerves eating away at her. Why were they being so nice to her? They had no reason to be. The only other time she recalled it happening was with Martha, but that was because Martha already knew Lex from before. Lex had already gotten into her good graces, so...

What was in it for these two? Plus, it was a minor thing, but it caught her attention as she glanced between Fiona and Eren. If they were brother and sister, why did they appear so different from each other? It didn't make sense to her.

She took the clothes and slipped inside, locking the door as she went. She glanced at the tub but shook her head, darting into the shower. She would usually take her time, but she felt no inclination to this time around. She quickly stripped, tugging the tie from her hair which was already slipping out and hopped in the shower, trying hard not to look at her leg, or the rest of herself, for that matter. However, as the water stung her and, as she wiped herself down, she noted the gash. It was sickly purple with a long breaking scab. Not pretty in the slightest. However, she paused, her movements slowing as the warmth of the water finally pierced her troubled mind. It did feel good. She shifted upward, shielding her eyes as she let the water pound down over her head and shoulders. Her tense muscles, taut with anxiety and pain, relaxed under the warmth and she let out a breath. Maybe she could take a few extra minutes to make sure she was cleaned up properly. She shifted, making sure most of the pressure was on her good leg and slowed, somewhat enjoying the shower she so desperately needed. Soon enough, once the water was mostly clear instead of brown or red, she stepped out. A chill wafted over her as she quickly dressed in the new set of clothes, only giving the undergarments a passing glance as she pulled them on. A simple t-shirt and a pair of shorts sat snugly on her waist. Even with the shower, she still felt off, chilled, but incredibly warm at the same time. Her stomach twisted and dizziness was never far off if she wasn't careful. She unlocked the door and peeked out. Fiona stood outside, leaning against the wall as she hummed a little tune.

Fiona glanced down, blinking in surprise. "That was rather fast. Are you done already?"

Karina nodded and Fiona smiled. "Alright, then let's get that wound checked out."

"You're not worried about being infected?" Karina spoke, her words soft. Fiona blinked, then shook her head.

"You don't appear sick to me, just injured. I've heard and seen enough about the Epidemic to understand the basics. If that was a wound from the third stages, there would be other signs as well. You don't exhibit any of those or other symptoms. So, I don't need to worry." Fiona shrugged and gestured to one of the rooms down the hall.

Karina stepped into the left-hand room to see that it was a bedroom. There was a four-poster bed set to one side of the room with couches, a TV and two bookshelves filled with books, games and more. Karina spotted a few gaming consoles and blinked. What? She'd only seen them once or twice when she went over to someone else's house while still living at home. She hadn't seen any since, even in Lex's place.

Fiona patted one of the couches and Karina walked over, taking a seat. Fiona poked at her leg before pausing, expression stern. "The marks around the wound, it's no doubt a bullet wound, but did someone force it out?"

Karina could only nod, startled as careful fingers darted over the area, never quite touching hard enough to hurt. Fiona's inspection must have satisfied her because she pulled back, reaching into a small box beside her that Karina hadn't noticed. She could see antiseptic and other medical supplies inside. "Crude, but I suppose it's functional if you don't have medical supplies nearby. So, where are you from?"

The question hung in the air for a moment as Fiona worked. She paused momentarily, glancing up toward Karina. "Uh, Reinmark," Karina sputtered out, realizing she wasn't going to be able to avoid saying something.

The woman acknowledged her for a moment before returning back to what she was doing. "I see. What was your name again? Karina? It's a pretty name for a pretty girl such as yourself. It's been so quiet around here. We don't hear much in this community. Just what comes on the news and radio." Fiona glanced up. "I think even the government forgot we were here. We are practically out in no man's land, after all."

"Where exactly are we?" Karina winced as the woman dressed her wound, the antiseptic stinging fiercely.

"Hm? Oh, we're in South Dakota. Only a couple miles from route I-90. I remember that used to be a main thoroughfare from Seattle to Boston, though I'm not sure if that's really the case anymore." Fiona shook her head as Karina stared toward the ground, shocked.

So, she went west? Well, northwest like she'd thought. Guess she got on the right train. She was already halfway across the country.

So then, where was he? Where was Maxwell? Was he okay? No. He was fine.

She shook her head, her long hair, still wet, slapped partially into her face, startling her. Right, she needed to put that back up. She would wait until it dried.

Fiona chuckled quietly and pulled back. "Alright, it's going to be painful for a while, but the infections should die down in the coming week. Here, take this for now, it's an antibiotic. You'll want to take one per day for the next few days. I'll have Eren give them to you accordingly. Is that alright?"

Karina stared down at the little pill, hesitating. She wasn't sure if she wanted to trust this person or not. What if swallowing this pill killed her or something? Or knocked her out? What then? She hesitated for a moment more before practically shoving it into her mouth and quickly swallowing.

Fiona seemed to relax slightly, a gentle expression on her face. "Thank you." She pushed herself to her feet. "As long as you take the medicine and keep your wound bandaged properly, you should be fine in about a week."

"Thanks," Karina muttered, pulling her leg back as she glanced at Fiona. "You had no reason to do all this for me. Why?"

Fiona stared at her quietly before starting to pack up her supplies, attention focused on that task. Now that Karina was paying more attention, it was surprising to notice just how much the woman had. She had all sorts of medicine, tonics and varying types of bandages and items such as tongs, scalpels, the works. Was she really just a medical student?

"Like I said earlier, I've never met anyone from the outer community on...good terms, then you came along. I just, wanted to know what it was like out there. I've only ever been to a few places and, while my memories tell me outer community people are bad, I can't help but wonder if there might be more to it. Why would someone destroy an entire gated community? What was in it for them besides just destruction? There are so many more people outside the community than in, so why haven't they all killed each other off? If they are so destructive, why aren't they all dead?"

Karina felt a chill at the woman's words, spoken in an honest and confused way. Speaking of so many people, so many lives, just...disappearing. Fiona examined her quietly. "Yet, you don't seem that way. Scared, sure, but not destructive. You could have shot us both as soon as Eren said something, but you didn't. Of course, that doesn't make sense with what I know, so..." Fiona shrugged. "That's beside the point. If you don't mind, I think you should stay until you're healed up. No one should find you here. Not many people come by anyway, and neither Eren nor I will talk."

"What would happen if someone learned about me and my connections to the outer community?" Karina could guess, but she was curious on what Fiona would say.

Fiona hesitated before shaking her head. "It's best not to think about it. After all, I'm not the only survivor from a destroyed community here. Others weren't as lucky and hold a strong grudge against those like you." Fiona stood up, patting herself down. "Anyway, this will be your room while you stay here. I know it's still early, but you should get some sleep. It seems like you haven't slept in days. Let me give you something light for your stomach, then you can get some sleep."

With that, she left the room, the flutter of her skirt the only thing Karina saw as the door swung shut. She bit her lip and stared down at the floor. Her leg throbbed, as if trying to grab her attention, the white flush against her skin. She slowly stood up, keeping her balance as best she could, though it was still a little unsteady, and carefully moved around the room, taking everything in. There was a balcony on the back that looked out into a surrounding forest and, below, a covered pool with deck chairs sprawled around it. The room itself was simple, a walk-in closet and nothing else, not like the separate chambers for servants that she and Maxwell stayed in while with Lex.

It was a little while later when the woman returned with a small bowl of soup and some soft bread. Realizing just how hungry she was, Karina downed it in no time at all. The woman smiled knowingly, picking it up and leaving with a soft, "Good night."

Karina stared after her before turning toward the bed with a strange, yet warm feeling. The food sat comfortably in her stomach and her thoughts, which decided to go over what to do next, were still more on the sluggish, if traitorous, side.

Could she actually stay here and rest?

What then?

What was she going to do, now that she no longer really had anywhere to go?

Chapter Eighteen

Maxwell stared out the window of the pick-up, watching the fields roll by like he'd been doing for the past day. After refueling the truck and resting for the night, Lex decided to take the interstate highway, getting on the road quite early in the morning and only stopping briefly for lunch. Maxwell hadn't known such a long stretch of road existed, but it wasn't a far-fetched notion, now that he thought about it. It would definitely make travel easier, as evidenced by the good time they were making, relatively speaking. Cars passed by at even intervals, moving alongside and zooming past. Maxwell felt another sigh coming on and, instead, reached into his pocket and pulled out his phone. The blank screen glared back at him and his mood sunk even more. How long would he have to wait before she could contact him? Would she? Speaking of, he knew her phone was dead, but wasn't there another way? Another way she could let them know she was alright? Was she okay? He was pissed at himself for letting this happen. How could he not realize?

"Stop thinking about the what ifs."

Maxwell jerked and turned to Lex as the phone fell into his lap. Lex glanced over to him briefly, hands firmly on the wheel as he turned back. "What do you mean?" Maxwell cut in, causing an unamused, frown to cut across Lex's face. "Did you get another text from her? Like earlier?" His words were harsher than he meant them to be, but he didn't retract them.

Lex seemed to twitch, more annoyed than Maxwell was used to. "You have asked me that at least once every five minutes. The answer hasn't changed." He let out a long-exasperated sigh. "But that's not what I was trying to say. What I meant was exactly what I said. Stop thinking about the what ifs." Lex's tone and expression was taut as he continued, "There is no point in wondering what's going on with your sister or what she is doing. Just think of what you need to do and what she would want you to do right now."

"You..." Maxwell fell silent as he realized the emotions behind Lex's words.

He glanced sidelong at his friend, noting the glimpse of frustration and sadness before he turned away. Of course, he was probably thinking of Caym. Maxwell berated himself. He'd only been thinking of his situation and yet Lex had been dealing with this for a lot longer. He WOULD know.

Maxwell placed his chin in his palm, elbow on the windowsill. Sure, he asked each time he thought about her. He thought about her a lot, but he couldn't help it. The landscape was speeding by, a blur to his tired mind.

"We'll be stopping in the next town. We need to grab something to eat and rest."

Lex let out a yawn and Maxwell jerked, blinking in surprise before shaking his head. Of course, if this was mind-numbing for him, just sitting there, staring, it must be tiring for Lex who was trying to concentrate on a single stretch of pavement for hours on end. He winced. Yikes, no wonder his friend needed a rest.

"That's fine."

Lex sent him a grateful expression before spotting something ahead. He hummed in contentment and pulled off the exit. The town they drove into seemed normal enough. the roads wide enough for cars either direction. However, it was small, so small that Maxwell almost could equate it to being just that one road. The houses were starting to fall apart, held together as they were with bits of plaster and wood. A dry heat invaded the place, soaking up sweat as soon as it emerged. Maxwell huffed out a breath as Lex turned the truck off, the rackety air conditioner going quiet in the process.

They wandered around town before spotting a building off to one side with a few posters and a hanging sign that showed a soup bowl, the letters faded over time. Maxwell hesitated, but Lex walked forward, opening the wooden door with a faint jingle. The inside was surprisingly quaint, a gentle murmuring filling the air with the few others around. Wooden chairs and tables were set up at even intervals with paraphernalia lining the walls. Some things, Maxwell decided to avoid looking at. He was not in the mood to be staring at a skinned animal pelt.

"Hello, how can I help you?"

A young woman spoke up from behind a counter, a relieved grin on her face. Probably happy someone was coming in to eat, or something to do, Maxwell figured as the two of them were led to a seat and given some menus. The woman winked at Lex before walking away. Maxwell chuckled as Lex just shook his head and perused the menu in curiosity.

Maxwell followed suit. The first thing that caught his eye was the little type under the curled name of the restaurant. "Nebraska?" He voiced out quietly, startled.

"Hm. We must have passed into the state a little while ago. Guess we missed the sign," Lex spoke up, not pulling away from the menu.

Maxwell just shook his head before returning his attention to the menu. A sharp pain filled his chest as he spotted a spiced jalapeno dish. His sister would have loved that. He wrenched himself away, forcing himself to decide on what he wanted.

He heard the screeching of chairs and glanced over to see a small group sit beside them. One of the men, an older man that looked like he might need a cane, spoke up. "You hear about them wildfires of late?"

Lex peered over his menu as Maxwell glanced around his own.

One of the women responded, slapping him lightly as she took a seat. "Of course, we've heard. With this here heat? It's no surprise them be starting up so much. It's dry as them peaches out back."

"You mean as dry as you." The other woman chortled, getting a glare back.

Maxwell glanced toward Lex who shook his head and put his menu down. "I really should have thought of that."

"Why?" Maxwell spoke up, causing Lex to glance over to him before sighing and swiping a hand through his hair as he leaned back.

"We're heading into Midwestern country. I've heard about it enough while in my studies." Lex grimaced. "Due to the amount of wooded areas and the dryness of the atmosphere, wildfires are pretty abundant around there, especially during summer."

"So..." Maxwell trailed off, unsure what he was saying.

Lex hesitated and shrugged. "We'll just have to keep an eye out. I don't know much more than you on it, but it really shouldn't be too much of an issue. We're not going to be around much longer. One or two more days should get us to the mountains and from there, we'll have to worry about other things, like hailstorms."

"If you say so," Maxwell muttered before looking up as the waitress returned.

He could hear the four at the next table, talking, but they were speaking about some sort of game. He figured it was best to ignore it. They ordered their food and, in no time, finished up. It wasn't anything grand, but it was a home-cooked-like meal and Maxwell could appreciate it.

"We'll head out after we eat. This town is too small to find someplace to rest and we still have a ways to go." Lex spoke up as he stood and, waving to the waitress, he passed her a tip. "Quick question," he asked as she took the money from him. "Where's the closest town from here with a large inn?"

"Oh, um, I know there is an inn about twenty miles from here, but a decent-sized inn is not for a good one hundred and fifty miles due west of here. Kinsen, I believe. Though be careful out there, it's been dangerous on the roads lately." The woman seemed hesitant as she took the tip. "I wish you safe travels."

"Thank you." Lex nodded before gesturing toward Maxwell.

Maxwell glanced at the woman as they left, watching her hurry away to the next customer. He shook his head and caught up with Lex's longer pace.

"So, a hundred and fifty miles?"

"Seems it." Lex rubbed the bridge of his nose in fatigue. "I don't want to stop in the first hotel we pass, it would be better to go as far as possible. Plus, a bigger hotel is safer to hide in if or when someone comes searching. It will give us more time to escape than something small and falling apart. Hopefully, that one should only take about two hours, but I hate traveling like this. Not only am I the only one able to drive, but the damn constant environment is just draining."

"I know what you mean." Maxwell grimaced, remembering the flatlands they'd been traveling through for hours.

As much as he felt bad for Lex, getting behind the wheel of that rickety old thing just scared him. He had no idea how to drive the thing or where to even start. Plus, they were trying NOT to grab attention on themselves, which left him pretty limited in what he could do. To keep himself entertained, they tried the radio, but it was busted and mostly static, so they gave up. It made it difficult to keep from being completely bored out of one's mind.

Maxwell groaned and pulled himself into the passenger side of the truck, leaning against the window frame as Lex slipped into the other side. The truck rumbled to life and, after a few jerky movements that Maxwell was unfortunately getting used to, they were off. It was a rough start and he still had the bruises from the seatbelt to prove it. Within no time, they were back on the highway and trundling along. The windows were cracked open to relieve a little of the heat. Even with the air conditioner blowing on maximum, he could feel a burning sensation. He groaned, placing his forehead against the window, hoping for it to be just a little cooler. It wasn't.

Maxwell glanced at his phone again before putting it away. It's been days and still nothing. Where was she?

~ * ~

Karina slowly opened her eyes, staring up at the ceiling in silence. The white glowed softly in the morning light. Sunlight sparkled off the glass and cast interesting shapes above. She sighed and pushed herself upward, perusing the room. It was about the same size as Lex's back in the gated community, lavish, but simple. The bed she lay in was soft. She winced, feeling uncomfortable that she got a soft bed when her brother probably hadn't. She swung her legs out of bed, wincing as pain shot up one. She glanced down to see a clean white bandage wrapped tightly around her upper thigh. Oh, right, she'd been helped by that gated community person. What was her name again? She frowned as she stood up, carefully putting pressure on it before peering around.

She heard a knock on the door and turned as the woman who'd helped her yesterday walked in. Fiona, that was her name, she reminded herself as the woman spotted her. "Oh. You're up." Fiona placed a tray down and walked over. "How are you feeling? Any better?"

"I'm fine," Karina muttered, unsure how to really respond.

The woman beamed and then gestured.

"Come, I made breakfast." She turned, heading over to the tray and taking a seat at the little table it was set upon.

Karina hesitantly followed suit, slowly lowering herself into the other chair as Fiona grabbed a Danish and began eating, humming quietly. Karina tentatively took a banana and bit into it. She eyed the oatmeal and Danishes warily before taking a nibble of one. She blinked before finishing it off, enjoying the treat.

She heard a chuckle. Fiona smiled widely, a sparkle in her eye. "I'm glad you like them."

"Thank you." Karina spoke up before glancing away. "Anyway, I should probably get going soon. I appreciate the hospitality, but..."

"Where would you be going?"

Karina glanced back as an odd expression shifted over the woman's face. Fiona must have noticed because curiosity quickly replaced it. Karina hesitated, yet responded truthfully. "Somewhere..."

She paused and sighed. She honestly didn't know. Where was she going? "West, I need to go west."

She decided. She didn't have a reason to stay with Maxwell, but maybe she could do something about this disease? It was a foolish thought, considering she wasn't sure if she had it, the cure, but she needed something to do, anything, or else she would go crazy.

"What for?" Fiona leaned forward, fist under her chin and head tilted. "You seemed to be pretty lost when we found you."

Karina stiffened before sighing. "I was. I guess I have a lot on my mind."

"Ah."

The woman didn't say any more, which Karina was grateful for.

They continued eating in silence.

After some time, she shook her head and glanced toward Fiona. "Thanks. I really appreciate you helping me."

Fiona smiled faintly before standing up and picking up the food. "That's fine. I'll go check on my brother, see how he's doing regarding all this."

"Oh." Karina frowned, vaguely remembering what the 'brother' called Fiona. It seemed so formal. "Eren, right? You two don't..."

"Don't look alike?" Fiona's smile shifted slightly, her eyes clouding before she shook her head and turned. "Now why would you say that? He's my brother and that's it."

Karina frowned, watching as Fiona left, slipping out the door with food in hand, or at least, what was left over.

That seemed so strange, Karina couldn't quite understand why she said it that way. Was she trying to tell herself that? It sounded almost like that was exactly what she was doing. She glanced toward the doorway before standing up, carefully putting some weight on her leg. It seemed to be okay for now. She sighed in relief and walked out the door after Fiona, examining the hall. There was no one there. No one she could see. Damn, that woman moved fast. Curiosity getting the better of her now that her leg was feeling better, she took a chance and wandered down the hall, deciding to explore the place.

Part of her mind wondered if she would find a charger for her phone, but the more she walked, the more her footsteps rang back to her, echoing in the quiet and almost lonely hallways. As she took turn after turn, keeping half a mind on the way back, she crossed her arms over her chest, fingers clamping on the upper arms. Vague light beamed through the windows, dancing over some of the dusty ornaments and vases. A shimmer sat in the air as coolness clung to her skin from the air conditioner. Yet, she didn't see anything, nothing that modern besides what was in her room.

The area she was passing through now barely seemed used, the rug clean, but worn under her feet. Dust danced in the air, causing her to sneeze as she peeked into a doorway on her right. Inside was a study that was neat and organized...and absolutely untouched in what appeared to be years.

Having heard no one else besides herself, a trill of fear and concern coursed down her spine, but she pushed it off. She briefly wondered where the kitchen or the entrance hall was. This place, while not quite as big and grand as Lex's place, still wasn't exactly easy to navigate. There were so many things to keep an eye on, it was hard for her to keep track. She shook her head and turned, only to start when she spotted Eren behind her. He nodded toward her, fingers clasped in front of him. "I'm sorry if I startled you. I noticed you wandering and wondered if you were perhaps lost."

"I might be?" she muttered. "Wasn't Fiona going to talk with you?"

"She already did," Eren spoke, before turning. "Anyway, your room is this way. Is there anywhere else you would like to go? We do have a lovely music room, as well as a pool out back."

"No, I'm good." She waved it away, feeling uncomfortable, her stomach twisting. "Um, I was wondering if you had a phone, or something to charge mine with or..." The sudden pitying expression on Eren's face made her stop short.

"I'm sorry. Ms. Fiona is badly startled by phones, ever since..." He shook his head. "I have a PDA if I need to contact anyone, but that is all."

"Oh." Karina briefly wondered how a phone can startle someone so badly that they don't have any, but she decided to let it go.

Shaking it off, she hurried after the man, grateful for the guidance. Especially when she realized she'd actually messed up her mental map of the place when she took a right when she thought she took a left. Frowning at that knowledge, she ended up back in her temporary room.

"Well then, I shall be off. There's an in-house phone on the counter if you need anything. Do try not to get lost here, the mistress would not like that."

With that, he left and Karina gulped. Wait, but there was an in-house phone? Wouldn't that startle her as well? Was it something different? Karina briefly glanced at the phone, noting there were no numbers or anything. She picked it up and heard a quiet sound outside.

She heard a knock on her door and jumped, dropping the phone back down. She walked over, peeking out to see Eren, standing outside with a slightly furrowed brow. "Did you need something?"

"No, I was just confused how the phone works."

The man stared for a moment before nodding. "As you can probably guess, it is to notify me. If that is all, please, have a good day." With that he closed the door.

Karina stared at the door, wondering, once more, what she had gotten herself into?

Why did he call her mistress?

Who was Eren...and was he really Fiona's brother?

Karina flipped through the channels on TV, her original clothes now cleaned and laundered. She took a nice long bath a little earlier which made her still smell of lavender. There wasn't really anything of interest. There were a few cartoons way too censored for her taste, sitcoms that still had canned laughter that made her want to chuck the remote at the screen and news channels that were going on about the weather and how it was another 'beautiful summer day'. It's like they were completely oblivious. She flipped the channel one more time, spotting a young woman with bright red locks, singing some music. The music and woman were, admittedly, quite pretty. She glanced at the name at the bottom of the screen, ignoring the screaming of fans. She must have been watching a concert recording. The name, Rose Thornfield, flitted over the bottom and she hummed in thought. She'd heard the name before. Glancing back up as the woman gave one more wave and left the stage, Karina shook her head and turned the TV off, getting up and stretching toward the ceiling.

There wasn't much to do at all. Her leg was feeling better now that she'd given it some rest, and lunch had already come and gone with a wide assortment of foods that she enjoyed, the taste surprisingly fresh. She peered out the window of her room. Spotting the sunny sky, her mood dipped as her thoughts flickered to her brother. Was he alright? She supposed he was probably fine, same with Lex. Unfortunately, it wouldn't stop bothering her, her worry. She knew she should stop, that it wasn't getting her anywhere, constantly thinking about it, but she found she couldn't help it. Though she knew it would only hurt to think about how she screwed up, her mind kept dragging her back, kicking and screaming.

She needed to find something to keep her mind off things. Though she had been failing for most of today anyway. Thankfully, she heard a knock on the door and called, "Come in."

The door swung open and Fiona peeked inside. She glanced at Karina and gave her a soft, kind smile. "Hello, I just wanted to check on you. How are you feeling?"

"Fine. You?" she asked.

Fiona blinked, seeming surprised before she shrugged, stepping inside. "I was talking with Eren. My dear brother is absolutely confused on how we can help you. You know...you look a lot like my little sister, did I mention that?"

Karina paused, trying to wrap her head around the sudden switch in dialogue. My little sister? Why did she say my and not ours? A distant expression came to Fiona as she smiled faintly. Karina frowned, examining the smile. This woman seemed to do it a lot and it was starting to bother Karina just a little, did she do much else? Then her brain caught up with what the woman was saying and she blinked. Seriously, sister? Where did that come from? Why the heck did Fiona bring it up? She felt a slight chill run down her spine as she spotted Fiona examining her, a strange expression on her face as the smile widened just slightly. "Fiona?" she called, her voice surprisingly high-pitched.

Fiona seemed to snap out of whatever thought she was in and she shook her head sheepishly. "Sorry, did you say something?"

"No... No, it's fine," Karina muttered, keeping the nervous tone out of her voice.

Fiona nodded. "Alright. So, let's get that bandage checked."

Karina stiffened, but Fiona quickly moved to her side, squatting down to get closer to the wound. Her fingers lightly traced over the healing scabs and the reddish, but no longer purple, skin. She hummed, changing the bandage with fluid and exact movements. "Seems to be healing alright. Good." She glanced up. "I know you are probably bored, being in here all by yourself. Can I get you anything? A game? Something?"

"No, I'm good," she spoke, her throat tight.

She wasn't sure she wanted to ask for a charger for her phone, hesitant to get on this woman's bad side.

Fiona blinked, a faint frown on her face. "Does it hurt?"

Noting the growing suspicion, Karina found a shaky smile coming on her face. Why she was so nervous around the kind woman, she couldn't understand, but she just felt uncomfortable, though the woman never did anything bad. If anything, she was helping Karina, though she didn't need to. "A little..." she lied. "It's better though so, thank you."

Fiona nodded, pushing herself to her feet, a little more at ease. "Alright. Eren will be by with food later. Get some rest and I'll check on you in the morning, alright?" She waved good-bye, slipping out the door.

Karina opened her mouth to ask, but then stopped. Of course, Fiona wouldn't be able to come by all the time. She was probably taking classes or whatever for her medical degree. Karina let out a breath she hadn't realized she was holding in, then promptly berated herself. What was she doing? Fiona was only being kind. Just like Martha. After all, she could easily just turn Karina into a servant or send her off like she saw happen before. Fiona hadn't though. She's been keeping an eye on Karina and making sure she was feeling better. Karina grunted, falling back on the couch, arm over her face. She was the worst.

Chapter Nineteen

Maxwell groaned as his hand fell from his chin, his head smacking into the hot glass of the window. Their air conditioner broke down about a mile back and he was sweltering. He knew he should roll down the window, but the wind was so loud as they traveled down the road and he honestly did not want it blasting into his face.

Lex had no such qualms. After making sure his hat was firmly on, he cranked the window all the way down and let one arm dangle over the sill, fingers tapping near the mirror.

Thankfully, the sun was setting, so the heat wasn't completely unbearable, just uncomfortable. He finally caved and cracked the window open a little, letting some of the cross breeze through. "How much farther?"

"I think only about another mile or two." Lex let out a huff, just as tired as Maxwell.

Maxwell thought he would be excited to be traveling. Even though his sister was more of the traveler, it didn't mean he couldn't still appreciate the journey. As they trundled along, he realized how much he hated the endless road and the same featureless expanse around them. It didn't help that the old truck smelled of gasoline and there were barely any turn-offs as they traveled. Plus, there was a distinct lack of anything interesting to do, which left him going crazy. He heard a heavy sigh. Lex hummed a strange tune before glancing over to him. "If I am to guess, we still have a few more days' worth of travel before we arrive."

"A few days?" Maxwell slumped then shrugged. "I can deal," he muttered, wanting to say something else, but feeling it was best to just seem optimistic.

Lex was probably getting annoyed with his sulky attitude, even if, in Maxwell's opinion, it was totally justified.

Lex noticed anyway because he huffed and leaned his head on his arm, chin in hand as the other lay over the steering wheel. His hair blew in the wind as he glanced sidelong for a moment. "No distracting you, huh?"

Maxwell felt uncomfortable as he faced away from his friend. Well, true...

"Oh, there's the turn-off. We'll rest there for tonight and head out in the morning."

Maxwell peered up and spotted the exit ramp a little ahead, the green of the overhanging sign shone, slightly dilapidated and run-down from time and weather. They turned off the exit as the sun began to set and quickly scoured around for an inn. Finding a dilapidated, but still in use motel, they decided to take a rest.

While the entrance was brightly lit, it was a strange combination of clean and cluttered. While Maxwell wasn't exactly fond of it, he knew he could tolerate it as Lex acquired the keys and they trudged upstairs. Ignoring the pastel and grungy orange of the wall, they tried their key. Maxwell frowned, pushing the key card into the slot while Lex waited, laden with bags. The light flickered back and forth between red and green, but nothing actually happened. Maxwell tried again, this time going a little faster. Still nothing.

Lex let out a groan and reached into his pocket, where he'd already put his card away, and tried himself.

Nothing.

"I'll get us a new set of cards, stay here." Lex plucked Maxwell's card from his grip and turned, walking back the way they came.

Maxwell watched him go before slumping against the wall, examining the ceiling without much care. He was starting to get annoyed, but it wasn't really an issue. He heard chatter and peered to the left as a man and woman stepped out of a doorway. Maxwell couldn't quite catch what they were talking about, until they passed by.

"...gated community?"

"Oh yeah, there is one nearby. Think the Resistance will attack it as well?"

"Don't know, what about the instigators, you know? The twins..."

The rest of the conversation faded away as they left and Maxwell frowned. Twins? What were they talking about? On top of that, there was a gated community nearby. He wasn't sure what he thought about that. And what did they mean by instigators? He shook his head and glanced over just as Lex headed toward him. For a brief moment, he thought of mentioning what he heard but quickly dismissed it. After all, he highly doubted it would do Lex much good to hear and would only worry them both. After another round of cards and another failure, they returned to the main entrance, beyond annoyed. Maxwell knew he, at one point, could be qualified as having a good amount of patience. That very same patience was running thin with both of them.

The woman at the counter seemed utterly frazzled and confused at the fact that the key didn't work. Maxwell was only really half-listening. His attention stuck on the radio playing softly in the corner. It wasn't anything special, the song, but it cut through the white noise. He heard Lex scoff and turned in time to note the way Lex's face twisted in anger. Lex took a deep breath, probably attempting to calm himself, before he waved the woman away. She took the keys, scrambling away with the same fervor as if Lex hit the fourth stage.

"What happened?" Maxwell asked, stepping forward, finding the tiredness dragging at his eyelids.

Lex muttered some choice words that Maxwell dared not repeat before turning to him.

"Of all the rooms here, we happened to get the ONE that had a dead battery. I didn't know motels used batteries for their doors."

Maxwell could not stop the deadpan expression from crossing his face. "You're joking."

"Wish I was." Lex shrugged before leaning against the counter. "They're finding a new room for us now. Shouldn't take too long, but still..."

Maxwell huffed and took a seat on one of the few chairs around the little entrance. A dead battery, of all things. How stupid could these things get? After a couple more minutes, they had a new set of keys and a new room. Maxwell followed Lex up the stairs, mentally cursing stairs as he stumbled on the top one. To his relief, this time, the card key worked. They both stepped inside.

Maxwell took in the little room and cringed, carefully dropping his bag on the bed. The hardwood floor under his feet was weird, almost sticky and cold. He could hear the air conditioner rattling and groaning as it turned on and the air smelled heavily of smoke to the point where he had to open the window anyway. Though he could have sworn they asked for a no smoking room. Just their luck, really, even the 'new' room was, well, crap.

"Well, it could be worse." Lex took a seat on the bed as Maxwell finished wrenching the window open to let in a little of the night time air. Maxwell turned in time to notice as Lex winced and patted the bed, feeling it over. "Though I would prefer a bed that didn't feel like metal pipes."

Maxwell raised an eyebrow and stepped over, taking a seat on his chosen bed. Ah, so that's what he meant. The bed was more lump than mattress. The pillows were okay, but the sheets felt scratchy. He sighed, well, it would have to do. Hopefully, he'd be able to get some sleep. Lex didn't seem too convinced though as he stepped into the bathroom. Maxwell glanced over as water started running.

Maybe he would wait until the morning to take a shower...he might need it to wake up. Huffing and deciding that was probably the best course of action, he slipped into his nightwear and pulled himself into bed. The air was stifling even after he threw off most of the sheets. Kari would be cursing about now... Maxwell weakly chuckled. If anything, she would probably be stomping downstairs to demand at least an air freshener, if not a total refund due to all the problems they experienced. Huh... He closed his eyes and groaned. He really needed to take Lex's advice and stop thinking about this, it was making him upset.

That's what he would do. Until Karina contacted him, he would just have to hold out hope that she was alright. When she did contact...he had a few choice words for her.

Nodding to himself, he curled into bed and convinced his body that, yes, he did actually need sleep. Thankfully, his body actually listened.

Maxwell awoke slowly, his body screaming with aches and pains. The air felt sweltering and pressured. He pushed himself up. Lex slipped out of bed, cringing a little, but seeming alright.

"How are you moving?" Maxwell muttered, trying and failing to swing his legs out of bed, the last of the sheets tangling into his limbs.

"I've slept on worse, though that's not saying much." Lex shrugged as he stepped over to the window. He closed it, letting the air conditioner take more control. "Just do some stretches."

"Right..." Maxwell huffed, but followed his suggestions, remembering when he and Karina first left home, she mentioned stretching before continuing on.

He tried to mimic what she did all that time ago, but it was hard to remember exactly. Still, it did help alleviate some of the pain.

At least he still had a shower to look forward to.

Which was good because he felt like he didn't sleep at all. Since they would be traveling most of the day, he had a feeling he was going to be stiff and tired later. He was not looking forward to it.

Maxwell was grateful when they grabbed something to eat and headed out not too long after he finished up his shower. The place still stunk and he was grateful to just get out of that cold feeling, but too hot, room. The sun was rising into the sky and the temperature was going up with it. It was another dry day that made Maxwell curse the fact that their air-conditioner was completely broken. What could they do about it though? Last time he checked, they didn't exactly have the money to fix it, and he highly doubted Lex would be willing to waste money on it with all the other issues they still needed to deal with. So, resigning himself, he peered out, letting his mind wander.

It was probably about midday when he noticed something strange. He blinked and sat up. Off to the right-hand side, still a good distance away, he swore there was something there. He couldn't tell what it was, but the air shimmered.

He heard a shout then screech. He scrambled, grabbing onto something as the truck swerved, pulling him sharply into the seatbelt and causing him to lightly smack his head against the headrest.

"What was that?" he gasped, catching his breath as his heart pounded.

Lex was frowning, gaze flicking into the distance. "Some idiot decided to speed past going the wrong way. You didn't notice?"

"I was watching something else," Maxwell admitted, feeling a bit sheepish.

How did he miss that? He shook his head and peeked back out. With his mind having wandered for so long, he hadn't noticed they had entered a thick forest. He blinked, surprised, and felt a smile tug on his lips. He hadn't seen a place like this in a while. The trees were densely packed, letting in little light, but it was pretty in the shimmering heat. Dark clouds rolled above, as if night was descending. A storm? He frowned, spotting a few deer bounding in the opposite direction from them, racing through the trees. He only saw them that spooked when a predator was after them...or when Karina was swinging between the trees as she sometimes used to do.

He would have dismissed it, if he hadn't noticed more animals racing away as well. He heard the shrill cry of birds and snapped his head up as a whole flock took flight, a cluttered clump more than the clean flight patterns they usually took.

"Something's wrong," Maxwell said as he sat up.

There were a few people traveling with them, but no one going the other direction.

"Hm..." Lex hummed, his tone indicating he agreed. His grip was tight on the wheel and he was perusing the long wide highway.

Maxwell heard the shrill sound of a car horn and jumped, gripping the door tightly as a car driving in front of them suddenly veered to the side. Coming the other direction, not caring that it was going against the flow of traffic, was a Humvee. Maxwell only got a glimpse inside as Lex cursed and once more dodged. There was a pair inside, the couple from last night. They must have left earlier then Maxwell and Lex. One person gripped a phone tightly and yelled into it while the other was white-faced and leaning forward, as if racing with the car.

Around the same time, they reached a bend and Maxwell realized why there weren't any cars coming the opposite direction. A large pile-up cluttered the left side of the road. An overturned trailer truck was caught between a few cars that had smashed into the trees and the concrete barrier that cut the highway off. Behind the accident were a few more cars, just haphazardly parked as if having drawn to a stop suddenly. With the whole other side of the highway blocked off by the initial pileup, it was no surprise there was a backup behind it. Yet it startled and unnerved him how far back the cars were parked, some with blinkers on and some at an angle as if they swerved suddenly, unable to stop fast enough. Lastly, there were the people weaving between and away from cars... A lot of people.

Maxwell's eyes widened as he spotted people struggling to get out of their cars, some going to help those within the accident and some just fleeing down the road past the accident, carrying only basics.

What were they all fleeing from?

He heard the squeal of tires and caught the faint smell of burning wood. Hoping that he was just imagining things and reminding himself that it did NOT remind him of the riot he and his sister got caught up in, or the burning destroyed gated community, he turned toward the sound, the acrid smell and paled. That shimmer he observed earlier wasn't a shimmer.

It was a heat haze. A heat haze that hid the billowing smoke of a blazing fire that was eating through the trees like paper a few miles down the road. The clouds from before weren't from a storm, they were smoke being blown by the wind heading in their direction.

The fact that it was a few miles away didn't seem to make anyone feel better. Lex twisted the wheel, the truck almost doing a one-eighty to avoid the car that slammed on its brakes in front of them. Maxwell yelped, smacking his head into the window, matching the throbbing at the back of his skull. Yet he ignored it, staring at the flames dancing and eating away just ahead of them.

"Shit," Lex spoke summarily, his monotone tone expressing much more than Maxwell's high-pitched squeak that he definitely did NOT let loose.

"Lex..." Maxwell choked, fingers twitching in panic.

Lex didn't respond. He just grabbed the wheel and yanked, turning them fully around same as the other vehicles were doing. The crash on the other side of the road made much more sense now. As well as the fleeing.

"Maxwell, call 911."

"WHAT?" Maxwell yelped, turning to him. "But..."

"That wildfire is already taking out a good portion of the forest. I'm not sure if anyone else has called, but there are towns ahead. It needs to be stopped as soon as possible."

Maxwell pursed his lips but did as Lex said. He grabbed his phone as Lex weaved out of the slight mess created by his and others' sudden halt. Maxwell glanced back as the phone clicked and began to ring. Across the road and past the median, most of the cars were abandoned and the people farther down the highway were stopped and staring in helplessness. Some continued to run, but others just stood there, deer in headlights.

"Lex..."

Lex glanced over to him then followed his gaze. "We can't help them."

"We could though!" Maxwell cut in before stopping as a line picked up.

"Hello, what is your emergency?"

"Hello? This is... There's a wildfire at..." Maxwell cut off as he realized he hadn't a clue where they were. He really should have been paying more attention

"About twenty miles west of exit 25." Lex's voice jerked him out of his thoughts.

Maxwell nodded and conveyed the information. He heard a pause and then the person responded, "Thank you. We have received reports of the fire. Emergency vehicles are on their way. If possible, please go to the nearest evacuation center, there should be one off exit 23. Twenty minutes or so from there. It should be safe enough."

"Alright." Maxwell pulled the phone away as he heard the click of disconnect and jerked forward as Lex slammed on the brakes and parked the truck next to the median. Maxwell caught the raised eyebrow and sent him what he hoped conveyed his gratitude.

He pulled himself out of the truck and vaulted over the median, hurrying over to the brunt of the accident where the stragglers remained. A few people fled past him. He just avoided bumping into a woman with a baby and had to stop so he didn't run into a man leading his wife forward. He muscled through the fleeing crowd and came up to where a different smoke billowed up, a lighter gray. The truck driver was crawling out of the cab, helped along by another man. Another car was in front of the truck, completely crushed. Maxwell had a feeling it was the car's fault for the accident more than the truck, considering the skid marks and the angle of the truck. Unfortunately, the subsequent cars weren't able to dodge either and he caught one smashed under the turned-over trailer.

He winced and quickly pulled himself out of his observations. Thankfully, most of those caught behind the accident had already fled past, so all that were left were those in the accident itself and the few stragglers at the end of the line. He hurried up to the first person he could reach.

It was an older woman, probably mid-thirties, early forties. She looked up from where she was on the ground, her leg twisted at an odd angle. "Wha..."

"I'm here to help." Maxwell squatted. "My friend is in the truck on the other side of the median. We're taking who we can."

"But..."

"Edith, go." Another voice croaked out and Maxwell jerked, spotting a figure lying on the ground, trapped under one of the vehicles. Maxwell winced, noticing the pooling blood. He had seen enough death lately to know the other person wasn't going to make it.

He heard footsteps and jerked, peering over his shoulder as a few people hurried toward the wreckage, crossing the barrier. While some of the cars that were with them on the road already fled, it seemed a few people stayed, just like himself and Lex, their cars idling on the other side of the median, ready to go.

In truth, the next few minutes were a blur. He remembered ushering a few people into vehicles that were accessible and operable and helping to carry others too injured to move themselves. The fire wafted closer and closer as they worked. The squeal of tires and the sound of shouts and cries rang in his ears as the cars, already laden with people, sped away to safety. Those who were still close to the scene joined them, loading anyone they could. Within no time at all, the truck bed was completely packed and there were still people. The other cars were gone, theirs the only one left with room and space.

The few that were left were clamoring to get in. Lex, who stayed in the truck so it wouldn't get stolen in the chaos, had to slam his door and lock it with all the people scrambling to get in.

"Maxwell, we have to go."

He didn't shout it, but his teeth were gritted and Maxwell could hear the slight fear in his friend's voice. Which indicated much more than everyone else's panic. Maxwell, who'd been helping the last person in, jumped into the front as one of the stragglers grabbed at his clothes. He turned, just as an older woman shoved a child into his arms. It was a little girl who hadn't been able to fit in the back. "Please. At least take her."

"Mama." The girl, startled, turned on Maxwell's lap as the woman slammed the door shut and pointed.

Lex got the hint, shifting faster than Maxwell ever saw him do before slamming on the gas. The tires squealed and he heard startled cries before they were off. Maxwell felt his heart leap into his throat as he caught sight of those left behind. The woman who'd thrown the little girl in his arms, two men who'd been trapped under their cars, those few who'd been closer to the fire and...

Maxwell turned his head as they sped, faster and faster down the highway. On the far side, across the median were those who tried to run.

Considering how fast the fire was approaching, how the flames flickered behind him at a distance that was still too close for comfort and the black smoke covered the sky like an encroaching thunderstorm, it didn't take much to realize that those with him in the truck might be the last of the survivors.

He gritted his teeth as the little girl in his lap sobbed. He glanced down and, more on instinct, pulled her close, arms tight around her little waist. The girl startled before turning and gripping his shirt, pounding her fists into his chest. He glanced sidelong at Lex whose lips were pursed into a tight thin line.

There wasn't much else they could do. He felt the tears and quickly blinked them away. No, he needed to be strong. It hurt, so badly, to see all the people they couldn't help. That they couldn't save.

Hell, they were in danger themselves. With the fire flickering behind them, almost upon the accident even as they rounded the bend, it was like hell itself was following on their trail, the black smoke completely obscuring the blue sky.

They were already a good mile away when the distant sound of sirens reached their ears. Lex clicked his tongue but ignored it, going as fast as the truck would allow while keeping watch on those in the back. The little girl went quiet, just a trembling ball in Maxwell's lap. He couldn't blame her, keeping his hold light, but warm. He understood why the mother did what she did. She must have been one of the ones trapped farther back on that side and so only got to them near the end. He knew his mother would do the same thing for them, if she had to.

He would do the same for his sister, he knew that without a doubt. They curved around another bend and shot forward. Up ahead, there were three firetrucks, sirens blaring and racing toward them. The firetrucks shifted, letting them pass as they continued on the way. Behind them, a police car wailed past, followed by another. The second did a sharp turn then pulled alongside the truck. Lex glanced over and slowed down, stopping. The police car stopped beside them and the person in the passenger seat hopped out. Maxwell flinched at first, before he noted the blue uniform, a member of the police brigade, glancing at the bed of the truck for a moment before turning to Lex. "Is that everyone?"

"Unfortunately, no. We couldn't carry any more. There are still a few runners and I don't know about those stuck at the accident," Lex responded, though Maxwell was only half-listening.

He peered over his shoulder, toward where the bend was, and frowned, wondering what that strange sound was. He could hear almost a high-pitched hissing sound, faint though it was, over the crackling of the approaching flames and smoke clouding the once clear sky.

"Alright, the other vehicles already left. There's a police barricade being put up a little down the road. Head there and they will lead all of you to safety."

"Alri—"

Maxwell covered his head with one arm while keeping a tight grip around the little girl with his other as a loud explosion sounded behind them. The ground shook, causing the officer to stumble. His head snapped toward the bend, almost fast enough to cause whiplash.

Another plume of black, acrid smoke billowed into the air.

"That must have been the cars. Many were leaking gasoline. I think the drivers probably got away, but..." Lex grimaced and turned to the officer. "Go and check if the rescuers are alright, we'll continue on."

The officer quickly nodded, recollecting himself before hurrying back to the car and hopping in. His partner didn't need to be told twice as he pulled a sharp one-eighty and screamed around the corner.

"Are they..." Maxwell felt choked as he dropped his arm. He knew the people in the back were in shock. Lex only shook his head and quickly shifted up to speed, pulling away once more.

"What are you doing? Go back." A woman, Edith, screamed as one of the men, who was holding his arm tightly to his side, caught her.

Maxwell turned noting the man holding the woman who appeared to be attempting to jump off the side of the truck, staring back at the billowing smoke, barely seen amongst the sheer black cloud. How he heard her voice over everything else, he wasn't sure, but he attributed it to how much he was focusing on everything. Every instinct screamed at him. His blood practically sang with adrenaline, fear and hurt.

The little girl in his arms just stared. Whether she understood what just happened or not, Maxwell wasn't sure. Part of him hoped, at least for her sake, that the mother got away from the accident enough that the rescuers could help.

He didn't hold out much hope on that. He hated it, but he was well aware that hoping for something like that would only bring more hurt and pain. If he was hurting, he could only imagine the others, separated from loved ones in order to be protected.

Still, Lex wasn't just sitting there. The truck was already up to max speed in almost no time at all. He could hear shouts and conversation from the back, followed by a faint thump.

That one caused him to glance back once more, and then sigh with relief when he spotted everyone still there. The only difference was the woman was now unconscious, laying between some of those rescued.

Lex quickly checked him before returning his focus to the road, his fingers tightly clasping the wheel. Maxwell wondered how far they had to go as he heard the crackling and snapping of the fire so far behind them as to be completely out of sight, but too close, just always too close.

"Mister...you can let go." The little girl's voice startled Maxwell into loosening his grip. She turned her teary-eyes toward him and he balked. "Mama... She's not coming, is she?"

Maxwell bit his lip, unsure what to say.

"Mama...she said it might happen. That she was sick, just like everyone else... Are you sick too, mister?"

Maxwell blinked and quickly examined the little girl, this time noting the way the girl held herself. She didn't appear injured, at least not more than the accident caused.

"She's not affected..."

Maxwell glanced sidelong at Lex, whose quick glance showed a hint of relief. "She's probably avoided it so far."

"No, I'm not, but what about you?"

The little girl curled into her side, holding her arms close. "Mama was careful. She wasn't sure what caused her problems, so she's been testing everything. She's really smart and is always working with really smart people, but..."

Maxwell sighed, and gave a faint smile. "She sounds like a good mother. She'll be glad to know you are alive."

"But... Mama..." The girl's lower lip trembled as tears trailed down her cheeks. She rubbed at her cheek and then let out another sob. "Mama told me, she might sleep soon, but..."

Maxwell bit his lip, feeling overwhelmed. His thoughts flickered to Karina, to his ma, before he gently started threading his fingers through the little girl's hair. "I'm sorry. Alright? By the way. What's your name? I'm Maxwell."

The girl sniffed. "Yvette..."

"That's a pretty name."

The girl nodded, leaning into his touch. They stayed that way for a while until Lex let out a heavy breath and started to slow. Maxwell glanced forward, spotting the barricade. It was a set of three police cars as well as a bunch of posts. A few firetrucks were nearby, already spraying down trees and setting some on fire. Maxwell blinked in confusion as he noticed this before frowning. Now that he thought about it, he did remember reading about it, a long time ago when he was still in Claremore. How, to cancel out a fire, you can set a new one that's more controlled. It would burn away anything that was burnable, creating a makeshift barrier. Considering the size of the wildfire behind them, it was no surprise to Maxwell.

Lex pulled to a stop just past the barricade. One of the officers hurried up, carrying a piece of paper. "You are the last to leave the area, correct?"

"Other than the rescue personnel, yes." Lex spoke, keeping his voice even as he kept a hand rested on the wheel, fingers twitching. Maxwell scrunched backward, reminding himself that they were from the police brigade and not Enthrope... It didn't help much and the little girl seemed to notice, curious.

"Alright, please follow us, we have a place for injured a few miles up." The officer hurried away and hopped in one of the vehicles off to the side. It turned on, rolling forward in front of the pickup. Lex pulled behind the vehicle, following after.

"What are we going to do?" Maxwell gulped, feeling the little girl's warmth seep through his t-shirt, her chest rising and falling as she leaned into his side, shaking. "We can't just leave, we have a lot of people injured, but..."

"We'll just have to do what we can. It should be fine still, but we'll keep watch." Lex drummed his fingers, the tone of his voice saying more than any expression. "We'll have to stay there for a bit, so as not to draw too much suspicion. Just don't panic and we should be fine."

Maxwell did not hold back on the deadpan that he sent Lex's way, which earned a chuckle from the older male. Maxwell let out a long breath, catching the greenery that passed outside the window. Maybe he was just being paranoid. The police brigade had been pretty good back in

Collern City, so...who knows. He would just have to hope that Caym hadn't decided to get the outside community involved. He wouldn't put it past the man, considering what little he recalled of him.

Chapter Twenty

Lex wasn't sure whether to be grateful or annoyed that they arrived to the safe house without much issue. His fingers felt stiff and tight. He was surprised he hadn't bitten clean through his bottom lip. He knew they would be safe now, at least from the fire, but that didn't stop his heart from racing. He took a deep breath, glancing sidelong at Maxwell as he pulled to a stop. The boy was trembling badly, his face pale and grasp gentle, yet firm on the little girl that had been shoved into his hands.

A little girl that, Lex realized, could help them blend in. After all, Enthrope would be searching for a set of twins and himself. Having a little girl in the mix and not having Karina would make it harder for them to figure out who they were.

He shook his head and opened the door, turning the truck off in the process. The sudden sound of the truck pittering to a stop caught the boy's attention, though he appeared confused. Lex slipped out of the truck to help the others. He mentioned earlier that they may have to stay for a bit.

If anything, he wanted to stay both to not appear suspicious, but also because both of them were exhausted from the mix of a lack of sleep and the sudden onslaught of the fire. A night's rest should be enough.

Off to one side, he spotted a golden gleam and frowned. So, there was a gated community nearby. He would just have to hope there was no Enthrope. Though he understood that the likelihood of that was low. With the emergency shelter being so close, it would be no surprise that some would come out just to make sure there were no 'issues'.

He cursed the fact, but pushed it off, reminding himself of Yvette when he noticed Maxwell finally slide out of the truck, the girl's hand in his own. Lex walked away, letting the last few help each other out. He grabbed Maxwell's attention and gestured toward the building. "Come on, let's get going," he said, shoving his hands in his pockets and heading inside with Maxwell hesitantly following behind.

The inside of the emergency shelter was simple. On either side of the hallway were lockers and little banners and so he guessed that it was probably a school of some sort, which was only reinforced as he recalled the layout of the long flat building.

They were ushered into a large entrance area. Lex spotted medical personnel hurrying up to them, quickly looking over each person before helping those most injured to a set of beds pushed off to one side. They all wore heavy garments, along with the masks everyone but themselves and a few poorer folks were wearing. Plastic shields covered their faces as their gloved hands worked almost tirelessly.

Everyone else was led to another room which was filled with chairs and people. Lex wasn't fond of the idea of being pulled around, but he understood the reason for them to do a check. Though they were probably free to go whenever, the doctors and nurses would want to make sure they were able to go safely. Lex glanced over his shoulder, thanking whatever luck they actually had that there were no Enthrope guards around yet. He wasn't sure how long that would last, but he would have to hope for the best.

He heard chatter and looked over as Maxwell took a seat, the little girl sitting beside him. The girl practically latched onto Maxwell, though it made sense, considering how young the little one was and how traumatizing that would have been.

Though, he was a little shaken by the experience, and he doubted he was alone. He leaned against the wall, arms crossed as he noted the lack of seats around the room. Not surprised. They probably didn't expect so many people caught up in the fire. It probably wouldn't have been an issue, if it wasn't for the accident that blockaded the road.

"Hey, Lex?" Maxwell's voice, weak as it was, still managed to draw his attention.

He glanced over, noting that the little girl was sleeping, leaning against Maxwell as he caught his gaze. "How long are we staying?"

He spotted the tiredness, the bags under Maxwell's eyes. With the lack of sleep the night before and all the panic, they were both drained more than they should have been. He sighed, dropping his arms and shrugging. "We'll have to stay the night anyway, just to make sure we're okay to move on."

Maxwell nodded, eyelids fluttering. It wasn't that it was late, it was just the adrenaline of the near brush was definitely wearing off the longer they stayed there. He suppressed a yawn and turned, heading for one of the civil workers. He heard Maxwell call in confusion, but he waved, indicating it was fine. He stepped up to the harried volunteer, who glanced at him before smiling. "We're handing out blankets, do you need one?"

"My...little brother, sister and I would, thank you." Lex nodded.

He had been debating on what to tell people if they ever asked, since it would be strange for two young men to travel across country by themselves. However, now that they had Yvette, they might be able to pass it off. Though then again, Karina traveling on her own would draw even more attention, but he tried not to think about that. Maxwell was doing that enough for the both of them anyway.

"Oh?" The volunteer reached back, drawing up three blankets. "Alright then, we're running low, so I hope this will do."

Lex took them gratefully, turning and heading back to Maxwell. He spotted Maxwell leaning back against the wall, half asleep. With a faint smile, he draped two blankets around the two before letting himself sit on the floor, his own blanket draped around his legs. He noticed Maxwell stir. "Lex?"

"I got us some blankets, it's not much, but it'll offer some protection." Lex waved. "If anyone asks, we're brothers with a little sister."

Maxwell blinked, humming faintly. "Alright..." He yawned and pulled the blankets close, curling them around him and the little girl. Lex chuckled before shifting so he was leaning against the seat. Not the most comfortable position, but better than being sprawled across the floor with the likelihood of getting trampled. He could deal. It wasn't the worst thing, after all.

~ * ~

It was sirens that woke Maxwell from his drowsy sleep. Sirens and startled yelps. He rubbed his face blearily and sat up, feeling the blanket shift around him. He turned his head, catching Lex's sleeping form leaning against their chosen spot. Well, once sleeping form. The young man was now awake, alert as he scrutinized the surroundings, posture somewhat on edge. Maxwell heard movement and turned in time to notice Yvette rub her cheek and peer up. She blinked at him before confusion clouded her face and she shifted around to figure out what that sound was.

Maxwell shook his head and stood, thoughts swirling. Now that he finally got some much needed rest, he couldn't stop all the thoughts from invading his mind, one of the foremost being, what now? What was he going to do now? He wanted to find Karina, so badly. Seeing Yvette, even though she was younger than him, stabbed him in the heart. He wanted his sister. He'd always been able to find her when he wanted to, whether it be in the forest or on the way to school. Yet he also knew Lex was right. That they needed to move west, and yet... The fire stopped them, right in their tracks, not only ending lives, but also sending Maxwell's thoughts into a frenzy once more. Realizing he was hyperventilating a bit and curious on what was going on, he shifted Yvette closer to Lex, blanket draped over her before he slipped outside, holding the backpack close to him.

Their truck was still where they left it, parked to one side. He glanced over, spotting what seemed to be emergency vehicles. The wounded were being carted off into a separate area, shouts and calls catching others' attention. A faint breeze blew through the air and he glanced westward, wondering at the state of the fire.

He decided he needed to know and now. He had enough of not knowing things. He gripped his backpack tighter, knuckles white as he hurried up to one of the emergency personnel who seemed to be directing the flow of traffic and other personnel. The man spotted him and scowled, but Maxwell didn't flinch. "Sir, what happened to the fire? Were there any other survivors? Is it out?"

The man glanced at him before shaking his head. "It is under control. We are busy right now I can't answer any of your questions. Now leave us alone so we can get our jobs done."

Maxwell felt a little disgruntled, but nodded, stepping back. He spotted another vehicle coming in and noted the burn and scorch marks on it. It wasn't hard to miss the way the workers scrambled and, to be honest, he wasn't positive if he could recognize Yvette's mom if she did come through. He winced and turned to head back inside. Only to pause. Off to one side, near the entrance on the east side of the building, closest to the gated community, there was a thin line of cars. He shivered at the sight, spotting a few Enthrope stepping out of the cars. Hoping against hope they didn't notice him, he ducked his head and hurried back inside to find Lex.

Lex was shaking his head in amusement while he held his hand out in what seemed to be a sideways v while Yvette held hers in a fist, giggling happily. Maxwell could faintly hear her cheer, "I won," as he came up.

Lex blinked as Maxwell raised an eyebrow, calming his pattering heart a bit when he realized Lex, Lex of all people, was playing rock, paper, scissors and losing. He bit his lip, feeling something bubble up as Yvette glanced over before turning back to Lex. "Again?"

Lex shrugged. Maxwell watched, covering his mouth this time, yet still unable to hold in the snort of mirth that slipped from his lips as Lex went with paper and Yvette did scissors. At Lex's bemused expression and Yvette's glee, Maxwell let out a bark of laughter, holding his sides as his brain finally managed to connect the image of Lex, his oldest best friend who could talk about death without batting an eyelash, to the same person who was frowning in annoyance after losing another round of a child's game. He could tell he was drawing some attention, but when he heard Lex's own chuckle, probably realizing why Maxwell was laughing, he sobered. Yvette giggled. He took a seat, shaking his head to get rid of the last of his chuckles. He wasn't certain why it was so hilarious, but he needed it, so badly. He hadn't realized how much until the laughter fully ebbed and he noticed his shoulders relax, a weight gone that he thought he knew about but hadn't really realized was so heavy.

Man, he was even being cliche...yikes.

He shook his head, letting a faint smile trail across his lips before it was wiped away by the sounds of doors opening. He tensed but didn't turn around. Lex glanced around him. "So, that's why you came back in." Lex pushed himself to his feet, pulling his hat low. "Stay here with Yvette and don't look over, got it?"

Maxwell gulped, nodding. He spotted the dark expression on Lex's face and decided to stay out of it. At least Lex now knew why he came back. It wasn't hard to guess since he saw everyone else gasp and clamor away.

Enthrope...

He shuddered at the thought before glancing toward Yvette. The girl was watching the exchange, the sadness once more returning to her gaze. "I'm scared," she muttered. "That nice man was playing with me, but now..."

Maxwell didn't hesitate. He reached forward, ruffling the little girl's hair like Karina would do for him. "It'll be fine. I'm sorry. A lot's been happening lately, but you'll be alright." The light-hearted mood from earlier helped him clear his mind, his thoughts no longer as frazzled. They were still there, lingering and waiting, but he could organize them, think them through. The thought of Enthrope, however, made him more than a little nervous. However, first, in all honesty, he needed to check that the little girl would be alright. It was what he could do in the here and now. He held out his hands, taking hers. "Do you have any other family?"

The little girl paused before shaking her head. Maxwell debated on his options before blinking and reaching into his backpack. He pulled out the bible, staring at the cover, preoccupying himself with not thinking about Enthrope. It was odd. Up until now, the bible had been Mother's. It meant them trying to find her and rescue her. Now it meant something else entirely, and he wasn't quite certain what it was. Was it for finding Karina? Or...

He shook his head and let it flop open. Yvette shuffled forward, peering over to examine it upside down. Maxwell could hear faint chatter behind him, but he daren't glance back. He peered down at the open bible, resting in his lap. His gaze flitted to a passage, Matthew? He noticed the number thirteen, but didn't think much of it as he read through the passage.

"Then people brought little children to Jesus for him to place his hands on them and pray for them. But the disciples rebuked them. Jesus said, "Let the little children come to me, and do not hinder them, for the kingdom of heaven belongs to such as these."

He felt a flutter and the faint smile from before returned. He wasn't sure why, but he was always happy to read from here. The passages always seemed to hold true to the situation, to what he was dealing with in some way. Maybe not explicitly sometimes, but still...

"What's it say?"

Maxwell glanced up before turning it around and pointing once more to the passage, deciding that it was an easier one to read. He wasn't sure if Yvette read anything from a bible before, but he figured he could read it to her.

She seemed curious and surprised at the words as she placed her hands together. "Just like Mama." Her expression fell. "Do you think...?" She tilted her head down, hair covering her expression. "Thank you, mister, for being so kind to me. You didn't have to..."

Maxwell shuffled just enough to reach an arm around the little girl, pulling her into his side. She snuggled in as he closed his eyes. The adrenaline from before was gone. Lex was keeping watch on the people from Enthrope. Karina would be fine, and he just needed to get his act together.

Once Yvette was in good hands, they would leave, find another route west. It shouldn't be too hard, not in this day and age. He wondered how long it would take. He glanced sidelong to the doorway that led to the medical wing. No one had been allowed in, so no one knew what the state of the patients was. Then there were those brought in recently. Were any of them from the scene of the accident?

If so...could he actually hope that, for once, luck was actually on his side?

Glancing down as he closed the bible and gently slid it back into its compartment, he was unable to think otherwise. He had to hope, for the little girl's sake beside him.

As well as probably for his own sanity...

Chapter Twenty-One

Caym gritted his teeth, his palms kneading his temples. He could hear the words of the letter echo through the room he'd given to the reporter. The descriptions of the twins and of those he recalled from the attack, including the mother. He at least had the cognition to NOT put Lex's description. He was well aware of what he almost did to his little brother with the resistance, recalling the gentle glow of red from the girl's lapel.

In his anger, he sent the resistance after his little brother.

He glanced out the window of his silent home. His mother was gone, somewhere he didn't know nor care. The servants were staying far away from his part of the house except for Machael. Caym didn't mind, he wasn't staying much longer. He had already made arrangements for a new home, or at least, a new base of operations. He was foolhardy to think it would be so easy to gain control of Enthrope in his father's place. His father was right in one aspect, the company was big and Caym didn't realize just the full extent of the enterprise.

It sent a thrill down his spine at the same time that it halted his breath in worry. He shook his head, pulling from those meaningless thoughts.

His thoughts flickered to the conversation with Machael, just a little while ago.

"My lord."

"What?" Caym snapped at the butler, his head racing with thoughts, his heart pounding as he mulled over what he was going to do to those damn twins, what he would do for Lex.

"You are not in a good mind. Don't you think you should rest before you do anything more? You've been running around since the incident. When was the last time you held a good night's sleep?"

"I'm fine," Caym spoke, flipping back to the cameras as he typed into them, collecting pictures of the twins to send, his words sounding surprisingly childish in his ears. Almost as if he was throwing a tantrum. He felt hands, falling on his shoulders and a faint sigh.

"Caym..."

Caym stilled, finding himself surprised at the use of his name, without any honorifics. Yet, he didn't turn around. "What is it?"

He could almost hear the faint smile in Michael's voice as he spoke. "Sir, Lex would not like for you to be in this state. You need your rest. Lex will be fine and, if you keep this up, you won't be able to find him. You know this as well as I do."

Caym stared at the screens, at the old recordings showing up clearly. Those twins, interacting with his little Leo without a care. Up until his point, it sent a bubble of anger and hatred...now he just felt weary. Michael was right. He was draining himself. With a sigh, he pushed himself away, being led away from the room.

He didn't even protest, the anger draining out of him with each step.

No...not quite right. It was still there. He was just too tired to care.

He groaned again, pulling himself back to the present.

At least he was right to speak of the Resistance. In all actuality, he thought the other communities had a right to know what they were in danger of. His father thought to keep it hidden, he saw no reason in it. If anything, it put pressure on the Resistance. It would definitely allow more people to know that there was something happening, but it would also cause a tension...a tension that had been building in this country anyway.

To be honest, once he found his brother and brought in those twins, he didn't much care if the world burned. The outer community were nothing but rags and blood, hatred and destruction, but the inner communities were almost no better.

He finished packing the last of his bags, finding not much was necessary. A few pieces of memorabilia here and there, a small charm from his brother...

His brother.

He gripped the pendant tightly, recalling Little Leo's gaze. Caym recalled those gray green eyes staring at him in worry, concern. His little Leo had grown, that was a fact. He wasn't that scared little kid anymore, the one that hid behind him. Caym tilted his head down. To Caym's surprise, Leo still had the pendant Caym gave him all those years ago.

He thought Leo would have gotten rid of it by now, left it behind like him.

Leo...Lex hadn't, and Caym wasn't sure if that made it better or worse. He sighed, dropping the item back into its spot and closing the case. He pulled it up, turning to the doorway as Machael stepped inside. Good, he wanted Machael with him. The man had been there to keep him mostly in check and he had no doubt that, if he saw those kids again, it would not end well.

He pulled from that thought and took one more gander around the home, noting just how cold and lifeless it felt. There was no singing, no giggling...

No one he truly loved was left here, would ever come back here.

So, it was time to leave, and he was not turning back, not again.

"Come now, Machael, I must be going." He turned, walking briskly toward the entrance, spotting the winged angels of the fountain, the water glittering in the bright sunlight. He slipped into the car, parked out front toward the golden gates as Machael got into the driver's seat. He needed to head west. Get more to the center of the country. It would make communication easier and quicker and would bring him closer to his brother. It would also centralize Enthrope just a bit more, crucial for what he could envision was coming. People were getting too bold, too rash like himself.

He needed to start preparing to not only find Leo, but also find a means to make absolutely certain that he was safe. His father worked from the east coast, one of the hubs of the people. He would work from the center.

The only way to do that? To make sure he would be safe from then on? Was to make it impossible for those from the outer community to ever be able to hurt him again.

~ * ~

Lex listened into Enthrope's conversation, briefly wondering if they noticed him. When they only gave him a passing glance, he pulled away, wrapping the blanket around himself from the slight chill in the air. So, Caym hadn't sent out a picture of him and father must have never gotten a chance to get it out west before his death. It was possible they were still okay.

However, from what he heard and how one or two men mentioned the twins possibly coming this way, he held no doubt they knew of Maxwell and Karina.

That was confirmed when one of the Enthrope workers glanced over and spotted Maxwell before gesturing to something on their pads. There was a discussion, so quiet, Lex couldn't hear, but the way they flicked their gaze to Yvette before turning away and ignoring them proved that it was probably beneficial that Maxwell had made fast friends with the little girl.

His hammering chest settled a little at the thought, grateful to note that the Enthrope employees were staying put, either talking with the workers, or staying to one side of the room as observers. They weren't wandering through the room, which Lex supposed made sense. They didn't want to mingle to much with the outer community.

He turned back to notice Maxwell talking with Yvette. Others sat around in their own groups, families with families, friends with friends. A few lost souls sitting here or there. It wasn't happy, by any stretch of the imagination, but it was manageable, and easily ignored if necessary. He walked back over, grateful that Maxwell was humming softly, gently swaying with the little girl in his arms, something more peaceful than his usually tense posture.

Admittedly, Lex was both surprised and gratified. The young boy sniggered, even if it was at his expense, with the earlier game. It hadn't been intentional, but he could admit seeing the amusement in it. He knew Maxwell needed it, the reprieve, and he couldn't deny he needed a little bit of amusement himself. He glanced at the little girl. She was strong for such a young child. Did she happen to notice the way they were struggling? Well, children were sharp like that, they were surprisingly adept at noticing the things adults often missed.

He took a seat beside them, catching Maxwell's attention. Maxwell kept his voice faint as he spoke. "Any luck?"

"Not particularly. I decided it was for the best I avoided speaking with them. It seemed having Yvette around was a good decision."

"Oh..." Maxwell furrowed his brow before turning away. "She's not a tool..."

"I know that." Lex took a seat opposite them as the little girl peered between them curiously. "But you can't deny, while we watch her, that it is beneficial."

Maxwell clicked his tongue but didn't argue. "So, what are we doing? I don't want to leave right now, not without making..."

"Idiot." Lex ruffled the boy's hair, earning a slight squawk and half-hearted glare. "We'll rest here for the day and leave tomorrow afternoon. We'll have to find another route. I believe we can get a path south from here. It'll take longer, but..."

"It'll have to do." Maxwell shrugged and Lex could tell he was trying hard not to glance over his shoulder.

Lex sighed and leaned against the chairs, staring up at the ceiling of the school. The whitewash wasn't pleasing per se, and it did not help with one's boredom, but he didn't particularly mind this time. There really was a lot on his plate. An interesting euphemism, considering the lack of food recently.

Actually...

"I'll be right back." Lex pushed himself to his feet. Maxwell glanced over before blinking in confusion. "I think we're all a bit hungry. I, for one, need something soon."

Maxwell blushed as a low growl sounded out. Lex smirked before turning and heading toward the exit. He should have thought about it earlier, but his mind was a bit distracted with the people from the gated community.

He found the cafeteria in due time. It was filled with different people, all vying for some food. It was orderly in a panicked sort of way.

That didn't make sense, but he didn't bother correcting himself. He grabbed some food from the helper who was handing out steady portions before returning, hands full. It wasn't much, just some sandwiches, but it was all volunteer and donation, which, considering how quickly it was put together, was rather impressive, he was okay with it. Giving Maxwell the food along with some smaller slices to Yvette, he sat down with his own sandwich. It wasn't anything spectacular, but it did the job. Once satisfied, he decided to just relax.

In all honesty, there wasn't much else to do.

~ * ~

Karina found a fond grin crossing her lips as she heard a knock on the door. Fiona slipped inside, letting out a sigh as she slumped into the seat across from her.

It was the second full day since Karina's arrival, or maybe the third? It was hard to keep track sometimes. Still, the last few days had been, admittedly, kind of nice. Other than the first day, she hadn't seen anything exceptionally strange and while Fiona was overly friendly, it wasn't anything she couldn't handle. If anything, the woman often left her alone to recover and she both hated and appreciated it.

"Ugh, I can't wait until I'm done with my masters. The amount of work is astounding." Fiona huffed before glancing toward Karina. "How are you doing?"

"It's been a bit boring, but good. Thanks." She meant it. Her leg was basically healed and, while her mind was a bit battered, the relaxation of the last few days helped her to just refocus herself. She hadn't thought things through, purposefully ignoring it, but it allowed her a clearer mind then she had in a while and she appreciated it.

"That's good." Fiona examined her, that familiar odd gleam in her pointed gaze.

She reached forward, startling Karina by ruffling her hair and chuckling. Karina yelped as Fiona pulled back, fingers in front of her lips. Karina huffed, but didn't say anything as she noticed Fiona's face light up in delight, almost like a little child, Karina analyzed. It was something she noticed in her time there. There were times Karina noticed Fiona more as a young child than the woman who was helping her and going for her master's degree in medical assisting.

"So, what are you doing today?"

Fiona hummed in thought before glancing outside. "Well, it is pretty nice out..."

Karina couldn't argue and, considering her leg was no longer tingling and she left the bandage undone, noting the slight scar, but not much else. She recalled the pool out back. That sounded like fun and would keep her mind off different things. Yet, she didn't recall getting a swimsuit and she felt awkward with asking for one. She was already intruding on them enough. She didn't want to bother them more.

"Karina?"

Karina jerked. Fiona stepped in, seeming tired, busy as usual with her studies, probably. "Oh, sorry," Karina muttered sheepishly. "I was just thinking."

Fiona simply shook her head and smiled softly. There was that smile again, Karina noted, she had so many different smiles. "No problem. You seem distracted though. What's up?"

"Oh..." Karina muttered, shrugging. "Well, since you mentioned how nice it was outside, I've been thinking of using the pool..."

Fiona slapped her head. "Of course, I've been lending you my clothes, didn't think of anything besides that." Karina glanced down at her clothes, reminded of how bulky they were on her, well, that made sense. "Anyway, it's been a few days, why don't we go out and get you some clothes?"

"Shopping?" Karina winced, not fond of the idea. Not only was she not keen on going outside in the gated community, but she wasn't a shopper. She got what she needed and left. Plus, the idea of going shopping...how long did Fiona expect Karina to stay there? Though, she did pause as a thought took over. She could get a phone charger while she was out. They would have something that would work for her phone...right?

"Yep. Would be fun, right? I need a break anyway. Hold on, I'll be right back." With that, Fiona disappeared behind her door. Karina blinked, staring at the doorway in stunned silence.

A minute or two later, it opened with Fiona holding a set of keys with a wide grin, hair combed and clothes adjusted. "Come, I'll let Eren know."

Karina didn't have time to argue as Fiona hurried down the hall, pulling her along. She yelped, but didn't stop. Was this how Maxwell felt? She gulped, her throat suddenly tight. She shook her head sharply. *Don't think about it,* she reminded herself. There was no point in thinking about it, not now. Taking a deep breath, she allowed herself to be pulled into the car from before. Eren, who seemed to be cleaning the car, glanced up. "Ms. Fiona, what seems to be the matter?"

"Eren, we're going out for a bit." Fiona waved, slipping into the car. "Mind watching the place for a little while? I'll pick you up something on the way."

Eren winced, much to Karina's surprise, before he stepped away from the car and nodded. "Of course." His gaze flitted to her and she frowned, spotting a strange expression flash over his face before he turned away, heading into the house.

"Come on, Karina!"

Karina shook her head and pulled herself into the car after the anxious woman. Fiona hummed and started the car, pulling away from the wide gates of the mansion. Karina peered back, actually getting a chance to examine the place. It appeared almost...sad. The windows were dark and curtains were pulled sharply across many. Her thoughts flashed to her time with Lex and she frowned.

She turned away as they moved around a corner, the trees blocking the image of the sad home. Why it was so sad, she wasn't sure, she just got that feeling.

"So, there's a mall right around the corner. We'll head there and grab some lunch. Sound good?" Fiona flicked her gaze over toward Karina.

Karina shrugged, not caring one way or another. She was just glad she was already wearing her shoes and everything before Fiona brought her out. She snickered at the thought. Fiona did seem to be impulsive.

It didn't take long for them to come across the shopping area. It was surprisingly full of cars and Karina suddenly felt very uncomfortable. She curled inward as she stared at the surroundings. She usually didn't mind crowds, but this was a different thing entirely. Thankfully, Fiona didn't seem to notice. She pulled her out and headed toward the doorway, chattering away about something Karina didn't particularly care about. Karina examined the area. The building was huge, a two-story thing that could hold most of Claremore. Well, maybe not, but still...

They stepped through the sliding glass doors into the coolness of the area. It was filled with people. A glass roof overhead shone sunlight down into the middle which showcased lines of stores and stalls. A fountain bubbled up in the center, shooting toward the ceiling before descending down.

On either side, Karina noticed the occasional flash of black...of Enthrope. It took all her will power not to react or stand out.

Fiona led her to one side, weaving around a family of four with two little kids. Karina gazed down at the boy and girl, the boy poking at the girl who swatted his finger away. Karina chuckled before letting it die. She felt that twinge that she couldn't push away crawling back. She viciously shook her head, walking after Fiona at a slower pace as she scrutinized the area with wariness. Other than the people giving them a wide berth for some unknown reason, there wasn't much to say. The Enthrope employees would give them a quick glance, but upon spotting Fiona they would quickly turn away.

The mall itself was similar, yet different from when she went out with Martha all those months ago. Beautiful and clean, yet almost clinical, where with Martha, it was empty and dying, but with a slight homeliness to the locations. Karina was pulled from her thoughts as they entered the first store, a clothing shop with a wide variety of clothing, all pretty expensive. Karina cringed, spotting a price-tag. Who would want a shirt for sixty dollars? Yet she could see people checking them out, and trying them on. Fiona gestured and grinned. "Pick whatever you like, okay?"

Karina blinked and turned to her as she waved and stepped away to peruse through the clothes. Karina tilted her head, finding herself at a loss of how to respond.

Deciding to ignore it. Karina wandered around the aisles. She stepped toward a shelf and pulled out a blue sweatshirt with a hood, noting how soft it was. Glancing at the price, she cringed. There was also the size. She had grown a lot lately, yet she was still just as small and skinny. More curves, much to her chagrin, but that's about it.

She put it back before pulling out another. This one was a bit smaller with black outlines. She hummed in thought before slipping it on, noting the pocket in front. It was comfy, she didn't mind it. Staying far away from the skirts and dresses, she grabbed a pair of jeans, some shorts, a blouse and a tunic that trailed a little past her shorts on one side. She briefly noted the warm smile blooming over Fiona's face as the woman watched her. Karina ignored it, ecstatic to find another pair of fingerless gloves, her old ones worn to the bone from use.

Leaving the store with a surprising amount of bags, they continued on. She waited as Fiona went into the jewelry store, coming out a few minutes later with a few bracelets, one of which she gave to Karina, to her surprise. It was a gold loop, simple yet elegant. Karina tried to return it, but winced at the dark glare Fiona sent her way. Deciding not to argue, she took it. Slipping it on, it sat delicately around her wrist. She was surprised at how light and pretty it was.

A few more stores later and Karina found herself standing in front of a rack of swimsuits, blinking in surprise at all the choices. Fiona was in another store, letting her be by herself, which Karina didn't mind. Karina bit her lip, examining them. Going swimming sounded great, but... She glanced down at herself, feeling a bit uncomfortable before groaning. This wasn't like her. She growled in frustration and, grabbing the first one she saw, stomped to the changing room. It was a simple one-piece suit. Nothing special or grand, thankfully. Slipping it on, she turned to the mirror and froze. She hadn't thought much about her appearance, not recently. There was no need.

In all honesty, she didn't expect the person in front of her. Dark eyes stared back at her, widening in surprise as black hair trailed around her pale face. Deep shadows and a furrowed brow decorated her features. She tried to force a smile on her lips, but it appeared more like a grimace. She lifted a hand, staring at it in mild shock. She was almost frail, something she never thought she would attribute to herself. She seemed so different. She recalled once peering in the mirror and seeing delight, interest...was that all gone? She bit her lip, hard. She shook her head, smoothing down the bathing suit. Though it was entirely unnecessary, it still helped settle her nerves. Is that what Maxwell saw?

Was that appearance the last thing she really showed him before she left? Before...

She abandoned him. She felt her legs crumbling underneath her, fingers curling into and tugging on her hair. She left him, thinking he would be better off without her, but...she'd only made it worse, hadn't she? She abandoned him, thinking of herself, thinking of how she couldn't protect him.

And now...she had no idea where he was, what he was doing, if he was even okay. The thing was, though, she was too scared to look. What would he say? What would either of them say? Would he hate her for abandoning him like she did? Would he just leave her behind like she expected? She should have talked with them, told them what she was feeling. The words probably would have only been condolences, but...

No, Maxwell would have known what to say, he always did. Yet she didn't want to burden him, didn't want him to worry about her.

She felt the tears right as a sob ripped from her throat. What had she done?

She managed to rein herself in after a moment or two, wiping away the tears harshly. Quickly throwing her own clothes back on, she bolted from the room and tossed the swimsuit on the counter, startling Fiona who'd come in to check on her. She raced outside, not caring where she was going, but wanting to be anywhere but there, away from that mirror. How could she let something like that affect her? Pathetic, she was so pathetic. A complete and utter idiot. She didn't realize where she was going until she slammed headfirst into someone.

Chapter Twenty-Two

Finnagen stumbled, barely keeping his footing as his arms naturally wrapped around the thin frame in front of him, feeling a breath ghost his collarbone. The person was light, and, though he was used to being hit, he was not as used to finding the hitter to be a girl around his age. Her palms pressed against his chest as she pushed away. Before he could think, the words, "Are you okay?" slipped from his lips. She had pretty blue eyes and long black hair that seemed soft to the touch. What got him though, was the faint red, a deep blush mingling with stains trailing down her cheeks.

"Fine," she said, her voice a little shaky, but light and warm. "Sorry, wasn't looking where I was going."

He shook his head. "It's fine. I wasn't...well..."

She hadn't hurt him in the slightest, he'd taken rougher hits in school. Being on the basketball team made it difficult to avoid. Though, well, he wasn't exactly the star player. He mostly warmed the bench, but still, he made the team which was an accomplishment in and of itself, so he couldn't complain too much.

He was pulled from his thoughts as his mom spoke up, a faint note in her voice speaking of amusement. "Finnagen, we do have things to do."

"Alright, alright, why don't you go on ahead. I'll be there in a minute." He waved, hoping his mom got his point.

"Well, don't let the little lady keep you." She hummed before walking away.

Mom. He wanted to yell after her, but stopped himself as he heard the girl's comment about "not being a little lady."

He let out a faint laugh as he made note of where his mother was out of the corner of his eyes. He could tell she was far enough away not to be listening. Good.

. "Yeah, that's her for you."

He examined the girl, spotting the baggy clothes. She held herself in a way that, if he hadn't run into her, he probably wouldn't have given her a second glance with how well she fit in, but she was so tiny. He shook his head. "I've never seen you before. Are you new around here?"

She seemed to stiffen, as if unsure how to answer. Deciding to ignore it, he reached a hand forward. "My name's Finnagen. Yours?"

When he spotted the hesitation, he started to pull his hand back, feeling uncomfortable. He could walk away, not bother, but he was a gentleman and he had walked into her as well. His thoughts flickered to his little brother's teasing and his younger sister's laughter and mentally snickered. They would be having a riot with how awkward he was acting. Thank goodness they were with Dad right now. He felt thin fingers grasp his and turned just as she pulled away.

"Karina. Don't let me keep you though."

The slight harshness to her tone made him wince with unease.

"Oh, ah, I didn't mean..." He grunted in annoyance before reaching behind his neck. "I'm sorry, this probably seems really strange. I wanted to apologize for running into you, that's all." He was a gentleman, after all, he reminded himself.

She shook her head. "Like I said, it's fine."

Finnagen stilled, spotting a mischievous smirk on her face. He felt a hint of relief. "That's good."

He peered over her shoulder before spotting a familiar woman, the crazy witch of the community, or so everyone else called her. Finnagen wasn't really sure, but he knew he didn't want anything to do with her. Yeah, he knew she was once related to a prominent family back a few years ago, but that family, while on vacation, was killed so...maybe she was a relative using the home? He had to stop wondering, it wasn't his place to ask.

"Karina? Karina, where are you?"

Finnegan's eyes widened as he looked toward Karina, who winced. Curiosity colored his voice as he glanced between the two. "Wait, you know Fiona?"

"Yeah..." Karina's voice was soft, hesitant.

Finnagen frowned. How did this girl know Fiona? No one got close to the woman and it was rare for the wit...Fiona to be out and about. He heard the rumors, the ugly rumors of screams, of people finding strange things near the house, bloody rope and upturned dirt. Even his mom moved away from the searching woman, still keeping half her attention on him.

"Oh...she's a strange one," Finnagen muttered as he peered toward the girl beside him who seemed to be debating with herself.

She had her hands up to her chest, as if subconsciously twisting at her heart. She seemed to come to a decision before deftly slipping away, heading away from the searching woman. More curious than anything, Finnagen ended up following behind. How did this girl relate to Fiona? They couldn't seem any more different, so...how did this girl know such a crazed woman?

The girl whipped around, pinning him with a glare. He took a step back, surprised at the sharpness of her gaze, the fierceness of her expression. She stood tall, almost older than she appeared. She regarded him for a moment, her expression flat, before flitting away, disappearing around the corner. He watched her go, finding himself intrigued despite himself. Who was that girl? He shook his head and returned to his mom. She raised an eyebrow and he couldn't stop the forlorn expression. She ruffled his hair, a soft tone of condolence. "You can't win them all. Now come on."

Damn, so she saw how badly he did. Well, if he saw that girl again, he could always try to speak with her, right? He pulled from his thoughts, glad to be without his siblings. It was nice to be out and about with just his mom, even if it was for school shopping. He shook his head, walking alongside Mom as both of them gave Fiona a wide berth.

~ * ~

Maxwell awoke with way too many cricks in his neck and back from the uncomfortable position. He heard hushed chatter floating around and observed as the room emptied out a bit. Some people must have left yesterday. He did vaguely recall hearing something about it being safe to leave, but he hadn't thought much of it.

He glanced over at Lex who caught his eye. "You're awake."

Maxwell nodded, shifting to look down at the little girl. She was still asleep, lying into his side. He was a bit surprised how attached she was to them since they practically ripped her away from her mom. Admittedly, not of their own doing, but...

He shook his head and stood, careful to make sure she was comfortable. More curious than anything, he headed to the infirmary. The walk through the school wasn't silent, but it wasn't warm or filled with chatter like in the sleeping area. The vague, disappearing moonlight indicated it was almost sunrise, still super early for him. He shook his head and spotted the nurses station set up. To his relief, there was a nurse there.

"Um, I was just wondering when we could check on the patients?"

The woman considered him for a moment, bags almost digging into her cheek, before she sighed. "Unless you have proof of relation, I cannot let anyone in."

Maxwell groaned. "Oh." He shook his head. "How many were lost?"

The woman paused, as if debating on whether to tell him. She was obviously tired of the situation and the questions which she had probably already received multiple times. "Last calculation was twenty-three dead, fifty-two injured."

Maxwell cringed. How many died in the accident, or because of it? He hadn't realized how bad it was, but everyone was in a panic, some probably got hurt while fleeing and it wasn't like they were the only ones. Some of the rescuers were probably included in that number. "Thanks," he muttered.

She observed him before nodding, her own lips twitching up into a gingerly grin. He turned, glancing out the window, noting the sky was starting to turn; deep yellows, reds and purples, a beautiful, yet harsh dawn. He felt his stomach growl. The sandwich from yesterday hadn't done much to curb his hunger and, while he knew why food was scarce, he was still peckish. They could probably leave to get food, but he couldn't stand leaving Yvette here alone. There were still too many people here, strangers. A little girl by herself like this was just a bad idea all around.

He felt a little uncomfortable as he glanced toward the doorway. Some people meandered back and forth, some wearing masks and others just wrapped in bandages. He shook his head and headed toward the cafeteria, hoping to grab something. To his relief, it was early, but not so early that there weren't already people there, or food. He grabbed a few bars left out by someone. He returned, resigning himself to a long boring day of waiting. He munched on his bar, keeping the backpack close. He learned from Karina's mistake not to leave it out of his sight after what happened last time. Since he didn't have a lock here, well... He sat down, trying to get himself comfortable once again. There wasn't much else they, or he, could do. Lex was resting to one side, shifting slightly upon his return before settling back in. Yvette was curled up beside him, relaxed and comfortable. Maxwell took a seat beside her, letting out a sigh as he ate.

Footsteps echoed through the room, not uncommon, but unique for this early in the morning. There was a thump and he jerked, glancing to one side.

A woman sat beside him, her sharp features and wide grin caught his attention first, but it was Lex's visceral reaction, knife already out and pointed at her that indicated this woman was a threat.

The woman let out a quiet laugh, legs crossed under her as she leaned onto one elbow, chin sitting in her palm. "Now, is that really a way to greet someone you've seen before?"

Lex had a slight tremor in his hand that Maxwell only noticed due to knowing the man for so long. Maxwell shifted closer to Yvette and Lex, eyeing the woman carefully. "Who are you?"

The woman hummed, staring at Maxwell with a curious gaze. A shudder ran down his spine. He did not like this woman, and it wasn't just because of Lex's reaction.

"Why, Maxwell, I suppose it's not too much of a surprise you don't know me, only this one and your sister have met me, after all." The woman smiled, her gaze flickering to Lex for a moment, who had not moved an inch, his posture tense. "I should introduce myself fully." She bowed her head. "My name is Priscel. I guess you could call me the adjutant of Wilma and one of the care-takers of Madeline."

Maxwell stiffened at the names, thoughts whirling at the sound of Madeline's.

Priscel leaned back, seeming quite relaxed. "I've been chasing you two with a comrade of mine for a while. Your sister is being handled by another group."

Maxwell stiffened and she shrugged, continuing, "Imagine my surprise when we catch up to you because of a measly forest fire." Her gaze flicked over the group, settling on Yvette. "So, you already replaced your sister. No surprise, she did abandon you two, after all, fled north by train and everything. I had to send less competent people after her. Hope she's still alive." There was no actual warmth to her words, just a cold almost calculated cruelness with an overlaid smile.

Maxwell stiffened, a growl thrumming in his throat. "Don't speak of my sister like that."

Priscel shrugged, pushing forward once more. "I don't want to make a big scene here, and neither do you, correct?"

"What do you want?" Lex's voice was slightly shaken. "I highly doubt you came here to talk."

Priscel analyzed him, expression shifting to a neutral one before she directed her gaze onto Maxwell, sizing him up. "So, Madeline likes you." The words were calm, but eerily monotone, compared to the more chipper words from before. "I was intending to wait until you all left with Huxley, but I had to meet the one Madeline is so smitten with, she forgets her duties." She tilted her head. "Hmm."

She examined him with a gaze that made him freeze. What was this woman? Her voice, her posture, everything screamed 'danger'.

She subtly frowned and let out a breath. "Well, to be honest, I wasn't sure what to expect." She shook her head. "Considering you were the one who caught my dear Madeline's attention, I figured you would be...something." She pulled back, pushing herself to her feet. She held out a hand, palm up. "I will convey anything you wish to say to Madeline.

After all, this was simply a meeting to figure out whether you were actually worthy of her. However, I cannot allow someone so uncouth to be by her side. So, to follow with her desires, I will not do anything to you now and allow you to say a final good-bye through word of mouth. Don't worry, I'll deliver your message. After that, you will not speak to her ever again, and next time I find you, you are coming with me, whether you like it or not." She smiled.

Maxwell felt a little offended, wondering how, at all, he was uncouth. What did he even do? "That's..."

Her expression suddenly shifted and Maxwell understood why he had the earlier feeling. A sadistic smile crossed the woman's face as she leaned forward. "I wouldn't continue arguing. My goal is to capture you two alive, but I have no qualms letting one of you disappear." Her gaze flicked to Lex before returning to him.

Maxwell snapped his mouth shut, pulling back slightly without meaning to. Priscel leaned back and shrugged. "Well, no matter. We will have you soon enough, this was just my little warning and parting gift." She smiled once more. The expression twisted to a hint of malicious glee as she shifted her gaze to Lex. "I can't WAIT to get a chance to mess with you, once this is all said and done. I will thoroughly enjoy myself." She gestured, as if miming caressing his face before she stood. "Well, it seems you have nothing to say to my dear Madeline and, like I said, I'm not in the mood to make a scene. You would no doubt fight me and I'm not so dumb to think I would not struggle a little in this situation." She waved and turned, walking nonchalantly out of the hall. "I will see you later, boys." Her words echoed back to them, not loud, but loud enough to be piercing as she moved out of sight.

Maxwell didn't feel the tension ease at all.

Lex seemed more than a little shaken, the knife almost clattering out of his tight fist as he pulled back in, eyeing the way she disappeared. "We need to go."

Maxwell couldn't help but agree, but he hesitated, glancing toward Yvette who had woken during the exchange but watched quietly.

"She's scary."

Maxwell couldn't argue with the sentiment. Lex seemed to relax a little at Yvette's words, slipping the knife back into wherever he kept it hidden. Good thing no one noticed he pulled it out because of the angle in which they were sitting. If Priscel planned that... Maxwell shivered at the thought. No, it was probably just coincidence and sheer dumb luck.

Lex's fingers grazed over his leg, which had healed quite a bit over the last few days. He let out a breath, relaxing a bit more, but still trembling just slightly. "Well, that could have gone much worse."

Maxwell nodded, peering back toward where the woman had disappeared. "What was that about?"

"Most likely her own curiosity and wish to talk with us privately before she did anything." Lex lightly rubbed his leg and winced. "Though, it also could just be because, like she said, she owed it to Madeline to at least give us a chance to escape or, well, prove ourselves. Note, she didn't say she would be dealt with if something happened now, only that she would struggle." Lex winced. "I think she probably meant it."

Maxwell gulped and couldn't help but agree. Her posture, her voice, the way she moved was almost predatory. It also didn't help his nerves one bit that the woman was still out there, waiting for them.

Lex shook his head, letting out a long breath. "Thankfully, my head is on a little straighter now." He glanced toward Enthrope, who stayed put, not noticing the exchange. Either that, or ignoring it like everyone else seemed to, not counting the few curious glances, but that was about it. "I know I said we have to leave right away, but..." His gaze flicked to the doorway once more. "I have a feeling we should wait a bit longer. That woman wants us to be rash, to make a mistake. Our best option is to not follow through and sneak out when we get a chance."

Maxwell wasn't keen on the idea, but he supposed Lex did know what he was doing. Plus, he didn't want to meet that woman again. To think, she was one of Madeline's caretakers, maybe? It seemed like it with the way she talked. If so, how did Madeline end up so caring after growing up under people like that?

He let out a long breath, nodding, getting a relieved smile in return.

For now, he would wait. He would try again later, maybe bring Yvette next time to check if her mom was in the infirmary, but, how much time did they have? To dawdle here? How long was the ticking clock going to go before it chimed? He berated himself on the stupid analogy, yet couldn't argue with it. Either way, it was a gamble, but it was worth a shot.

Chapter Twenty-Three

Finnagen tapped at the desk in front of him, outright ignoring the math assignment he was working on. His room was serene, the window open to the morning breeze as a few curtains billowed back and forth. His bed was already made, though he suspected it wouldn't stay that way with his two siblings out and about. Every book and article of clothing was in their rightful places. Neat and orderly.

"Hey, Finny?" a soft voice called.

He glanced over as his little sister peeked around the doorway. Her deep brown eyes peered up at him.

"Hey, Annie," he called, unable to hide the fondness from his voice.

She slipped inside and hurried up to him, crawling into his lap. He chuckled and wrapped an arm around her waist, placing the pen into its holder. "Oh geez, you're getting heavy, you know that?"

Annie puffed out her cheeks and stuck out her tongue before scrutinizing the floor, squirming. "Big brother, I'm bored. Caleb is being mean and Momma is busy with Papa."

Finnagen sighed and tilted his head enough to catch her eye. "What do you want to do?"

"I want to go outside." She snapped up, clapping. "It's pretty outside. I'll be careful not to go near the golden gates. Okay?"

"You..." He shook his head and stood, pulling her up with him. She squeaked in delight as he put her on his hip. "You would just keep bothering me anyway, wouldn't you?"

"Yep." she chirped and he laughed before an image flashed through his mind, of the girl from earlier. He wondered where she was now.

He shook his head and grinned at Annie. "Alright, let's go."

He walked outside, heading down the steps. His parents' two-story house gleamed behind him, the gardens overflowing with his mom's flowers. He was partially surprised he didn't notice his mom actually working in the garden, but it made sense. He placed Annie on the ground and held her hand, finding himself struggling to hold up her weight. She was growing up fast. They slipped past the white wooden gates and down the road. It was beautiful out, with a clear sky and crisp, yet warm air blowing at him. The neighbors' kids played a game of baseball off to one side.

He knew for a fact that they weren't the wealthiest gated community, but he knew that they weren't destitute either. Off in the distance, the glass of the greenhouses sparkled in the sun. The farmland beyond that, which held the produce for other communities, could just barely be seen on the horizon. He hummed as he continued down the road, swinging his sister's arm as she surveyed the area in a sort of childish glee. It didn't take long for them to arrive at the wooded area still left in the community. Admittedly, it probably wasn't the smartest idea to go there, since it was getting close to Fiona's place. Unfortunately, that was why it was the only place left. Most of the other parts of the gated community were residential, malls or something else. The few available parks were on the other end of the community and he wasn't in the mood to try walking all the way over there. Plus, at this time of day, there were probably games happening in them. He didn't want Annie getting caught up in a rough game of football or something, so...

He was pulled from his thoughts when Annie slipped out of his grasp and ran up to the trees, hopping up and down and turning to him with glee. He chuckled, following after her. "Hey. Wait up," he called, earning a giggle from his sister as she darted into the trees.

He rolled his eyes, a hint of affection running through him as he followed after her. Annie really enjoyed the game of hide and seek. He stumbled over a branch and inspected the area, hoping to avoid that a second time. Spotting the subtle brush of brown hair as Annie stared at him from around a tree, he ignored her. He decided to exaggerate his movements even more by peering under bushes and picking up pebbles. He sighed, as dramatic as possible, earning a faint giggle. He placed a finger to his lips, pretending to be deep in thought. Honestly, it wasn't hard to find Annie, ever, but it was more fun to make it so both of them acted as if it was a game. He turned, heading around the tree from the opposite direction before suddenly whipping around and surprising the girl who'd been creeping behind him, bopping her on her head. "You're it."

"You cheated."

"Nope." He shrugged before taking a step back. "Do I ever cheat?" he called innocently as he spread his arms out wide.

"Yes, you do."

"Alright, alright, no cheating." He placed his arms behind his back. "I'll look for a place to hide, you find me, alright?"

She nodded and covered her face. He wasn't going to go too far. Carefully stepping back, keeping his attention on her the whole time, he lost track of his steps and tripped.

Letting out a yelp, he glanced back as he overbalanced and tumbled down into a ditch. He felt the breath get knocked out of him and coughed. His back hurt, especially his shoulder blades and he could tell his clothes were a mess. He carefully pushed himself up and winced. He'd fallen farther than he expected. He glanced over and froze. Peering down at him was the old ruins of Fiona's manor. Well, not ruins. They never were ruins, but they were just as eerie as ruins might be. He would have fled, right then or there, if it wasn't for the fact that he recalled that girl from the mall. Finding himself curious, he peered up the slope just as Annie poked her head over the edge and grinned. "Found you."

He chuckled and then winced, garnering her attention. "Yeah, you did." He stood up and leaned on one foot. He must have bruised his leg on the way down because it stung greatly. He shook his head, his attention shifting back to Annie. "You coming?"

Annie glanced past him, uncertain, before nodding and sliding down. He quickly grabbed her up before she hit the bottom and she cried out in surprise. "That was fun."

He just shook his head, placing her on his good hip as he crept around the gates, peering at the house all the while. He knew there had been a few dares among the others his age about ringing the doorbell as a test of courage. He wasn't one of those, but it wasn't so much fear as he didn't want to bother her.

No, he wasn't being a coward, he was a gentleman, thank you. He just didn't want to be rude. At all. It's not because she was creepily grinning all the time, nope.

"Finny?" His sister's voice caught his attention and he glanced down. She was regarding him in that silent way she sometimes did, gripping his shirt. "Are we going inside? It's scary."

"No, I just want to look around, alright?"

He got a nod from Annie and pulled her up, swinging her onto his shoulders. He winced, but she giggled, her mood lightening, so it was good enough for him. He crept along.

He was almost near the back of the house when he heard a splash. He froze, giving the surroundings a once-over before he heard more slightly muffled splashes and shifting water. He carefully stepped forward, only to stop when he spotted where the sound came from. It was a pool, a rather large one, actually. Something moved in the water and for a split second, he back-pedaled, thinking it was a shark.

He berated himself on his idiotic deduction a moment later when he noticed it was human-shaped. He leaned forward, fingers curling around the wire of the gate. The figure came up, catching a breath and his eyes widened. It was the girl from before. Karina. She hauled herself out of the pool and his breath caught. He spotted a deep gash on one of her long legs. Her hair trailed down her back as she turned and dove back into the water with one fluid motion. He watched longer than he probably should have before he felt a sharp tug on his hair. "Who is that?"

"Karina." He spoke, his voice surprisingly breathless. He coughed and turned away. "I met her the other day, but what is she doing here? Doesn't she know the rumors?"

He moved away, suddenly feeling incredibly embarrassed that he'd been staring for so long, it didn't hurt that she was nice to look at, nope.

"Finny? Rumors?"

"Hmm?" he hummed, hurrying away. "I haven't told you?"

Annie shook her head.

He peered over his shoulder. "I'll tell you later."

~ * ~

He was back at the house the next day, this time without Annie in tow. Karina didn't appear to be outside, not this time. He felt a hint of disappointment before pausing, wondering why he'd felt it. It was just curiosity, right? Shaking his head, he went to turn and leave, only to freeze when he heard a call.

"What are you doing here?"

The voice was familiar and, slowly, he turned. The girl stood before him, attention firmly on his. She had her hands on her hips and she appeared better than the day before. Like some rest helped. He gulped, unsure how to respond, fumbling slightly. "I, ah, was wondering if you were staying here and, well, I wanted to..."

"If you're here to apologize, don't worry about it." She sighed. "It's no big deal."

"Oh, ah. Okay." He stumbled over the words, massaging the back of his neck. He knew he should have brought his little sister. She would have been able to say something.

Karina stared at him; arms crossed. She was leaning on her good leg. The fence broke up the view, metal gleaming sharply in the sunlight. "So, obviously, there is another reason you're here, isn't there?"

He stiffened and coughed before looking askance. "I was just wondering. Since, well, I didn't recognize you from anywhere and..."

A flash of something flew over her face at his words before she turned. "So, you just found yourself curious." It wasn't a question.

She turned to walk away and he quickly pressed up onto the links of the fence. "Wait." He wasn't sure why he called out to her, but at least she did stop. "Would you like to come over sometime?"

What are you doing? he mentally screeched. *She doesn't know you and you don't know her.*

She peered over her shoulder, seeming amused before hurrying away.

He slumped down and slammed his head against the links for a few minutes. That went so badly, it almost hurt. He grunted and turned away, hurrying away from the house. The sun shone in the sky and he was grateful it was a long weekend. It felt weird that school was starting up again tomorrow. Thankfully, because of that, no one else was around to see how much of a fool he made of himself. Not that there was anyone else around, but still.

He returned home to Annie and Caleb playing in the driveway, though it was more Caleb laughing as Annie yelled at him to wait up. Finnagen shook his head, finding himself amused as he walked up. He scooped up Annie, who yelped before calling his name in glee. Caleb stopped, bumping into his leg before snapping his head up, arms crossed his chest.

"Finn."

"Hey, little bugger, you aren't messing with Annie again, are you?" he chided, causing Caleb to glare.

"Annie started it."

"You are older, you should be a role-model, like me."

"Says the one who completely forgot why I sent you out," Mom spoke up, stepping outside, watching in amusement. "Weren't you going to pick up some milk?"

Finnagen couldn't repress the blush as Annie chuckled behind her fingers and Caleb gloated. "Okay, I get it." He coughed before shrugging. "I'll go get it." He went to put Annie back down, only to stop when his mother cleared her throat.

"Oh no, you are taking both of them. I need some peace and quiet around here."

His mother's words hit his ear as Annie cheered.

"Mom, I took care of Annie yesterday and it's a Sunday. Can't I have a little time without these squirts before school starts?"

"I would have, if you hadn't forgotten what I sent you out to do. Plus, you know how busy your father is and this is the one day I have off. It won't take long, just there and back, and you'll have the rest of the evening to yourself, alright, sweetie?"

Finnagen groaned, hanging his head. "Fine." He let Annie down while reaching for Caleb. "Come here, squirt."

He wrapped an arm around Caleb as Annie leaned around his waist, poking at Caleb's head. Caleb slapped her finger away playfully before struggling to get out of his grip. Finnagen let go, causing Caleb to stumble. Caleb glared. Finnagen chuckled before holding out a hand for Caleb to grasp. "Come on, before Mom throws us down the street."

Caleb hesitated before taking the peace-offering, muttering under his breath. Finnagen smiled before heading back out. He was distracted, wasn't he? Man, he needed to get his act together. If only he had remembered the milk. Though, he supposed, it wasn't an uncommon occurrence to forget things. He did tend to go off into his own little world.

"Hey, Finn?"

Finnagen glanced sidelong to Caleb, who was watching him.

"Do you think we have to worry here?"

"Hm?" Finnagen frowned, humming a bit in question as Caleb began to fidget nervously.

"Well, I heard a gated community a few days away was burned to the ground. Mom and Dad were talking in all those hushed whispers and such. Everyone seems worried. Are we going to be alright?"

Finnagen hesitated. He knew well enough what Caleb was talking about. In truth, he'd been trying to ignore it, but it seemed his brother was taking the opposite avenue. He sighed. "We'll be fine, remember? Our community was created to protect us. We were chosen to be safe and we will remain that way, as long as the government is around."

He was saying the words, but he wasn't sure how much he believed them. Hadn't the government abandoned this place? That's what he heard. That they were left to rot, yet, because of their location as a farming community, those in the community survived and expanded. Eventually, they started to dump the survivors from other locations here, to be forgotten. He shook his head. That's what happened to Fiona. To many others.

He was lucky to have been born here, but he knew of many who hadn't had that fortune. Which returned him to his thoughts of Karina. Where was she from? Another community?

He frowned, finding himself thinking that was wrong. He was brought from his thoughts when he spotted the grocery store. He chuckled, realizing he'd been completely lost in his thoughts again. He stepped inside. "Now, where was it?"

"This way." Annie cheered, pulling forward.

Finnagen followed after as Caleb yelped, glaring.

They weaved through the aisles, arriving at the correct one in no time. Annie reached in and grabbed a bottle, stumbling slightly before beaming up to him.

"Annie, you're going to drop it," Caleb called, reaching forward and pulling it toward him.

Annie yelped before shaking her head and tugging back. Seeing where this was going, Finnagen groaned and knelt on one knee, carefully pulling Caleb's and Annie's grips from the bottle.

"Caleb, I know you want to help, but that's no reason to just take it, got it?"

When Finnagen got a huff and crossed arms, he shook his head and turned to Annie, who was examining the tiles as she scuffed one shoe forward and backward. "Annie, you know that's too heavy for you to carry."

She pouted and Finnagen sighed before standing back up, holding the bottle himself. "Come on, let's go."

The two hesitated before following him as he threaded through the aisles. He was almost to the front when he stopped, spotting a familiar woman ahead. It was Fiona, to his and the store clerk's shock. She was holding a bag of jalapeños and was humming some strange tune. He peeked around the corner, his siblings seeming to understand and falling behind him to watch from either side of his legs.

"Oh, the poor dear, she rarely eats," the woman muttered, whether she was talking to herself or the cashier, it was hard to tell. "She's so thin. I know I was not going to tell anyone, but she does need some things Eren can't provide." She shook her head. "I'm blathering on, my apologies." She passed the food over to the confused and nervous store clerk.

Jalapeños? That seems so strange. Finnagen continued to watch, Annie tugging at his shirt while Caleb glanced between him and the woman. Finnagen couldn't say anything.

"What are you doing?"

Finnagen, at this point, was berating himself for jumping to the same comment twice in one day. He was doing way too much sneaking lately. He whipped around, keeping his siblings behind him, much to Caleb's protest, before relaxing. Behind him was Fiona's butler, though no one knew what his real name was, considering she always called him Eren.

The butler scrutinized the three of them quietly before peering toward Fiona. "Do you need something with my mistress?"

"Um..." Finnagen hesitated. The man's expression pinched slightly and he found himself stammering over his words. "I thought I saw someone with her at the mall the other day that was my age. I was just wondering who it was. I wanted to meet her, that's all." *Gosh darnit, brain, you could have just said you were startled to see her out of her home. That would have been more than enough.*

The man regarded him with a strange expression before nodding and walking right past.

"Finn? What was that about?"

Finnagen just shook his head, unsure how to answer Caleb. Though, when he turned toward the counter, he was at even more of a loss for words. Eren went up to Fiona and spoke in a hushed whisper to her. Before Finnagen could hide behind the corner again, she turned, her curious gaze catching his. He felt a trill of fear trail down his spine before he forcefully looked away.

"Come on, you two, let's get going." He kept his voice steady, ushering the two toward the cashier, avoiding the woman's gaze.

Caleb crossed his arms over his chest, standing perfectly still while Annie clung to him, regarding him in confusion.

"You three."

Finnagen stiffened, hearing the words trail behind him, as he managed to tug Caleb forward and put the milk on the counter. He slowly turned, slipping an off-center smile onto his face. "Hello, Ms. Fiona. What brings you here?"

"I've heard from my dear brother that you wish to come over."

Her words were firm and Finnagen gulped. "I am leaving now, so do come along. I'll have Eren drop you off afterward."

"No, no, we're good."

"What? But I'm hungry," Caleb complained.

Dammit, Caleb, Finnagen thought, of course he would get hungry now. No sense of self-preservation, none.

Though he wasn't exactly much better because he sighed and reluctantly nodded. "Let me get these two home and..."

"Oh, no need for that, I bet your parents are quite busy. I have no doubt that they would be fine with you three staying out a little longer, right?"

Before Finnagen could say anything, Fiona had a grasp on his arm. It was painfully tight and he winced. Eren gestured to his two siblings as Finnagen was tugged forward. Why did part of him want to scream and run? "Seriously, Ms. Fiona. We appreciate your kindness, but we really should be going."

"Nonsense, come along now."

Like that, Finnagen was pulled into the back seat of the car with Caleb on one side, scanning it over in surprise, and Annie silently sitting next to him, biting on her finger. He half-heartedly pulled her fingers away from her mouth and shook his head, but felt his tongue was too thick to say anything. This was not what he expected to happen today. Part of him briefly wondered why the cashier hadn't said or done anything. That thought was brushed away as the car hummed to life.

They wove through the streets, approaching the house he'd been to not twenty minutes prior. Maybe he was being ridiculous, but the stories he'd been told for the last few years, the tests of courage he'd, rightfully, ignored. It all spoke of something he should be afraid of.

He peered out the window as they pulled up to the luxurious house. The irony being that it was both one of the saddest and nicest houses in the community. He shook the thought away as the gates opened and they pulled in. Annie shuffled next to him, holding him tightly as Caleb grew quiet, no longer jumping up and down in his seat. They pulled to a stop and, though he didn't want to, he dragged himself out of the car. He held onto Annie tightly and placed the other hand on Caleb's back as he followed Fiona up the stairs, warily watching Eren. The inside was beautiful; marble, glass, exquisite paintings, definitely higher class than his family. He took a deep breath as they moved to another room. A dining room, it seemed.

"Eren, can you go fetch Karina? I think she would like some company."

Damn curiosity. It was eerie, his siblings all shifting uncomfortably while Fiona stared at some papers, reading, yet not reading, it seemed. It didn't take long for a door to open and Fiona to look up. Finnagen blinked, surprised as Fiona's entire being seemed to shift to delight and contentment.

Finnagen turned just enough to spot Karina standing in the doorway. Why would Karina's appearance change the woman so much?

He shook his head, that wasn't his business. So instead, he returned to inspecting the girl. Her black hair was pulled into a high ponytail, a pair of shorts sat snugly on her waist, a blouse just trailing over the hem. She spotted him and she blinked, eyes widening slightly before a faint frown crossed her face. She observed the situation quietly before tentatively taking a seat.

"Karina, dear, did you want anything in particular?"

"Dear?" Karina muttered, a flicker of confusion on her face before she spoke up loud enough for Fiona to hear. Finnagen still caught it anyway, pursing his lips. "I don't care. By the way, what's going on?"

"Oh, this boy was interested in coming over." The expression on her face twisted slightly and he felt a shudder wrack through his body. "Maybe he wanted to meet you?"

Karina glanced sidelong at him, seeming uncomfortable and a little wary, unsure. "Possibly," she muttered, locking eyes with him.

Her expression was filled with utter confusion.

So, she had no idea what was going on either.

Fiona clapped her palms together and they all sat to eat, sort of. He wasn't sure when Fiona handed over the food, but the butler, Eren, stepped in with a few piles of plates. Most of them were filled with different types of pastries. One bowl held some jalapeños which was set near Karina.

Bless his little sister, she was oblivious to the awkward air, swallowing down the food greedily. Caleb, while still a little nervous, seemed to not notice anything once the food was on the table. Finnagen chuckled lightly at his siblings' antics before carefully taking a bite himself. The pastry was flaky and warm, maybe just out of the oven? How? Was it baking while they were shopping? His attention slid to Karina, noticing she was picking at the jalapeños, munching on them quietly as she watched. Okay...so she preferred that hot stuff over pastries? Maybe she felt as awkward as he did. His heart pounded in his chest. This was so strange, uncomfortable. He wanted to scream. What was going on?

He'd been buying books for school just two days ago and now he was eating lunch in the witch's house with a strange girl sitting across from him. Shaking himself, he smiled nervously. "So, uh, you coming to school tomorrow?"

He almost slammed his head against the table at the sheer idiocy of what he said, but it seemed to have amused the girl across from him. She raised an eyebrow before shaking her head. He frowned, spinning his spoon. "Oh, well then, that canceled out any and all conversation I was thinking of."

A short bark of laughter came from Karina and he jerked up as Karina shook her head. "You're pretty open, aren't you?"

He felt heat rise to his cheeks. "I say what I think. What's the harm in that?" he sputtered out.

A cheeky grin flashed across her face. "Nothing."

He definitely did not pout, no matter how much the frown tugged at his face. He stuffed a large bite of pastry in his mouth, some of the cream going over his cheek that he quickly wiped off. Fiona seemed to be watching them with a careful eye, but he decided to keep ignoring her for his own self-preservation. "Okay, so, do you do any sports? I'm on the basketball team."

"Really?"

"Oh, are you going to make jokes on my height too? Because I've got a real good leap for you," Finnagen snapped back, not really offended.

At this point, he was used to people's incredulity. He wasn't exactly the tallest player, but he wasn't short by any stretch of the imagination.

"Oh." She leaned her elbow on the table, chin in her palm as she spun her spoon, seeming intrigued.

"Yeah. Finny is the best. He helps keep the seats warm for everyone." Annie chirped as Caleb snorted.

"Yeah, Finn has a great fumble."

"Shut it, you two." He felt the heat rise more. "Anyway, enough from these pipsqueaks."

He tugged at Caleb around the neck while ruffling Annie's hair. Annie giggled while Caleb squawked, slapping his arm away. "What about you?"

Karina shrugged, her fingers playing with a napkin. "Not much," she mumbled hesitantly, her gaze flickering to Fiona, who seemed to be talking with Eren.

His attention snapped to Fiona before he lowered his voice, just a bit. "How are you related to Fiona? I know I asked earlier, but you never gave me an answer."

"We're not. She's been helping me."

He sat back, stunned. Fiona, the witch, was helping someone?

Karina scrutinized his face, wariness clinging to her expression. "Why does that surprise you? Because of those rumors or whatever you told me about?" Her voice was low, unease dancing across her face for a moment.

He bit his lip, massaging the back of his neck.

Thankfully, the two pipsqueaks kept silent.

"Well, I'm going to be off. Eren will see you three out, alright?"

Finnagen practically jumped out of his seat as Fiona clapped, smiling. She stood and gestured. "It was nice of you to join us. Our door is open if you'd like to come again." With that, she swept out of the hallway, Eren stopping near the door, just standing and waiting. Finnagen frowned.

Huh? He wasn't sure what to think of the strange woman and her butler. He turned to his siblings, seeing Caleb patting his stomach, content. He spotted a little spill on Annie's mouth and gently brushed at her face with a towel. "Geez, Annie."

She pouted and he chuckled before standing up and glancing over to Karina. "Well, I guess introductions are, well, necessary. My name is Finnagen, though I might have already told you. This is my little sister, Annie, and this here is Caleb. Sorry for the intrusion, but she kind of didn't allow no for an answer."

"Sounds about right." Karina rolled her eyes, but stood, hesitantly examining the two children before catching his gaze. "Why were you so nervous though?"

"Er, well..."

"She's the wicked witch of the community," Caleb called, wiping his mouth with his shirt sleeve as he hopped down from the seat, getting a sharp look from Finnagen.

"Witch?" Amusement and concern flashed across Karina's face.

Finnagen sighed, picking up Annie so she was holding onto him. "She's always been a strange one, ever since she arrived. It was only recently she's come out from the house. Every so often for the past few years, we've heard screams resonating from the place, but no one has seen anything, except for odds and ends."

A shiver seemed to run up Karina's spine as she frowned. He glanced over his shoulder and grinned. "Though that doesn't mean anything much, considering some of the people in town. I swear, half the town is full of crazies." He spun his finger near his temple. "I think it comes with the territory."

"You seem fairly..."

"Sane?" Finnagen grinned, mentally cheering as a faint smirk pulled on the other girl's lips. "I'm as sane as they come, as expected from yours truly." He placed a fist to his chest, puffing it out proudly.

She rolled her eyes and he almost slumped as the smile faded.

She had a nice smile.

He shook his head, what was THAT thought? "Anyway, I should get these little pipsqueaks home. Though..." He hesitated, unsure how to continue. He spotted Caleb scrutinizing him before a mischievous look shone in his eyes. Oh no. The little brat.

"Finn has a cr..."

"Finn is going home and so are you." He slapped his palm over Caleb's mouth, causing the boy to roll his eyes while Annie giggled.

Karina raised an eyebrow, a strange expression on her face. He swallowed heavily, suddenly feeling uncomfortable. "I'll come by later?"

She stiffened, expression shifting into one of surprise. "Why?"

"Uh, I mean, aren't you lonely here?"

He wanted to slam his head against the table. That was NOT what he wanted to say! He was a gentleman. Gentlemen weren't rude like that.

He noticed a shift, her shoulders slumping that littlest bit. A smile that didn't seem right danced on her lips. "No, I'm fine."

"Can we come see you?" Annie clapped, tilting her head with a puppy dog look practically oozing from her. "We would really like it."

Way to go, Annie. That's my little sister for you.

Karina seemed to debate before shrugging. "I guess," she muttered, as her posture shifted once more, more confident than earlier.

He felt a sense of contentment before nodding sharply.

"Alright, I'll come over tomo—"

"Didn't you say you had school though?" Karina pointed out, hand on her hip and smirking widely.

Finnagen felt that heat rise once again as he turned away, whistling. "I..." He massaged the back of his neck. "I guess, I'll come over after school?"

Why did he leave that as a question? Why was he having so much trouble with this?

Karina hummed before nodding. "Alright."

He almost threw his arms up in the air in a whoop, but managed to refrain as he spotted Caleb roll his eyes, arms crossed and glaring at him. Right, he should probably let his little brother go. Finnagen scooped up Annie, who giggled and then held out a hand for Caleb to take. Caleb took one scan around the place they were in before tentatively taking it. Finnagen could feel eyes on him, but tried hard to ignore it. "So, I'll see you tomorrow. Take care of yourself." He turned, heading out the door, half-walking, half-fleeing from her intense gaze.

His curiosity only heightened more with each moment seeing the strange girl.

Chapter Twenty-Four

Mom had been, admittedly, a bit worried when he returned home much later than thought of with the milk. He had to return to the store and apologize. Thankfully, the clerk seemed to understand and apologized for not doing anything. Still, once he got that taken care of, he was admittedly, unsure what to tell his mom, knowing she would probably freak out if he gave her the truth. So instead, he said he lost track of time.

It didn't help that Caleb started singing something along the lines of "Finn has a crush. Finn has a crush."

Damn that little pipsqueak. Mom chuckled before gesturing them all inside. Thinking back on it, he guessed he was thankful for Caleb a little bit. Just a little. He didn't have to explain nearly as much. Though Annie cutting in every now and then about the nice lady they met certainly made the conversation interesting.

He stared out the window of the school room, hearing the ticking clock over the door. The pencil flipped through his fingers as he got lost in thought once more. Oh, he'd completely forgotten he had practice tonight. They wouldn't need him, right? He kind of didn't want to go. He wanted to meet up with Karina. He wanted to get to know her more and all that. He did NOT, as his younger sibling seemed to think, have a crush on the girl. Nope, not at all. He was curious about her, that's all. Nothing more.

He couldn't get himself interested in the normal subjects. They were talking about history and the formation of the gated communities. He knew he should be paying attention, but he didn't much care. He knew the basics from the readings. No need to go into detail about what president enacted what edict in order to legalize the creation of such places.

Thankfully, for both his boredom and his mind, the day finally came to an end and he raced out the door. Missing one practice wasn't going to be a problem. He made sure to drop by to say he needed to be home. Thankfully, since it was just a toning day, they were okay with it.

Finnagen hurried home, throwing his backpack onto the table as he called out to his parents that he was heading out. He faintly heard the canned laughter of one of his mother's favorite reality TV shows as he threw open the door. Without waiting for their response, he dashed outside. In no time at all, he was back at the house, staring at the imposing mansion before swallowing heavily. What was he doing? Taking a very deep breath, he tapped on the intercom to one side. The intercom crackled for a moment until the gates eerily swung open without a word. Trying to mentally laugh it off, he gingerly stepped down the walkway. "Okay, Finn. You can do this. You've already been here before." He ignored the fact he was talking to himself. More saying it out loud to distract from the sad environment. "You can do this."

Sadly, within no time, he arrived at the door, which swung open to reveal Eren.

"Uh, I'm here to see Karina." He almost shouted the end, his nerves getting the best of him. Eren didn't really react, just turned and led him through the halls. Stopping in front of a doorway that appeared to be like every other one, he gestured.

"This is her room. If you need anything, I will be right outside."

Finnagen watched as the man stepped to one side, watching. He paused for only a moment, gave himself a sharp nod, and knocked. A soft "Come in" echoed from the room and he could already feel his face heating up. He stepped inside, peering over in time to spot Karina staring at a phone she was cradling. She looked up, then started, almost fumbling with the phone. "Oh, you came." Her startled voice was pitched awkwardly.

He rubbed the back of his neck, feeling sheepish. "Well, yeah? I did say I would." His gaze flicked to the phone, curious. "Is something wrong with your phone?"

"No, it's fine." She quickly stuffed it into her pocket before she turned to him. She hesitated before her expression softened. "Still, thanks," she muttered.

He beamed, deciding to ignore the phone like she seemed to want. "No problem."

He shuffled over and took a seat on the couch, ogling the richness of the room and how out of place she appeared in it. "So." Finn fidgeted, not quite sure what he was trying to say. He hadn't really thought things through before coming here, though that wasn't unusual.

"Yes?" Karina prodded, appearing both amused, by her upturned lip, and annoyed, with her arms crossed over her chest. She was leaning back against the couch with intense eyes boring into him.

He shrugged, feeling awkward. "How are you doing today? Your leg any better?"

A moment of silence ensued and he forced himself to face her, only to wince when he caught her wary expression. "I took the bandages off the other day."

He paused, thoughts flitting through the past few days. He paled on realization. The only time he saw it was when she was in the pool. She'd been wearing pants at the mall.

He coughed awkwardly and turned away. "So, nice place you have?"

Why did he ask that as a question? He mentally banged his head against the wall. At least he wasn't stuttering, that would make it worse.

"It's not mine."

"Er, uh, I meant..."

There went the whole not stuttering bit. He shook his head and peered back at her, massaging the back of his neck. He was making this awful and it all started because he wanted to apologize, which he still hadn't really done. He sighed. Now it was more than that. He basically intruded into her life out of his own curiosity and now he was in her room.

In her room. Alone.

He quickly snapped his head in the other direction, roving over the bumps and swells in the bubbled ceiling as he tried to get rid of any pleasant thoughts. He. Was. A. Gentleman. Gentleman do not think those things.

"Is there any reason you're here? Because if not, then..."

"Why are you here by yourself? What did you mean by the wit...Fiona saving you?" He quickly interrupted, not wanting the conversation to end.

She stared at him in silence, as if evaluating him quietly before letting out a breath. "You seem," she hummed, as if lost in thought. "Maxwell would know what to say."

Maxwell? Who was Maxwell? It was a guy's name, that was for sure. He felt a faint frown cross his face, his lips turning downward even as he tried to hide the annoyance and ignore it. "Who is that?" he ended up asking anyway, causing the girl to blink and peer over, startled.

She paused before her expression grew outright downcast. Her posture slumped, yet everything else seemed so taut, almost white from the grip, her legs curling up slightly. "No one you would know."

"He's obviously important to you." Finnagen pushed gently.

He didn't like seeing this type of Karina. For some reason, it didn't feel right to him. Every time he saw her, she was so confident.

"It doesn't matter," she snapped and he backpedaled, waving defensively as if to ward off her words.

"I'm sorry. I won't ask. How about you tell me how you met Fiona? You said she saved you, right?" *Okay, note to self, don't ask about Maxwell. Got it.*

Karina unwound a little, nodding slightly. "I guess? I haven't really gotten a chance to talk to anyone about it."

He felt a hint of pride at that, but pushed it away as he leaned forward, hands trailing between his legs to listen more intently.

She glanced up and shrugged. "I got lost. Fiona found me outside the community and took me in. She's been helping me heal up ever since."

Wait, outside? As in...

He froze, his mind coming to a halt. She was an outsider. He gulped, catching her eye. She seemed to be waiting, seeming to know full well what she said.

She was waiting for his response and, considering how tense she was, as much as he wanted to respond instinctively by screaming and running, he took a deep breath and gave a sharp nod. "Okay... Okay. I can deal with that. I can deal," he said.

A hint of surprise showed on Karina's face.

He knew anyone else would have left, would have called her out, had her hanged, something. But he couldn't. Everyone said Fiona was a witch, but while she was a little intense, she'd only been nice to him. He knew Father always said she was probably fine, but everyone else spoke so many stories about her, it was hard to believe him. While Karina was an outsider, she didn't appear sick or evil, per se. She wasn't a demon or devil. She didn't seem keen on arson and considering he knew full well that Fiona was from a community that burnt to the ground, for the woman to take in and heal up someone from outside the community was something that he had to keep in consideration.

So, against all his learnings, against everything he'd been told, he found he wasn't sure he believed it. Similar to how he never joined the others in those games of ding dong ditch or tests of courage.

"You're not going to do anything?" Her voice was quiet, muffled almost.

He stilled. For a brief moment, he almost thought he might have mistaken it, he saw a hint of fear cross her face. Her shoulders tensed as her fingers crumbled into her shirt. She seemed to almost be holding her breath. Was she scared? If so, why?

Because of him?

The words rang in his head and he shifted back, his side digging into the arm of the couch. A moment later, he leaned forward, fisting the cushion as realization swept over him. She expected him to run, screaming. To call her out or something and yet all he'd done was sit there.

He shook his head, both for her sake and his own. He could almost feel the tension in the air fade. He briefly caught the pretty smile that crossed her face as she slowly relaxed. She chuckled and shook her head. "I do not know how Maxwell does it."

That name again. He gritted his teeth. No, he promised he wouldn't ask her. At this point, he wasn't sure if he wanted to ask. Both because it would hurt her and himself. "So, outside?"

"Yep." She popped the P.

Once more in a more chipper mood. Was she happy that he was tolerating it? He couldn't say he was happy about the idea. He was curious, however, so it was only fair that he not judge when his curiosity was somewhat sated.

"Who are you?" he voiced out, unsure what to do with himself.

His mouth was dry, the air tickling his nose with the faint scent of spring and honey. Strange, but endearing smells. She raised an eyebrow and he cleared his throat, rubbing the back of his neck as he realized he'd gotten distracted. "I mean, who are you really? You're an outsider, yet you're not freaking out about being in a gated community. You're okay with telling me and you know someone who seems to be used to those situations. Fiona, whom everyone is scared of, seems to dote on you."

"I don't get the last one either..." she trailed off before smiling softly. "Yet the other parts are a bit more interesting, if you are willing to listen."

"Of course." He smiled, relieved. He could still feel those hints of panic, but he tried hard to ignore them. "I won't tell anyone."

"Good." She grinned cheekily. "I'm from an area quite far from here, actually, to the northeast, to be precise." He leaned forward, intrigued. She hummed, amused. "So, this is what Lex thought when he talked with us. Jeez, now it makes sense why he had such a tense relationship with Caym. Strange."

Wait. His eyes widened and he jumped, standing up and staring down at her, mouth open in shock. He'd heard that name. He KNEW that name. Hell, everyone knew that name. Especially after Mr. Askren's latest broadcast, about how his brother was kidnapped, so, then, wait, how did Karina know him? "You know the man who came back from the dead?"

"Huh?" Utter confusion hung in the air. Her head tilted just a little bit to the side.

He shook his head, arms spread out wide. "You know Leonard Askren. I heard he returned to the gated community about half a year ago after being lost to the outer community for years. He's practically a prince of the gated community."

"Prince?" Karina snorted.

Finnagen glared, feeling a hint offended by her lackadaisical summary of Leonard Askren. While he might not have been the one most fascinated by the prince's return, he was definitely excited at the idea of meeting him, or hearing someone talk about him. Especially since so many were worried for his safety. He could only imagine how his brother must have been feeling. Still, it was frustrating, that the first person he met who knew him spoke of him so lightly. "Yeah. Enthrope are the protectors of the gated community. They also have connections with most of the government and maintain good connection with most communities, better than the so-called president."

"So, what, they basically control them?" Karina said in a tone of voice that practically screamed displeasure and disdain.

Finnagen rolled his eyes. "That's absurd. They don't control the president. The president has say in what Enthrope can and can't do and they have to listen. It's just that the president doesn't deign to pay attention to communities like ours. That's Enthrope's job."

"Uh-huh." Karina didn't seem impressed, once more on the defensive. "Also, how did you know I was talking about that Lex? After all, that's not his actual name, but a nickname. Aren't there more than one out there?"

Finnagen stilled. He hadn't thought about that. He's mostly guessed from her using Mr. Askren's name. He'd heard the nickname in a rumor mill months ago when everyone was talking about it at school. He shook his head. "That's beside the point. How do you know Leonard Askren?"

"Lex, actually. He hates being called Leonard." Her face twisted strangely at the name. She spat out the words. "God, that does not fit him at all. No wonder he hates it."

Finnagen plopped back down, in slight shock. The girl in front of him knew the practically prodigal son of the gated communities and was shrugging it off? Was she aware that he was kidnapped?

She shrugged. "To answer your question, we're friends." She hesitated. "Well, were. I'm not sure if he is really too fond of me right now. I know Maxwell probably hates me."

He grit his teeth, trying not to bite his tongue at the name. "How?

Did you? Become friends?" he forced out, trying to get his mind onto the next topic. So, maybe she didn't know. He wasn't sure he wanted to learn the answer of that question right now, partially for his own sanity.

Karina hummed, swaying back and forth in thought. "Maxwell and I met him a while ago, while he was in Reinmark. He helped us out, though he didn't have to, and we've been with each other ever since. I never did thank him for all the help he's given Maxwell and me. There's another thing to add to the list."

Reinmark? Wait, she'd said northeast, but that's practically the other end of the country. "What are you doing all the way out here?"

He was feeling dizzy with all the information she was giving him, though she was being quite vague for the most part.

She shrugged, fingers twitching as she crossed one leg over the other, pushing back into her chair a little more. "No reason," she muttered, once more in a down mood.

He nodded as he tried to process all the information. This girl met Leona...no, Lex. She had someone named Maxwell whom she cared for deeply, and that annoyed him. She was practically doted on by Fiona, of all people.

To top it all off, she was an outsider.

He had NOT expected this when he realized he was curious about her. Not at all. Yet, he was still curious, even more so now. Plus... He grinned wildly. "You're talking to me," he cheered, causing her to start and scrutinize him strangely.

He turned away, rubbing his neck nervously. "I mean. You seemed so closed off and intense. I wasn't sure if you would want to talk to me. I wanted to talk to you. So, I'm glad you're talking to me?" He found his bangs blocking part of his view, but didn't push them to the side, feeling increasingly sheepish, warmth practically making him sweaty and shaky. "Does that make me strange?"

"Strange?" She trailed off, seeming unsure how to respond. "That's one way to put it."

"Oh."

He knew it. His grin fell and he gulped, his chest tightening. He always did this. He wished his siblings were here, at least he could use them as bait or a distraction. They were good at both. "I, ah, I'm glad to see you're doing better. You answered my questions, so..." he trailed off and inspected his empty hands. He hadn't gotten her anything. Nothing. Once again, he leapt without thinking. This time, he basically leapt himself off a cliff.

It hurt, a lot.

"I'm sorry." He bit his lip before taking a deep breath. Okay, he could do this. Making sure that he had her full attention he spoke. "I'll be right back. Can you wait for me?"

"Wait for you? Where do you think I'll go?"

He shook his head. "I meant, can you wait and meet me again later today? I..." I want to get you something, he decided, firmly snapping his mouth shut before he said the rest of the words. His foot was already through his mouth and down to his stomach, no point in pushing it farther.

She analyzed him for such a long time and, he wanted, for a brief moment, to shift and quell under her gaze. Her intense blue eyes were so filled with different emotions, but he held still, like his father taught him. To be a gentleman, he had to first know how to respect women and that meant making sure she knew she had his full attention.

It didn't make it any less difficult.

Finally, when he thought he would burst from his held breath, she nodded and he let out a breath of relief before shooting to his feet. "I promise. I'll be right back. Okay?"

With that, he darted out the door and was gone without another word.

~ * ~

Karina blankly followed a butterfly as it flitted back and forth on the other side of the window, chin in her hand as her mind raced. She learned so much in the last few days. Mostly from that strange boy. He fluctuated so much, from childish to respectful to firm. He was a good listener, for the most part. Though she was still struggling to figure out how he knew she was talking about Lex. She knew there weren't a lot of Lex's out there, but still. Maybe she shouldn't have mentioned Caym.

The thought was settled when she once more went over her earlier interactions with the boy. He did tend to speak recklessly with his mouth more than his mind. She'd never been that bad, but she could recall doing that a few times.

She knew she should be freaked. This strange boy, whom she crashed into at the mall, was now everywhere. She wasn't an idiot. She could tell that he found her interesting and wanted to know her. She wasn't sure if she wanted to talk to anyone, but admittedly, it was kind of nice to talk to someone her own age besides her brother about everything that was happening.

Fiona was nice, strange, according to both her own observations and Finnegan's, but nice. Of course, her thoughts flicked to her phone and the strange woman. She still felt uncomfortable with asking Fiona for things, mainly because she didn't want Fiona asking her any odd questions. More specifically, she didn't want Fiona asking why she needed her phone charged and who she would call. That could open a can of worms she was not prepared for. She could probably ask this strange boy, but...

Speaking of, she heard a knock on the door. Fiona opened the door, head poking inside. "I saw that boy run out earlier. Did something happen?"

"No." She shook her head. "He needed to run to..." she trailed off. She didn't even know.

"Did he leave you?" Fiona's eyes glinted.

Karina couldn't hide the annoyance as she said, "No, he was listening to me talk."

"Sounded like yelling, actually."

"Whatever," Karina muttered.

She was too tired to deal with Fiona right now. The last few minutes were so taxing on her nerves, and she knew it would be just as taxing when he came back. But she didn't mind. He was sincere. She could see that. He had that same innocent and soft expression as her brother. That was only verified with how he was with his siblings, who obviously adored him.

It made her smile as she recalled the trio, his fond smiles as he watched his two younger siblings. He was a good brother, a good sibling, unlike her.

She curled up, burying her head into her lap, noting that Fiona must have stepped back out at some point. It was a minor thought, pushed to the side. She was so done with all of this.

Chapter Twenty-Five

Finnagen panted heavily, sweat practically gripping the hair to his face. He brushed some back, trying to pat it down so he appeared somewhat nice. He fixed up his clothes and took one more scan of his gift. It was secured in a box wrapped with a hastily found and done bow. Would she like it? He nodded to convince himself and then started back down the stairs, heading for the front door of his home. He slunk forward, not sure why he was creeping.

"Finnagen Andrew Cornwall."

Finnagen stiffened before slowly turning enough to see over his shoulder. His mother stood there, arms crossed over her ample chest and nose tilted downward in disdain. His father stood behind her, hand on Mother's shoulder and looking at him with a neutral expression. Neither upset nor happy.

"Yes?" he choked out before clearing his throat. "Is something wrong?"

"Is something wrong?" his mother outright growled. "You've been gallivanting off to who knows where for the past few days, skipped practice, which your father and I were both here for by the way, left the younger ones alone even though you KNOW we're both busy for work and you try sneaking out of the house without letting us know you came back. What do you think, Finnagen?"

"Your mother's right. You have a lot of explaining to do, young man." His father spoke tersely. "I've heard from Caleb and Annie that you went to Ma'am Fiona's house yesterday."

Finnagen winced as his mother's gaze sharpened. "Speaking of. You couldn't have, I don't know, tried calling? We waved it off because

Julie Boglisch

things happen, but too much of this has happened at once. The teachers called today, saying you were more spaced out than usual. You can't graduate if you keep this up."

Finnagen bit his lip. His parents didn't usually yell like this. His mom was usually pretty chill, but he must have worried them more than he thought.

He heard a sigh followed by faint footsteps. His father come up to him, placing a comforting hand on his shoulder. Brown, almost amber eyes, much like his own, stared back at him. "You know we're just worried about you. With Ma'am Fiona acting out of character the past few days, we've all been on edge, and to hear you've been over to her place, we feared the worst."

"She's not that bad," Finnagen found himself saying. "She's taking care of Karina."

"Karina?" His father mouthed, confusion shining on his face before he glanced toward Mother.

Mother frowned thoughtfully before giving him a careful look, her anger still rolling off her, but slowed slightly. "Would this Karina happen to be the girl you ran into while we were at the mall?"

"Oh? This sounds like it would be an interesting story." His father perked, a mischievous smile on his face.

"It's nothing major, and yes, Mom." Finnagen shifted from foot to foot.

His father examined him quietly, before understanding fell onto his face. He shook his head, pulling back. "I see, son. I'll hear that story later. As for your previous comment, you are right. No person is inherently bad, it's just Ma'am Fiona can be unpredictable in certain circumstances." He hesitated for a moment before shaking his head. "She's a sweet enough woman, but trauma does a lot to a person. After all, aren't we all a little messed up in the head?" He tapped his head.

"That shouldn't excuse him from leaving like this." His mother spoke up, drawing both their attention to the woman who was no longer fuming, but still seemed to be on the defensive.

His father nodded. "Yes, it doesn't, but remember when we fell in love?"

257

"I'm not in love," Finnagen shouted, heat rising on his face. "I find her interesting and want to know more about her and she's pretty and..." He cut himself off and groaned, pushing his palms into his face. "Oh god."

He heard a faint sigh before his mother pulled him forward in a hug. "I'm sorry, sweetie."

"That's...but I can't be in love. I only met her three days ago," he whispered, admittedly appreciating his mother's embrace.

Sure, he'd experienced crushes before, and even dated a girl a few months back, but it was a quick thing, and both of them agreed to remain friends. This felt different and he wasn't quite sure what the word was to describe it. Love seemed so...there was no way it could be that.

"Love is strange, that's for sure. It causes people to act and do strange and sometimes terrifying things." His father spoke up, slowly prying his mother off him. "Doesn't mean you are off the hook though. When you get back, you are grounded, understood?"

Finnagen groaned and hung his head.

"Finnagen, when did you have another chance to talk with her? I haven't seen her around," Mother piped up, confused.

"Here and there." Finnagen shrugged, feeling uncomfortable lying to his mother.

She waited, as if expecting more before letting out an annoyed sound and turning to Father. "Speaking of Fiona, has she seen you yet?"

Finnagen blinked at the non-sequitur, spotting his father shaking his head.

"No, she's seen every other psychiatrist though. I've been so busy with my own clients that I haven't been able to go to her yet, besides the initial perfunctory consultation visit."

"The poor dear."

"I know, but she's one of the latest to arrive. I can only do so much. I do know one of my patients should be good soon. I'm checking on her now, actually. Maybe, if she's good, I'll head over to Fiona's tomorrow morning."

Finnagen bit his lip. Right, he hadn't thought about that. What would his father say about Karina? Part of him didn't want his father to meet the girl, the other part did. He knew his mother would probably not mind her, they were both strong women and, in all technicality, they met once before, sort of.

"So, I'm okay to go?" he managed to get out, inching toward the door. His mother put her hands on her hips and frowned.

"And what, young man, are you going back out for?"

"I, ah..."

"I would assume he wants to give this Karina he's infatuated with a little gift," his father put in, smiling knowingly as his gaze flickered to where he was holding the little box.

"Oh?" His mother's eyes brightened slightly, a faint smirk on her face. "What are you getting for the little lady?"

"It's none of your business, Mom," he muttered, shuffling from foot to foot. "I'm simply apologizing for running into her and bothering her. That. Is. All." He enunciated each word, his voice and posture firm.

His mother sighed before reaching a hand up and ruffling his hair. "Be careful, okay? I don't want you hurt. Let her know, I want to meet her."

"I will." He beamed, relieved. He turned and hurried out the door, shouting a bye to his parents. As he swung out the entrance, he could barely see his father shake his head before closing the door.

Hurrying down the brightly lit street, it took him no time at all to return to the manor. He hesitated at the intercom then frowned, feeling uncomfortable. He didn't want to bother the butler again, so, deciding to take a different route, he walked around the mansion, scrutinizing the windows carefully.

Okay, which one was Karina's again? Maybe he could throw a rock at it? Stuff like that always worked in the romance movies. Though it would probably shatter the window in real life. Ah well, worth a shot.

He spotted a window up on the second floor, the light still on inside. He mentally thought through what he saw of the house. Yeah, that was probably the right room, plus it was facing the pool.

He squatted down, picking up a rock. He tossed it up and down to get a feel for its weight. His brother was right, he was great at fumbles. He hoped his chances weren't as bad. He did have those few three-point shots, so...

Judging the distance, he took a step back and flung. It sailed through the air and clanged off the sill...of the first-floor window.

He cringed and flung himself into the bushes, hiding in place. That did not go as planned.

Thankfully, Karina must have noticed because he spotted her inching toward the window, her shape outlined in the light, though she was low down, as if creeping.

He sighed and stood back up, waving up to her with both arms flung into the air. Thankfully, in his lighter-colored clothes, she spotted him before shaking her head. He watched her disappear and he slowly let them drop to his sides. Oh god, he hoped this wasn't a mistake. He contemplated the chain link fence in front of him, half-tempted to bang his head against it. Thankfully, for what few braincells he knew he had left, the door opened toward the pool. In the warm glow, Karina stepped out and walked over.

More like stomped. He flinched and shuffled his feet.

"What the hell was that?"

He grinned sheepishly at her, rubbing the back of his neck. "I wanted to surprise you? Plus, it was late and I didn't want to bother the butler or Fiona."

She stilled before sighing. "Come on, I'll let you in."

He nodded and followed her as they walked around the premises, her on one side, him on the other.

Considering the fact that she was an outsider, this made it feel so strange and part of him found himself hating the fence that was separating them.

Finally, they arrived at the front and she opened it, letting him in. He stepped in and turned to her. "So, not as nice as I would want, but I wanted to give this to you."

He held out his hand, opening his palm which had been tightly clasped around the little box. She took it confused, glancing between the box and him. He waited, pulling his hand back as she carefully undid the bow and opened the box.

Inside was a beautiful antique wrist watch. She stared, startled and he found he couldn't hold her gaze. "I noticed you were constantly looking at your phone and you didn't have a watch on you, so I figured I could give you one of mine. I have a few at home. This one is pretty heavy-duty. I mean, I don't know if you like this sort of thing but I figured it would help you."

She shifted, her hair covering a part of her face for a moment, as if she wasn't sure how to respond, before shaking her head and letting out a faint snort. "Geez," she muttered, but took it anyway. "I guess I should cut Maxwell a little slack next time we see Madeline." She gently traced the metal links with her slender fingers. "Thank you. I appreciate it."

He let out a breath of relief before grinning widely. "No problem."

Karina rolled her eyes before flipping the watch onto her wrist and clasping it. The silver encrusted numbers gleamed in the moonlight, as a faint ticking could be heard.

"I replaced the battery, that's why it took so long. It should be good as new now."

Karina stared down at it in silence for so long, Finnagen wondered if he'd messed up again.

"So, did you want to know anything else?"

Finnagen beamed before nodding. "You probably have all sorts of stories. I know what I've been told, but..."

"I bet it's quite different than what it is like out there." She waved, tilting her head. "It's been a while since I've had someone to talk to. I'll show you to the lounge."

She turned and Finnagen hurried after her, beaming in giddy pride. Yes. He hadn't messed up. First victory.

He would take it.

Chapter Twenty-Six

Finnagen listened with rapt attention as she began her story. He noted she didn't mention where she started, but she did mention about the Resistance. "Maxwell, Lex and I all managed to leave the place, but I ended up getting shot, which is why I got hit in the leg." She gestured down to her leg and he nodded. "We ended up moving west because it was away from both the Resistance and someone else who was after us." She waved, ignoring the vague statement.

He would have pressed, but he was simply thankful that she was saying anything. Though, it did make him wonder. Did Mr. Askren lie about Lex's kidnapping? The way Karina spoke, it was so genuine, it made him wonder which story was actually true.

"After arriving in this small town, I decided to leave them. Not my best decision," she muttered quietly and he frowned, noting her downturned expression.

He reached up and stilled before dropping his arm back down. He wasn't much of a comforter, there wasn't really much he could do. "So, you left and what happened after?"

"Oh, right. So, I hopped on the nearest train out of town. Just to tell you, train-hopping without an open carriage is NOT fun, especially when it's raining. I got so sick and wet from it, even when I did manage to find a way into a carriage."

"I bet." He grinned.

She clicked her tongue softly, making sure he could tell how annoyed she was, even as her lips twitched upwards a little bit.

"Anyway, it was about half a day later or maybe a few days. Everything after the train kind of blended together. I found myself near this gated community. While Fiona was out and about, she spotted me. It took some convincing, but I eventually went with her. She mentioned how she was a medical student. Considering her knowledge, it seemed to fit. Not having many other options and barely able to do much else, I let her bring me here. I've been recovering here since. I believe that was, five days ago, I think?"

"Really?" The word tumbled out of his mouth, stunned.

He hadn't known Fiona left the community. How did she get out? Did the guards let her out? Why did no one know about that?

"Yeah. She's been nice to me. I haven't—done anything for her, so it feels a little strange."

"I know that feeling," he muttered, pointedly avoiding her gaze.

"I bet." A cheeky voice spoke up and he glared back at the grinning girl.

"Geez, try to be nice for a second." He huffed, before grinning. "Guess that means I have to try harder, sound fair?"

Karina leaned back, amusement dancing on her lips. She glanced at her wrist and paused. Bringing it up, she peered at him worriedly. "Don't you need to head home?"

Finnagen couldn't hide the confusion he was feeling, as he leaned forward to examine her watch. It was eleven o'clock, not really an issue. "No. Why?"

"Don't you have, I don't know, school?"

Finnagen blinked once, twice and then yelped as the realization hit him and he groaned. "Oh god. I completely forgot. My parents are going to kill me when I get back." Considering how they were when he went out, then again, it was already late when he left, so maybe they expected? Who even knew? "I guess I should head back."

He didn't want to. He wanted to stay and talk. He hadn't gotten a chance to figure out who Maxwell was. She was always hesitant when saying his name, that was the only way she described him. Who was he in relation with her? A friend? A boyfriend? A relative? He hoped to God that it wasn't the second one.

"Yeah." Karina shrugged. "I guess you do."

For a brief moment, he thought he caught a glimmer of sadness, or maybe it was just his mind playing tricks on him. Probably just wishful thinking. He sighed and pushed himself to his feet. "See you tomorrow," he spoke, letting the warmth slip through into his words alongside his smile.

He would have to wait until after practice. He couldn't skip again, then he could meet her. It would be late, but... He stopped and outright groaned. Right, he was grounded. Dammit.

"Huh?"

What was he going to do? He said he would see her tomorrow and he wasn't about to back down now. He was finally getting her to open up to him. Dammit, Mom.

"Yeah, tomorrow. I know my dad is probably coming to meet Fiona in the morning, so maybe you'll see him? If not, I'll come after practice is over." He let the words out slowly, trying desperately to think over how to work it.

Maybe he could go straight after practice, or hitch a ride with Dad? No, he couldn't do that. Dad respected Mom too much to do it. He would have to wait until after school. Actually, if he avoided practice again. He grasped his hair, tugging in frustration. Ugh, and he probably looked so stupid right now.

"You don't have to, you know," Karina butted in, interrupting his thoughts, her expression guarded.

Oh, hell no. He finally got her to open up. He wasn't going to let that victory slide away just because of one foolish mistake.

"I want to." He turned his head up, making sure his gaze didn't waver from hers. "I'll talk to my parents, see if they'll let me come."

She shook her head. "No, really. I've been feeling better lately, so I think I'll speak with Fiona and leave tomorrow. If I stay any longer, it might be a danger for you and Fiona. There are people who would not be happy about me being here. Anyway, I need to meet up with..." She trailed off.

She reached into her pocket, grasping tightly what was probably her phone. He remembered seeing it with a black screen. Was she going to leave it off like that? Why?

"I need to go west. There is something I need to do."

What did she mean? That they would be in danger? Part of his heart leapt that she included him, but part of him felt like his heart was being torn. She was leaving? Was tonight the last time he would see her? No, he would have to come by tomorrow, before she left. He wasn't going to leave it at this.

"I'll come by anyway," he spoke, conviction filling his voice. "I'll skip school. I don't care. I can't let you leave alone."

She jerked back, startled before raising an eyebrow. "What? Are you going to come with me? Don't be an idiot."

He rubbed his neck, sorting through his thoughts. What were his options? "I..."

She watched him for a moment before letting out a breath. "Fine, I'll wait for you to come by tomorrow, but you are not coming with me. You have your parents and siblings to take care of." She bit her lip, almost choking over those words. "I'll ask Fiona or Eren for a car, or some means to bring me out west. I'll be fine."

He felt his heart wrench, something lodged in his throat. He didn't realize how tightly he was curling his fingers into his palm until he felt a sharp pain. He winced and slowly forced his mind to command them to loosen. Those words... "Alright," he whispered. "I'll come by tomorrow." He smiled weakly. "Anyway, I should probably go home."

She examined him quietly before nodding, a faint, tired smile on her lips.

He turned and, glancing over his shoulder once, walked out the door into the hallway. To his surprise, the warmth of the living room only shed a little light into the dark, cold hallway. It was quiet from the late night and he found himself scrutinizing everything, as his teeth grit tightly, so tight, he could almost swear he heard cracking. What was he going to do? Just come by to wish her good-bye? Could he leave it at that? Even now, he barely knew her. He didn't know if she already had a boyfriend, or girlfriend, he wasn't a stranger to those things. Was she interested in him? Plus, she was right, if he did leave, what about his parents, his siblings? No, he couldn't think of them right now.

He pulled from those thoughts and paused, realizing he'd gotten turned around. Very little moonlight shone through, blocked by trees and clouds. Why were the lights not on? Was it because of power usage? It would make sense with how big the house was. He shook himself from his thoughts, trying to quell the rising worry as he worked to remember the way to the entrance.

"Where are you going?"

He let out a scream, noting how pitched it was, before searching wildly around. From one of the doorways with a candle in hand—why a candle? his mind supplied as it calmed from jack-hammer to normal—stepped Fiona. The candle cast her face in a strange light and he frowned, uncertain. "I, uh, home?" he responded, gulping.

"Ah." She stayed silent and he fidgeted for a moment.

"Well, I best be going. Take care?" He didn't mean for the last sentence to sound like a question, it just seemed to come out that way, much to his chagrin.

"Of course."

A little weirded out and admittedly freaked by the mix of darkness and the eyes glowing softly at him, he quickly bowed and hurried away. It wasn't rude to leave like that. He'd said his good-byes, right? Dammit, his mind was a mess tonight.

He didn't want to meet up with Fiona again in the dark. A woman walking around with a candle in this day and age was just screaming bad vibes.

Really bad vibes.

He glanced over his shoulder, noting a flickering shadow from the corner, the faint sound of footsteps reaching his ear. Dancing flames indicating it was probably Fiona.

Deciding against just standing there, he scurried down the hall. He would find a way out soon enough.

Spotting the door that led to the entrance, he let out a breath, hand to his chest, berating himself on being so paranoid. He walked toward the door.

The crackle of flame was the only warning he received. He heard a whoosh and yelped as he stumbled forward and turned. Behind him was Fiona. She held the candle extended, a serious expression on her face and wax dripping down the candle in rolls onto the floor.

"Ma'am?" he called, unsure what happened.

"You hurt her, didn't you? My cute little sister. How could you."

Fiona's voice was even, her gaze distant, often flickering to the candle where wax slowly dribbled down the side, heated by the tiny flame. Finnagen shifted backward, ready to bolt as the words rang through his mind. Hurt? What?

"Don't worry. I'll make sure you are kind. That you won't ever leave her."

Finn took another step back, letting out a nervous laugh. "I wasn't planning on it. Plus, don't people usually NOT want someone near their..." He couldn't say sister. Karina wasn't related and he believed her when she mentioned it.

"She likes you. I think you could be very nice." She smiled just a little too wide. "So, can you come with me?"

"No thank you, ma'am. I have to get home."

"Oh, it's no issue." Fiona beamed and reached forward.

Deciding the best course of action was NOT to get grabbed, Finnagen yelped and darted away. For once, he was grateful for his shorter stature, it made running away much easier and his lanky frame helped as he pushed a doorway open and raced through. What the hell was up with her? Was she as crazy as he thought? As everyone in the community thought?

Not realizing where he was going, he ran smack dab into someone. The light body and familiar yelp caught his attention as, once again, his arms wrapped around whomever he'd hit. He stumbled and found himself pushed against the wall. He reached up, back smarting as the other person let out a hiss.

"What the—Finnagen?"

Finnagen blinked and turned to see Karina step away, as if she'd been about to do something. She held a flashlight, seeming both annoyed and uncomfortable.

Finnagen shook his head and pushed away from the wall, wincing. "Sorry," he mumbled.

God damnit. Nothing was going right tonight. He slammed his head backward and let out a laugh. Not anything exuberant, but a laugh.

267

"What are you doing?"

"Who knows." He let his laugh die, his nervousness coming to the forefront once more. "I, uh..."

He didn't want to mention he was running from a creepy Fiona. He wasn't sure how much Karina trusted him and he highly doubted she would trust him if he mentioned something like this. Why did he have to run into her after what happened earlier? "Why are you using a flashlight anyway, don't want to turn on the lights?"

Karina's deadpan expression made him chuckle uncomfortably, hand reaching the back of his neck. After a moment she moved around him, gesturing for him to follow. He hesitated but stepped beside her. "The power is off. I think they cut the power every night since it's just Fiona, Eren and myself. Considering how big this place is? It makes sense. After all, no point in going to the other end of the house because you forgot to turn a light off." Karina shrugged. "None of my business though. It doesn't really bother me."

Finnagen peeked over to see Karina wave dismissively, the light bouncing with her movement. He couldn't get rid of the nagging feeling, sheepishness foremost on his mind. He was looking pathetic, wasn't he? Geez. First, he gets lost and runs into Karina, again, then she ignores the very thing that was scaring him out of his wits.

After all, being a scaredy cat, especially when you basically outright said you were leaving, was not gentlemanly at all.

Feeling a bit of a need to sulk, he turned his face away, examining the surroundings. He must have been running blind because he didn't recognize where he was. Distracting himself from his thoughts, he turned to Karina. He might as well ask, considering he already was in the dumps anyway. "So, why do you stare at a black screen? Is your phone dead or something?"

Karina hesitated for a moment before nodding. Her voice came out faint, a little lonely. "Yeah, I left my charger with Maxwell."

Maxwell, eh? He should ask, part of him supplied, he should find out who this Maxwell was. However, even with his pride battered and bruised, he wasn't sure he could do it, he wasn't ready to deal with the final blow, if that was what it was.

Finnagen smiled, smacking a fist to his chest. "I'll get one for you. I'll bring one tomorrow to use, sound good?"

She examined him for a moment before nodding, her lips upturning just a little. "Sounds good."

After a few more turns, they arrived back at the dining room, though whether Finnagen was relieved or not was up for debate.

"What were you still doing up anyway?" Finnagen asked sheepishly, his tone quiet in the echoing chamber.

She shrugged. "Just exploring. I couldn't find it in myself to sit still and I didn't want to sleep, so I figured I would take a walk around the place some more. Kind of like, a safe adventure." The last few words were soft, almost barely perceptible, but Finnagen caught them.

"Safe adventure?"

Karina seemed to debate with herself for a moment, her mouth moving without words as they passed through the doorway he saw earlier. She nodded, as if having come to a decision. The sound of their footsteps echoed off the wooden walls and ceiling, the rug only slightly dampening their sound. "Yeah, I haven't had one since..." she trailed off, deep in thought before huffing. "Since Claremore. Wow, it was that long ago?"

Claremore? He didn't recognize the name. Maybe it was a small town? It would make sense. Still, he thought she'd said Reinmark. Maybe she traveled there and met Leona...Lex? He wouldn't be able to ask, for a moment later, they arrived at a doorway that he knew led outside. He didn't want to go, he realized. Going meant he might not be able to see her again. Going meant he would be grounded. Stuck at home.

He put his hand on the door, hesitating before letting out a long-drawn breath. Did it matter though? She already said she didn't want him coming with her.

"I'll see you tomorrow." Karina spoke up and Finnagen's thought process outright froze.

He whipped around, earning an amused expression. "Wha...really? You'll wait? I've made such a fool of myself today and..."

"Shut up." Karina's words, while harsh, were said softly, a faint smile on her face. "You've done nothing wrong. You've been nice to me since you met me and still are. Yeah, you may be a klutz, but..." She shrugged. "It's been nice to talk. So, thanks."

He felt the heat shoot across his face and he quickly wiped the back of his hand over his mouth, unable to keep eye contact. How embarrassing. He coughed lightly and turned back in time to spot the amusement shining on her face, as he found himself unable to hold back the joy he could feel thrumming through him. "Alright. I'll see you tomorrow." He waved before hurrying away.

If his parents yelled at him or his siblings nagged him, he didn't care. Nothing could ruin his good mood right now.

Except maybe lack of sleep from too much excitement. God he was tired. He continued his vigilance of the ceiling, his thoughts racing. What was he going to do today? His dad would be leaving soon to go to Fiona's place. If he didn't go early, he might not have a chance to see her before she left, though she did promise to wait, and, since Dad actually finished up with the prior client, that meant that she would be having to leave soon anyway. If he waited till after school, she might be gone. So, what was he going to do? Stay here or... There was no point thinking of that, first things first. He needed to decide what he was going to do to see Karina.

He clicked his tongue as he threw his legs over the side of the bed and stood. It was still early enough. If he left now, he might be able to get there before Dad, maybe in time to ask Eren about how Karina planned to travel. He would just have to wing it. He took a deep breath, nervous. He usually wasn't one to do things like this, but he felt no inclination to go to school and knew, without a doubt, that if he left this alone, it would bother him for a long time.

He pulled his clothes on, patting down his unruly hair into some semblance of nicety before slipping downstairs. His siblings' classes weren't until the afternoon due to being part of the second set of students, so they were sleeping while his mom could be anywhere. He kept his senses on high alert as he carefully opened the door and rushed outside. The car was still in the driveway, which meant Dad hadn't left yet. Made sense, the sun wasn't fully up and a gentle breeze was the only thing that stirred the lazy morning air. He walked down the path, the phone charger in hand and thoughts flying a mile a minute without any actual ending or response. After all, he still didn't know what he wanted to do besides see her.

He heard quiet sirens and glanced over to see an Enthrope car drive slowly by. He hadn't seen one in a while, so it startled him to notice as it drove past, sirens quietly churning above the black car.

Strange, I wonder why they are out and about today?

Wait, they didn't somehow find out about Karina, right? No, that wasn't possible. She kept to herself and Fiona didn't seem like someone who would rat on Karina, especially after last night. Worries abated, he continued on.

He came to a stop in front of the house and took a deep breath, centering himself. Right, he needed to calm down, relax.

He reached a hand up and rang the doorbell, hearing it chime faintly through the large, sad mansion. Silence fell for a long time, causing him to fidget, but eventually, he heard movement.

Eren's formal gait caught his attention as the man bowed and opened the gate. "Finnagen, sir, what brings you here so early?"

"I heard Karina was leaving today. I..." He trailed off before examining the man quietly. "Actually, what vehicles do you have?"

He raised an eyebrow, but didn't argue, amusement dancing in his eyes, as he turned and led the way to what was definitely the garage.

~ * ~

Karina packed the last of her clothes, making sure everything was properly sealed. She felt kind of bad. She hadn't done anything for the boy, though he was going to so many lengths to help her. It made her a little uncomfortable, yet she couldn't hide the hint of fondness she felt. She peered out the window, seeing the sun just barely peeking over the horizon. She struggled to get any sleep last night, but that was common. She was starting to get used to it. As unfortunate as that was.

She watched the sun rise quietly, letting the warmth of the early rays wash over her.

She heard a faint knock on her door. Puzzled on who it could be, she turned and walked over, opening it enough to peer out.

A bright grin and a shock of reddish gold hair caught her eyes and she yelped, jumping back. "What are you doing here so early?"

Finnagen winced, his proud expression turning sheepish as he rubbed his neck. "Yeah, sorry about that," he murmured, one hand pushed in his pocket, fiddling with something. "I just couldn't sleep and I knew my parents wouldn't allow me to come, so I..."

"You left without telling them?" She wasn't sure whether to be amused or resigned. Geez, what was up with this boy?

He grimaced, expression disappearing off his face with a snap. "Right," he muttered before pulling out a wire. "As promised, here is a phone charger for you."

She took it, hesitating before letting out a sigh. "You know, I'm not leaving for a while and no one else is up. I did promise to talk with you today so do you want to stay?"

His eyes lit up and she could almost imagine a tail wagging behind him in his excitement. Geez.

He seemed to realize what he was doing because he coughed and pulled back, returning to a more neutral expression, though she couldn't miss the happiness. "Thank you, I would appreciate that." He caught her gaze before gesturing to one of the couches. "Should we take a seat?"

She rolled her eyes, but did just that, getting comfortable on the sofa, back pushed against the arm and feet digging into the cushions. He took a seat on the far end, his posture straight and gaze curious.

So, what was she going to say today?

She paused, peering over at him for a long time. He just sat there, waiting patiently, curiosity shining in his eyes, but staying quiet, giving her time to decide. She closed her eyes, letting out a breath. She wasn't seeing him again, so was there any harm in telling him? In giving him her story? She wouldn't mention the cure, but everything else was fair game and, she knew, it would help with the heavy weight burying her chest.

She nodded and felt a faint smile cross her lips. That was exactly what she was going to do, as thanks.

As well as a good-bye.

Chapter Twenty-Seven

"So, it's kind of a long story." Karina's voice pulled Finnagen from his worried thoughts, he snapped to attention only to blink, confused. Wait, was she going to tell him her story? He opened his mouth, but promptly shut it, gesturing for her to continue.

She sent him a thankful look before speaking again. "My brother and I are from Claremore. It's a small town near Reinmark. Our mother was taken from us."

Finnagen blinked before he leaned forward. "Wait, brother? Taken?"

She nodded, an affectionate, sad smile on her face. "Yeah. I'd dragged my brother out though I knew he was tired. It turned out to be a bad thing since when we returned home, our mom was gone and the people who took her were returning, searching for us."

"Bad thing?" He spoke up, voice soft. "It sounds like it was good that you brought your brother along. You seem the type to go off and do your own thing so maybe you saved your brother too?"

She trailed off, staring at the floor in thought before shrugging. "Well, either way, we managed to escape and went to Reinmark. That's where we met with Lex." She chuckled. "He definitely liked to call us idiots and, looking back on it, I agree. We were stupid, traveling the way we did. I never thanked him for his help. Anyway, to sum things up. He helped us to find our mother, who was in Collern City."

Collern City? That name sounded familiar. He spotted her watching him and she tilted her head just slightly, her hair flowing over her shoulder. "It's the city that the Resistance attacked."

His eyes widened and he leaned forward. "You were there for the attack." It wasn't a question. The fact that she was bringing this up, mentioning it. He knew she'd talked briefly on it yesterday, but...

She nodded. "You're right, we were. We found our mother and were trying to get her out. It didn't go as planned. At least for my brother and me."

Finnagen stilled, spotting a thin stream of blood trailing down her lip, hands white with how clenched they were.

He stopped long enough for his neurons to finally fire. "Wait. Who is your brother? Why isn't your brother or Lex with you?"

She laughed, her voice hollow. "I couldn't protect..." She jammed her mouth shut and pulled her legs up closer to her chest, arms curling around them. "No, that's not right. I abandoned them. I couldn't stand being with them, not after how badly I messed up. I'd almost gotten them killed and they'd gotten hurt protecting me." She smiled morosely. "I figured it would just be better if I left and now, I can't face them, either one of them." She closed her eyes and let out a breath. "I have no idea what to do now. Part of me wants to go back, to see my brother, but another part of me is..." She trailed off before slowly lifting her head enough for him to see her distraught face. "Sorry. I haven't told anyone this."

His fingers clutched into his lap as his mind raced. Centering his thoughts, he took a deep breath and gave a sharp nod, smiling. "It's alright. It sounds like you've dealt with a lot." He turned away, drumming his fingers for a moment before stilling. "I don't have anything as interesting. I've lived here my whole life with my two younger siblings and my two parents. My mom is an assistant nurse while my father is a psychologist. I've practically lived the most normal life you could imagine. Seems strange to me that someone could, well, deal with everything you've told me and I highly doubt that's everything." He glanced at her before looking away, rubbing his neck. "You never mentioned your brother's name or which of you two was older?"

She didn't speak for the longest time, and when she did, her voice was soft and somewhat choked. "He's my younger brother, my twin. His name is Maxwell."

He suspected his brain shut down then. Twin? Maxwell? What the hell? Because it sure as heck wasn't making sense to him. The air felt heavy, weighing in his mind. Maxwell was the name she'd been using, the person he might have been jealous of. No, he had definitely been jealous, now that he thought about it. Jealous because of how close the two seemed. Now that he knew, it made sense. If anything, it made it even more disconcerting. Karina had a twin and she left him because of something. She obviously dearly regretted it and missed her brother.

As much as his younger siblings bothered him, he wouldn't want to leave them for the world, but he knew they would be safe. She didn't.

"Is that why you are going out west?" His words seemed to pull her from her own thoughts.

She hesitated, mouth opening and closing with indecisive words before she finally nodded. "Partially, yeah."

Now he felt almost dumb. He had not, in fact, been jealous, he denied. He'd been curious, but now it felt different. Knowing that the person she held with such high regard was her brother was both relieving and worrying. What would her brother think of him? Why was he wondering about that?

After all, she was an outsider. He found himself scrutinizing her quietly as his brain decided to connect the dots. She was an outsider, but for some reason she didn't appear ill at all. Which was strange, from the sounds of things, she'd been in the outer community for months. He knew why Leon-Lex was able to avoid it, due to his inner community genes, probably, but what about her? What about her brother? Not only that, but... His thoughts flickered to the news report he saw with a couple of his friends over a week ago. It was Caym Askren's report. The report talked about how two twins were part of the resistance that caused the demise of the gated community and kidnapped Mr. Askren's brother. Here he was, sitting in front of someone with a twin brother and who was the Prince's friend. Her story, it both fit with what Mr. Askren said and didn't. So, who did he believe?

His thoughts flicked to the Enthrope car he noticed on the way here and that worry came back once more. "Do you think Enthrope would be after you?"

She jerked up, watching him warily and he quickly held up his hands. "Just asking. As I said, I have no intention of saying anything. You're trusting me with this information. It would be outright cruel to betray that trust."

She didn't relax, but she did settle back down a little. "I wouldn't be surprised. I don't think they know I'm here, but that's why it could become dangerous." She smiled sardonically, a hint of pain crossing her face.

He wasn't sure what to say to that. He decided to focus on something else, anything else, but his mind betrayed him, instead drifting to how it was possible that she wasn't sick. He'd read up on different reports regarding the disease out of curiosity. What little was known made it out to be a genetically modified organism that affected the very genes of a human and spread quickly. It was inconceivable for someone to avoid it unless their genes were already developed in such a way and even then, why her and why not someone else from the gated community? Plus, she was from the outer community, which didn't have an excuse.

"You know? I never thought I would envy someone with a normal life."

Jerked out of his thoughts by Karina's voice, he turned, noticing her watching him.

"When I lived in Claremore, all I wanted to do was get away. To explore and find new things and get out of the normal, I guess. Funny how things change." She chuckled faintly, a somber sound more than anything.

It really is. He leaned forward, examining her. She seemed so tired and drained, now that he was getting a good long look. To think, she already went through so much and...

"You feel alone." He slapped a hand to his mouth, realizing too late he'd spoken out loud.

She watched him, but didn't say anything, lost in thought.

"Not..." She trailed off. She huffed and pushed herself up. "True. Not true."

He mentally decided to just screw it, and stood. "No, that's exactly it. You miss your brother and friend. It's nice here, but it isn't what you're used to. You've already gone through a lot and now you're separating yourself from people you care for. I know, if it was me in your shoes, not knowing if my siblings were safe, if my parents were home and alright, I would hate it. I would hate being away from my siblings when I think they hate me. I would hate knowing I couldn't protect them. Still, that's not the point. I'm not going to be able to protect them all the time, just like you, but that doesn't mean..."

"Doesn't mean what? That I can just abandon him and leave him to suffer more?" Karina shot up, anger flashing on her face. "I left him to fend for himself and got stuck here. Only to put you and Fiona in danger. I don't know how to get to him and I can't face him. What am I supposed to do?"

"I don't know." Finn threw his hands in the air, frustrated. "I don't know who he is or anything. Maybe he'll actually want to see you. Hell, if I was him, I would be probably finding some way to climb over the damn fences just to see you."

Karina, who'd been about to let out another shout, suddenly choked and took a step back, staring at Finnagen.

Finnagen drew in a shaky breath. When had he stood up? His heart pounded, blood singing in his ears. The words rang back at him and he almost choked himself. He couldn't believe he said that.

"You're right, you don't know Maxwell, but..." Karina turned away, arms crossed over her chest. "You're not wrong either."

Letting out a breath when he realized she took it the way he intended instead of the way he felt, he stepped forward, hand rubbing his neck. "So, why don't you try contacting him?"

"What?"

"Well, yeah? If not him, then maybe your friend. I did give you a phone charger, after all. Plus, wouldn't it be nice to see how everything is going?"

"I can't...not..." Karina let out a breath and turned to him. Her face was set, though her eyes were shimmering. "I have nothing to say. Nothing to tell them. I can't help them, because I don't know anything. Maybe if I could warn them about something, something I can only find out in the gated community, then..."

"What? You'll be the big hero? The one who saves the day simply because she was in the right place at the right time?" Finnagen stilled.

"I'm sorry. That's not—"

"No." Karina cut him off. Voice almost cold. "You're not wrong. I guess I deluded myself into thinking I could do something to apologize. Give them information as a cheap way of calling. Maybe even hope Lex would just throw the phone at my brother and he'd pick up without me knowing. Maybe I was hoping he would talk me out of it. Call me out on everything and..." she trailed off and faced away. "Whatever. Don't you have somewhere to be?"

Finnagen frowned, the tension in the air thick enough to fill the basketball court at school. What could he say to her? He clenched his fists. He didn't want to leave on this note, not like this. The thing was, though, did he have an option?

Did he ever have an option to begin with? They were two very different people with two very different lives. He still had his whole family and she was down to practically one with whom she had a rocky relationship.

He didn't know what to do.

~ * ~

She hadn't meant to say all of that to him. She could see the pain twist in Finnagen's face and she felt more than a little uncomfortable. He'd only been nice to her, patient, and now she was yelling at him, practically shrugging him off and telling him to get out. Once again, she couldn't find it in herself to do anything.

She wasn't a coward. At least, she didn't think she was. This was starting to make her feel like one. She heard hesitant footsteps and half-expected to hear the door open. Instead, she felt a hand on her shoulder. She stiffened, but the hand didn't move. She felt something brush against the back of her head, warmth seeping into her back from his presence before he stepped away. Before she could turn, before she could figure out what happened, she heard the door open and close. He was gone.

She felt the tears she'd been trying to suppress finally trail down her cheek.

She was such a liar.

She trembled. For a brief moment, she wondered if he would be able to find his way, only to mentally slap herself. The place was much easier to navigate with it so bright out. He would be fine.

That didn't help though. Did she want to leave it like this? She already decided she needed to leave, to move on. She figured this conversation would be her way of saying good-bye. She clutched at her shirt tightly, feeling all sorts of emotions bombarding her. She needed to go, she knew that, but she was so tired of leaving someplace on a bad note. It happened every single time and she was sick of it.

She felt the arm of the couch dig into her back as she pushed against it. She let her head fall over the arm so that she was able to follow the patterns of the ceiling, letting her thoughts flow.

She wasn't sure how long she sat there, lost in thought. It was the sound of a knock that jolted her out of her melancholy. She lifted herself enough to see the door swing open. Fiona stared at her, surprise shining on her face before a mix of anger and worry clouded her expression. "What's wrong?"

Realizing Fiona caught her crying, or whatever the hell she was doing, she shrugged and put an arm to her face, leaving it there as she flopped backward once more. "Nothing," she muttered, her voice slightly hoarse.

"Dear, it's not nothing."

Footsteps sounded in her ears before a set of arms curled around her. She felt a hand press against her neck, pulling her closer. She dropped her hand, letting herself rest against the woman's shoulder, unsure what to do. She could just barely tell she was kneeling beside the couch, pulling her up so she was no longer craning her neck. "What happened?"

Karina stayed silent as she realized she wasn't really sure. She knew the argument occurred, but... "I—" She took a deep breath and pulled back. She hated it, but she needed to admit to herself. "I made a mistake."

Fiona's eyes widened as she pulled away, head tilted slightly. "Mistake? How so? With that boy?"

"No." Karina reached into her pocket and pulled out the charger Finnagen gave her, the phone pushed up against her thigh as she shifted.

The doorbell rang and Karina jumped. Fiona turned, as if unsurprised. "Let's go see who that is, shall we?" Fiona gently pulled her along and Karina, deciding to allow herself a distraction, followed.

They walked down the steps, spotting Finnagen standing in the doorway, a weak smile on his face. An older man, appearing remarkably like the boy, stood there. The two seemed to have just finished conversing when Fiona reached the bottom step. Finnagen glanced over, hesitated, then left, hair hiding his features. The older man watched him go, a fond, if sad expression crossing his face before turning, not to Fiona, but to Karina. He examined her for a long time, and, if Karina was being honest, she felt like she was in a court of law or something with how he seemed to be analyzing her every movement. What did Finnagen say? Did he hate her that much to pit his dad against her? This was his dad, right? Damn, she'd messed up, but then again, what else was new lately.

Still, she didn't back down. What reason did she have to? She faced scarier people.

He seemed to spot whatever it was he was searching for, because he finally let out a long breath. "As I thought. You are that Karina."

"That?" She found the word tumbling from her mouth worriedly.

He seemed to notice the concern. "Nothing, just the Karina my son has told me about. He can't stop talking about you." He stopped, and she got a sharp feeling of 'knowing' from the man. "It is a pleasure to meet you, though I suppose many would not say the same."

Karina stiffened at his words, though she couldn't help but let her gaze flit to the still open doorway where Finn slipped through.

"Well, I wanted to speak with Fiona. You should be going."

The man turned to Fiona. "By the way, it is good to see you are doing well."

"You too, doctor. I did not know you were to be arriving."

The man smiled gently. "My apologies, I was much delayed. I would like to speak with you in a moment, if that is alright."

Fiona examined him for a long time before giving a faint nod and turning into the nearest room.

Karina wasn't sure she felt comfortable, and that feeling was reinforced as he turned his full attention onto her. The smile dropping slightly as he examined her quietly once more. "If you are who I think you are, I'm surprised you are by yourself, especially so far from Reinmark."

Alarm bells rang through her mind as she pulled back, ready to sprint. Tension ran through her muscles, taut with worry. "What are you talking about?" She managed to hiss out.

He raised both hands with a sigh. "I'm just confirming some suspicions. Fiona never had anyone before you then, a few days after the attack on the gated community in Reinmark you show up, injured. I wouldn't have thought otherwise, if not for this." He reached into his pocket, pulling out a phone before turning it to face her.

On the screen was a news article and two very familiar faces.

Shit, Karina mentally cursed.

His expression softened and he sighed, slipping the phone away. "However, I can tell there must be more that I'm missing."

Karina didn't respond, but the tension did ease slightly. He smiled. "My son may be impulsive, but he has a good heart. I trust him to make the right decision. He wouldn't care for you otherwise."

Karina slowly straightened up, feeling confused. "I'm sorry, I'm...what are you talking about?"

The man shook his head and waved. "It's nothing for you to worry about. Just know that my son, while impulsive, isn't rash. He's a smart boy. Now go, you need to talk with him. After all, he already has his mind set and I don't think anyone will be able to dissuade him at this point."

"That's..." Karina felt her shoulder slump, standing upright once more. "Thank you?"

"No need to thank me. Now go. I need to speak with Fiona."

Karina stared at the man as he walked after Fiona. There were so many strange people here. They were all somewhat nonchalant and almost innocent? No, that wasn't the word, especially since he figured out who she was just by meeting with her once. It was actually somewhat terrifying how quickly he figured it out, even with the picture.

She took a deep breath and shook it off. He seemed fine with her and she was leaving soon anyway. She turned and stepped toward the doorway, only to stop. What could she say to Finnagen? An apology? Why?

Deciding to think of it later, she raced out the door.

Chapter Twenty-Eight

He was so STUPID! He cursed to himself, still feeling the heat on his cheeks as he shuffled down the road, past the gates. He was glad he was able to talk to his father though. It was a surprise to come down the stairs, only to run into him. Dad had been right on the verge of ringing the doorbell.

He certainly had a few words to say in regards to Finnagen's choices, but ultimately kept his cool, as usual, through most of the conversation. Thankfully, Finnagen was able to convey what he wanted to do and that his father couldn't stop him. It took some doing, but he managed to convince his father.

Dad laughed softly, ruffling his hair with a fond sort of gesture as he said, "You take after your mother and me too much. I trust you, whatever you decide to do. Your mother will understand eventually. Just be careful out there, understood?"

Finnagen nodded, somewhat relieved. It was then Dad turned and rang the doorbell. Finnagen shifted, uncertain, should he just leave? Or...

His decision was made for him as he noticed Karina descend the stairs and the way his father's expression shifted to one of surprise, briefly flickering to him, before straightening once more. Finnagen didn't think much of it as he raced away.

His thoughts returned to the present, though he almost regretted it as they swirled around and around without answer. Why did he say that? Why did he call Karina out like that? Why did...? He felt the heat rise even more and put fingers to his lips. He moved instinctively again earlier and, luckily, she didn't seem to notice. He was acting like a damn romantic from some cheesy sitcoms Mom loved to watch or something.

Letting out a breath, he slumped his shoulders.

Well, at least he achieved something, right?

Maybe?

Who was he kidding? He let out a weak laugh as he tilted back enough to examine the sky. "This is a cruel joke, isn't it? You're laughing at me right now, aren't you?" he yelled before dropping his head and groaning. "Great, now I'm just shouting at nothing."

"You seem to talk without thinking a lot, don't you?"

So lost in his thoughts, he hadn't heard the set of footsteps that came up behind him. As a result, his feet practically leaped off the ground as he stumbled to turn toward the voice.

Karina stood there, hands on her hips. She seemed almost a little uncomfortable, but... "Well, I guess it isn't a terrible thing." She sighed. "I want to apologize, okay? I've not been in a great mood lately and I took it out on you, so..."

He watched her silently, mouth opening in surprise. What was he supposed to say? Unfortunately, she seemed to take his silence as meaning something else and she turned, huffing.

"Well, I said my piece. With your father here, I guess that probably means I should leave." She seemed to frown for a moment, as if lost in thought. "You are free to do whatever..."

Recognizing the goodbye for what it was, his hand shot out, almost unconsciously, and gripped her arm. THIS was why he'd talked to his father. THIS was why he'd come to a decision. The movement caused him to stumble and her to falter in her turn, her head snapping to face him. He gulped and quickly let go. "I'm sorry, okay? I do want to see you again and, well, I didn't mean to call you out and all that. I wasn't thinking."

He looked to the ground. He could stay here, continue his life and let this go, just like his father said, let go of his feelings, his curiosity and interest. He paused, or he could say goodbye to everything and try something new. Considering he spoke with his father about this very topic and he seemed to understand. It was a viable option and yet, would Karina let him? After all, she'd argued the idea before he even thought about it.

He took a deep breath, chest expanding as he came to a decision, turning to Karina with an expression that he hoped conveyed his determination. "I want to help you find your brother."

~ * ~

All movement stilled. Karina's breath caught in her throat. The air was silent for a brief moment, as if holding its breath and then she blinked and the spell was broken. She huffed, turning away, but not outright saying no. "This came out of nowhere."

"Not really." He shook his head, grinning as he massaged the back of his neck. "I've been debating for the last little while, actually. After you told me about your brother and everything, especially after what we both said."

"The argument?"

"I wasn't going to say that," he muttered before letting a grin cross his face. "My father's going to be helping Fiona, so this would be a good time to head out, right?"

"Huh?"

"Well, we get your phone charged and you grab your things while I say good-bye to my family, then we will head out. I've already asked to borrow Eren's car."

"Wait, really?" She raised an eyebrow. "Were you thinking of coming even before you heard the rest of my story? Plus, you can drive?"

"That's all you're asking in all that?" Finnagen blinked.

Karina shrugged. "Well, it's not the strangest thing I've heard, so..."

He shook his head, laying a palm on his neck. "Well, I did just get my license, so yeah, I'll be able to drive. I just don't do it often."

"Alright then, sounds good." Karina nodded to herself. "Thanks."

He beamed, giddy with joy. "My pleasure."

Deciding to go back to see Fiona after everything was arranged, since Karina wanted to meet Finnagen's family, they made their way down the street. Karina was shocked at how relaxed and normal everything seemed. Whenever she thought of the gated communities, she recalled the harshness of Lex's abode or the flames of Collern. Even the majestic houses bordering Reinmark and Claremore. Here? This was the epitome of a middle-high class town. People played and laughed in the streets as cars moved to and fro. Houses were beautifully done up, but still spaced well enough to have room without feeling like they're in separate time zones. She could appreciate this. It was simple and beautiful. It definitely looked so warm and inviting. So different from all the calculated and cold people she knew of from the other communities. She wondered whether other communities were like this, if any, or if this was an exception. Either way...

She turned just enough to look at Finnagen who seemed to be humming to himself, swaying his head side to side in a cheerful melody. She was admittedly quite surprised by his comment, though at this point, she suspected she shouldn't be. He was a very straightforward boy and persistent, that was for sure. So different from her thoughtful and quiet brother.

Once again, it made her wonder how her brother would react to meeting him. What would Maxwell say? Seemed like her question was probably going to get an answer. Though in a way she wasn't sure she was ready for.

She pulled out her phone and scrutinized it, clenching it tightly. The black screen was just as dead and lifeless as it was every time she pulled it out. She finally had a charger, maybe she should have just plugged it in, but she didn't want to just leave it in the house if she was gone. She didn't want to be away from it. She huffed and stuffed it back into her pocket, stomping to catch up to the oblivious boy. Was she prepared to bring him along? That was the other question now on her mind. Was she ready to try to take care of someone else? After she so miserably failed at taking care of her own twin? How he, instead, had to take care of her. It hadn't bothered her much when he bound her wounds while still at home but now? Now the thought of it hurt. He shouldn't have to worry or deal with that.

"So, where are we going anyway?" Finnagen called, glancing back at her sheepishly. She stared at him, feeling a deadpan expression cross her face.

As usual, he was an idiot. Though she couldn't completely fault him for it, growing up in these types of surroundings.

Wow, she was sounding more and more like Lex by the hour. She was going to have to work on her cynicism. She pulled herself from that thought as they stepped up to a nice two-story home with a basketball hoop out front and a beautiful garden off to one side. "West, toward California. My brother should be heading that way, hopefully."

"Why California?"

Karina's gaze drifted to Finnagen, unsure what to say. She knew, sometime, that she would have to mention her situation entirely, but... "It's not something I can just tell you."

He stared at her for a long time before smiling. "Alright."

She jerked as he continued, not noticing her reaction. "That's fine." He turned to her. "Just let me take care of the driving, you lead the way. Sound fair?"

Her words got stuck in her throat, not for the first time with this boy. Turning away, feeling a little uncomfortable, she nodded, unable to say anything.

"Anyway, we're home. Well, I mean. I'm home. Er, this is my house." By the end, he trailed off, rubbing his neck as he shuffled from foot to foot.

She felt the edge of a smile, which expanded slightly more when the door burst open and two young children came barreling out. The little girl from the other day, Annie, flew into Finnagen's arms, causing the boy to stumble back as he caught her. The other one, a slightly older boy, that she recalled was named Caleb, walked over and looked up at him with relief before spotting her. His eyes widened as he hurried next to Finnagen.

"Okay, pipsqueaks, enough." Finnagen laughed as he pulled his sister off him and checked his brother. "I wasn't gone that long and I thought you two would be enjoying your day off."

"We missed you!" Annie piped up as she pulled away from Finnagen, hands draping in front of her dress. She peered up at him, head tilted slightly.

He huffed and ruffled her hair. "Yeah, yeah. I know. Is Mom inside?"

"Yeah, she was wondering where you were. She was really mad.

She said something about sending out a search party."

"Oh, right." He grimaced as the door to the house opened and a middle-aged woman stepped out.

The woman had her hands on her hips and appeared outright furious, if her demeanor and expression were anything to go on.

Wisely deciding to stay out of the way, Karina pulled back a little as the woman stomped up to Finnagen and sharply tugged on his ear, causing him to cry out in pain.

"Finnagen Andrew Cornwall, what were you thinking? How dare you just leave without telling me, though I specifically told you that you were grounded? I was worried sick. Not only that, but you've missed half the day of school. You're damn well lucky your father was out or he would have something to say as well."

"Sorry, Ma, and uh, Dad already gave me an earful."

The boy winced and the woman's features softened as she let out a sigh and shook her head, releasing her grip. Finnagen reached up, massaging his ear as the woman turned toward Karina, finally noticing her.

"Ah, you're the girl from the other day..." she trailed off, examining Karina for a bit. A slight frown crossed her face, and a surge of nervousness threaded through Karina. Did the mother recognize her as well? It seemed not, because the woman shook her head and muttered something under her breath. "Sorry for that display. My idiot son can be a handful sometimes..."

"Mom," Finnagen cut in, voice strangled and annoyed.

The woman blinked, as if surprised, before a faint smile slipped onto her lips.

"Well, anyway, come inside. I'll get you some breakfast and then you two can head off to school..."

"Er, actually." Finnagen rubbed the back of his neck, shuffling from foot to foot in that familiar awkward way.

Karina decided to take a large step back, realizing what was coming next.

Finnagen looked his mother in the eye and, without missing a beat, said, "I want to head west with Karina to help her find her brother, so I won't be going back to school."

Silence, utter silence filled the air and Karina found she didn't want to move an inch for fear she would break it.

"I'm sorry, what did you say?" The woman spoke up, tone icy.

"Well, I, kind of want to go with Karina and help her find her brother. You know, outside?"

"Absolutely not." His mother shook her head, arms crossed and expression stern. "I don't know where or how you decided on that madness, but you are not going, you understand me?"

"This would be my only time to go," he argued, his nervousness once again gone. "I can be helpful. Plus, well, I like her, as a friend." He quickly seemed to add the last few words. "I want to help her. She can't stay here. With Dad taking care of Fiona, she would have no place to go. Come on, Mom. I know you're worried about me, but I can take care of myself."

"No is no. Now get inside, young man. As for you..."

She turned to Karina who stared back, trying to hide her nerves, but didn't move or stiffen. The woman paused, as if noting Karina's posture, before her expression softened. "I'm sorry about that."

"No, you're not." Finnagen cut in, a frown on his face.

"Finnagen Cornwall, get in the house right now or I'll..."

Finnagen's face twisted into something similar to a sneer, but it quickly washed away as he turned his focus on his siblings, anger rolling off him in waves. "Come on, Mom's throwing a hissy-fit, let's get inside."

"I want to play."

"We'll play house or something, just let's get inside." Finnagen paused for a moment as he glanced over at Karina. For just a second, he seemed lost, but it disappeared as he guided his two younger siblings inside as the two started to bicker between themselves.

The mother watched them go before letting out a long and tired sigh. "I'm sorry for my son."

"Why?"

"He's a good boy, but he's impulsive. I don't want him making a decision that might..."

"Cost him his life?" Karina put in and shook her head. "No, I'm sorry. I shouldn't have said that. I've been very cynical lately."

The woman turned to her, scrutinizing her up and down before she let out a breath. "No, no. I can understand. You are not wrong. If anything, you are quite wise for your age. Say, where are you from?"

Karina paused for a long time. "Reinmark."

The woman examined her quietly. For a moment, surprise colored her expression and her whole body seemed to tense up. *Recognition was a very obvious emotion sometimes*, Karina thought. "I see," was all she said, the words just that little bit strangled.

She glanced toward where Finnagen disappeared then back to her. "I will go." Karina spoke quietly.

At this point, she didn't want to intrude, not anymore. It would be better for her to just go, after all. It hurt, seeing someone that almost reminded her a bit of her own mother examining her with a heavy, almost angered suspicion.

The words seemed to cause the woman's demeanor to soften, and she shook her head. "No, no, dear. It's alright." She hesitated for a moment. "I have to ask. How old are you?"

Hm? Karina thought, watching the woman quietly. She didn't seem to be doing anything. She just simply stood there. "Fifteen."

A flicker of horror caught Karina's attention before the woman shook her head and gestured. "You really are around the same age, if only a little younger," she said. "Please, come inside. I'm sorry about that. I'm just worried about my son is all."

Karina hesitated for the longest time, thoughts spinning through her head faster than she could keep up before she turned to follow after the woman.

"Thank you." Karina's voice was faint, but it seemed the mother heard.

"No, no, thank you."

Karina nodded and glanced over her shoulder toward Fiona's place, partially realizing she had yet to eat this morning, but that was only a small fragment of her thoughts, quickly washed away by another. From the sounds of things, she wouldn't be able to stay with Fiona much longer. Why? What was going to happen?

What made Finnagen's mother let her in? Especially if she recognized her, just like the father did? Would Maxwell trust them? What would he do if he were here?

Could she trust this woman? She would have to, for now. She had to trust someone.

Her mind called out to her, berating her and pointing to the fact that she was already trusting Finn. If she could trust Finn, why couldn't she trust his parents? Was she that broken?

Chapter Twenty-Nine

Maxwell peered through the doorway, noting that Priscel was right there, leaning against the truck as she was earlier. She seemed to be examining her nails in a way that spoke of disinterest, but her manner was anything but nonchalant.

He pulled back, grimacing as he met Lex's gaze.

"So, she's still there." Lex seemed more than a little frustrated.

Not surprised, Maxwell thought. They intended to leave earlier. After all, Lex managed to convince the staff that he was related to Yvette and requested to learn about the girl's mother.

Lex's expression when Maxwell asked later was all he needed to know. Yvette was all alone.

Maxwell pulled himself from that thought, gaze flickering to the little girl who was standing beside Lex quietly. Her expression had fallen and she was holding onto his pant leg tightly, as if grasping onto something solid.

"I don't think Priscel is going to let us just waltz back out to the truck."

"No, she's most likely done something to it," Lex muttered. "Even if we got to the truck, she's probably made it impossible to drive."

His gaze flicked around the shelter which had been steadily emptying as the forest fire subsided and people were allowed to go on their way. They couldn't stay any longer, but they had no means of leaving either.

Maxwell almost wanted to curse out loud.

Not only had he STILL not heard a word from his sister, but now they were stuck like mice in a cage. Enthrope was starting to get suspicious as well, Maxwell noticed, as his gaze caught one of theirs. He quickly looked away worriedly.

They had been paying more attention lately.

Lex let out a tired breath, as he peeked outside, "I have an idea, though I don't like it."

"I'm all ears." Maxwell gestured. "Because I have nothing."

Lex pulled away and turned to Maxwell. "It's almost night. I suggest we wait a little bit longer and use the night time to leave, but not with the truck."

Maxwell's eyes widened and he hissed. "Wait, then what? You intend to just run out of here?"

Lex shook his head, a flash of pain in his gaze. "No, I intend to borrow one of Enthrope's cars."

Maxwell narrowed his eyes at Lex's words. Borrow? No, that wasn't right. "Steal, you mean?" He kept his voice low, but it wasn't accusatory.

At this point, he could understand and, to be honest, he didn't much care. Though, he would slightly miss the truck. It at least had some charm to it over the plain creepily black Enthrope cars.

Lex nodded. His gaze flicked to the Enthrope employees. "I've been keeping my attention on them since they arrived. A few are a bit more lax, compared to the others." He glanced down to Yvette. The girl paused and turned to face him. "Yvette? Can you help me with something?"

The girl just nodded and, while Maxwell felt a little bad, he understood what Lex was doing.

He couldn't go over there to help distract like Yvette would be doing, not after what Priscel said. If they really did have his picture, getting close wouldn't be good.

Lex, however, knew what he was doing. He would be fine and Yvette was a surprisingly smart child. Distracting a guard wouldn't be too difficult he supposed.

Maxwell shifted to one side, leaning against the wall, trying to stay to the shadows as the sun set in the distance, the last tendrils disappearing over the horizon.

He decided not to watch. Just because he understood didn't mean he wanted to be involved.

It did make him wonder what Lex had to deal with to get those skills, just like how he always seemed to wield weapons with a certain ease that showed way too much use. Though, did he want to know? After all, his sister had a gun that she kept secret from him. She kept a lot of things secret from him, actually.

Annoyance flared through his veins once more, though who it was directed to, he wasn't sure.

He heard footsteps and glanced up, expecting to see Lex.

He was startled when one of the Enthrope employees walked over. It was the same one who caught his attention earlier. He seemed a little disgusted with walking past those from the outer community. Maxwell almost snorted at that, if it wasn't for a trill of fear that sang down his spine. He was stopping at each person, talking quietly and gesturing to a picture.

The people just shook their heads and he moved on.

Maxwell almost shifted away, but the man locked onto him and walked over. "I saw you earlier. With a young child and an older man."

"My sister and brother," he replied, forcing himself not to stumble over the words. "We were caught in the fire, sir." He barely remembered to get the last word out.

The man watched him for a moment before pulling out a paper. "I don't suppose you recognize this person then?"

It took all of Maxwell's willpower not to react when he noticed two pictures side by side. One of them was from when they were at Lex's home, so long ago, the maid outfit snug around his sister as she held a broom, which seemed so unlike her even now. The other was a picture of Karina next to a strange woman, walking in what seemed to be an upscale mall.

"No. I don't." His voice was flat, though whether from overwhelming amounts of emotion or just shock, he wasn't sure what to think at that point.

The man examined him warily before nodding. "Well, if you see this person, let us know." He watched him quietly. "She had a brother as well, appeared a lot like you." With that, he turned and continued talking with the other people.

What...what was that? Where was she? Was she hurt? Was she okay? Why did they have that picture? Was it recent? If so, she was probably safe, because it seemed they were looking for her but Maxwell had no means of contacting her, no means of warning her.

Pain stabbed through him at the thought. The thought that there was nothing he could do.

He heard footsteps and jerked, only to relax when he noticed Lex walk over, Yvette continuing to hold onto him.

Lex furrowed his brow, seeming to notice something off. "Did something happen?"

"Enthrope is walking around, asking if anyone recognizes a picture of Karina." Maxwell pushed away from the wall. The words were once more neutral, tired.

It sounded nothing like himself, he mildly noted.

Lex winced, gaze flicking to the wandering Enthrope employee. "If they are searching here, Caym probably has his people out in force. Wherever she is..." He shook his head. "She's smart, I think she will be fine."

Maxwell nodded, but it felt more subconscious than anything.

"Well, then, let's head out."

Maxwell jerked, glancing toward Lex who flipped a key from his pocket before letting the key disappear back into it. "We have what we need. Let's go."

"I'm not going to ask how you did that so quickly."

"Don't worry, it's a skill I would rather not have." With that, Lex headed out the door. Maxwell followed a few paces behind. He noticed Priscel was gone and tensed.

"She's still here. Her and whomever she is with." Lex spoke quietly. "They would expect us to move at night, after all."

Maxwell nodded, keeping half an eye on things.

He heard a faint beeping and peered to one side, noting how one of the Enthrope car's headlights sputtered for a moment. Lex met his eyes and nodded subtly.

The two quickly redirected their movements moving closer to the car.

Unfortunately, the car was completely opposite the truck. It was probably obvious they weren't heading for the truck anymore.

That was confirmed when headlights suddenly flashed on from near the truck. The beams piercing over the tarmac and almost directly into their faces.

"Run." Lex didn't shout, he simply scooped Yvette up and dashed toward the car. Maxwell barely a step behind.

What Maxwell noted was an SUV swiftly drove forward, tires faintly squealing on the pavement as the high beams cut through the darkness. Maxwell glanced over just as something gleamed in the faintly beginning moonlight. He ducked as something whistled past his shoulder. The yelp that left his lips was enough to draw Lex's attention.

He heard a curse as Lex swung to one side, practically throwing open the door, ignoring as it slammed into the car next to it.

Maxwell scrambled into the other side as something hit the side he was on. Were those maniacs trying to capture or kill?

He pulled the door shut, ducking his head down as something shattered against the window frame. Something stuck to the glass, splintered with thin spiderweb tendrils. Lex, already in the other seat, threw the car on and into gear. Yvette was between them, her expression startled and scared as she held tightly to Maxwell.

"Hold on," Lex called as he slammed onto the gas, shooting out of the spot and twisting the wheel, just avoiding the SUV. Another sound splintered against the metal.

"I hate when they have silencers," Lex growled, frustration clear as he slammed on the gas.

Maxwell felt the car jerk before they were racing down the road.

He glanced back and gulped. "Uh."

"Yeah, I noticed, they are still on us." Lex's gaze flitted to the rear-view mirror. "Well, time to see if these cars are worth anything."

Maxwell practically heard the roar as the car kicked up in gear, just barely dodging around an incoming car.

Horns blared as they swerved left, almost on two wheels before slamming down and shooting forward. Rubber burned as they raced down the freeway. Something splintered against the back window.

Maxwell looked back. A moment, barely a breath passed before the glass shattered. He ducked his head, pulling Yvette with him. Something slashed past his cheek, but he ignored it.

Curse words rang next to him as the whole vehicle swerved right. He peeked up slightly, careful to keep his head low as he noticed the vehicle behind. The lights were on high beam, almost blinding him. The SUV seemed to be keeping pace as Priscel leaned out the window, holding onto the roof, gun in her grasp.

"Maxwell, I don't suppose you have a weapon?"

If Lex was asking if he had a gun, he had to say no. Though he was starting to wish he had something, at least.

"What about that?" Yvette's voice caught his attention and he glanced down, gripping the car seat as they took another swerve.

Between the seats, strapped to the back as if in easy reach to grab, was a gun.

He pulled it out, unsure how to hold it.

Lex flicked his gaze. "Of course. Hold onto the wheel." With that, he pulled the gun from Maxwell's grip and rolled down the window.

Maxwell yelped as the car swerved wildly. He quickly took the wheel, half of his body practically sprawled over the driver's seat. Yvette scrambled to the back and Lex imitated Priscel, half out of the window. The only problem, Maxwell barely noticed, was that Lex was leaning out the driver's side while Priscel leaned out the passenger. Maxwell could only hope Lex had a plan as the wind whipped by, pulling at hair and clothes. He turned the wheel, suddenly wishing he paid more attention to Lex's driving. He heard a loud bang followed by a click and another loud bang.

Silver flashed in the distance.

"Hang on." Maxwell twisted sharply, feeling the car swing, just barely missing the metal girder.

There was another click.

Smash.

Skidding sounds echoed behind, but he didn't pay much attention.

He shifted enough so his foot was on what he hoped was the gas. Lex pushed against his side as another gunshot rang out.

Another swerve, another car horn as they missed the metal of a car by inches.

Swears rang through the air followed by another shattering bang.

A screech sounded from behind before Maxwell felt himself shoved to the side. Lex pulled back in, sweat coating his face, a slight tremor in his otherwise stoic posture.

Maxwell peered back and let out a heavy breath.

There was no longer anyone following them.

He slumped into the seat, the pounding ringing in his ears, catching his attention as much as his stuttered breath.

Silence filled the car between them for the longest time as they sped down the road, the howling of the wind through the open or shattered window a persistent discordant melody. After a few good miles they finally started to slow down.

It was Lex who let out a breath of relief, dropping the gun between the seats and pushing fingers through his hair, keeping it there as if to focus on something else.

"That could have gone better. Is anyone hurt?"

Maxwell, just catching his breath and slowly allowing himself to shift, shook his head. "I'm fine." He peered back toward Yvette who sat up, blinking.

"That was scary."

"Yeah, it was," Maxwell responded, peering through the shattered glass of the back window. "That was just one person, maybe two." His thoughts drifted as he stared down at the gun between the seats, thoughts drawing to a halt.

If Karina were there, she would have known what to do.

He, though, had been unable to do a thing. He barely managed to drive, through sheer dumb luck. Yvette caught his attention and his heart ached. Not only that, but they dragged Yvette into their mess. His mind spun with thought after thought and he could do nothing to silence it.

The howling of wind only worsened his mood as they made their way westward.

Chapter Thirty

Finnagen could see some of the neighbors moving about outside the window of his room as the sun beat down through the pane. Another Enthrope car passed by just as slowly as before and that feeling arose once more. He could hear the faint hum of the air conditioner, his room chilled just enough to be comfortable. Annie was playing on the floor with Caleb who seemed to be frustrated with his losing streak. The little ones already ate and wanted to play instead and he was not in the mood to face his mother, so instead grabbed up a piece of toast and completely ignored her calls for breakfast in favor of taking care of his siblings.

Finnagen laid his chin in his palm as he closed his eyes. He was hungry, but it was too awkward to go downstairs now. Plus, he had no idea whether Karina left or not, what his mother was doing, anything.

He glanced toward his siblings as Annie threw her arms in the air with a cry of "Yay." while Caleb buried his face in the floor, fist pounding the rug. He shook his head. At least he managed to avoid going to school. His mother was obviously preoccupied and she hadn't said anything so... He didn't mind school, but it wasn't something he loved. Unfortunately, he was so absentminded that more often than not, it went in one ear and out the other. He let his head drop, hitting the desk with a jarring crack. His head hurt, but he couldn't convince himself to sit back up.

So, he stayed that way, only turning his head slightly to the side so he was facing the doorway. He blinked as his brain back-tracked through his thoughts. Wait, his mother HADN'T gotten on his case about not going to school. Though he'd been grounded, she hadn't done a thing.

"Hey, Is Finny upset?"

Finnagen jerked around to face his sister while Caleb barely gave him a second glance. "Finn's probably fine. He's just being all, you know." Caleb threw his hands in the air, causing Annie to giggle.

Finnagen chuckled weakly, thoughts racing. "Yeah, sorry, Annie."

Annie pouted before tilting her head. "Finny is upset."

"Yeah," Finnagen trailed off as he finally realized what bugged him about what happened earlier.

He'd been able to go to Karina and bring her here. Yes, he had sort of gotten yelled at, but his mom wasn't doing anything. She wasn't locking him in his room, though she would never really do that in the first place. He could almost feel a weight lift off his shoulders as he nodded to himself. He'd only been worried about Mom. His conversation with Dad worked out fine. Now, though, Mom was so against it...

She couldn't stop him.

He pushed himself out of his seat and sat down cross-legged in front of his siblings, garnering both of their attention. "What do you think of your big brother leaving for a while?"

"Leaving?" Annie tilted her head.

"For a while?" Caleb leaned forward, a hint of curiosity on his face.

Finnagen nodded, his attention shifting toward the doorway, yet not really seeing it. "Yeah. I was wondering, if you two would be alright if I go away for, maybe a few weeks? Maybe a month or two?"

"Where would you be going?" Caleb spoke up, surprisingly subdued.

Finnagen turned back to him, chuckling quietly. "Out west somewhere. Your big brother wants to help someone..."

"Can we come too?" Annie piped up and Finnagen shook his head.

"No, Annie." He leaned forward, pressing a palm to his chest. He was going to get this next point across. "Finnagen," he emphasized, "is going alone, or, well, not completely alone, but..."

"You're going with that girl." Caleb spoke up bluntly, sounding hurt and angry. "You're going to leave us for..."

"Caleb, I want to help her and you don't need me. You're old enough to take care of yourself, right?"

Caleb's arms crossed over his chest. "That was mean."

Finnagen couldn't stop the soft smile from falling onto his face, as Annie tried to grab his attention, her tiny fingers curling around his bicep. He turned to see Annie holding him, big eyes filled with sadness met his own. "Do you have to?"

Finnagen let out a breath. He figured it would be hard, telling his siblings, but... "Yeah. I do. It won't be forever, I'll be back."

Annie's grip tightened for just a minute longer before she let go and stepped back. "Alright. Annie thinks she'll be fine." Annie put a fist to her chest, other hand on her hip. "Annie will take care of Mama, Papa, and Caleb until you get home. I promise."

Finnagen chuckled, reaching forward and ruffling her hair.

"Hey. Me too." Caleb spoke up, getting in front of Annie, a firm gaze shining clearly and assuaging any last-minute worries Finnagen held. "I won't let anyone hurt Annie or anyone else. You need to promise that you will come home safe, okay?"

Finnagen reached out, startling his siblings. "Alright, I pinky promise, will that do?"

Both children glanced at each other before nodding and reaching out. Finnagen could feel his siblings' warmth as their fingers curled around his before they let go.

"So, are you leaving?" Caleb crossed his arms, averting his gaze.

"Yeah, I'm going to say good-bye to Mom once more. I've already said good-bye to Dad and made some arrangements." He grimaced.

Finnagen stood, packing a small bag with clothes and other things with his siblings' attention on him the whole time. Finally packed, he slipped out the door, waving goodbye one more time before his siblings were out of sight. Before he could have time to think or reconsider, he was downstairs. Karina was sitting at the table with a cup placed in front of her. She seemed out of it, listlessly spinning a spoon in the probably now cold liquid. Thank God she hadn't left yet. Mom was busy cleaning up, stopping only when she heard his footsteps. Both sets of eyes glanced toward him.

"Finnagen, what is that on your back?"

Finnagen took a deep breath, steeling himself and reminding himself of his earlier realization, before making sure he had his mother's full attention. "I'm heading out. I just wanted to say good-bye, alright?"

His mother stilled before clenching her fist hard enough to splinter the wooden spoon in her grip. "Alright? Alright. No, I am not alright with this. I thought I told you..."

"You've always told me to do my best. Dad has always told me to be a gentleman. I'm just doing what both of you said. Plus, I'll learn more being out there than if I was stuck in here."

"You don't know anything about what's out there. You could..."

"I don't, but..." Finnagen glanced at Karina, who averted her eyes. He pursed his lips and returned his focus to his mother. "Seriously though, Mom. I'm not backing out of this. I've made my decision and even Dad's okay with it. He gave me the go-ahead." That caused his mother to freeze. He walked forward and wrapped his arms around her. "I'll be safe. Okay? I'll come back with stories to tell. I'll make you and Dad proud." With that, he stepped back and turned to a stunned Karina, grin on his face. "Well, shouldn't we be going? I bet our ride is probably already outside."

Karina's brow twisted in a way that practically screamed confusion before shaking her head and standing up. She turned to Mom and bowed her head. "I'm sorry. Thank you. You are very kind." With that, she hurried out the door, ahead of Finnagen.

Finnagen turned, following after, only to freeze when he heard a soft, "Wait." He stopped, unsure on what to do. Finally, gathering whatever emotional stability he had, he turned. His mother reached around her neck, unclasping something before gently pulling it around his. "I know it's girly, but I want you to have this."

Finnagen hesitantly picked up the locket. He scanned the silver chain draped around his neck. He clicked it open to reveal a small, but clear family picture. He smiled weakly and closed it, stuffing it carefully under his shirt. "Thanks, Mom... I love you."

He nodded before hurrying out the door. He wasn't going to cry, but boy, did he definitely feel a turmoil of emotions.

"Are you sure?"

Finnagen peered over, noting Karina's expression. It was taut, tired and concerned, which only hardened his resolve. "Yes. Now let's get going."

He turned forward, hearing the sound of a car. He glanced down the road, the sound of tires indicating what appeared to be a SUV pulling to a stop.

The butler, Eren, stepped out and gave a short bow. "I was told to pick you up. I believe the mistress would like to say good-bye."

Eren slipped back into the car, Karina hesitantly following behind. Finnagen turned just enough to spot his mother standing out front, his two siblings on either side with her hands on their backs. He gave a faint smile before hopping into the car.

"You know, this isn't going to be easy. It's dangerous out there. You can get sick or..."

Finnagen turned toward Karina before focusing on the car ceiling. His palm smoothed over the cool leather as he, for once, thought through his words. He knew he was being reckless, but... "I know. I'm likely to get sick or hurt, but... I..." He couldn't seem to get the words off his tongue.

It was strange, his sudden inability to speak. He wasn't sure what was worse, not speaking or speaking without thought. Time seemed to pass in that silence before he shook his head. "I WANT to. I don't want you going alone and now that Dad is working with Fiona, she'll need to stay at the clinic with Eren so the place would be empty and I don't want that for you. So... "

"Oh." Karina put her elbow on the windowsill and leaned her chin against her fist. "Is that so? Don't blame me if you wind up hurt."

"I won't because I'm protecting you, or, well, we're protecting each other? Either way, I won't get hurt. Can't protect you if I'm dead, and vice-a-versa, right?"

Katina stiffened, shock clear on her face.

He rubbed his neck. "Well, that's how I feel, at least. So..." he shook his head. "Anyway, we're here. "

The change in topic was very much on purpose as he slipped out of the car, face burning. He examined the house, spotting his father outside with a car parked in front. Eren slid out of the car, leaving it to idle and walked over, sending a genuine look of gratitude to Dad before getting in the other car.

Finnagen caught his father's attention. He sent Finnagen a warm, sad expression before his father got in the car behind Eren. Fiona stood outside, attention glued on Karina.

Finnagen felt a chill run down his spine. "I'll be in the car. Just let me know when you're ready. Alright?"

Karina's lips twitched upward as she let out a quiet snort. "You are so strange."

She spun and walked up to Fiona as Finnagen let out a laugh, unsure how else to respond before slipping into the driver's seat and getting comfortable. It was an SUV, with comfy seats. Plus, it was clean and fully fueled. He could enjoy this.

Chapter Thirty-One

Karina stared at Fiona whose hands were clasped over her chest. "This is all so quick. Are you leaving already?"

"Yeah." Karina felt a grin cross her lips once more.

As strange as this place was, she was going to miss it. However, she was getting restless and she missed Maxwell. Deeply. So, since this was an opportunity she couldn't pass up, she would take it. It was a gamble, but what else was new? "Thank you for..."

Arms wrapped tightly around her as Fiona shook. Her voice was choked as she spoke. "I...I don't want you to go."

Karina's breath caught, before she wrapped her arms around Fiona in return. "I'll be fine. Thank you for all your help, Fiona. I really appreciate it. "

The grip tightened briefly before Fiona pulled away, tears trailing down her cheeks. "My little sister's growing up. Elliot already talked to me, telling me you were leaving with his son. He reminded me that you should decide, so I'll support you." She reached forward, hand gently holding Karina's cheek. "My dear sister, Elsa. If you ever need anything..." She reached into her pocket and pulled out some paper. "Here... My number and a passport to get into any gated community. "

Karina's gaze shot downward to her palm as she thought over Fiona's words. Elsa? Why did Fiona call her Elsa? Who was Elsa? She shook the thought off, focusing on the item Fiona held. A small white booklet sat nestled right there. What? She'd never heard of this.

"It's used for outsiders. Those from the community don't need them, but people from the outside like you? This is their only way in."

"Lex never mentioned that."

"Hm?" Fiona's voice hummed with confusion before she shrugged. "It's possible he didn't know. It's a more recent thing."

That would make sense. Karina hummed in thought. It wouldn't have been the first time Lex didn't know a policy change in the gated communities. "Thank you."

Fiona nodded sadly and, giving her one more hug, slowly backed away. "Go ahead and get your things."

Karina nodded gratefully and headed inside. She'd only been here a few days, yet it had been some of the safest days in ages. She would miss it greatly. Shaking her head, she went to her room and finished packing. Her bag was practically bulging, but she felt satisfied. New clothes and gear were carefully folded inside. The bag was still sturdy even now. Taking one last look around the room, she pulled out her phone. She still hadn't gotten a chance to charge it and now, the charger sat in her bag, unusable. Gripping it tightly, her gaze caught on the black screen. Was she really ready to leave? Was she ready to contact her brother? She wasn't sure. Ever since Finnagen entered her life, she'd been thrown for a loop. He was so strange and kind. He seemed so willing to jump in to help her. Why though? Why was everyone being so kind? She couldn't understand and yet she could appreciate it. The warmth and reprieve.

Yet she doubted she would ever fully enjoy it until Maxwell was with her and safe. The only way to do that was to keep moving. Keep going. She wasn't over everything, not in the slightest, but... She pulled from her thoughts as she stuffed the phone in her pocket and headed out the door. No point thinking about it. It was time to go.

She stepped outside, shading her eyes from the bright sunlight. Fiona stood next to the car with Finnagen in the driver's seat. Finnagen appeared a little pale, but was laughing in a way that seemed strange, hesitant almost. Did Fiona say something to him?

Walking up to the car, Karina managed to catch Fiona's and Finnagen's attention. Fiona turned and smiled gently toward Karina. She walked over, pulling Karina into another hug. "I hope you find what you're searching for and stay safe out there. After all, the Resistance does not make things easy for people like you." With that, she pulled away.

"I'll be here if you need me. I hope to meet everyone someday."

Karina, unsure what to say, nodded. "Yeah. I hope so too." She gave Fiona another quick hug before pulling away. With a wave, she slipped into the passenger seat and glanced at Finnagen who gave her a relieved grin, his window rolled up and hands on the wheel, taut and white.

"You're sure?" Karina pointed out one more time, glancing toward his tightening fingers.

He blinked before relaxing and sending her a soft expression. "Yeah, I'll be fine."

They watched as Eren pulled out before Finnagen shifted the car into drive. Karina peered over the area one last time as they drove out past the gates of the place she could almost call home. She watched as it swung closed behind them, shutting with a clang. She let out a breath. It felt so strange, leaving like this. In a comfortable car without fear. It was almost surreal.

"So, have you explored much of our community?"

Karina blinked, not sure how to respond. She saw some of it, but... Finnagen seemed to realize, but waited as she thought through her answer. "Not really."

"Ah..." He turned back to face the road.

Karina watched as Eren turned off a side road and disappeared around the bend. She turned and faced the golden gates in the distance. Well, off she went yet again. She had a feeling she was starting to understand how Maxwell felt whenever she pulled him away. Fantastic...

Finnagen's heart was pounding in his chest, thumping away enough to put a drummer to shame. Fiona's words rang in his head every time he turned sidelong toward Karina. Fiona's face still in his mind's eye.

Fiona had held a smile on her face that belied a sharpness that was in her tone as she said, "So. Finn, dear, you'll be taking care of my sweet little sister, right? My sweet little Elsa. No matter what happens, no matter what you discover, you won't leave her, right?"

"What...?"

"I'm trusting you with Karina. If I find out she gets hurt or, God forbid, dies," the whole time the expression never left her face as she leaned in closer through the window, "well, I am called a witch for a reason." With that, she pulled away and he had never been more grateful.

Her words caught him and made him gulp. Witch? So, she knew about what she was called and agreed with it? He shuddered at the thought, quickly moving to the next unnerving part of the whole short exchange. What did she mean by, "Whatever he would discover?" While it was true, he didn't know much, he was willing to learn. So, he would have to try his best. He would have to be careful not to get sick, but he hadn't heard of a gated community person getting it. Even the prince who had been away for so long hadn't gotten it. He would probably be fine.

Though the name Elsa also caught his attention. Why did Fiona call Karina Elsa? Did Karina know? He wasn't sure and he couldn't find it in himself to bring it up. He certainly had other things to think about.

He shook his head and stared up at the golden gates, his fingers tightening as they slowed to a stop near the gates. They passed a few Enthrope cars, which caused Karina to cringe downward. After a second, she reached up, pulling her ponytail out, letting her hair trail around her face, obscuring her pretty blue eyes. He wasn't sure how to respond, so he sent her a warm grin, hoping to calm her nerves a bit, and his own as well. "So, a new adventure. This should be fun."

She jumped, long black locks falling softly over her slender shoulders before letting out a huff as her lips twitched upward. "Seems it. So how do you leave?" Her gaze flicked outside once more.

"Not that hard, actually. Mainly 'cause no one is usually willing to leave." He shrugged, glancing forward as they approached. "Well, at least almost no one. I didn't know Fiona left."

A guard glanced his way and Finnagen noticed Karina bend her head down, once more hiding her face. Was it because of all the Enthrope people out and about? Sure, maybe she was a criminal, but he didn't think so. He passed it off, waving his ID to the guard. The guard nodded.

Julie Boglisch

Finnagen could hear a faint creak before one gate slowly swung open. He gulped, swallowing heavily as he slowly pushed down on the gas, almost crawling out of the gates. This was it, no turning back any time soon.

His fingers were cramping as they gripped the steering wheel. The golden gates passed behind them and he heard the gates close with an echoing, grinding crash. He scrutinized the outer world, suddenly feeling uneasy and almost scared. Realizing his emotions, he let out a faint laugh and shook his head. What was he doing? He wasn't going to go regretting his decision now. He slowly loosened his grip on the wheel and pulled out his phone, placing it near the odometer.

"What are you doing?"

Finnagen glanced at Karina, who was examining the phone in confusion. "I'm pulling up a map. You said we need to head west, right? Well, I wanted to check if there was a way to get us on the main interstate highway. That's all. Speaking of, can you grab the car charger? I know I threw one in my bag for you to use. Since the one I gave you won't work in a car."

He turned back to the road, listening to Karina shuffle around, grunting slightly whenever they hit a pothole. He grimaced. The roads were so much worse out here. No wonder. He knew of the destitution, disease and death in these parts. He supposed he hadn't really thought much past that. He had a feeling he would be witnessing a lot more in the coming days, but pushed the idea away when he heard a thump and exhale. He spotted Karina shoving the phone charger into the slot before hooking up her phone. She seemed lost in thought as the phone hummed and connected to the charger. Good thing his worked for hers, that was fortunate.

Finnagen glanced at his, taking a turn as they approached a light. His fingers twitched as he decided to lock the car doors. Outside, past the windows, were the beginning signs of houses. He knew there was a small town about two or three miles away from the community, but... He took a deep breath and slowly let it out to help calm his nerves. It wasn't like he was diving into some monster's belly, though he certainly felt like it. He was just traveling, learning more about the world through hands-on means, that's all.

309

Even with that thought process, he wasn't able to calm down much at all.

He heard a sound and glanced over. Karina's phone was up and practically exploding with missed calls and texts. He shifted, deciding to give her a bit of privacy as he glanced at the map and took another turn, not long until the highway, then he could relax a bit. The houses were becoming denser and he cringed, noting the state most of them were in. If this was what it was like just outside the community, he couldn't imagine what it was like in the city proper or other areas.

He knew well that his region was okay with the epidemic, not great, but not quarantined either.

He jumped when the phone went off, his foot jerking and slapping the pedal, causing the car to jolt. Karina yelped, fumbling with the phone before finally clasping it tightly, staring at it in a mix of panic and fear. He bit his lip, trying to calm his racing heart. That startled him. Soon enough, he found a spot where he could pull to the side and threw the hazard lights on before turning to her right as the ringing died.

"You're not going to pick up?"

Karina twitched, but didn't really respond beyond that. The phone went off once more and, almost on instinct, she clutched it tighter, knuckles white. "I..."

Finnagen swayed a little in thought before leaning forward to look up at her. "Well? I think it wouldn't hurt. They probably realized that your phone is back up, now that it's not going straight to voicemail. If your brother is anything like you, then he'll probably keep calling."

Karina bit her lip, staring down at the phone as it rang and rang before once more cutting off. She hissed before slamming the power button down, forcing the phone off once more. She placed it in her lap, slightly trembling. "Are we going?" she muttered.

He watched her, feeling more than a little shocked, before he let out a sigh.

Clicking the hazard lights off, he pulled back onto the road and continued on in silence. Within no time at all, they reached the highway. He couldn't stop the smirk from forming on his face as they picked up speed. The quiet hum of the engine, the faint blowing of wind rattling the metal, the landscape flying past. It was all so exhilarating. He picked up speed to match the other cars, something he couldn't do in the gated community with its winding roads. Feeling almost giddy, he took a deep breath and glanced over to Karina once more, allowing one hand to fall from the wheel. "You know you need to talk to him eventually."

"I know that," Karina snapped before slumping and turning away.

Finnagen peered back at the road in a mix of awe and uncertainty. Deciding not to bother her anymore, he was startled when she continued. "I know I need to talk to him. But I..."

"Need to call him on your own terms?" he put in then slammed his mouth shut.

She chuckled before her voice sobered a bit. The sound of cloth shifting, followed by a light tapping indicated she was once more probably taking in the outside world, head against the window. "You're not wrong."

He let out a breath, relieved he hadn't put his foot in his mouth again. "So?"

He didn't hear anything except for soft breaths followed by a shallow grunt. A car sped past, the whistling of the wind faintly trailing through the closed window, the air conditioner almost at full blast. The roads were mostly empty, but there were enough cars to tell it was still well traveled. He leaned back, shifting to get comfortable with not much else to do. This decision had been spur of the moment, and maybe he could have thought it through more, but he knew he wouldn't have changed anything, so it was best not to think about it. He switched his hands, letting his other one lean against the windowsill, tapping gently on the plastic. His mind veered off to the next realization which did not help the situation.

The fact that he was alone with a very pretty girl. He gulped, quickly pinching himself to get out of that thought. Yes, she was pretty, but he was a gentleman. He was not going to think of that, nor do anything regarding it.

Feeling the wallet dig into his leg, he let out a breath. At least he had a good chunk of change so he could probably get separate rooms at hotels. The only thing he would have to worry about was during travel and he was otherwise preoccupied, so it wouldn't be too much of an issue. Though, he briefly wondered if Karina worried about that. She didn't seem to be upset with him joining her and...

He bit his lip, but the words slid out anyway. "So, you're not afraid that I'll do something now that we're alone?"

Dammit, mouth. He made sure not to turn, feeling his fingers tense up, his palm smarting from how tight his fist was. "I mean that I don't PLAN on doing anything, but... uh..."

Silence filled the car and it took everything in him not to face her, not to peek over.

He heard a long-drawn sigh before a quiet voice spoke, wary. "I won't say I'm not. I don't think you would do anything. I've seen others...been in those situations and I could tell you don't mean me any harm."

"Others? Those situations?"

His voice came out in a squeak as he jerked his head over, startled. She smirked before shaking her head and clenching her fists.

"When Maxwell and I were in the last city, there were a couple...incidents that made it quite obvious where people's intentions lay. If we hadn't had help, Maxwell and I, well..." She shrugged before peering through the front window. "Let's just say you don't give off the same vibe. Of course, I'm not as good as Maxwell at telling those things, but I've learned a few things here and there while on the road." She glanced over. "Unless you give me reason to not trust you, then it's fine. Plus, in all honesty? I think I would be able to protect myself just fine if you try to do anything."

He winced, recognizing the dig for what it was before groaning. "Yes, yes, my apologies on not being..."

"Geez, you're something else."

Finnagen stiffened, peering over at Karina who chuckled and grinned. "You're not a bad guy, you know. Just lacking a bit in the confidence, at least, most of the time."

Finnagen winced. "Yeah."

She shook her head and peered forward. "Still, thanks."

"No problem," he muttered.

Silence descended on the car, but, to Finnagen's surprise, it wasn't nearly as heavy or choking. The hour passed into the next without much happening other than a slight change of scenery. It was undisturbed, quiet, almost serene.

He could appreciate it, quietly humming to himself as they continued down the road. He knew they should probably stop for lunch soon, but he wasn't ready, not yet.

He was enjoying the time with Karina too much to disrupt it. Though he knew it wasn't going to stay like this much longer.

Chapter Thirty-Two

Finnagen wasn't really sure what to expect when he pulled into a little town in search of food. He'd gotten hungry and he could hear Karina's stomach groaning so he could guess, though she stayed quiet, she was as well. Still, what could they eat? He heard a plaintive groan before following Karina's pointing finger. A sign with a burger glowed with luminescent light, indicating the location of a restaurant. Most likely one he'd never tried before. He pulled up, curious on why Karina made such a noise and frowned upon noticing the small lines of cars off to one side. Deciding to get in line, he heard a faint chuckle from Karina.

Karina's amused tone spoke volumes as she shifted back in her seat to get more comfortable. "I'm not really fond of the idea of food right now, at least, not this, but it was the best option I could find that lets us get back on the road."

"Ah." He blinked, but dismissed it as they moved forward bit by bit. "Do you think they would have restroom?"

"Probably, but I wouldn't count on them being that clean." She shrugged, earning a grimace from Finnagen.

It was only when he saw a line of menus and what seemed to be a speaker that he put two and two together. He'd heard of them, but they weren't exactly common in gated communities due to certain conditions. "A fast food joint?" He perked up, intrigued.

"Yeah, though hopefully..."

"Huh?"

"Just order whatever."

"Well, that's not ominous," he muttered before pulling up to the speaker and taking a quick peek at the menu.

He conveyed Karina's order which turned out to be a chicken sandwich, fries and a drink. He perused it for a bit before deciding on just a simple cheeseburger with all the fixings, onion rings and a chocolate shake. He heard an amused snort and could just imagine the raised eyebrow. She was probably thinking how strange it was for him to be ordering such outlandish things. He shot her a smirk. "When in Rome."

"That's, ugh, never mind." She huffed and shook her head; amusement clear in her voice.

He chuckled and pulled up, handing over the change. At least, he prepared to. He drove up to the window and, money already out and ready, faced the cashier, only to jerk back as he noticed a young woman with a mask over her face and a wound trailing down one side of her neck. A strong smell of spice and perfume hit his nose. She spoke with a slightly hoarse and quiet tone, watching him warily. Karina pulled the money out of his hand, her soft fingers jolting him out of his reverie.

He was completely unable to react when she reached over, her body practically on... oh shit. He gulped heavily as her warmth seeped through him, a faintly pleasant smell of spring and honey gently wafted to his nose, her hair just grazing his clothing, falling over her shoulder as she passed the money over to the cashier before pulling back and flicking his forehead. Thankfully for his addled brain, he'd had exact cash because he quickly pulled forward, fingers reaching up to massage at his forehead.

"I guess I should have warned you, but I kind of did, so..." She paused, fingering her hair, before tying it back up into a ponytail.

He gulped heavily, hand dropping from his forehead to his mouth as a faint laugh of panic slipped out. "Is everyone like that out here?"

Sure, let's go with that question. That was fair.

"Eh. A good portion, at least she had a mask on and was mostly healing, I think."

He felt himself pale before shaking his head. "Well, thanks. That was really rude of me."

"It's fine." Karina waved it off before raising her eyebrow. "Just never thought you would freeze up like that when just interacting with someone."

"Sue me." He bit back with a deadpan.

He gathered his nerves and pulled up, ignoring the honk of the car behind him. The window was already open, the person seeming annoyed about the wait. He tried hard not to flinch as he accepted the bag and two drinks. If he was acting like this just through drive-through, maybe he was better off just finding a place at the side of the road...yeah, he'd do that. He handed the food to Karina and drove away from the window. He let out a breath as Karina perused through the bag.

"Yep, seems like everything's here."

"Alright, I'll eat when we get back on the highway."

Karina nodded, sitting back as he focused on finding the entrance ramp. Once on, he took a breath before grinning over at her. "So, thanks for the save again, didn't expect you to lean over me like that though."

She rolled her eyes. "How else was I supposed to get your ass moving? Here, your sandwich."

She thrust it almost onto his lap and he yelped, managing to drive and catch it, somehow. He opened it up, dripping in grease. This was his first meal outside the gated community. He'd decided to go all out, but... He gulped, before taking a bite.

He blinked in surprise, grimacing as it slid down his throat. In a strange combination, it made his gag reflex react, even as he found the flavor not that bad. Was it the texture? He wasn't sure, but he ignored it in favor of focusing on the decent scent and flavor, as well as his starving stomach.

He downed the food, sipping at the drink in relief as it cooled his throat that he'd almost burned in his speed.

"Geez," Karina muttered, amused. "I guess this is what Lex...wow, I've been repeating myself a lot." She shook her head.

"You talk about the prince a lot," Finnagen groused, taking another bite.

"What can I say? He's my friend."

Finnagen nodded, slowing his pace as he heard the faint crinkling of a bag. He bit into his straw, pushing it back and forth in his mouth before sighing and taking another long drag as they continued down the freeway. It was getting later in the day and he knew he would have to pull to a stop soon to find someplace to sleep, but...

He groaned. If the restaurant was any indication, he wasn't sure if he wanted to sleep in a room. He blinked as he saw a sign that mentioned they were leaving South Dakota. So, did that mean they were already entering Wyoming? He grinned at the thought. He was leaving the state, his home. While part of him was terrified, another was thrilled. He hummed at the thought before hearing a choked sound from beside him, garnering his attention.

Karina seemed to be glued to watching the sign, her head swiveling to follow it even as they passed.

He frowned. "You okay?"

"Yeah, Yeah, I'm fine. Just a little..." she trailed off before shaking her head, arms crossed. "So how far are we going anyway? We can't just keep traveling, as much as I wouldn't mind the idea." The last bit, she muttered in a low voice that he almost missed, the tone wistful.

He chuckled sheepishly, rubbing the back of his neck. "I just figured I would keep driving until I got tired, needed to run to the bathroom or something, then we'd find a hotel."

She gave him a deadpan look and he turned away, feeling even more sheepish. She let out a huff and faint chuckle. "Fine, that'll work.... Though, if you can. I do want to learn how to drive myself."

He blinked and spared her a bit of attention, grinning widely in delight. "You want me to teach you? I can do that." She must have heard the enthusiasm in his voice because she pushed back against the seat, giving him such an unamused expression, he wilted. "Well, if that's okay, I'm not the best driver, but I can tell you the basics."

"That's fine," Karina murmured, relief clear in her voice. "I appreciate it."

He nodded, feeling the grin return to his face.

It was a few hours later when they stopped for the night. As he promised himself, Finnagen got a separate room for each of them, both to Karina's and the hotel manager's surprise. It was a bit on the expensive side, but not exorbitant, which was a relief to him. He stepped inside the little room, only to spot how cramped it seemed. The hallways, painted a warm red, had been one thing, but here, where he was staying, was quite different. To his right was a door that led to a bathroom. He frowned as he noted that it was maybe the size of his closet at home. The room itself? Closer to the size of his bathroom. Yet he didn't mind it. It was still warm and cozy, a gentle noise rattling from the air conditioner as he took a seat on the quilted sheets, groaning in relief as his body sunk a little into it. They weren't nearly as comfortable as his, but they were still comfortable. He didn't think he minded staying in a room like this for a short time. He let his bag down and dug into it, pulling out a change of clothes, the car keys sitting in sight on the side table.

He paused upon seeing his phone sitting to one side and let out a sigh. He should probably call his mother to make sure she knew he was alright. He wasn't sure if he wanted to, but he picked up the phone and flipped to her number.

It barely took two rings before his mother picked up.

"Finnagen? Are you alright?"

"I'm fine, mom. I'm just calling to let you know I've made it out of the community and am in a hotel right now."

"Oh...so you are safe? She hasn't...?"

"Mom! I'm fine. Actually, it's been kind of cool getting a chance to be outside of the gated community. I got to try some fast-food. Seriously though, I'm safe. I just wanted to send a quick call before I get some sleep."

"Alright, honey. I'm glad to hear you are alright. Stay safe out there and please be careful."

"I will. I'll call you in a few days, alright?"

There was a long pause followed by a sigh before the quiet, "Alright," echoed through the phone.

"Good-night, mom." Finnagen spoke softly, happy.

"Good-night, sweetie."

He closed the phone and let out a breath. It was good to know Mom wasn't too upset with him. It didn't take long to change, nor to fall asleep as his tiredness from the long day finally caught up with him.

Chapter Thirty-Three

The next morning led him to being a little less accommodating to the abode. His head hurt and he figured it was due to the dryness of the room, but his throat felt scratchy and dry. He hadn't slept too well, his stomach twisting painfully in a way that made it hard to tell if he needed to burp or shit. Finally, he managed to get some necessary sleep, though there wasn't much until the sun woke him for the final time. Shaking off the sleepiness, he quickly got changed and met up with Karina. She was dressed in simple attire with a white blouse trailing down to mid-thigh, a pair of jean shorts peeked out underneath. A set of gloves trailed past her wrists and the same boots he saw her in before sat snugly on her feet. He'd changed into a pair of jeans, a t-shirt adorned with broken clocks shattering against each other and wearing his favorite wristwatch. He noted she had her watch on as well.

She examined him before chuckling and gesturing. "So? Shall we go?"

He grinned. "Yep."

He hurried down the stairs, humming in relief when he noticed she was still there. Part of him was worried that she would take off, now that they were outside of the community, but it seemed his fear was unfounded. Quickly grabbing something to eat, a sandwich for her and a bagel with cream-cheese for him since his stomach was feeling a little queasy, they were on their way. He winced as his stomach decided it wanted to do a loop-de-loop and he groaned. The bagel was almost sticking in his throat, the cream-cheese somehow having a scratchy texture contrary to the savory taste.

Shaking it off and hoping the fresh air might help, he continued down the road, opening the window a little as a result.

He noticed Karina's concern, but he ignored it, trying to focus. Deciding the lack of changing scenery wasn't doing him any good, he turned his attention toward Karina, who stiffened. "It's been a day. Wouldn't it be better to try calling him?"

She turned away, lips pursed. Finnagen groaned, tempted to throw his hands in the air. "I mean, come on, you're so strong most of the time, so why are you struggling so much with this? I get it, I know what you said, but at the same time, I don't see any reason for why you are so scared."

Finnagen almost felt the jerk as Karina whipped around to face him. Her mouth was open in either shock or a need to argue. However, no sound came out and she snapped it shut, grimacing. "I don't..."

"Don't give me that," he snapped, his head aching and causing him a moment of irritation. Realizing, he grimaced. "Sorry, I'm not feeling all that well."

"Are you feeling sick?" Her words were a mix of panicked and concerned.

He quickly waved the thought away. "No, I'm fine, my head just hurts, that's all. I think I slept wrong since it was a different bed and all."

It was true. In his head, he hadn't slept well because of both his stomach and the lump he kept finding in the originally comfortable bed. "It's not like I got the epidemic. Not only would it be ridiculous to get it this quickly, but those from the gated community do have a higher immunity. I mean, even the prince was without the sickness."

He sent her a warm smile, only to blink when he noticed her grimace at his last words. That was strange, why would she grimace? Wasn't what he said good?

Shaking off the thought, he continued, "Well, I figured, since we would be traveling most of the day, there isn't much else to do. We could talk, but I think you need to talk to your brother first, right?"

He heard her shifting back and forth, the air almost uncomfortable with the silence. Finally, she sighed. "I... Fine. Fine. I'll do it. Happy?"

He shook his head, worried. "I'm not, actually." His words startled her as she almost dropped the phone she'd pulled out.

"What?" She breathed, fingers trembling around the phone.

He groaned and shifted on the leather a bit so he was leaning against his fist, his elbow propped against the windowsill while his other hand lazily sat over the steering wheel. "I'm just worried. You're bull-rushing into this. I know I said you need to call him, but if you call him now when you're annoyed, either at me or the situation, it'll only end badly. I know my words probably don't mean much, considering I run my mouth way too often for my own good, but..." He groaned, slumping a little. "I just think that you should THINK about what you're going to do instead of just doing it to stop me from annoying you." He shifted slightly, expression grim. "Because I know me annoying you is the only reason why you decided to do it."

She didn't argue. She sat, tracing over the glass of the phone for a while before letting out a long breath. "Geez," she mumbled before picking up the phone. After a second of hesitation, she turned it on and watched as the screen flickered to life. "Don't worry, I know what I need to say." Her words were almost vacant, lips barely twitching up in the facsimile of happiness as she dialed the number. "Hopefully, he picks up."

Finnagen held no doubts that he would, considering how much he called the one time she'd turned it on. Still, he bit his lip in worry and concern. He could hear the ring as loud as Karina, though he wondered how it sounded to her, a death knell? A chiming clock? He wasn't sure. "Hey, can you do me a favor?" He spoke up, voice unusually quiet. She shifted, but didn't really say anything so he continued, "When he picks up, can you put it on speaker? I want to get a chance to meet him."

She almost got whiplash with how fast she turned to him, mouth open, only for a "Wha...?" to breathe out past her lips.

He hesitated, noting how long it was taking to pick up the phone. Why were these two siblings so bad at picking up a phone-call? Did her brother drop it in surprise or something? He reached behind his neck, rubbing it as he tilted his head away. "Well, he's probably going to realize I'm here anyway so..."

She seemed to debate, but whatever she decided was lost when the ringing ended with a click. He wasn't sure if she did anything, but the faint buzzing from the phone grew louder and there was a sense of gratefulness of a warm feeling in his chest that she'd listened to him.

"Karina? Is that really you?" A hesitant voice filtered faintly through the phone, clearly heard due to the speakers. A male's voice with a faint tremor to it, soft and gentle in a way.

Finnagen could almost feel the way Karina stiffened up, the air liable to snap as her fingers slowly clenched around the phone. "Come on, just say hi," he whispered quietly. He would introduce himself later, for now...

To his surprise, it was the boy who spoke first, his words loud and coarse. "Karina, who is that?"

"Maxwell. It's..."

She took a breath, interrupting Finnagen before he could respond and assuage the other boy's concerns. Unfortunately, it seemed Maxwell was on a roll, because he didn't let her continue.

"What the heck, Karina? I've been worried about you for a week now. A freaking week and you can't call me once? I know you turned your phone on. Are you just ignoring me? What did I do wrong?" As the voice continued, it seemed to pitch up and up, a slight sob cutting off the end. "I'm sorry. Whatever I did that made you leave, that made you go with someone else. I'm sorry!"

Karina choked, covering her mouth as a tinge of blood slipped down her chin, possibly from how hard she was biting her lip. "Why are you apologizing?" she whispered, voice hoarse. "You have no reason..."

Finnagen knew, KNEW he shouldn't interrupt. It was not his place. Yet the words came out anyway. "Karina, just talk to him." He kept his voice low, this time soft enough for only Karina to hear. "He's right there, listening."

Whatever words Maxwell said were lost as Karina cleared her throat and, with a hardness in her tone and her knuckles white as clouds, she said, "I know. I..." She cut off, wetness staining her cheeks. "Dammit, I want to apologize," she cried out, her voice shaking. "It was my stupid fault. I shouldn't have left you like that. I should have told you and..."

"Karina, why didn't you—?"

"How could I?" Karina's voice screeched, causing Finnagen to jump. "Look, I'm sorry, okay? I was stupid and reckless like usual. I was just, you've gotten so strong, so..."

"Why do you think that?" Maxwell muttered. "I'm not strong, you're deluding yourself. I have my strengths and you have yours. Do you think we could have lasted this long without the other person? Excuse my cheesiness, but we're two halves of a whole. You're my twin, my other half, what do you think I would feel if you're not there?"

"I..." Her stammering seemed to fade, her fingers catching at her clothes, tugging it upward. Finnagen averted his gaze, trying to keep his focus on the road as she continued, "I don't know, alright? I don't know. I didn't know and it was my fault—"

"Karina," Maxwell cut in, his voice echoing around the car. "Stop it. Please. You don't...you don't have to..."

"Really?" Karina chuckled morosely. "We both know that's a lie. But, don't worry. I'm fine."

Finnagen almost jumped when he felt a tap on his shoulder, having been starting to tune the conversation out so that they could have their privacy. "I have someone here who would like to say hi. I'll...I'll talk to you soon, okay?"

"Wait, what?" Maxwell's voice rang out as Finnagen cried, "Come on, what the heck?"

Both voices caused Karina to curl inward.

"I can't talk to him anymore right now, alright?" Karina murmured; voice low enough for Maxwell not to hear. At least, Finnagen hoped.

"Why did you get me involved now?" he hissed, annoyed.

He took a moment before raising his tone so the other boy could hear, said, "Uh, hey?"

Silence filled the other end of the phone and Finnagen almost felt his breath dissipate in his lungs from the wait. Finally, a harsh, cold voice spoke up, very different from the gentle pleading from before. "What is going on? Who are you and why is my sister not talking to me?"

"Er, the latter part I'm not sure of, you'll have to ask her." He winced, realizing what that meant before clearing his throat. "But, uh, for your first question. My name's Finnagen. We're traveling west right now. Is there someplace you two were planning to meet up?"

"Planning?" Maxwell's voice pitched before quiet enveloped the other side, a whispered conversation ensuing that neither Finnagen nor Karina could hear.

Who was Maxwell talking to? Finally, Maxwell continued, a faint creaking heard through the phone indicating more than his monotone voice ever could. "Sacramento. Now, Karina, I know you are there."

Karina grimaced, but didn't react beyond that. Silence followed for a while before Maxwell continued, the monotone gone and only a heavy sadness remaining. "Please, talk to me? I miss you. I don't know what I did wrong to make it be this way, but even though you said I don't need to apologize..."

There was a faint click of a tongue and rustling, causing a staticky sound to crackle through the phone. A hiccup, similar to a cut-off sob sounded before Maxwell said, "I will talk to you. We will talk. When you get out here, when you meet us out here." A deep breath sounded before Maxwell bit out, "You will talk to me and we will get this cleared up because, by god, Karina, you are being such a stupid idiot!"

Karina pulled into herself and he heard a sudden choked sound from Maxwell, as if a panic overcame the boy before he spoke once more. "Wait. Karina, that's not what I meant. It's not like last time, please, believe me!" The desperation coloring the other's voice was almost painful. "You're not stupid. I was just angry, please, believe me."

Karina seemed to be unable to say anything, her mouth moving up and down in something resembling the words, "I'm sorry," but no breath leaving her lungs.

Did she actually hear his pleas? Finnagen wasn't sure.

"Karina? Karina, please...please talk to me? Please tell me I didn't screw up again." The cold voice was gone, only a pleading despair filling the car.

Finnagen wasn't sure what to do at this point. Karina seemed to be on the verge of breaking down and from the sounds of it, so was Maxwell.

He let out a tired breath and turned away, his full focus on the road. "We'll meet you in Sacramento. I'll introduce myself properly there, and make sure she gets to you safely, okay?" Finnagen cut in, deciding to end this mess.

Silence filled the other end before he heard the sound of rustling, followed by another voice. This one was smoother, a deeper tone filled with a tiredness and strength that sounded familiar. "This is Lex. It seems we should be meeting up soon." There was a slight pause as Finnagen caught his breath in shock. "I need to ask. How do you know Karina?" The words were said calmly enough, but Finnagen couldn't help but feel a chill run down his spine.

"Uh, well. I happened to run into her at the mall in my home town and then things just kind of happened from there." He gulped and then spat out. "I'm sorry, but are you Leonard? I mean, Lex, the prince?"

"Prince?" Lex responded, this time sounding more than a little bewildered over the phone. There was a long pause followed by what almost sounded like a snort, but that couldn't be. "Ah, I understand. While I am Lex, please do not refer to me as 'prince'. I will ask later how she ended up within the gated communities, but for now that information will work." There was some shuffling and shifting before he continued, "Considering the situation at hand. I'm grateful there is someone able to talk. I don't suppose she is able to speak at the moment, correct?"

Finnagen glanced sidelong to Karina whose head was buried into her knees. "Uh..."

"I'll take that as a no." Finnagen let out a breath, only to stiffen as Leona...Lex continued, "I don't have the time to ask more, however, if I learn that she was somehow hurt while she is with you..." The silence between them was tense enough to feel even over the phone. It was finally broken when Lex said, "However, for now, just make sure she gets here safely. When you get closer, call us and we'll set a more specific location. Understood?"

"Clear... Clear as day," Finnagen stammered out.

There was a pause followed by a faint chuckle. "Relax, kid, I'm just making sure she stays safe. I'm well aware she can take care of herself."

Finnagen felt his entire body relax at those words. "Right, yeah. She can."

"Alright, I apologize, I have to focus on the road for now. We will talk soon."

Finnagen just nodded, unsure what to say. Thankfully, it seemed he didn't need to say much because the phone clicked shut, ending with a long tone.

Karina slowly took the phone back and closed it, but didn't put it away, head down, legs pulled close to her chest as if she was hugging the seatbelt.

He let out a breath he must have been holding for way too long with how dizzy he felt. The air itself was thick and warm and uncomfortable as he rolled the window back down a crack. "So, I'm sorry, but I'm going to ask a stupid question here. Did that help?"

Silence. Utter quiet filled the car for what seemed like forever. Finnagen waited, figuring she needed time.

He would, after something like that.

He'd never heard such a messed-up call before and it made him somewhat grateful he at least left on good terms with his family.

Finally, Karina seemed to shift, the sound of her quiet breathing catching his attention. His attention drifted briefly to her, noting as she relaxed slightly, head leaning against the window. "Did that help?" He waited a moment for her response, which lingered in the air as he turned his attention back to the road, feeling a little unnerved. "No."

Finnagen winced, fingers clutching the steering wheel. "You know? I still think it was necessary." No response, though he wasn't really expecting one at this point. "If you don't mind me saying, he cares about you."

"I know that."

"Well, of course you do." Finnagen sighed. "Because you care deeply about him as well." *Very deeply*, he thought. He shook his head, pulling his thoughts back together. "Siblings say stupid things to each other. I know I've done it." She twitched at his words, but he continued, "Yet, no matter how angry we are at each other, how much we might want to yell and scream and throttle each other, at the end of the day, they are still my family. Unless they did something absolutely terrible, then I would forgive them. I know they would do the same for me."

"But I screwed up."

"So did he." Finnagen snorted. "I'm not denying the fact that both of you screwed up. Both of you were trying to reach out to each other and just, well, missed the mark I suppose." He winced. "We're heading that way anyway. I'll call when we get closer and you will talk with him then as well. This time, listen."

"I..." she trailed off and didn't say anything else, arms crossed tightly over her chest.

Finnagen felt his whole-body slump. "Well, at least we know they are okay, in some sense of the word, and they know you are fine. That helps, in the long run. Plus, well, I got a chance to talk with the prince...I mean Lex. That was cool, if a little short."

He got a quiet weak chuckle from Karina. "Yeah, he's pretty curt."

"I noticed, but I guess I'm not too surprised." He smiled before a thought crossed his mind and he felt the blood drain from his face. "Oh, I probably made a really bad impression there."

"How so?" At this, he noticed Karina glance toward him.

That blood surged back in as he stumbled over his next words. "Well, I mean, your brother as well as Lex might be thinking I kidnapped you or something awful. I don't want that, but it's not like I can change the conversation. Oh man, now I don't know what to say and I really should shut up."

This time, she was outright staring, bemusement slowly curling over her lips. "Oh?"

"Well, I want him to at least like me, you know? I mean, especially since..." He jammed his mouth shut, screaming at his brain to shut up.

The faintest of smiles crossed her lips. "You really are something. Still, thanks."

"Huh?"

Karina's fingers grasped onto her shirt, fabric tugging lightly over her skin. "I don't think I would have had the courage to call if you weren't here." She shook her head. "I guess I just appreciate the fact you're here, that's all."

For a brief moment, Finnagen's heart soared, before he quickly tugged it down. She was just happy he was here, as a friend, nothing more.

For now, he supposed, he was fine with that. Maybe someday, she would want him there as something more, but not right now. Not like this.

Chapter Thirty-Four

Exhaustion slammed over him like a wave, but relief didn't follow. Maxwell wasn't surprised. The anger he felt earlier, the desperation, it had all just disappeared. In its place was just, nothing. He was just so tired.

"That could have gone better," Lex voiced out, no longer having to shout now that they had some plastic and duct tape over the broken back window. It was at least comforting not to hear the whomp, whomp, whomp of the wind anymore. Lex lightly tapped the steering wheel before continuing, "It seems that she found someone from the gated community. We can only hope things turn out well enough that they make it."

Maxwell just stared at the phone, almost cracking it in his grip. The thought of the boy being so close to Karina, who talked so hesitantly yet with a certain awe to Lex, just made him want to break something. What was his sister thinking? What was he thinking? He screwed up again.

That moment of lacking emotions disappeared as anger surged once more and he slammed the phone down. He heard a yelp from the back, but ignored it as a scream begged to rip from his throat. His whole body shook, as he felt hands carefully take the phone out of his grip.

He ignored it, frustration, anger, hatred swirled around and around in his head and he realized, with a heavy sadness, that none of it was directed outward. He felt white hot tears trail down his cheeks.

Dammit. Dammit, dammit, dammit! He brought his hands up, palms digging into his eyes as he hiccupped. He finally got a chance to talk with his sister, and instead of checking on her, instead of making sure she was alright and making sure he would speak with her again safely, he yelled at her. He'd done the same thing as before. He KNEW better and yet...would she head west now? What about that GUY she was with? Was he actually someone safe?

Safer than him at the moment, it seemed.

The thought caused him to snap his jaw shut tightly. The emotions swirled and slowly settled, eating at him quietly.

"Maxwell?"

Yvette's voice caught his attention and he slowly took a breath, hands dropping to his sides. Yvette was leaning up between the seats, precariously poking her head forward to stare up at him with a worried expression.

"Sorry," he muttered.

Leaning his head back to stare up at the ceiling, the heavy exhaustion took over once more. The sound of the tires rolling over the tarmac, the faint smell of ozone and gas leaking through the shut windows as the sun struggled to peek through the cloudy sky, they all only worsened his mood. That man, Finnagen, he said they would meet up in Sacramento, but...

"Ugh," he moaned before slapping the back of his head against the headrest.

The scenery flashed past outside the window. He heard a sigh and slowly turned toward Lex who only spared him a moment before focusing back on the road.

"Well, at least we know she is somewhat safe and able to contact you. She must have gotten a charger at some point and if that boy held ill will, I doubt he would have let her call you."

Maxwell knew Lex was right. He knew it, and yet he couldn't help but keep questioning himself. "Why didn't she say more?" His words were soft, so soft, he almost worried Lex didn't hear.

However, Lex proved him wrong by glancing over. "I think it's just like you, why didn't you say more?"

Maxwell snapped his mouth shut before turning away.

"I'm not saying everything you said was bad, but you didn't actually listen to her."

Maxwell pulled inward at that as realization dawned on him. Lex was right. He'd mostly been saying what he wanted to say. It didn't help him feel better.

Yvette leaned forward, peering up at him with a surprisingly wise air to her. "Max, that was someone you care for, right? Like Momma? I don't think you should be upset, right? She's not sleeping like Momma is."

Maxwell bit his lip wanting so badly to pull Yvette into a tight hug, only to remember the awkward angle both of them were in. Still, he felt a hiccup escaping as he tilted his head forward. He was surprised he had any tears left. "Right, right, Sorry," he whispered. The little girl didn't say anything, just wrapped her arms around him as best as she could from where she leaned and buried her head into his side. "I'll try to stay more positive. Thank you, Yvette."

The little girl giggled softly, a sad sound before pulling back, tired. He couldn't blame her. They had been traveling for a long time already with barely any stops.

"Sorry to interrupt." Lex's tone indicated he was only slightly apologetic. He turned his gaze ahead once more. "While I'm glad to hear from her, we have our own issues. For one, we need a new car, especially if we do want to meet them in Sacramento at least somewhat safely. I have no doubt this car is being tracked."

Maxwell nodded. Lex was right. They needed to get a new car or else. If they meet with Karina, she would be in danger because of them. He couldn't risk that, not now. "What do we need to do?"

Lex glanced over before turning forward once more. "We'll have to ditch the car and walk for a bit. Once we get to a town we'll search around. Hopefully we can get a new one."

"Can't we just go to town and do that?"

Lex shook his head, frustration clear in his expression. "I wish. No, if they track the car to a specific location, like a town, it wouldn't be hard to find how we left or what type of car we picked up from the local dealer. If anything, I almost wish we could find a bus stop and go from there."

Maxwell let out a tired breath, that was fair. He peered out the window. "We'll look for a bus stop then. I would rather not worry about this car being the reason we're caught."

Lex nodded, picking up speed slightly to dodge around a slower moving car.

Hopefully, it would be enough.

Chapter Thirty-Five

Caym peered around the new base of operations with a practiced scrutiny, Machael a few paces behind him as he became accustomed to do. Caym didn't mind. It was a reminder of Leo, one of the only ones left. Enthrope employees bustled around as he strode to his office and slipped inside, piles of paperwork and folders almost burying the desk. He clicked his tongue before glancing askance at Machael. "Any news on my brother's whereabouts?"

"The only report we've received is from a small town out west. Due to the wildfire that destroyed most of the area, their focus was protecting the community." There was a pause. "However, just recently, there were reports of a stolen Enthrope vehicle in the area. They are trying to trace its coordinates right now."

"Interesting, and were those twins with him?"

"From the reports, there was a young man and a child, but they didn't recall witnessing an older girl."

Curiosity clung to his thoughts. Did they separate? For what reason? Caym shook his head, annoyed as he took a seat, filing some of the paperwork away. With his acquisition of the business, he'd admit, he'd been a little surprised on the actual extent of what his father hid from him. He thought he knew, from the get-go, just how entrenched his father's people were. That was not the case. Looking over the reports, he spotted numerous military assignments amongst them. Word of planes being shot down off the Floridian coast and reports from scouts that had been to other countries. He hadn't realized they had anyone outside of America, but it seemed his father had been involved with everything, from the global situation, which did not appear promising, to the internal situation which was less so, even for the gated communities. He winced as he read another report regarding a community that had been under siege for the past year, finally breaking down. His father would have probably kept it under wraps, but he didn't see the need to. The country was already on the brink, he didn't particularly care if it went over.

"Caym, sir."

Caym directed his attention to Machael, who seemed to be hesitating, something he only recognized due to the slight tightening of the man's jaw, before waving for him to continue.

"I have been meaning to ask, but you have yet to state what your plans are for Sir Leonard's charges if you are to acquire them."

Caym sat back, elbows on his chair and attention straight ahead. Ah, yes, those devils. "Considering the extent that Little Leo is protecting them and how it will no doubt devastate him, I am not sure. However, I can't deny the necessity in making use of their gift."

Surprise flittered onto the man's face for the briefest of moments before returning to placid. Caym observed him, but didn't comment on the reaction. "That, I'll decide at a later date. We still have to set the prerogative on finding and bringing back my brother. Make sure that it is done." He grimaced. "I have paperwork to attend to."

Machael's reaction was a brief smile before nodding and departing. Caym watched him go before turning to the mound of paperwork. He felt his lip curl at the sight. He could ignore it all he wanted to. He could throw his hands in the air and just let it all crumble. A part of him KNEW he couldn't. Knew it would only hinder him to let it fall. Knew that it was one of the only ways to get his dear Little Leo back. So, resolving himself to the task, he delved into it. The more he knew, the more he could protect him, after all.

Chapter Thirty-Six

Finnagen downed the water, his throat feeling dry and scratchy even with the cooling liquid. They had been traveling most of the day and both of them were tired. Karina yawned, a faint, if weak smile on her face. "You seriously managed to fumble a shot when you were right on top of it?"

Finnagen huffed. "Yeah, yeah. That's why I'm not a main. While I do get lucky occasionally..."

Karina chuckled. "Well, if it's any consolation? Maxwell wouldn't have been able to make the team if he wanted to. Not to worry about that, he's too much of a bookworm."

"Really?"

Finnagen chuckled, focusing back on the conversation as they continued along. After the initial bout of silence brought about by Karina's call, they finally decided to delve into normal conversation. Well, normal in that he got a chance to tell about his life and she told him bits and pieces about what it was like in Claremore. Well, sort of.

"Yeah, he would be sitting at home, reading all day and into the night. He was so out of it, I got a chance to switch his alarm clock with a fake spider. He was so freaked out, it was hilarious."

"That's mean." Finnagen grinned. "Sounds like my little brother." He pulled away, humming. "Sounds like it was a pretty quiet place." She nodded and he continued, "As you can tell, our area has more of a small-town vibe. We don't have a city nearby because of our farming capabilities. Most communities do though, from what I've heard. Something about being easily able to get goods and services? Don't know." He shrugged, only to blink when Karina cringed, rubbing her arm.

"Is that so." Her voice was quiet, sounding uncomfortable. She shook her head, her lips tilting up slightly in what he hoped was amusement. "Still, must be hard to leave that behind."

Finnagen tilted his head, hearing a faint wistful sound in her voice, but shrugged. He turned the wheel, shifting over a lane so the car behind them could pass, speeding along. "Don't know. I haven't been gone for long and I know they're all still there and fine."

He couldn't stop the fond smile from crossing his face as his attention drifted sidelong to Karina, who raised an eyebrow. Her blue eyes glowed in the evening light as a faint smile tugged at her lips. He flushed, cheeks heating up as he turned away and cleared his throat, both to help with the scratchiness and to push away the not unwelcome thoughts. "I don't have much to complain about, plus..." he trailed off, bringing up his watch for a moment which clicked to show it was five thirty-two. "I didn't have much going on at home. Sleep, go to school, watch my siblings, eat, rinse and repeat. You know?" He chuckled as he returned his gaze to the road. "This is the most excited I've ever been and I'm going out and about with a pretty cute girl as well."

Silence invaded the car and he almost choked as he realized what he said. He almost went to respond when he heard a snort. He briefly pulled his attention away from the road and spotted Karina covering her mouth, shaking violently.

"Pft..." He didn't have to wait even a moment before she tilted her head back and started a pure outright laugh. "Hahahaha." She gasped, arms wrapped around her stomach, a hint of tears on her cheeks from her laughter. "I'm sorry." She grinned. "Your expression, the way you said that. It was just funny. It was kind of cute." Her grin widened and she leaned forward. "You are so different from Maxwell and Lex, it's an interesting change." Her expression softened. "Still, thanks. I needed that."

"No problem."

He coughed sheepishly and diverted his attention away from her beautifully bright expression, feeling like he was going to burst from embarrassment and a bunch of other muddled emotions. It wasn't the first time, true, but boy was it a powerful feeling each time. Still, he appreciated her laugh, her strong personality and her brashness. Maybe he was observing her through rose-colored glasses like some might call it, but he didn't particularly care.

He let out a breath, clearing his throat in the process. His head still ached, though not as fiercely as it did that morning. He'd forgone taking Advil, deciding just to deal with it. It helped that he also didn't HAVE any, but... He centered his thoughts, frowning a little. He was getting off track more than he usually did. He wasn't sure what was causing it. "So, do you want to stop soon to grab something to eat and rest? Do you want to eat and keep going? I'm open for either."

Karina paused for a moment, watching him quietly. "How far do we have left to go?"

"Um, not sure?" He glanced at his GPS and shrugged. "I would say we'll probably get there sometime within the next day or two. I think we'd probably be going through the Rockies soon."

"The Rockies?" Karina became quiet for a moment, staring into the distance as it began to fill with more trees.

In the far distance, hard to see with the setting sun and cloud cover, Finnagen could just barely spot a string of mountains. "I guess we can stop for tonight and go through the mountains tomorrow." Karina watched as they grew closer, voice wistful. "I bet Maxwell has already seen them. I wonder what he thought about it."

Finnagen kept quiet, firmly clamping his mouth shut as his attention stayed caught on the distant horizon. Another sharp pain slashed through his head and he grimaced. "Alright, let's find someplace to stop and rest for the night."

He could hear Karina hum in agreement and, with a barely held back sigh of relief, he found the nearest town and stopped. After a quick dinner of chicken and chips, they found a motel and got some rest, or at least, tried to.

Finnagen curled into his bed, his face burning and his throat hurting like hell, or like when his little pipsqueak of a sibling decided to try stuffing jalapeños into his sandwich when he wasn't paying attention. Just not nearly as funny. He let out a cough and frowned. Did he catch a cold? Damn, what timing. He hoped Karina didn't think it was the epidemic. He closed his eyes, trying to even his breath, only for another cough to come out. Maybe some sleep would help? He wasn't sure. Should he call his mom? No, it was only a cold. It would be utterly stupid to call her because of a cold. He had some pride.

~ * ~

Karina frowned as she waited outside Finnagen's doorway, arms crossed over her chest. They agreed to head out early so as to get to the Rockies when the sun was high in the sky. However, she hadn't heard a word from his room and she didn't have a key. She'd already tried knocking, but it didn't seem to be doing much good.

A hint of worry flared over her face. He seemed a little red-faced yesterday and distracted. She tried to laugh it off, but when he agreed to stop for the night, she noticed him grimace and for his fingers to twitch for a second as if indecisive. She let out a huff and rapped against the door once more. "Finnagen," she called, annoyed.

She heard a faint yelp before dragging feet sounded faintly through the door. The handle turned and she peered in, only to stop. Finnagen seemed exhausted. His eyes were red-rimmed as he wiped at them. His hair was messier than usual, his clothes hanging off him oddly. He blinked up at her, seeming confused. As if it was taking a long time for his brain to process what he was witnessing. After a moment, he jerked back. "Wah?" he croaked, stumbling back. Karina quickly grabbed the door and pushed it open, pulling herself inside as she held his almost too warm arm. Did he have a cold? Was it the Epidemic? What was it?

He chuckled weakly and slumped against her arm. "Er, sorry. I didn't..." He coughed before wiping his mouth with his sleeve. "Don't I look pathetic?" He let out another laugh before grimacing. "Damn, this cold is hitting me harder than I thought."

Karina didn't say anything as she closed the door behind her. She gently led him on the bed, noting how much he was shaking as they moved. "Did you get any sleep last night?"

He hummed for a moment as she helped pull the covers up. "I don't think so. Head hurt too much." He groaned.

She blinked, only slightly annoyed. Well, seemed they wouldn't be heading out today. She reached into her bag for a moment, hesitating, only to shake her head and pull out one of her water bottles. She wasn't going to get sick, so it was fine. She held it out and he stared at her, seeming confused before spotting the bottle. He took it and started to drain it, taking tiny sips as he went. Karina sat back, frowning. She would have to keep checking on him, it seemed. Maybe now he could get some rest?

He blinked blearily before letting out a yawn. "Are you staying here?" Karina went to respond, but he only chuckled. "Haha, what am I thinking. This cliche. One person taking care of the other in sickness, typical." He huffed, his eyelashes fluttering. "Not that, I particularly..." He slumped downward, Karina quickly grabbing the water bottle from his loosened grip. She observed him for a long moment finding herself a mix between amused and bemused.

He was so cheesy sometimes, but it wasn't necessarily a bad thing. The fact that he could still somewhat joke about it made her feel just a little bit better. She sat there for a moment then blinked. What was she supposed to do now? She never had to deal with someone being sick before and, if it was the epidemic, which she desperately was hoping wasn't the case, then any medicine would only make it worse.

She leaned back on the other bed, not really doing much besides watching the light play over the ceiling. She could get something to eat for them. Where was his card key? She scanned the room. Unable to find the card, her attention turned back toward him. Sweat coated his face and he was breathing heavily, chest rising and falling as his hair clung to his cheeks. She groaned. Okay, she could deal with this. It wasn't like he was dying, not like...

She grimaced, scanning the room once more. There was his suitcase and on the side table was the card she missed earlier. She picked it up then paused. She had no actual reason to stay with him besides transportation, but she couldn't just leave him. Not like what she did to Maxwell. She wouldn't do it again.

She nodded to herself and slipped out the door, hurrying down the stairs to the breakfast buffet. She stopped by the front desk to pay for another night before she grabbed some simple things like toast, bananas and some eggs for herself. Bringing everything upstairs with her, she brought it to Finnagen's room, noting he was still asleep, though sleeping more soundly this time around. He seemed comfortable, no longer panting for breath like before. Maybe the sleep was helping. She munched quietly on her food as she sat back, lost in thought. There wasn't really much for her to do, but it gave her a moment to think and for once, she didn't hate the idea. She was going to find her brother.

Her little brother was waiting for her. She knew that now. As much as it hurt, she couldn't deny that what Finnagen said was right. She was just as much at fault as Maxwell was for that conversation, but there was relief. Relief that in the long run, he was alright. That Lex was still with him. That was the only thing she could hope for at this point. It helped to know she would at least have some support from Finnagen like earlier. She bit her lip. She still felt kind of bad about dragging Finnagen into their conversation, but...

She heard a cough and jerked toward Finnagen, who seemed to be awake again. A goofy grin crossed his face as he seemed to finally notice her. "Ah." He let out another cough. "You stayed."

"Idiot." She decided to steal Lex's word and mentally wondered if Maxwell had simply been doing the same. Finnagen only chuckled because of it.

"Yeah, yeah, I am." He grimaced before watching her quietly. "What time is it?"

She brought up her watch, checking the time on it. "Ten thirty."

"Okay, so we still have time." He tilted his head. "I should check out..."

"Nope. I already paid for another night and, anyway, why is that your first thought? You should be resting," she chided him.

He stared for a moment before he chuckled faintly, letting off a not so quiet cough. She watched, unsettled. He probably was going to need more time to rest. She heard a rustle and spotted him pointing shakily to his bag. She smiled. "Didn't I just tell you to get some rest? Geez," she muttered, picking up the bag and pulling out the money. "I told you, I already took care of it, okay?"

He chuckled once more, eyelids fluttering before he snuggled into the bedspread, pulling it close around him. She would have found it kind of cute, if her mind wasn't so filled with worry. She mentally berated herself. This wasn't getting her anywhere.

Chapter Thirty-Seven

Maxwell stared out over the city, taking in the tall spires, and in the distance was a horizon filled with water. The sound of the bus trundled underneath. Yvette sat beside him while Lex lingered behind. The carriage was moderately packed with people of all ages, so they didn't stand out much.

Not that they had for the last few bus rides either. Lex decided it might just be easier going bus to bus instead of trying to find a car outside of the city.

Maxwell could only be grateful that they had at least been relatively close to Sacramento when they decided to abandon the vehicle. A day of travel by bus was something he never wanted to experience again. Thankfully, for his sanity, they found a hotel quickly.

The air smelled rich with salt and fumes, a strange mixture. Part of him wanted to head toward the water, actually get down toward the beach, but he couldn't. Another part of him didn't want to. It felt wrong to be here without his sister beside him. He turned, facing away from the sparkling waters so far in the distance and instead focused on the small hotel they were staying in. Yvette was to his side, grasping his arm tightly. Lex was busy inside, speaking with the receptionist. Maxwell knew he could go inside, but he didn't want to. He peered around the bustling city, taking in everything Sacramento had to offer. The fluorescent lights beat down at him from above, searingly bright even in the sunlight. Even so, the streets were dirty and crowded. People hurried to and fro and cars honked loudly in the traffic jam that already started to form. There was a construction site off to one side that seemed to have been there for ages.

"Maxwell?" Yvette's tiny voice caught his attention, causing

Maxwell to squat down beside the young girl.

"Yeah?"

"How long do you think we'll be here? It's kind of scary."

Maxwell followed her gaze, spotting a group of men sauntering on the far side, masks covering their faces, but with a distinct design on them that made Maxwell shiver. It wasn't Halloween, there was no reason to be wearing something that showcased a bony jaw. Farther down the street, there was a screech as a car whipped out of line, partially driving over the sidewalk before whipping around the far corner. Yeah, not the safest place.

"Hopefully not long. Once we get some information on Mrs. Girshwin, we'll leave, alright?"

Yvette hesitated, confusion flashing across her face for the briefest of moments. She seemed to tilt her head at the word, as if deep in thought before she shook her head, grasping his hand tightly. He stood back up, making sure his back was to the building. It was disconcerting. In some ways, the city was beautiful and in others... He shook his head. This wasn't exactly new. He saw it all the time while traveling. He heard a faint chime and turned as Lex exited the building, a frown clear on his face.

"So?"

Lex huffed, reaching into his pocket before stopping and shaking his head. "I managed to get us a room, but not more than one. Supposedly, it's been busy around here since there's some sort of event or concert going on a few blocks from here."

"Concert?" Maxwell perked up, curious.

Lex waved it off. "Well, of course. They do still have concerts and such, it's just that the celebrities usually stay on the stage, protected by reinforced glass. After all, most of the celebrities who still do concerts are from gated communities."

"Oh," Maxwell trailed off, before frowning. "Why do they still come to outer communities anyway?"

"A fanbase is a fanbase." Lex tilted his hand left and right, as if in a so-so gesture. "It's still extra income and, to be honest, gated communities do sometimes need that."

"True."

"Well, either way, as much as it is actually beneficial for both sides, it is best that we stay away from the area. Lord knows they would somehow recognize me which wouldn't end well at all."

Maxwell chuckled as Lex's face twisted into a discontented scowl at the thought. True, that would be their luck and, unlike with the fire, they wouldn't have anything to distract Enthrope or any associated party. He could only hope their trick happened to waylay Priscel as well. "So, where to now?"

Lex hummed in thought, tapping his lip before shrugging. "I'll be honest, I'm not sure. I'm going to look around to pick up a cheap car, so when we figure out where to go, we don't have to worry as much about getting there. Other than that, though, I'm aware that Mrs. Girswhin is a prominent figure in medicine around these parts, but..."

"Yeah, that doesn't mean much." Maxwell felt a faint tug and glanced down toward Yvette, who was lightly biting her lip.

"Can I help?" she asked, hope blooming on her face.

He squatted down once more, ruffling her hair. "Sorry, yeah, you can help. Have you been here before?"

"Nope," she chirped, smile wide. "Momma and I actually live away from the ocean, not that far from here."

"Ah." Maxwell shifted, feeling uncomfortable at the momentary comment before shaking it off. It seemed Yvette was doing alright. "Okay, so we'll need to ask around, think you can handle walking for a bit?"

She nodded her head vigorously, hair bobbing with the movement as she beamed. He chuckled and stood back up, making sure he had a firm grasp on Yvette, before turning to Lex. Lex's amusement quickly vanished as he scanned back over the busy streets. "Well, we might as well get a start on things. Sitting here isn't going to help."

"True, so..."

"I don't trust you going off by yourself." Lex tilted his head just enough to peer over his shoulder as he moved forward. "I think we both recall what happened last time."

Maxwell flushed and glared. "Well, I'm sorry I got lost."

"You got lost in a small town with one street when we were trying to get to the only bus stop there. You were lucky I happened to notice you before the bus left."

Maxwell averted his gaze, grumbling. He hadn't realized how much he relied on his sister's sense of direction in new locations. He couldn't blame Lex though, every time he went off alone, something seemed to happen. He let out a tired breath and slumped. "That's fine," he muttered, hearing a chuckle from Yvette. Too tired to berate her, he followed after Lex.

"Good, so first we find a library for you and Yvette. Maybe there might be information on the computers in there." He pushed his fingers through his hair, appearing nonplussed. "I would call my uncle, but he hasn't been picking up since before we saw Caym. Though I highly doubt he would know, considering the distance. I don't have anyone around here that I know, so that's a bust."

Maxwell didn't argue. Maybe he could also check out some of the stores while they were at it, maybe pick something up for his sister? He shook his head, dispersing the thought. He would worry about that later. For now, he needed to remain focused. Either way, his sister and his mother were counting on him.

Chapter Thirty-Eight

Finnagen let out another cough and blearily blinked. Karina's face hovered over his, worry shining clearly. Ugh, this cold was hitting him hard. Maybe it was a good thing he'd let her buy them one more day. "Sorry."

She shook her head. A frown caused her lips to twist downward in annoyance. "Why are you apologizing? Seriously, every boy I know apologizes way too much."

Finnagen shrugged. "What can I say?" He let out another cough and settled back into the sheets, smiling as warmth wrapped around him. "I should be fine soon, we'll get going after that."

He wasn't sure if Karina responded or not, because he was out the next moment.

When he came back around, he could feel something cool on his head, water dripping down his face. Ah, that feels nice. He hummed and allowed himself to drift off once more, faintly hearing a distant sound of rummaging.

The third time he awoke, he could already tell he was feeling much better. His head still felt a little woozy, but the sleep did wonders. He shifted, opening his eyes to stare at the ceiling. His gaze was no longer blurry and he felt almost too hot under the sheets now. He quickly threw them off and sat up, letting out a yawn.

He heard a yelp and turned as Karina bolted upright. She was sitting in the chair, probably having dozed off at some time. He mentally pouted. He missed a chance to observe what she was like when she was sleeping... He promptly slapped himself and groaned, did he seriously just have that thought? "Hey," he spoke, relieved to hear his throat no longer sounded, or felt, like a rake was going over it.

"You're awake. How are you feeling?"

He glanced up through his fingers. "Much better, thank you."

She nodded, a faint relieved smile forming on her face. "That's good. You were out of it for most of the day. I had to extend our visit to a second night just to cover. To be honest, I think we should rest tonight and head out in the morning."

"Yeah, and you do realize I was awake for that, right?"

She hesitated before grinning toothily. "Maybe, you were quite out of it."

He snorted, shaking his head and swung his legs over the side of his bed, picking at his night shirt which was positively dripping in sweat. He grimaced, feeling heat rising to his face. "Did you take care of me the whole time?"

"Not much else to do." Karina's voice sounded nonchalant, though he faintly heard a teasing note at the end. The heat rose even more and, if he was staring in a mirror, he wouldn't be surprised if he appeared more red then pale.

"Oh, uh. Thanks."

"No problem."

He stood up, swaying a little as his head berated him on the sudden movement. Seemed he wasn't completely recovered, but that was fine. The rest was just left-over. As he took a step toward the bathroom, gathering up a change of clothes, he paused. "Wait, you said the whole time?"

He heard a hum of agreement and turned to stare at Karina as she swirled her fingers around, staring listlessly up at the ceiling.

He swallowed heavily and fully turned to face her. "Aren't you afraid you might catch whatever I did? Plus, didn't I say anything awkward?"

Her finger stopped, hovering in the air for a moment before she let it drop into her lap. Her gaze met his, a mix of surprise and uncertainty. "No." She sat up a little, swaying back and forth in thought. "As for the awkward parts? Well, I didn't change you or anything and you didn't say anything except for your usual babble, and maybe a little bit of talking about cliches?"

He coughed, hurrying into the bathroom to hide the full-out blush he knew was on his face. Oh, dammit. He heard a laugh from the other room and shook his head, relieved to at least know she wasn't sick. That would not be fun and, hey, at least she didn't try to change his clothes.

That would explain why they were so sticky with sweat. He grimaced as he pulled them off, looking forward to the hot shower that awaited him. He scrutinized his appearance in the process. He knew he didn't have anything to be ashamed of. He had a decent build, even for his shorter stature, and he was mostly healthy.

Didn't stop the embarrassment though, nor the uncomfortable feeling of her actually SEEING him like this. God, that would just be the worst. Thank the heavens she decided to let him recover himself. He stepped into the shower as soon as it was hot enough and sighed, relieved to feel the warm water trail down him. It was refreshing and, while a little bit of a headache clung on, it was manageable.

Still, he noticed how late it was when he was talking with her. So, he'd spent most of the day out of it like she said. He grimaced. Well, there went the promise of getting through the Rockies today. He would have to wait until tomorrow. Maybe he could also teach her how to drive? It wasn't exactly difficult and the SUV Eren gave them to use was actually very smooth to travel in.

Yeah, that's what he would do when they left tomorrow. He would show her how to drive. Though he would make sure to get through the Rockies before he actually LET her. He wasn't nervous, more excited about the prospect of winding roads along with beautiful scenery after the long hauls of nothing except farmland, plains and straight roads. Didn't mean he was reckless enough to have someone who didn't know how to drive going through such an area. That would be suicide.

He turned off the water and got into a new set of clothes, letting out a breath of relief. That felt so much better. His stomach twisted in a familiar way as it let loose a loud growl. Chuckling sheepishly, he stepped out of the bathroom and glanced over toward Karina. She was waiting for him, leaning against the wall, legs and arms crossed. She pushed away from the wall, relaxing. "Feeling better?"

"Of course. After all, you took care of me." He hummed happily.

She raised an amused eyebrow as he blinked, realizing what he said. "Uh, well, that is... Are you hungry, because I'm starved." He turned, grasping the handle to the doorway and throwing it open.

Her laughter followed him as he hurried down the hallway of the hotel and took the steps two at a time. Dammit, mouth. Still, it wasn't a lie and she took it fine, so he could still feel a smile slowly forming on his face anyway. After making sure they were good to go for one more night in the rooms—Karina just rolled her eyes when he went to check, he did feel a little disappointed that she'd kept them split, but he quickly pushed that away—the two of them hurried out to grab something small to eat.

They decided on a diner not that far from the hotel. It was homely and comfortable even in its cheapness. Cheesy music played over a stereo system as a waitress came over to take their order. The plastic of the seats and tables was fascinating to him, so different from home. As he waited for the food, he poked at the seat, grinning.

The food came out in no time, a spicy chicken sandwich for Karina and a Reuben for him. The fries were a little on the saltier side, but, this time around, everything went down much easier. Maybe he was getting accustomed to the food outside the community? Who knew? He was grateful to be able to enjoy both the texture and taste.

He felt a spike of pain through his head and grimaced. Hopefully, an actual night's sleep would get rid of what was left of this stupid cold because, by gosh, were those headaches annoying.

~ * ~

Maxwell groaned as he flopped onto the bed, throwing his arms in the air. Nothing. Absolutely nothing. They hadn't found a single thing so far and it wasn't for lack of trying. They'd spent ages in the library, going through all sorts of texts and websites. Even with Yvette helping by literally using her childish persona to talk to whomever entered the library, they were having trouble learning anything about Mrs. Girshwin. It was as if the woman was a tightly kept secret or something. Considering what he did learn about her, though, that made sense. She was seen as a miracle worker for those on the coast. Helping rich and poor alike. Her medical practice was well-renowned, but she also despised the government, so much so that she had some sort of spat with them. They wanted to recruit her, she didn't want to be recruited and thus the people, more willing to help someone who saved them, kept their word and kept her out of sight.

It was a pity that this included anyone who was asking about her, like them.

He heard a grunt and tilted his head. Lex rubbed his hair under the hat, tiredness practically shining through him. "Well, that was a waste."

"No kidding," Maxwell murmured, curling into the sheets before sitting up. Yvette blinked blearily, before giving up and relaxing once more. "What now?"

Lex clicked his tongue and ruffled his hair once more till it was an outright mess. "I don't know. I'm thinking of maybe checking out some of the bars to obtain any information I can. Drinks and loose lips are pretty synonymous."

Maxwell grimaced, he couldn't exactly help with that, plus he didn't want to take Yvette into an area like that, but he felt bad having her just stay in this room. He felt his shoulders dip as he nodded.

Lex's expression shifted as he took a seat on the bed, emotions flashing across his face, indecision foremost. He let out a long breath. "This is probably an incredibly stupid idea. However, I do know the concert is tonight. Maybe you and Yvette could go around there. Ask around and try to enjoy yourselves."

"Huh?" Maxwell whipped around to fully face Lex, flabbergasted. Was he nuts? "Why? You warned me about that being a bad idea."

Lex shook his head. "It is, yet it isn't. If you and Yvette go without me, they won't be as likely to notice you. They would recognize me in a heartbeat, but you?" Lex shook his head. "Even with the pictures floating around, with so many people, you would just mix with the crowd, especially with Yvette with you. Plus, the concert isn't until later. You can decide in the next few hours. Tickets are more than likely sold out, but you can probably watch from outside on the television screens. I do know for some of the major concerts they do that."

Maxwell pursed his lips, debating before slowly nodding. "Alright, yeah. I can do that."

"If you can't find anything, just try to enjoy yourself, alright?"

Maxwell bit his lip, but didn't respond. Could he enjoy himself? He might as well try, like Lex said.

"Meanwhile. I'm going to get us a vehicle and try some of the bars. Hopefully, I can find something before they get too rowdy."

Lex's brow furrowed in annoyance and Maxwell could only imagine. Those places seemed out of his league and not to his taste. Though, the one time he did have alcohol, he was more than a little talkative and touchy so that could be part of it. Either way, he was staying far away from those places for now.

Chapter Thirty-Nine

Maxwell peered up at the stadium in awe. Lights flashed as night fell around them. Streams of people, their voices echoing off the street, headed toward the open glass doorways. More out of curiosity than anything, he crept up to the desk. Yvette moved beside him, shifting closer so as not to lose him in the crowd, or so he suspected with how tightly she was gripping him. The line moved along until they arrived at the window where there was a harried teller. Maxwell gave her a faint smile. "Sorry, ma'am, but I was wondering if there are any tickets left?"

She gave him a despondent expression as she spoke, words said in a way that indicated some regularity. "The Rose Thornfield concert has been sold out for weeks. I'm sorry, kid."

"It's fine. Thank you."

He nodded and she sent him a tired, if appreciative smile. Right before he left, he paused and quickly faced her once more.

"Oh, quick question. Do you know where I can find someone named Doctor Girshwin around here?"

He heard someone stiffen behind him, but the woman just shrugged. "Sorry, kid, can't tell you. I'm not from around here, I travel with the band." She lightly knocked on the window. "It's a good gig for someone from the outer community, that's for sure."

"Right, thanks."

He nodded and hurried away, deciding to follow Lex's advice and watch from the TVs set up around the outside of the building. There were others like himself standing around. Some were sitting on the back of pick-up trucks, others setting up chairs and such. He chuckled. It was quite amusing to watch.

The screens hung high above, huge and clear. He could see a stage with flashing lights on it and could faintly hear instrumental music. A pre-concert event maybe? It wouldn't be far-fetched.

"Hey, kid."

Maxwell jumped and turned as an older man walked over, scrutinizing him quietly. He was wearing a bony-jawed mask. Maxwell took a step back as Yvette clung to his leg, peeking around his hip. "Yeah?" he asked, feeling his voice pitch a little from his surprise.

The man seemed to find his reaction amusing. "So, you searching for Ma'am Girshwin?"

Maxwell blinked before nodding.

"I can't say much, but I know some of my boys might know. Unfortunately, we're all pre-occupied with this here concert. You won't get any of them talking. Tomorrow, however, you might have better luck. Anyway, enjoy the concert, lad. It's sure to be a good one."

With that, he waved and walked away. Maxwell gulped, feeling sweat trail down his neck. That was just out and out creepy as hell. He shook himself and peered back up toward the concert as a countdown started to sound out. Might as well enjoy it, right?

The countdown finished and, with a shout, the stage blossomed with smoke. It cleared away just as quickly in time for a beautiful woman with bright red hair to appear. She was dressed modestly, but it fit her well.

"Hello, everybody! Thank you for coming," she called out into the microphone, her voice faintly echoing out here, the TVs amplifying the sound. Maxwell grimaced as a loud cheer erupted around him.

"...my first song!" Whatever she said before had been drowned out by the ringing in his ears. He winced, massaging his ears as Yvette swayed beside him, seeming a little dizzy from the sound. He chuckled, only to pause as a powerful string erupted from the sound systems, followed by a lovely voice. He smiled faintly. The woman, Rose, he reminded himself, did have a very pleasant voice. Pushing what the man said earlier to the back of his mind, he watched in awe and amusement. He could feel the energy of the crowd as the concert progressed and he found himself beginning to enjoy himself just a little. Yvette seemed to as well, if her cheering along with everyone else was any indication.

It probably would have continued that way, if there wasn't the sharp sound of shattering glass and the distinctly familiar sound of gunshots. Screams cut through the air as Maxwell whipped around. A group of about six to eight men walked calmly forward. They wielded what were probably high-caliber guns. One man was carrying something strange, similar to a long tube. He took a knee and aimed for the entranceway. Maxwell didn't stick around to find out what happened next. Sweeping Yvette up into his arms, he made a dash away from the ruckus, along with everyone else who finally came to their senses.

He heard a click, followed by a loud whooshing sound. Seconds later, an explosion rang out, buffering him, though they were so far away. He stumbled, but tried hard to keep his footing, as he smacked shoulders with another person. Yvette clawed into his sweatshirt, shaking violently.

"Glory to America. Home of the free." A cry echoed over the crowd and Maxwell grimaced. What the hell?

"Any who consider events like these good for America are just being swallowed in lies. We, the Resistance, will set you free."

Maxwell highly doubted that was the best way to set people free, but didn't have much time to think of it. He was grateful that he wasn't stuck inside the location like so many others. He briefly glanced over his shoulder as fire blossomed up from the shattered glass front as the men surged inward. Another man, the one he met before, stood off to one side with a megaphone, counteracting the gun that was held at his side. "Enthrope and all her agents are just using you. None of this is for your good, your pleasure. It is only being used to fuel the divide between rich and poor."

Maxwell shook his head, hurrying around a corner, away from the fleeing traffic. He leaned against the wall for a moment to catch his breath, placing Yvette down since she was getting heavy. She grabbed onto his side, wrapping her tiny arms around his leg with a tight grip. He briefly noted the movement and her shaking, but his mind drifted to other things. The Resistance? Was that really who they were? He hoped to God that wasn't the case, but at the same time, it wasn't far-fetched. They burned an entire community to the ground, but that was the gated community. This was the outer community, so...

Were they just rioting to riot?

He heard screams and carefully peered around the corner, wrapping one arm around Yvette's shoulder, trying to keep her as calm as possible. The entrance area was practically empty except for those hit originally. He made sure not to look down as his attention shifted to the TVs. There was an uproar going on inside the stadium. Rose was being hustled off stage, though it seemed as if she was struggling to reach the crowd, a conflicted expression on her face. He recognized the ones hurrying her away as those from Enthrope. Still, what was all that about? What was the point?

It hurt more of their own people than anything.

He grimaced as he noticed the teller from earlier, slumped over the desk, glass sparkling off the interior approximately where she'd been sitting. Trying not to upheave his entire stomach, he turned and hurried away.

He hoped Lex had better luck than he did.

Yvette's grip tightened and he winced, pulling her closer. "Sorry," he muttered quietly, his heart aching.

He hadn't been able to do anything this time around, plus, he didn't understand. Why did this happen? He would have to talk with Madeline. She had to tell him what that was about. That it wasn't actually the Resistance.

Because if it was, he wasn't sure he would be able to look at her the same again.

~ * ~

Karina's palm pressed harshly against the window pane as they passed a crook in the road, slowly climbing up the gigantic structures of rock and stone before them. The sheer size of the mountains startled and amazed her more than anything. The peaks spearing into the clouds as wind whistled through the valley, she could only guess was up ahead as they took another winding turn. Water glistened far below as trees swayed in the breeze. It was absolutely beautiful.

She heard a faint chuckle, but decided to ignore Finnagen in favor of quickly rolling the window down and popping her head out far enough to see ahead without the glass. After a good night's sleep and leaving early this morning, she was able to appreciate this environment even more. The wind whipped at her hair as a large grin flew onto her face. She heard a squawk as birds took off into flight, gliding over the water in the distance. Another turn led them farther up the mountain. Exhilaration pumped through her veins. This was what she'd always wanted. These views, these sort of locations. The air was fresh, though it was still a little on the warmer side, and the sun was high in the sky, cresting above the clouds that adorned the mountain peaks.

"Hey. You might want to get back inside."

Karina peered over her shoulder as Finnagen, face beet red as his gaze flickered from her back to her face, said, "It's not exactly safe to be leaning out like that, even if the roads are empty due to how early it is."

She rolled her eyes, but pulled herself back in, rolling up the window so that only a little bit of wind pushed through. "Fine, fine. I was done anyway."

She was definitely lying, she could watch this scenery all day, but she figured she might as well assuage Finnagen's worry. She wasn't in the mood for him to get sick again because he was worried about her.

Finnagen clicked his tongue, fingers tapping erratically at the wheel as he took yet another turn, sticking close to the line so that he wasn't near the railing. For a split second, his hand stilled and he grimaced before it disappeared just as quickly. She frowned. Was he not fully over the cold? He was only out of it for a day. Did it take longer than that to recover? Probably. Honestly, she was starting to wonder why she agreed to have him come. He has been sick almost the whole time and it was somewhat annoying. She pushed away the thought. He wasn't used to being outside the gated community. She shouldn't be surprised.

She peered out over the landscape. As she watched, her amusement and joy died. Maxwell probably already saw all of this. What had he thought? Was he able to enjoy it, or was he too worried about her? She would have to bring him back through here so he could see it with her. That way, they could both enjoy it. It would be one way to make amends, right?

"We should be passing through the Rockies in a few hours. When we get through, I'm actually going to have you drive."

"Huh?" Karina perked up, leaning over, palm pressed firmly against the middle panel. "Really? I can drive?" Her enthusiasm returned tenfold, along with amusement as he jerked back, almost hitting his head to the window. The car swerved for a second before straightening.

"Geez," he yelped, correcting his process before reverting his attention back to her. "Yeah, once we get through here, it's practically straight land and the best time for you to learn. I'll be honest, I'm getting a little si...tired of driving." He grinned sheepishly. "Plus, you seem to be interested, so..."

"Of course." She almost sang the words in her excitement, leaning back to relax. "It seems like fun and it would make getting around a heck of a lot easier. I doubt Maxwell would be interested, so..." She felt her mood sour at the thought and quickly pushed it away. "I've been kind of watching anyway. So, it shouldn't take too long to figure out."

"Nah, it's actually pretty easy." He waved, slowly pulling the wheel to the left, giving them a gradual turn. "This car handles really well. As long as you stay aware of your surroundings and know generally where the gas and brake are, you have the basics. Though literally just the basics, you would fail a driving test with just that, but..." he cut off, probably spotting Karina's expression.

After all, she couldn't stop the deadpan from crossing her face at the idiocy. "Why would I be taking a driving exam when I'm trying to NOT be seen by those types of people?"

"Uh, I don't..." he trailed off before gulping and facing ahead. "Anyway, so yeah. I'll tell you more when we get through here. For now, just sit back and relax, 'kay?"

She smiled, nodding. "Alright. Sounds good." She leaned back, turning once more to examine the scenery. She would be entertained for quite a while anyway.

~ * ~

Lex let out a breath as he returned to the hotel room, relieved at least that he found a vehicle. However, that was where the relief ended. The city had been in a panic, but he wasn't sure what it was until one of the stations in the bar he was in switched to the local news. He was quick to call Maxwell, only to hear that, though a little traumatized, both of them were fine. After making sure they returned to the hotel safely, he continued his search. Yet, nothing.

He did get a lot of commentary about the event though, and it was quite divisive.

"Good riddance. The Resistance did right to take down that company of sell-outs."

"How could someone do something like that? Was it really the Resistance? Seems a little extreme."

"HURRAH. Sucker punch that bitch. She and all those who support her are scum."

"Oh, I hope people were able to escape. Will the Resistance actually get punished for this? Probably not. Dammit, where is the police brigade when you need it."

"Someone's going to get arrested."

Lex shook his head. Whether the ramblings had been because of drunken stupor or shock he wasn't sure. He grimaced. What happened was terrible either way and he knew Maxwell was only taking it worse because of everything else going on. Poor kid.

He let out a sigh, looking up at the gleaming sun. It was morning and he'd been out all night, trying to find information.

Maxwell mentioned something about talking with a person with a bone-jaw mask. Maybe he would have to dig into that. He let out a yawn and walked to the end of the street. Off to one side, he saw a group of guys talking and laughing, beer cans clinking together with distinctive masks on their faces.

He hesitated for the briefest of moments. He was easily recognizable right now, but mostly by Enthrope. These thugs already looked drunk off their asses. He should be alright. Hopefully, if luck was actually on his side for once, they wouldn't recognize him.

Well then, worth a shot.

Chapter Forty

Finnagen grimaced, relieved when they finally got back on the straight-away. His GPS said they were only about a day's worth of travel away from their location and most of the roads seemed fairly straight-forward. Plus, as he told her earlier, he was pretty tired of driving. The headache, much to his chagrin, hadn't gone away. It still hung there, like a guillotine. Yikes, deadly thought. He chuckled morosely as he pulled to the side of the road. Wasn't he supposed to call someone when they got closer? "So, ready to learn?"

She nodded, almost childlike in her enthusiasm. It was really cute. As in, really, really cute. He returned her smile as he shifted the car into park and got out. A small part of him wondered about the fact that she didn't have a driver's license. What if they were pulled over? He wasn't sure he could convince the cops that he was training her when he was really only a little older. Maybe they would be alright? His thought was silenced, slamming to a halt as Karina scrambled out, pressing into his side to peer in. He gulped and gestured for her to get in. She obliged, slipping into the seat and scanning over the different panels and levers. He pointed out each, one after another, before explaining what they did. She nodded along, fingers tracing over each thing.

Once he was sure she got everything, he slid into the other seat and directed her on how to shift it into gear. Her fingers twitched as she gulped, seemingly nervous. Her foot was firmly on the brake as she slowly pulled the lever into drive. Both hands clasped around the wheel and she peered over to him.

He smiled, feeling warm that he was able to help her with this. "Now, gently release your foot from the brake. Yep, just like that. Put on the left blinker to show you're going back into traffic. Alright, now gently press down on the gas..."

He was cut off as the car lurched forward and Karina yelped. The car rolled a bit as she let out a breath before hissing, annoyed. He watched her, surprised as she peered through the windows before nodding to herself and pushing forward once more. This time, the car didn't lurch. It picked up speed as she slowly turned the wheel. He could feel his lips turning upward, hearing her whoop of joy as they finally pulled into the lane and were off. He winced, as he leaned back, keeping half his attention on what she was doing, the other half distracted by the growing throbbing in his skull. While she was a bit jerky in her movements at first and, while she was definitely taking it slower than he had, she got the hang of the car pretty quickly. Still, he knew he needed to stay awake, watch her. Yet, no matter how much he struggled to keep his eyes open, they just kept sliding right back shut.

He gritted his teeth, rubbing his temple to keep himself awake. He couldn't fully sleep now, even if a bit more sleep would help him get rid of this damn headache. Karina was still learning. He focused on continuing to watch her. Every so often, he would point out when she could move over or when she should slow down. He laughed when she accidentally hit the gas too hard while in the slow lane and ended up speeding past a car or two with a yelp. She glared at him, but managed to slow down at a reasonable rate. They continued this way until a little after lunch where he carefully guided her off the closest turn-off. She let out a breath and grinned as they pulled into a parking lot. She zipped through, pulling straight into a parking spot and practically slamming it into park.

He chuckled, yet sent her an expression that he knew was filled with warmth. "Nice job for your first time. How was it?"

She sat there for a moment. Indecision settled over her face before she smiled back. "Not bad, actually. A bit nerve-wracking, but fun. It is a bit difficult keeping attention on the road though, there are so many places to watch out for. Still, I'm starved. Let's get something to eat."

"Can't argue with that." He slipped out of the door, glancing briefly at the way she parked. He would have to teach her to park before they left. She'd done a great job taking up two spots. She seemed to notice where he was looking and blushed. Her cheeks glowed red as she hurried toward the restaurant.

He followed after and winced, a sharp pain just like before shooting through his head. Damn this headache. Maybe he should grab an Advil while they were there. It would probably help, at least a little. His head swam for a moment and he quickly shook it off, catching up to Karina. She watched him with a bright grin, blush gone. "Thanks for showing me, by the way. What are you in the mood for?"

"Something simple," he admitted, his stomach twisting uncomfortably.

He shook his head, fingers twitching. What was wrong? Wasn't he recovered? It was only a cold, after all. Karina would have reacted more if it was the Epidemic.

Unless...did she know the symptoms? Damn, he shouldn't ask, but he never got around to picking up the newest phone while he was still home. His old thing didn't have internet connection. Though, he figured it would probably be pretty crappy out here even if it did, considering it was a gated community thing. Deciding just to deal with it instead of ignoring it, he turned to face Karina. "Hey, uh, Karina. Don't mean to bother you, but quick question. Do you know what the symptoms are for the Epidemic?"

She stiffened and slowly turned to face him, her smile fading. "Why? Are you not feeling well?"

"Oh, no, I'm fine." He forced a smile on his face as another shot of pain slammed through his head. "I'm just curious is all. Let's not worry about that. We should probably eat first. No point talking on an empty stomach."

She nodded, but he could tell she was no longer feeling as relaxed, or as comfortable. She kept eyeing him nervously and he couldn't blame her. Stupid, why had he brought it up? He knew he should have listened to his gut instinct. Lunch, as a result, was incredibly awkward, and he was glad when they left and were getting situated in the car again.

"Hey, I was going to mention, next time you park, take your time. There's no rush to get into a parking space," he made sure to point out, resting his head on the cool glass. "That should help you park straight."

She only nodded, sending him concerned expressions as she carefully pulled out of the parking lot, taking her time like he suggested. He let out a breath. "I'm just going to take a nap. Wake me if you need anything, okay?" he muttered, the food sitting heavy in his stomach. The warmth of the sun made him feel drowsy and, this time, he decided not to fight it. Maybe he was just still tired, yeah, that was it.

If he got more sleep, he would feel better, then he could...could...

His mind trailed off, as a shiver trailed up his spine, which he quickly suppressed. Huh, was it really that cold? Maybe he should ask her to turn down the air conditioner. It was on, right?

Maybe?

The sun felt so warm and the glass was cool.

Huh...

Tingling, he felt tingling pulling its way through his body, flitting between veins. Wait, that's not supposed to happen. Was everything supposed to feel this fuzzy?

Why am I not thinking right...straight? Was it straight or...?

Sleep. Yes. I could do that.

Huh, wonder if Karina would be alright.

She was so cute when she blushed.

What did she think when I did?

Was I blushing now?

My head hurts.

Sleep...

~ * ~

Karina's heart beat strongly as she continued down the highway. The sound rang exceedingly loud in her ears. The traffic was getting a bit busier and she was still incredibly nervous. She let out a breath, trying to relax. She had this. She'd gotten a feel for it earlier. She briefly glanced sidelong toward Finnagen, noting he was fast asleep. She felt a frown cross her lips. He was supposed to be paying attention. Sure, she was a fast learner, but not that fast. She clicked her tongue, noting how his head was leaning against the glass pane, eyelids fluttering and face red. He had somehow pushed back as much as possible into the seat.

The annoyance faded as she bit her lip, noting a shiver tremble through his body. His lips contorted into a grimace. She snapped her attention back to the road. He was just tired, maybe it was just a nightmare? Yeah, who hopes that someone is having a nightmare?

She tapped her finger against the steering wheel as she sped forward. The sun obscured her vision in exceedingly awkward angles, making it difficult to spot the approaching signs. She was still a hundred miles out from Sacramento, but at least she was closer.

Though she could feel herself pulling back on the gas, slowing down inch by inch. Was she ready to see Maxwell again? She was the one in control right now. She could turn them around or stop for the day or...

She shook her head, pressing back down on the gas to pick up speed once more. No, she wasn't going to keep running. Didn't mean she was going to rush into it either.

She would call them when she was ready, and when they were a bit closer.

She heard a grunt and peered over as Finnagen shifted in his seat, causing his head to slip from the window. He jerked awake. His gaze flitted to the sign and he seemed to stare at it for a long time before turning to her. "You doing okay?" he muttered, head falling against the back of the seat again. He seemed to want to fall asleep once more.

"Yeah, I'm going to have to stop to get gas soon, but..."

He nodded, mouth firmly closed tight. His fingers were twitching against his thigh in a way that made her worry spike. His breath seemed a little uneven again. Was he still sick? Was he getting sick again?

She reached for his head, only to be slapped away as Finnagen shifted again, cheek pushed against the glass. "I'm fine," he muttered. "I'll be fine."

Alarms rang through her head and she jerked the wheel, speeding toward the nearest exit, outright ignoring the blaring of horns in her ears. She didn't care, she was focused on the exit. She screeched down the ramp and whipped into the nearest parking lot before quickly shifting the car into park. She unclipped the seatbelt and pushed herself over the center console and, against Finnagen's weak protests, touched his head, or at least tried. She could feel the heat brush her fingers before she hit the skin. His breath hitched and, now that she was scrutinizing him, his eyes were blurry and tired. He was shaking badly.

She felt his skin against her fingers for a moment as he pushed into her palm, letting out a sigh before he seemed to realize what he did. Yet, he didn't move.

She jerked back, stumbling out of the car and wildly scanning the area. Was there a doctor around here? Please, by God, she hoped it was just a fever from the stress of being outside. She fumbled with her phone, pulling it out before stopping dead in her tracks. Her options were limited. She didn't know the area. How would she know?

She heard movement and spun around to see the passenger side door push open. Finnagen slipped out, leaning heavily against the car. His gaze met hers and he grinned sheepishly. "Really, I'm fine. I just need to sleep."

"Are you kidding?" she snapped, stomping up to him and watching as the grin faded from his lips. "You. Are. Sick."

He pursed his lips, shaking, though she had a feeling that was more from fear than anything. "It's got to be just the remainder of the cold, right? Just a bit of fever from a lingering cold." He lurched forward and grasped her arms tightly, causing her to stiffen as he bowed his head. "I can't... I've only been out here for a few days, why would it be anything else. Right? Karina? Please." She could hear a faint noise and froze.

She slowly tilted her head down to see his face. He wasn't crying, no, but he definitely appeared like he wanted to.

"Please just let me continue to believe that it's just a cold. I'm fine."

She bit her lip hard, feeling her teeth almost pierce the skin. "I..."

He shook his head and pulled back, arms dropping to his side. "How about this? Worry about me after you meet up with your brother, alright? I should be recovered by then. Okay?" He smiled weakly. "I mean," he gulped, shaking as he slowly curled his trembling fingers into fists. "It's just a cold, right?" His words were firm and pleading.

She wanted to tell him, no, it could very easily be something else. Heck, the epidemic itself, but she found she couldn't. She didn't want to believe it and neither, it seemed, did he. She let out a breath and nodded, forcing a faint smile on her face. "Right. Right, yeah." Her smile fell as she glared at him. "But as soon as we get there, we are getting you to a doctor, alright?"

He grinned and slowly walked back to the car. The short distance seemed to drag at him as he slumped into the seat.

She wanted to yell, to tell him he was being stupid, but she felt like she could understand. Understand the desire to ignore it. After all, it was simply a cold, right? Nothing more.

Chapter Forty-One

Caym heard a knock on his door before it opened. He didn't respond, just continued working on the reports in front of him, recognizing the footsteps with ease. "Any news?"

"We have confirmed sightings."

Caym attention snapped up to Machael, whose face was impassive. "And?"

"There was a riot in Sacramento. Some of our men were searching for the culprits and spotted Sir Lex disappearing into a hotel. They notified us right away, but are too busy with the recent attack to set up a perimeter."

Caym pushed his pen into his holder, thoughts racing. So, Leo was in Sacramento? Why was he all the way out west? He turned toward Machael, noting the man's expression shift to one of worry as Caym spoke. "Oh? Then let's make sure we have some reinforcements, right?" He felt a grin twitch at his lips. "We can't have him escaping again. Make sure the squads are aware of the situation. We have a man-hunt on our hands, after all."

"Sir." Machael paused before nodding, keeping it bowed down. "Any restrictions?"

Caym turned away from Machael, one leg crossing over the other. "Bring little Leo back by any means necessary. If you have to quarantine the damn city, then do it. I don't care. I'm tired of waiting. This is the first definitive thing we've had in over a week, don't waste it."

He heard shuffling before the door clanged shut, indicative of Machael's departure. Caym's fingers clasped tighter as he stared at a picture, one he'd managed to scrounge up of the time when Leo was still at home. Leo was talking with those twins, smiling faintly. He'd grown up but... Caym's eyes narrowed as he spotted the weariness and age, the damage this place did to him. Caym had been patient, but his patience was wearing thin. He knew it would take some time to obtain the necessary people, but...whatever it took, he would get his brother, if not there, then he would sweep the damn country.

It wouldn't be difficult to pull in the military, the skirmishes on the outside were dismal. After all, which idiotic country would try to invade another that had such a devastating illness destroying everyone but the best?

No, he could use that manpower, but not yet.

He would give his sibling one last chance, then he was bringing him home, one way or another.

~ * ~

Madeline felt her heart tremble as she kept firm in front of her mother. Her mother was smiling widely, humming. "So, those twins are in Sacramento? After they escaped Priscel that first time, it's good to know they managed to track them down. Oh, how beneficial." She turned and Madeline did everything to stop the wince as her mother's stormy expression met hers. "Organize the search party, we won't have much time to acquire those twins."

"And the Richie?" Madeline carefully spoke up, keeping her voice neutral as she could feel herself internally shaking with emotions. Priscel and Huxley, even after losing them, managed to track them down again because of those extremists.

Her mother tilted her head up, looking down at her. "What do you think, Madeline? That is up to you, our main goal is those twins. We acquire them, we won't have to worry. The researchers have collected enough data. We are not going to waste it."

Madeline bowed her head and hurried away. As soon as she was out of her mother's presence, she raced through the hallways, heart hammering in her chest and tears welling up, just barely refraining from trailing down her cheek. Maxwell saw that, didn't he? Saw the destruction of the concert. Would he blame them? Blame her? They destroyed so many lives and, if it was a few months ago, she wouldn't have cared. It was for a good cause, at least, that is the thing she would have told herself. Now it pierced at her heart.

In no time, she was back in Veronica's room. The woman slowly lifted her head. She was still pale and, much to Madeline's consternation, she wasn't doing any better. Her skin was taut, her eyes sunken. She smiled softly before spotting Madeline's expression. She gently gestured and Madeline hurried over. "I..." Madeline stopped, slowly sitting down in the seat placed next to her bed. "I don't know." She sighed.

"It's fine, you can tell me as soon as you feel up to it."

Madeline hesitated for only a second. "Mother. She found where Maxwell is. She's setting up a search party right now but it's not just that. One of the radical groups attacked and..."

She found she couldn't continue, but she didn't seem to need to. It was as if Veronica understood. For a split second, panic flashed across the woman's face before she slowly let out a calming breath. She gently reached out toward Madeline, who held on tightly.

"Was Karina with him?"

Madeline paused and shook her head, noting the flash of worry and fear before the woman continued, "Alright, they will be alright. But there is something else your worried about, isn't there?" Madeline could feel the way the woman examined her, searching her from head to toe before squeezing, just enough to be a reassurance. "You're scared."

Madeline gulped and could feel her nails digging into her palm. This woman...even her mother hadn't noticed. True, she hid it from her mother, hid her emotions for the last few weeks. She hadn't realized the amount of pressure her mother pushed onto her, however, until she took a distant stance and observed it.

Her mind flitted to Maxwell, his warm smile, his soft laugh. She missed it, but she was afraid. Would he glare at her? Turn his back to her? She was part of an organization that instigated riots and killed. While Richies, she might not care about, that didn't mean she hadn't come to realize the importance of the loss of life. Did she need to do anything to prove to him that she wasn't like her mother or the rest?

"So, this is where you are. I should have guessed."

Madeline stiffened as the grasp on her hand tightened for a moment before letting go. She stood and turned to see one of her mother's followers. She wasn't sure about the woman's name and, at this point, she wasn't sure if she wanted to bother to know. "Shouldn't you be setting up a search party instead of whiling away time with this woman?"

Madeline turned her gaze back to Veronica, finally allowing herself to see the wires connecting the woman to different computers, only a few of which were actually helping her. Would this be Maxwell? Karina? Would they strap them down and just take IV after IV? Test after test?

"Go," Veronica said, a faint smile on her face. "You know what you need to do, right?"

Madeline would admit that, at first, she was completely confused by the statement. However, once she thought about it, that confusion flipped to surprise, followed by a faint smile crossing her face as she realized the decision she would have to make. "Yes. Thank you."

She turned to one of the people she probably once called a co-worker, back stiff and smile firmly in place. "Right, thank you for reminding me. I needed to center my thoughts."

The woman examined her before turning, obviously not noticing the facade that she threw up. After all, Madeline was a master at hiding. She wasn't going to fail now. Not when Maxwell's and Karina's freedom were at stake.

No, she knew the exact thing she had to do, just like Veronica said. Her decision, her choice was to make sure her mother NEVER got Maxwell or Karina.

She would find a way to apologize to Maxwell someday. She just had to hold to that idea firmly.

After all, it was the only thing she had left to hold onto, that flimsy hope.

Chapter Forty-Two

Maxwell curled up on the bed, Yvette pushing into his side in a hug, face buried in his clothes. The sounds from outside weren't really helping his nerves either. It seemed that, after the initial attack on the concert hall, things escalated. He wouldn't be surprised if Enthrope was roaming the streets as well. It had taken a while to get back to the hotel with everyone running around, but they finally made it around midnight. He'd tried to sleep, but he'd found himself unable to as the sun rolled into the sky. After all, not only was everything a mess, Lex still hadn't come back and he was starting to get deeply worried for his oldest friend.

He heard a click and jerked around to face the doorway as it swung open and shut again. Lex stood in the doorway, an anxious expression on his face and his skin pale as he stepped forward and took a seat.

"Well, that was an endeavor," he spoke up, his voice holding the faintest of tremors that Maxwell only recognized from having known the man for so long.

Maxwell felt Yvette shift and pull away, hurrying up to Lex. "Are you okay?" she asked, body pushing up against his knee, face in his. "You were gone for a long time."

Lex seemed to relax, a faint smile trailing on his lips as he ruffled Yvette's hair. "I'm fine, thank you." His attention flipped to Maxwell, who stiffened at the firmness he was practically exuding. "Actually, better than fine."

Maxwell scrambled off the bed. "Wait, did you find the information?"

"Did I find out where she is? Yes," he said as he reached into his pocket and pulled out a slip of paper. "Wasn't easy, that's for sure, but that information you gave me definitely helped. Turns out they are extremists in the Resistance and don't completely conform to the Resistance we met earlier." He waved. "Though they are part of the same group. The guy I talked with was pretty loose-lipped after a few drinks, though I'm a little worried about his buddy who'd arrived around the time I left." He grimaced before shrugging. "Still, they completely oppose all aspects of Government relations, including anyone who associates with Richies. Good thing I'm not, right?" Lex grinned as Maxwell gave him a glare, pulling the paper from his hand and reading it over. He didn't recognize the location, but he figured Lex would know.

"So, what now?"

Lex peered out the window, wincing. "We should try to call your sister now that we have a location. However, considering the uncertainty of the situation at hand, I will admit I am somewhat hesitant to say anything quite yet." He paused and shook his head. "Though, ultimately, I guess I'll leave that up to you. Either way, we wait until evening. We both need some rest, from the look of things, and the city is in upheaval. As much as I hate the idea of sitting around, more activity will be accomplished in the evening than in the middle of the day." He glanced down at Yvette. "You'll have to stay with us just a little longer, okay?"

"Okay." Yvette nodded, letting out a yawn as she curled against Maxwell. "But then... after that?"

Maxwell found his mind coming to a halt realizing that he wasn't quite sure how to respond to Yvette. He turned to Lex who seemed to be deep in thought. "Well, you can't stay with us, so—"

"But I want to stay with you." Yvette suddenly sat up, fear on her face. "I don't want to be alone."

"You won't," Lex interrupted. "We'll find someone to keep you safe. You can't keep traveling with us—"

"But I like traveling with you." She frowned. "People can be scary, but you're nice. I don't want to leave. Plus, I mean, I can be helpful, right?"

Lex let out a breath, glancing toward Maxwell before turning back to Yvette. He reached forward hesitantly before ruffling her hair. "Fine. For now."

Yvette furrowed her brow but seemed to accept the words, once more relaxing against Maxwell's side.

Maxwell glanced down toward Yvette before turning his attention to the paper Lex had shown. He slowly thought over Lex's words before reaching into his pocket. He hesitated only for a brief moment before pulling out his phone.

"So, you decided to call?"

Maxwell tilted his head up just enough to catch Lex's gaze before returning his attention back to the phone. Was that what he wanted to do? No.

If he was honest, he didn't want to talk with her, not right now. His emotions were in utter turmoil and he was afraid he might make their already rocky relationship worse. He gently placed the phone in his lap. His thoughts raced. He could feel disappointment, anger, frustration, sadness, even hints of despair eating away at him, just like it had been for the past few days...no, weeks. All the emotions were vying for his attention, demanding it. He knew he needed to tell her not to come here, but...

As much as he needed to warn her, he wanted to see her and talk to her face to face.

"Can I have you do it?" The words came out soft, even to his own ears, and almost listless.

After a long moment, he heard a sigh before Lex pulled the phone and paper out of his sight. He heard a click and then faint tapping. He couldn't help but to assuage his curiosity, returning his attention to his friend just as Lex hit the send button. He blinked before biting his lip. Why hadn't he thought of that? Dammit, brain.

"Why don't you get some sleep. I'll wake you when we need to leave, you're not thinking straight."

Maxwell went to argue, but he realized he really couldn't, not right now. So, with a sigh, he slipped into bed and curled onto his side. At this point, he was almost afraid to see his sister, because he was almost afraid of the way he would react if, no, when he saw her again.

Chapter Forty-Three

Karina remembered hearing the text go off in her pocket, could feel it vibrate against her leg, but she couldn't reach down for it, and, up until a few minutes ago, as the sun descended into early afternoon and she was no longer putting all of her attention on trying not to crash, she remembered it. She was going to have to find a place to stop soon. They'd stopped around lunch to grab food and fuel. Had she gotten the text around then? Before that? She couldn't remember. Maybe she had, it was hard to tell with her thoughts flitting to Finnagen and learning to drive which was one part exhilarating and one part petrifying. Finnagen directed her through fueling, too tired to move from his seat. Though she had a feeling both of them didn't think that it was just tiredness.

She turned toward Finnagen again, unable to keep her eyes away for a reason she wished wasn't the case.

His breaths had only gotten worse as the day progressed, sweat trailing down his face and soaking his shirt. He seemed both pale and flushed, which was something she hadn't thought was possible. He could barely seem to move.

She returned her focus and sighed with relief as she noticed a rest stop. It was a little after three thirty so not a bad time for a break. Pulling in, she parked and let out a breath, digging into her pocket. As great as it was to have the freedom to drive, she was enjoying it a lot less than she thought she would.

Though she figured she knew why.

She glanced down, pulling out the phone that she had held off looking at for a while. She noticed the text was from Maxwell. Damn, had she really ignored it earlier? Was she that distracted? Probably, plus there was the whole fact that she wasn't sure if she really wanted to talk with him... She flipped it open and stared.

Hello, Karina, this is Lex. We came into a bit of a situation and so can't call you. All of us are fine, though Maxwell is a bit out of it. Anyway, because of that, we'll have to change locations. I'll leave the address here. We'll rendezvous there. I do hope you are having better luck on your end and, really, your brother misses you greatly, so you better not do anything idiotic. I'll talk with you soon if anything else comes up.

Situation? She pursed her lips.

"Everything okay?" Finnagen muttered, garnering her attention. She nodded and he smiled faintly. "Alright. How far do we have to go?" He carefully pushed himself forward, glancing at the GPS.

"Actually, I was given a new location to meet them in. Do you know this place?" She showed him the location name, something she didn't recognize and he frowned before shrugging.

"No, but I can input it easy enough." He reached over and slowly transferred the information into the GPS. In no time, they had everything up and working. Karina examined everything noting it wasn't too bad, a couple hours away. She let out a breath of relief.

Only for that breath to cut itself short, a metaphorical string snapping at her side. A second later, she felt a body fall onto her. She jumped, shoving the slumped body away. Only to still as Finnagen crumbled against the seat. He was hot, burning. His arms spasmed as she reached over the center council, berating herself for pushing him away. Only for panic to start thrumming through her as her brain finally, against her will, told her the exact thing she was trying to ignore.

Finnagen. The kind, gentle and energetic boy that had been helping her this whole time, that seemed so healthy only a few days ago had the epidemic. She scrambled out of her seat, bolting to the other side of the car. She opened the passenger door before glancing toward the back. She had to lay him down.

She opened the back door and, with trembling hands, managed to dig at the seatbelt holding him, hearing it click open. She tugged, fumbling as she tried to pull him out of his seat and out of the car toward the back. After some maneuvering and panicking at how heavy his unconscious weight was, she managed to lay him down flat in the back seat, whatever blankets and stuff she could find wrapping around him. He was gasping, as if unable to pull air in, and her thoughts flashed to Arik, Mitchell, even the woman on the street all those months ago. No!

He hadn't hit the third stage yet. He wouldn't hit the fourth, right? Right? She couldn't stop it, couldn't stop herself from remembering Lex's words from so long ago. "That stage is the stage that can last anywhere between a week to a year, some never move past that stage, though one or two have skipped that stage altogether."

"No," she shouted, trying to calm herself. No, it wasn't going to be like that. She wasn't going to allow that.

Was there anything she could do? She didn't have the cure, right? Not like Maxwell. She was helpless. Her thoughts flicked to Finnagen's parents and horror slashed through her. Oh god. His parents. She reached into his pockets and bag, finally finding the phone. She would apologize to him later. If there was a later. She flipped through the phone, noting it wasn't locked. She pressed the first one she could find, which seemed to be Finnagen's father. That might work. He did medicine, right?

She shuddered, trying to make sure Finnagen was comfortable as the phone rang over and over and over again. Over the past few days, the past week, the boy had grown on her and, of course, she only realized this as she watched him struggle for each breath. She bit her lip so hard, it broke skin, unable to stop the tears from pooling without her consent, especially as the phone clicked over into voicemail. She turned it off, not wanting to say anything. She couldn't just say that she caused their son's possible death. No, that wasn't an option.

She shook her head and, making sure he wouldn't roll by carefully strapping him in, she jumped into the front seat. Her gaze flitted toward the GPS.

That's where Maxwell would be, and that had to be where Mrs. Girshwin was as well.

If nothing else, then she would save Finnagen. She was NOT going to let the epidemic take him as well. So, with that thought in mind, she spun the wheel and peeled out of the rest stop, her mind focused on the task she needed to accomplish NOW. She would get to Mrs. Girshwin and then...then she would beg Maxwell to save him. After all, there were no other options.

Chapter Forty-Four

The hours passed and Maxwell found himself struggling to sleep. Finally, he gave up and sat up, looking out the window. It was late afternoon, the sun beginning to set, but that was fine, it meant it was time to leave. He could feel the sheet stirring and turned to see Yvette pull herself next to him, tugging the sheets with her as she rubbed her eyes. She yawned tiredly.

He smiled weakly. "Hey," he whispered, trying not to wake Lex, who was fast asleep.

Yvette yawned. "Hi," she mumbled. "Where are we going?"

"Oh, right. I never told you, did I?" Maxwell stared down at the sheets, mind drifting. "Well, you know the sickness?"

"Ah-huh." Yvette slowly nodded, blinking tiredly. "Momma told me, remember?"

"Yeah." Maxwell peered out the window, lost in thought. "We're going to meet someone who should be able to help. We know a way to cure the sickness and we want to do that."

"We?"

Maxwell found his thoughts coming to a halt. He'd said we, why? Lex didn't care too much one way or another, and in all honesty, had nothing to do with it. He'd said we including his sister. His twin.

She would want him to do it, but could he accomplish that without her there? He turned his attention to Lex, recalling the memory of giving Lex his blood. He'd had to donate almost a pint of blood to cure Lex. He couldn't do that, not for everyone. What options did he have? His lip trembled as he curled inward, the sunlight washing over everything in dull oranges and purples. Could he wait for Karina? Would she be able to help?

He felt something tugging on his sleeve and he slowly turned his head. Yvette was holding his sleeve tightly, concerned. "I'm sorry," she said softly. "You were sad and..."

He let out a breath. Right, this wasn't getting him anywhere. He heard a faint chime and jerked, turning as Lex grumbled and sat up, rubbing his eyes as he peered down at his phone. With a sigh, Lex swung his legs over the edge of the bed and stood. He gave him a searching glance before heading toward the bathroom. "It looks like you're up. Get ready, we're heading out."

Maxwell gripped the sheets for a moment before sliding out of bed. Right, he needed to stop. One thing at a time. He was getting overwhelmed again. He took another deep breath and smiled down at Yvette. "Ready to go?"

She seemed to debate with herself for the longest time until her lips pulled upward. "Un," she grunted out in delight.

He wished he could have some of that childish fortitude. He shook himself and got ready. Once Lex stepped out, he hurried in and got changed, cleaning up.

Not long after, they grabbed something to eat and left, hurrying down the street with bags on their shoulders and heading toward whatever vehicle Lex managed to grab. For a second, Maxwell thought Lex somehow managed to acquire the one they had, then he noted the slightly dulled shade of blue instead of whatever color the other one was. Well, he supposed another truck worked. He winced but slipped inside with Yvette. Lex swung in on the other side.

Things seemed to calm down a little, at least on this road. Though Maxwell was sure stuff was still happening in other parts of the city, closer to the concert hall, for instance. Shaking that morbid thought off, he gripped the door handle tightly as Lex pulled out and hurried down the lane.

The ride out of the city was nerve-wracking. The buildings soared up into the sky, blocking the remaining beams of the falling sun. The air was choked with smells and sounds that only added to his unease. Traffic wasn't moving in the slightest, more of a crawl than movement forward.

Maxwell caught something off to the side and gulped. An older woman was standing seductively on the corner, clothes practically nonexistent. He heard raucous laughter, even through the closed windows and locked doors and cars honking with abandon.

Lex cursed, causing him to jerk from his observations. He followed where his friend was looking and froze, eyes widening. Off to one side, he could see Enthrope cars hurrying around the traffic, only half of them had their sirens blaring. He curled inward as Lex pulled down his hat. "Shit." Lex deduced. "I might have misjudged."

"We'll be fine," Maxwell muttered more to himself than anything before turning toward Lex. "They shouldn't have completely blockaded the city yet, we might still be able to slip out."

Lex sat quietly, inching forward with the truck. He let out a sigh. "We'll just have to take it slow and hope for the best." He glanced sidelong toward Maxwell. "Just hold on to the door, kid, we're going to have to make sure they don't see us leave. After all, if that's the case, we'll be leading them right to Karina and the good doctor."

Maxwell grimaced and gripped tighter.

"Is something wrong?"

Maxwell jumped and turned toward Yvette before blinking. "Actually, Lex, would you be able to hide your face?"

"Without looking like some hoodlum?" Lex responded sardonically.

Maxwell rolled his eyes. "I was just thinking, if I keep my hood up and have Yvette do the talking. If anyone comes up, we might be able to slip through."

Lex hummed in thought. "Not foolproof, but if worse comes to worst?" He pulled at his hat, tugging it down a little more to cover most of his hair and forehead. He let out a sigh. "Let's hope it doesn't come to that." He paused before glancing toward Yvette. "Yvette, if any officers pull us to the side, play it cute, alright?"

Yvette blinked, confused before she seemed to realize what he was saying. "Oh. Just like when we were in the school?"

"Just like that, yeah." Lex's expression was a mix between a smile and a grimace. "Use your cuteness to distract them for us, would you?"

Yvette put a thumb up with a smile before glancing out the window, curious.

Maxwell hoped it wouldn't come down to that. Hopefully, they could get out before Enthrope completely closed things off.

With their luck, who knew.

He hung on to the idea that Enthrope was too busy with the remainders of the riots to bother with them. A pipe dream, but a dream nonetheless.

~ * ~

Everything hurt. Finnagen didn't know everything could hurt like this. His body throbbed and screamed at him. Lava pooled through his veins, making whatever heavy thing was draped over him feel cool. That wasn't right. It couldn't be right.

He just had a cold yesterday or was it two days ago? Three? It was so hard to tell. He let a groan slip through his lips as his head lolled to one side. The car, he could tell from the smell of the gas and the faint humming filling his ears, was moving along. Did something happen? Why was he lying down? He was sitting up earlier, right?

"We're almost there, only an hour or two, alright? Maxwell will be able to help. I promise."

Maxwell? Why would Maxwell be able to help? It was just a fever— cold— Oh, who was he kidding. He was trying so hard to deny it, terror filling his stomach and head with panic, not helping his twisting stomach and aching limbs. He couldn't have it already. Not the epidemic.

He couldn't stop himself from wondering. Was he already at a certain stage? He couldn't be affected, he just got out here. He promised that he would be alright, that he would make it home. He was from the gated community. They should have a better immune system, right? Right? Please...

He didn't realize there were tears trailing down his face until he turned his head and felt the wetness push into his cheek from the leather of the seat cushion. "Ka..." His voice was hoarse, no sound escaping except for wisps.

"You'll be fine. I'm— I'll get you somewhere safe. I won't let you die." Karina's voice was choked, and he could hear her sharp breathing. "I didn't think... There was no way. I thought there would be TIME."

He couldn't even chuckle, lips trembling as he tried to open his mouth.

"You've already done so much and I can't let it end like this. Not again. I don't care if I sound insane. You've become a friend to me, I can't let you die. Not like they did. I just can't."

A faint sound echoed around the car and Finnagen found his mouth closing, tired despair clinging to everything, his mind, his thoughts...friend. Of course, he was only a friend. He would be.

Was he going to die as simply someone who'd been foolish enough to chase a dream? He didn't want to die. He promised he would help Karina. He'd promised his siblings he'd be alright.

Help.

I don't want to die. Mom? Dad? Could he call them? He had his phone, right? His fingers twitched and trembled, but barely moved, doing nothing more than pooling at his side. He couldn't call them. He couldn't reach them.

He could feel the darkness tugging, sleep calling him and he was outright scared of it. If he fell back to sleep, would he wake up? So many people got struck with this and lived for days, weeks, months, some even years. Is he just not that lucky?

He could feel his fingers curling, trying to clutch at the blanket, but unable to grasp. Was he at the second stage? Third? He didn't know it would hurt this much. Yet hurting meant he was alive, so did he want it to STOP hurting? Or...

He didn't know, he honestly didn't know.

~ * ~

Karina choked as she heard a quiet sob from behind her, gargled as it was. She wasn't really paying full attention. Her gaze was firmly on the GPS and road. She might be new to driving, but that didn't mean a damn thing right then. She knew where the gas pedal was and she knew of a way to steer. In that moment, it was all she cared about. She also didn't much care when she flew past a familiar police brigade car. After all, hers was faster. She flashed past another car, speedometer higher than she ever saw it while Finnagen was driving. The GPS beeped, barely keeping up with her movement, the clock ticking down the mileage.

Would it be fast enough? Would Maxwell be there? She prayed to everything that he would, that someone would. She might not know much about the epidemic, but the speed in which Finnagen was being affected was terrifying. Would he skip the third like she thought or would he finally transition to the third and settle out long enough for her to DO something?

She heard a honk as she jerked the wheel, barely avoiding the car ahead of her and zipping between two cars on her right. At one point, there might have been sirens behind her, but they faded from her thoughts. Reckless driver or not, she was getting where she needed to go and that was all that mattered.

"Come on," she said.

Her heart had been pounding for way too long, draining her with worry and fear. She was past the point of terror and was more in a desperate tiredness. The sun hung low in the sky, disappearing as night came around and it finally started to clear up, traffic diminishing, both to her relief and worry. She'd tried to console Finnagen earlier when she heard him awaken, but she wasn't sure if he heard her. His voice, breathy as it was, sent a spasm through her heart and lungs.

No wonder so many people were terrified of this thing. If she didn't have the cure, if she didn't know about it. If Maxwell ever got affected. It would outright kill her. She thought she understood the desperation before. How many people would vie for their blood? Now, watching as someone she'd grown to respect and somewhat care about suffered through the very thing she'd heard about while she could do NOTHING, hurt a hell of a lot more than she thought possible.

Even IF she had the cure in her blood, did she have any way to give it him? For a brief, very brief moment, she thought of all the different ways she could inject her blood into him, as gruesome as some were... She quickly shook her head. That wasn't an option. Neither of the boys would forgive her if she did that.

She put on another burst of speed, hearing the car rattle around her as she kept her hand firmly on the wheel, zeroed ahead on the oncoming travel. She could only hope she would be able to make it in time.

Chapter Forty-Five

Maxwell almost cursed as they were flagged down by the nearby police brigade officer. It would explain why the traffic was going at crawling speed, but... He kept his head down as the officer stepped up to their window, thankfully staying on his side instead of Lex's due to Lex being in the roadway itself. With the window rolled down, it was obvious to see that the man was exhausted, bags sat under his eyes and it was quite evident that he'd gotten very little sleep yesterday. "Hello there." He seemed to at least pretend to be chipper as he sent a smile toward Maxwell and Yvette, Lex specifically looking the other direction. "Sorry to stop you, but we've been ordered to search every vehicl—"

"Mister, are you alright?" Yvette spoke up, and Maxwell found himself almost on the receiving end of wide-eyed innocence.

The officer, however, definitely got the full version as he hesitated. "Did you know? My brothers and I are going for a trip and we've been trying to get out of this city. Have you been trying too, mister?"

"Well, that's—"

"Oh. Is that why you seem so tired?" Yvette leaned over Maxwell, causing him to mentally cringe at the same time as he was thanking the girl for hiding his face. Deciding he'd had enough and was not in the mood to keep up with Yvette as she started to chatter away to the befuddled officer, he tuned out the rest of their conversation in order to exchange a hint of relief with Lex that it was the ONLY jam they got into on their way out of the city.

As he turned his attention back on Yvette, he found himself thinking that, if he didn't know any better, he could have sworn Yvette was the cutest little girl around, but he knew well enough that she was laying it on, even for such a little girl. She was incredibly smart, he noticed, and quite willing to help them. Lex didn't have to say much for her to understand. He saw the officer chuckle and pull back, waving them forward. He still appeared exhausted, but a little cheered up and, from the little Maxwell caught before they were waved on, the officer was mentioning that it was 'impossible' that terrorists would have such a smart little sister.

Even with that comment, they were out of the city by the time Maxwell finally let out a breath of relief and smiled at Yvette.

She giggled.

"Good job there, Yvette." Lex spoke up, his voice calm and, since Maxwell was listening for it, relieved.

"Thanks," she chirped before her smile fell slightly. "But I don't like it."

"We know." Maxwell ruffled her hair gently, garnering her attention. "Hopefully, we can get you someplace soon, alright?"

She blinked up at him, furrowing her brow. "You promised..."

"Hopefully WE can get someplace soon."

Lex's gaze caught Maxwell's and he blinked.

Oh, right. He nodded. "Sorry, we." He smiled toward Yvette who frowned before letting out another yawn and nodded, burying into his side. He curled his arm around her before facing Lex. "So, how far do we have to go?"

"Thankfully, not too far. We should make it within the hour if we keep up this speed."

Maxwell groaned in relief, slumping back in his seat. To his surprise and utmost relief, the Enthrope employees were just setting up barricades as they slipped through. Talk about cutting it close. Good thing they didn't wait until night proper.

He peered at his phone and let out a sigh before sitting back, relaxing. He would probably be seeing his sister soon. Did he know how to react? The things he should say?

He wasn't sure.

As Lex said, they arrived about an hour later and, to Maxwell's surprise, the area was in complete shambles. He could see long lines of people, barely surviving, waiting at food shelters while buildings, more ruins than anything, practically enveloped the area. Maxwell got out of the car, holding Yvette close to his side as Lex followed, locking the door and peering at the paper before pushing it in his pocket and heading down the street. This area, now that Maxwell was actually paying attention, was much closer to the water, something he'd been hoping to avoid. It almost seemed like an earthquake devastated the area, and recently too, if the cracks on the wall and the injured people were any indication.

"It sounds like she moves up and down the coast. We were lucky she was nearby when I asked," Lex said quietly, answering Maxwell's unspoken question.

It wasn't long until they arrived at one of the few places still standing, noting that it was emptier than Maxwell thought it would be. Maxwell and Lex exchanged glances before knocking on the door.

Silence filled the area as they waited.

"She is on her break." A man spoke up from the right, glaring at them. "She works hard for these people and they leave her alone when she asks, especially in the evening like this. Don't go bothering her."

"We have a letter for her." Maxwell spoke up, digging into his pocket.

Thankfully, he grabbed the letter earlier while they were traveling. He showed it to the man who humphed but didn't bother them anymore, simply moving back to his seat up against the wall. Maxwell frowned, but shook his head and turned his focus back on the door, knocking on it once more.

"Who the hell is it, waking me? Better be a damn spleen ruptured if they—" The door swung open to showcase an older woman. She was well past her prime, but held herself in a way that spoke of experience and pride. Her dark complexion melded in the night, though the blackness that caught his attention was filled with a sharp intellect Maxwell didn't want to guess at. She peered out at them. Grayish black frizzed hair was pulled back in a loose bun, some strands falling around her wizened face in braids as if she'd just thrown it up. Her gaze flitted to the letter in Maxwell's grasp before her keen gaze caught his. "Who's the letter from, sonny?"

"Er, Dr. Girshwin in New London City. He asked me to give this to you since we were heading this way anyway."

"My son, eh?" The woman spoke up, scrutinizing the letter for the longest time. A strange flicker of emotion slid over her face before she tentatively folded it up. "That idiot son of mine. Of course, he would make the decision to stay there."

She shook her head before turning her attention to Lex. "Now, come on boy. My son seemed to like you and your friends."

Her attention shifted to Maxwell. "He asked me to keep an eye on you, you know." She waved the letter before slipping it in her pocket. "He's a bit trusting, but has a good heart." She turned. "Well, let's get inside." With that, she walked away and Maxwell let out his held breath, following behind with Yvette surprisingly hurrying ahead and Lex following.

"Dr. Girshwin. Dr. Girshwin," Yvette called as Maxwell examined the ruined walls and the makeshift doctor's office that they stepped into. "You're a doctor, right? Like my momma. I heard my momma talk about you. Maxwell told me we were coming to meet you, but I wasn't sure if it was really you."

"Dear, slow down, you are speaking too fast." The woman raised her arm, palm outward, causing Yvette's gushing to stop. The two scanned each other for a moment before Dr. Girshwin outright smiled. "Ah, you must be little Yvette. Your mother was Anna, right?"

Yvette nodded as Maxwell stared in shock.

Yvette knew Mrs. er, Dr. Girshwin? What were the chances of that? It would certainly explain her strange confusion and silence whenever they talked about her.

Dr. Girshwin seemed to notice his shock. "We doctors know each other on this coast. We're the only ones we can rely on after the earthquake destroyed the coastal cities. I know her mother. Though, why she is with someone I don't know makes me a little worried."

Maxwell winced as Yvette sobered, fingers clenched into her dress. "Momma's sleeping now."

Dr. Girshwin's expression saddened before she sighed and patted

Yvette's head, turning part of her attention onto Maxwell and Lex. "So, other than that letter, what brings you two here?"

Maxwell went to open his mouth when he heard distant cries, followed by a screech of tires. Everyone exchanged glances before Maxwell found himself darting outside, just in time for a car to swerve around the corner. It skidded on the road before slamming to a halt at an awkward angle. It seemed to pause there for a moment before the car shut off and the door swung open with a bit too much force.

It was then that Maxwell's brain froze as he caught the familiar form of Karina, darting out of the car, her attention snapping to his.

If Maxwell didn't know better, he would have thought that the whole world just up and disappeared with how quiet everything was as soon as they locked gazes.

That moment was shattered when Karina bolted forward and grasped his arms tightly. "Please. Maxwell. Tell me this is Mrs. Girshwin's place." Her voice was pitched and shaking, tears on the verge of tracing down her cheeks.

He wasn't sure how to respond. This wasn't what he'd expected. He could only nod. She seemed to crumble right then and there.

"Oh, thank god. Please, Maxwell. You have to help him."

What the hell was she talking about? He must have been quite out of it, because he heard a gasp and turned. Dr. Girshwin wandered over to the open back door of the car. "Oh, dear. I'm sorry. There really isn't anything I can do for this boy."

Wait? What?

"No. Maxwell is here. Maxwell, you can save him." Karina pushed herself to her feet, pulling him over to the car in a desperation he'd only ever seen occasionally.

Then, he understood.

Laying in the back seat of the car, barely gasping for air, was a boy only a little older than himself. He knew, almost without being told, what was afflicting him and could only guess it was the same boy he had talked with only a few days ago.

Was this really the same boy he heard over the phone? He sounded fine then, what could have happened?

"Let's at least get him inside and comfortable." Dr. Girshwin's resigned voice caught Maxwell's attention and, spotting the desperation and dismay in his sister's expression, turned to Dr. Girshwin to help. They hurried inside, carrying the practically burning form of the teenager. The boy whimpered quietly, a pitiful sound to Maxwell's ears, and one he hoped to never hear again.

Karina kept even, smiling shakily. "We'll get you help soon."

Dr. Girshwin shook her head, but didn't say anything as she led them into the office and laid him on the only bed in the room. It was then that Maxwell turned to her. Karina stayed beside the boy as Lex and Yvette moved to the edge of the room, Lex keeping half his attention on the surroundings while the other half watched the proceedings with a strange wariness. Maxwell took a deep breath and then stared right at Dr. Girshwin. "Do you have an IV drip for blood transfusions?"

The woman gave him a strange look but didn't argue, just simply nodded.

"Alright, hook me up with him. We might be able to save him." Maxwell paused for a moment before glancing at his arm. "Oh, and I am O negative, so blood won't be an issue."

The woman narrowed her lips, her gaze flitting between the boy, Karina's pleading gaze and Maxwell's expression which he knew was practically shining with determination as he turned his head back up.

Without a word, she procured the items as well as another. "If we're doing what I think we are, we need to drain some of his blood as well." She gave Maxwell a long look. "I'll have you explain after we get this all set up, understood?"

"We will." Karina spoke up, voice hoarse, and eyelids fluttering from what was obviously stress and weariness. The room was filled with the sounds of humming and movement. Maxwell sat down to one side, practically next to the boy with what little room they had as Dr. Girshwin hooked them up. Within no time, blood was flowing and Karina seemed to finally collapse, falling asleep with her head rested on the bed. Maxwell watched her with a frown. He never got a chance to say anything when she first arrived, but now that everything calmed down, he couldn't say anything again. He examined her, noting her harried expression. She seemed to have grown while she was away.

He turned his focus on Dr. Girswhin who was reading through the letter he gave her earlier once more, as if trying to memorize the contents. She was keeping half of her attention on the transfer while she read. Finally, she let out a sigh and once more folded up the letter. "Well, that is my son for you." She shook her head. "It's his decision." She let out a breath before her stern gaze turned to Maxwell. "Now, explain."

She left no room for anything, her gaze not sliding an inch.

Maxwell shifted, examining the cracked ceiling, listening to Karina's soft breathing, Lex's quiet shuffling, the wind whistling through the cracks... "It's quite a long story."

The woman simply shifted once more. "Well, go on, I don't have any more patients today since it was supposed to be my time off, but I suppose I can listen." Her gaze drifted to the connected IV slowly dripping from one to the other before returning her focus on him.

He nodded and let out a breath. "Well, it started when our mother went missing...."

He was only about halfway through the story when Dr. Girshwin reached forward and disconnected the IV's, bandaging them both up before taking a seat once more, never saying a word, for which Maxwell was grateful.

By the end, she was staring at the boy Karina brought with a quiet and thoughtful expression. "Well then, if what you say is true, then this boy will be proof enough. We caught him just in time, from what I could tell of his condition. He is one of the unlucky ones."

"He was about to skip the third stage then," Lex called from the other side of the room, causing Maxwell to jump. He completely forgot that his friend was standing there.

"You are correct. So, if he truly does end up being cured, then..." Her gaze moved to Yvette, who was holding onto Lex's leg before Dr. Girshwin chuckled faintly. "Well, I always do love giving a big Fuck You to the government, so what's one more thing to add to the list?"

She looked Maxwell dead in the eye. "If he survives, then yes. I will help you all develop the cure. After all, if that is the case, I can utilize it as well." She smirked and tapped her leg. "I might have managed to avoid it; doesn't mean I won't be completely immune to it like it sounds you two are." Her gaze focused on Karina before she frowned. "Though I wonder why she didn't donate the blood herself after we were all settled in. She obviously knows the boy, so why would she leave it to you? Didn't you say your sister..."

"I don't know," Maxwell cut in, pursing his lips. "She should have it like me, but maybe she doesn't believe that to be the case? Maybe she thought that, even though you have the equipment, she, well..." He couldn't help but to phrase that as a question. "And, when you say...that about the government, do you mean the gated communities?" He asked carefully.

Dr. Girshwin scrutinized him with a piercing gaze before the tiniest of smiles slipped onto her lips. "No." She shook her head. "Outer community, gated community, that doesn't matter to me. I'm talking about the government itself. I hold no allegiance either way."

She turned her gaze toward Karina's sleeping form. "If everything you've told me is the case, then you're going to need to talk to her and I'm going to have to run some tests. Do you mind?"

Maxwell hesitated before shaking his head. "No, that's fine. Thanks for asking."

Dr. Girshwin nodded before getting up and walking over to Yvette. "Come on, Yvette, you are probably quite hungry. Let's make something for everyone."

Yvette's enthusiastic response was cut off as the door swung shut and silence enveloped the area.

Now all he had to do was sit and wait for everyone to wake up. He spotted Lex getting comfortable and decided to do the same. It had been a long few days and knowing that Karina was alive and not even a few paces away, lifted the weight that he only semi-noticed, leaving him exhausted. So, now that everything was done, he let himself fall into a shallow sleep.

Chapter Forty-Six

Karina slowly awoke, something soft and warm draped around her shoulders. Her fingers were clasped into a plastic-like material similar to something she saw in the nurse's office at school. The ones laid out on those makeshift beds. She rarely used the nurse's room since Mom was the one who took care of her anyway. Huh. Was her mom here? Maybe Maxwell had gotten hurt again because... She blinked, frowning as she realized she could hear faint breaths not that far from her head, warmth gently flowing toward her. She shifted before sitting up. Only then did the memories from the day before slam into her and she reeled, attention darting toward the figure laying before her which was definitely not Maxwell. All the breath left her as she realized he was breathing normally, the flush already disappearing and it took everything in her not to slump back down and curl up in relief.

Something she would have done if she hadn't already caught the OTHER familiar form in the room. Green eyes stared back at her, distant and closed off. Not that she could blame him. She took a deep breath and pushed herself away from the bed before walking over. "Okay, look. I'm sorry..."

"Save it." Maxwell spoke up as he stood, just that little bit taller than her. His expression was stormy and outright miserable. "Just save it," he muttered, the exhaustion evident in his voice.

Karina pursed her lips and followed the lines of the floor. "What do you want me to say, Maxwell?" she finally said, garnering what fortitude she had to tilt her head back up. "You don't want me to apologize, but..."

A torrent of emotions flashed rapidly. Finally, they settled into a

393

blank expression that hurt more than she thought it would. She shook her head and stepped forward, fists clenched and nails digging into her palm. "I don't know what to tell you. I've tried to apologize. I've tried to figure out how to talk to you. What do you want from me? I was an idiot, okay? I'm well aware of that."

"That's..."

"Yet the only thing I can do IS apologize for my stupidity. I know I hurt you, I know I messed things up even worse and—"

"Karina," Maxwell cut her off by pulling her into a tight hug, his arms wrapping around her as he shook violently. "You are a damn stupid irresponsible thoughtless sister who..." Maxwell swallowed heavily, clutching her tighter. She could do nothing but stare up at the ceiling, her mouth more a fish than anything. That movement ended, snapping shut when he finished, "I dearly missed. We both screwed up. I know that and, I know, so do you."

Karina, hesitantly brought her arms up, emotions whirling and shifting. She thought she needed to protect Maxwell and failed. She thought Maxwell would yell at her, ignore her, give her a good hard slap, but... She felt tears dripping down her chin before she let out a sob, burying her face into his shoulder. She didn't need to protect him, she knew that, but he was still her family, the only person she had left in this ludicrous world that was with her. Mom was miles away with people she didn't trust anywhere near enough and Dad— no, there was no point in thinking of her father. There hadn't been for a long time. Though she'd known that, she still abandoned her brother, her twin. She felt herself slump down and could feel Maxwell fall with her. The dust clung to her skin and wood scratched at her knees, but she didn't care. How much had she held in all this time?

"I'm sorry I wasn't there for you, Kari," Maxwell murmured, voice scratchy. "I saw you breaking and I ignored it."

She went quiet, as the tears kept sliding past her lips.

"I ignored it because I was scared. Scared that, if you were breaking, then I wouldn't be able to stand it either."

"What?" Karina muttered.

Part of her wanted to pull away, examine her sibling, but the other part didn't want to let go. She could feel the grip around her tighten for a second before loosening.

"I've... I look up to you, how strong you always portray yourself as, and I let it blind me when you were hurting. We've dealt with so much that..." He gulped.

Karina pulled him closer, feeling his warmth beside her, his beating heart calming its rapid pace as she hummed. "Alright."

"Alright?"

She couldn't help the smile as she carefully pulled back, one hand reaching up to his face, blotchy as it was. "We both screwed up. We both have amends to make, but you're still my little brother. No matter what, got it?"

He examined her expression for the longest time until he gave a subtle nod, lip quivering. He bowed his head, grasping her fingers, still cupped to his face as a hiccup escaped his lips. "So, is it okay to cry then?"

Karina rubbed away the tears, laughing softly. "I think we're allowed to."

"Good," Maxwell muttered before once more burying his head into her shoulder as she held tightly onto him. The tears wouldn't stop falling, but this time, she couldn't help but feel the relief flow through her, the worry and weight disappearing with each hiccup and drop.

They still had a lot to talk about. They hadn't fixed everything, but at least she could talk with Maxwell once more and that was more than enough for her. It would take some time to make amends, on both sides, but she wasn't too worried.

For now, she just let herself cry alongside her twin as the warm air gently curled around them.

Chapter Forty-Seven

Finnagen felt the blackness. There was no other way to describe it. The blackness that dragged at him time and time again over the past day or two curled around him and yet, he was too tired to feel the fear that raced through him so often before. He heard faint voices, could hear his name ringing around and around in his head as the blackness slowly, finally, started to fade. Gentle hues of oranges and yellows filtered through him as aches and pains surfaced back into his mind. Something scratchy touched him and pulled as he shifted.

The conversation stopped. Soft fingers gently grazed his head as a faint groan slipped through. Was that his voice?

Was he alive?

He heard more talking, a different urgency to it, but those fingers never stopped and he found himself pushing into them, hoping to feel more.

"Agen... Finn... Finnagen." The voice echoed around and around in his head until he finally realized it was his name. He needed to know who it was, why it felt familiar. With that, feeling like he was moving with all the speed of molasses, he blinked, everything blurry before he spotted a mop of black hair. The form slowly clarified as a mop of brown came into the left side of his vision. His fingers twitched as he tilted his head, a faint smile pulling at his lips.

"Hey," he managed to croak out as the figure solidified into the worried and relieved form of Karina.

Her eyes were red and puffy, her cheeks blotchy and wet. She must have been crying. He slowly bent his arm up, his senses coming back to him piece by piece. "Cute," he muttered, rubbing a thumb over her cheek, brushing away some of the tears.

"Hey."

He heard a voice and then an arm reached over, pulling him back as Karina shot a glare over to the one who spoke.

Huh? His brain muttered as he turned toward the other blotch he saw in his periphery. The blotch was now a boy, a little taller than Karina, with brown hair and an annoyed green gaze. He was thinner than Finnagen and with a bit less muscle, but he held himself in a way that definitely indicated who he was related to.

Plus, Finnagen couldn't deny that the boy appeared remarkably similar to Karina in every other way. The way his brows furrowed as he glared at Finnagen was reminiscent of Karina.

"Maxwell, leave him alone."

Karina spoke up faintly and Maxwell, Finnagen's mind supplied, glanced over before wincing, the fingers that had been clasped around Finnagen's wrist loosened as Maxwell pulled back and let out a breath.

He shook his head and turned back to Finnagen with a guarded expression. "Sorry about that." His voice was soft as he spoke. "I'm just not used to people touching Kari like that."

"Sorry." This time, the word came out a little clearer and then, his brain caught up with him and he blinked. "Wait, why...?"

Maxwell's expression shifted into a faint smile as Finnagen caught a bandage wrapped around the boy's arm. He tilted his head down enough to note the IV, blood dripping into him before he turned toward Karina. "Can someone please explain how I'm not dead?" he admittedly pleaded.

Karina chuckled, fingers finally pulling away from him as she hid her mouth. "That would be because of Maxwell. I managed to get you to the doctor in time." Her lips narrowed into a thin line as she leaned forward, practically butting heads with him, causing him to let out a faint "Meep" and push into the pillow behind his head. "You better not do that to me again though, you understand?"

"Yes, ma'am," he squeaked out and she grinned before pulling back.

"Good."

"Kari." Maxwell's tone was more than indicative of the amusement that he was portraying. "You're scaring the poor guy."

Silence enveloped the other end and Maxwell winced, seeming uncomfortable for a moment.

Finnagen flopped fully backward, feeling his smile widen anyway. "Well, whatever it was, thanks for that..."

He froze, mouth opening wide before he shot upward, pushing away the momentary dizziness as his head snapped between the two twins as they jumped. "Wait. I KNOW I had the epidemic. Something happened, but, wait. Is there really a cure and..."

Karina's palm slapped over his mouth as Maxwell grimaced.

Maxwell seemed to hesitate before shrugging. "Yeah, you HAD the epidemic. Just don't question it right now, alright?"

"Don't question," Finnagen mumbled around Karina's grasp, sounding more like gibberish than anything.

Karina's sheepish chuckle drained what energy he had left and he groaned, flopping backward. "Fine, I won't ask. It's good to know you two talking though. So, you're Maxwell, Karina's twin?"

Maxwell seemed to be shaken from his thoughts when Finnagen spoke and he turned toward the boy. "Yeah."

"Karina talked a lot about you. It's nice to finally meet you."

"Oh?" Maxwell's words were half-hearted at most as he scrutinized Karina.

"So, I talked about you a little," Karina said in a quiet voice. "It's fine, right?"

Maxwell opened his mouth to say something before snapping it shut and shaking his head. Were they not getting along? That wasn't good. He felt the sleep drag at him once more and he let out a breath. Thank the heavens he wasn't scared of it this time because he definitely needed it. "Either way, thank you," he murmured, as the blackness swept over him once more.

Chapter Forty-Eight

Maxwell wasn't sure what to say as the boy fell asleep again, breaths even. He was a strange character, that was for sure, but he still felt the faint smile tug at his lips. While part of him was automatically feeling overprotective, another part couldn't help but sigh in relief. Finnagen, as strange as he was, definitely appreciated Karina. Much like when he recalled meeting Lex, Emma and Dr. Girshwin all that time ago, he found himself content. He knew neither of them would be hurt, he could just tell that the boy was honest and that was enough for him.

He let out a sigh and stood. "Alright, so he's recovering. I'll tell Dr. Girshwin..."

"Maxwell. What are we going to do next?"

Maxwell stilled as he caught Karina's gaze. She was once more tracing her fingers through Finnagen's hair, as if without thinking about it as her gaze locked onto his. He pursed his lips, unsure what to tell Karina. He hadn't thought that far ahead. He hadn't really been thinking ahead at all, to be honest.

Karina seemed to realize as she grimaced and turned away. "Sorry. I guess you wouldn't know either."

Maxwell groaned, palm slapping then trailing down his face. "Look," he mumbled. "I wasn't thinking that far ahead, I'll be honest. I do know one thing." He pulled away and pointed toward her, as his brow furrowed. "Why didn't you do anything for him? Why me? I wasn't going to ask, at least not until later, but he's awake now." He waved to the side, indicating the dilapidated little room they were in. "This isn't any different than if you sa—"

"I..." Karina bit her lip before shaking her head. "What if I didn't have the cure? We KNOW you do, we KNOW that, but I don't."

Maxwell stilled as he listened to his sibling pour out her thoughts. "I might have at one point thought I did, hoped I did. But I would still get infected, those around me still died, I didn't and still don't know. I didn't want to risk it. What if I was only a partial cure like Mom? Enough to keep me alive, but that's it? I didn't want to believe that, but I didn't have any proof otherwise. I know Dad's letter said we were both the cure, but I wasn't sure I could believe that."

Maxwell heard her voice peter out, almost dead by the end and he, honestly, wasn't sure how to respond. Unfortunately, he knew he should respond. It made sense to respond. Yet, as he stood there, he couldn't think of anything. How would Karina have known? There wasn't any instance for her to find out and while he himself managed to avoid it, she saw those she thought of as friends die by this thing. Was watching as... He turned his gaze on Finnagen, watching his slowly rising and falling chest, his wild hair falling all over the pillow. Karina watched as Finnagen was dying.

He let out a breath. "Why don't we have Dr. Girshwin test you? Is it so far-fetched to believe you might have it too? I don't want to do it alone," he muttered the last bit, but she still seemed to hear him anyway.

She went to open her mouth, just as a sound ripped through the once quiet room. Karina yelped, fumbling as she pulled out her phone and snapped it open. Maxwell swayed, ears ringing at the sudden loudness. Other than a grimace, Finnagen kept sleeping, though he couldn't say he blamed the boy.

"Hello?" Karina said, pushing back in her seat so she leaned backward. "Who is this?" Had she not thought to check first? Then again, who would have her number?

Maxwell found himself pattering over just as Karina's jaw dropped in surprise, before snapping shut with a hiss of worry.

"Really?"

"Karina, who is it?"

Karina opened her mouth to respond and then raised an eyebrow. "You sure?" She spoke into it for a moment before letting out a sigh. "Fine, fine, but thanks." She smiled faintly. "It must have been hard."

Who was she speaking to?

"Yep, I'll tell him. Yes, yes, we're back together again. Oh, come on, that's not what I meant." Karina threw her arms in the air, a wide grin dancing on her lips as she chuckled faintly. "Don't you have somewhere to be?"

A long moment of conversation ensued and Karina's expression softened. "Oh." She winced. "That makes sense. Thanks for telling us, and thank you for keeping an eye on Mother for us."

Mother? Wait... "Is that Madeline?" Maxwell lunged forward, grasping for the phone. Karina, probably having realized, quickly pulled it away, shouted a good-bye and snapped it shut. He stared at it, frozen, before glaring at his sibling. "What the hell, Karina? I wanted to talk with her."

"She had a feeling you did. She doesn't have the time right now, and neither do we." She examined Finnagen for a moment before she stood. "We need to talk to Lex. It seems the Resistance has figured out where we are." She glanced sidelong to Maxwell with a pained expression. "They saw you in the city."

Chapter Forty-Nine

Lex clapped the phone shut just as Maxwell and Karina hurried out of the side room they were in for the past few hours. Sure, they had eaten something with Yvette and Dr. Girshwin, but the two left soon after. Noting their expressions, Lex let out a sigh. "Let me guess. The Resistance has found us? At least, what city we were in?"

Maxwell blinked as Karina's expression shifted to surprise. Both of them glanced toward the phone still hanging in his fingers before understanding flashed between them.

"As you guessed. I just got a call from my informant, though I'm not sure who yours is, but anyway," he let out a sigh, pocketing his phone. "Caym has also sent employees into this region and there is talk of military movement as well. It's possible he may also be pulling the military in."

"What?" Karina yelped as Maxwell gritted his teeth.

"The military? There's no way we could avoid that." Maxwell's expression couldn't be any more disheartened if he tried and Lex understood why.

"Exactly. If Caym actually pulls in the military to do a sweep of the country?" He grimaced as Karina and Maxwell exchanged wary frowns. "Yet, we're at the cusp of you two creating a serum. I highly doubt you guys will be able to move once testing on that begins, which doesn't leave us many options."

Maxwell seemed to realize first because he jolted forward. "Wait. What do you mean? Are you...?"

Lex examined the two of them, his once swirling emotions slowed as a faint smile pulled his lips upward. "There's not much more I can do for you two. You have everything you need and, once the serum is created, you should be safe. No one will go after you two, after all, they would have the cure." He leaned back against the wall, scanning the bumpy and cracked ceiling. "You two aren't the idiots I met all those months ago. Plus, you two have realized your mistakes and are back together."

He tilted his head down, spotting the shock from both of them. "I really can't avoid it though. Caym isn't going to stop."

"You're going back to him." Maxwell deduced, a slight hitch to his tone. "You—"

"You can't." Karina stepped forward, fists clenched. "You—"

"Aren't needed here." He pointed downward as he pushed away from the wall. "As you can recall, I joined you to keep a promise and I kept it." He smiled faintly. "I also am making a new one now. I'll do what I can back in the gated community, just like I've helped you both to this point. I may not be able to do much with the Resistance, but if I can pull one of the groups off you, at least for a short time, it should be fine and who knows?" A full-blown smirk fell onto his face. "With Enthrope's position, I might be able to have some say in this country, now that Father is gone." He shrugged. "Am I fond of the idea? Hell no. However, I also need to find some things out for myself and I can't do that here."

Karina bit her lip hard as Maxwell turned his head away, nails digging into his palm. Lex sighed and stepped over, patting them on one of their shoulders, jerking them out of their thoughts. "I'm not dying or anything," he said, drawing both of their attention. "I just need some answers and I can't get them here. Neither can you two."

"So, we are splitting up again," Karina said, her voice cracking. She hesitated for the briefest of moments before, to Lex's shock, pulling him into a hug. "Stay safe."

She pulled back as Maxwell grabbed his hand with a faint smile. "We'll see you again, right?"

"No promises." Lex's expression softened. "But I'll try."

The twins peered at each other before nodding and taking a step back. "We'll head out. I'll tell Dr. Girshwin. Hopefully, we can find someplace a little safer to make the serum. Take care, Lex."

Lex pulled back and, for a split second, found himself hesitating. When the determined gazes met his—though he could tell both of them were still upset—he nodded and turned.

He took a deep breath and slipped out the door, heading toward the pick-up. He stopped, noting that Karina's car seemed to be gone. Not surprising, she probably left the key in the ignition in her panic. He pulled himself inside the truck after unlocking it and rested his hand on the wheel as his head fell back against the headrest. He was really going to do it, wasn't he? It wasn't going to do much, at least in the long run. However, for this moment, for a few days, Caym's attention would be diverted, Enthrope's forces focused on his return.

So, he was going to find Caym.

He was going to meet his brother again.

Chapter Fifty

Karina couldn't believe it. Lex was gone, just like that. She finally got a chance to talk with him, to thank him, and then he left.

She was able to say good-bye, Maxwell hadn't when she did the same thing. She pulled in on herself, noting how Maxwell already left to talk with Dr. Girshwin and Yvette as she continued to stare at the door. She understood why he left, she got it, but it didn't mean it wasn't still hard to bear. "Thank you," she muttered, biting her lip hard. She tilted her head back, searching the ceiling for answers that weren't there.

With the Resistance and Enthrope so close, they had to move, but would they be alright? Finnagen was still recovering and, while she and Maxwell talked through their differences... She winced as she remembered Madeline telling her about the concert attack and how she didn't want to talk with Maxwell. She could understand that desire. After all, Maxwell probably wasn't too keen to speak with Madeline if, no, when he found out that Madeline's family was behind the attack that he'd gotten caught up in.

She was glad she hadn't panicked when Madeline mentioned it, but it seemed that she'd been sort of numb to the whole thing. Either way, she would let Madeline tell Maxwell at her own pace. Plus, she didn't think Maxwell needed the added stress right now. She had a feeling he had no reason to distrust Madeline, but, well...

She shook her head to clear her thoughts. Either way, it was so familiar in regards to feeling uncomfortable that she could understand Madeline's decision. Maxwell was in enough turmoil. She wasn't going to compound it. Her gaze moved toward Finnagen's closed doorway.

A faint ringing caught her attention and she reached into her pocket, startled to remember she pocketed Finnagen's phone. She pulled it out, noting someone was calling. She stared for so long, debating, that the call hung up.

Right, she forgot she called Finnagen's parents. She glanced at the time, noting there was a call earlier that she must have missed in her panic. She jumped as the phone rang again and this time, she picked up.

"Finnagen? Son? Are you alright?" The sound of a familiar male voice rang through the phone as Karina found herself heading into Finnagen's room.

"Hello, this is Karina." Karina spoke up, taking a seat next to Finnagen. "Finnegan is sleeping right now."

"Karina? I'm sorry, but why do you have Finnagen's phone?"

Karina stiffened, brain jamming to a halt before she mentally scrambled to figure out a response. "Well, he tried to call you earlier and you didn't pick up. He left it on the table when he went to bed."

"Really?" The father hummed, a hint confused before he sighed. "Well, he's probably exhausted. It is late. I was just worried when I couldn't get a hold of him after he called me earlier." Karina winced but didn't respond. "Well, as long as he is alright. Speaking of, what are you doing up at this hour?"

"I couldn't sleep," Karina admitted truthfully. "Too much on my mind."

"Well, that is something we all struggle with." Finnagen's father chuckled before cutting off a yawn. "Well, tell him to call me when he wakes up and next time to leave a voicemail so I know what's going on, okay?"

"Yeah." Karina glanced down at Finnagen, noting his calmly rising and falling chest and just smiled. "I can do that." She noted fondness in her voice and it seemed the father had too because he let out a breath.

"Well then, take care of Finnagen for me and please, don't swipe his phone again?" The man chuckled as Karina stiffened before he continued, "Still, thank you for letting me know. Get some rest. The brain isn't always useful when it's running a hundred miles per hour."

"I'll try." Karina let a weak smile cross her face.

There was a hum from the other side before the man said a quick, 'good night' before hanging up.

There really wasn't a reason to thank her. She caused the situation to begin with, but... her gaze flipped to the IV drip and she relaxed.

Lex was right though. If they created the serum, there would be no reason to be scared anymore. They wouldn't have to keep running or worrying about those around them.

She could take care of Finnagen and he wouldn't have to worry for his life like she, Maxwell and Lex had.

Yeah, that's what she would do.

"So, he's healed." Mrs. Girshwin's voice pulled her from her thoughts and she turned toward the older woman as she entered, awe and a hint of hope in her expression.

There was a little girl that she thought her brother called Yvette. She stepped behind Dr. Girshwin, holding onto the doctor's leg. Yvette let go and took a seat, watching the surroundings carefully before eyeing Karina with a curious expression. Maxwell hung back a bit, taking a seat next to the little girl. Dr. Girshwin stepped next to the bed and peered down at Finnagen. Her scanning and scrutinizing made Karina shift uncomfortably as she poked and prodded at Finnagen before pulling back, only a flicker shone in her posture of the surprise she must have been feeling. Her voice, however, indicated it far more than her expression. "Unbelievable. This has happened before?" Her gaze turned to Maxwell before shifting to Karina. "Alright, I am convinced. I will help you."

Karina didn't realize she was holding her breath until it all came out in a whoosh. While her thoughts were still on Lex, another part of her grinned in delight at the new help.

"Do you know someplace we can go? It's not safe around here." Maxwell spoke up, garnering everyone's attention.

Dr. Girshwin pulled back, thrumming her index finger against her leg before nodding. "Firstly, before we leave, I need to check your sister. I have the equipment already set up and it'll save us time in the long run."

Karina grimaced, but didn't argue as she continued, "As for where we will go? I do know of a location farther north, it's my old lab. I haven't used it in ages, but everything should still be there. I highly doubt the government will expect me going back there, and I also highly doubt they are aware of my involvement." Her expression grew vicious. "Plus, with this, we can definitely give a big Fuck You to the government and save those lives that I've been unable to do a thing about." Her gaze flickered to Finnagen before turning to Maxwell and Karina.

"Anyway, girl, I need you over here." She gestured toward the bag that held Finnagen's blood that she was working to disengage from his arm. After making sure the bandage was secure, she gestured for Karina to follow.

Karina hesitated, only to feel a light push on her back. A warm smile filled with encouragement crossed Maxwell's face. "Go."

She bit her lip before nodding and following after the woman. They ended up in a separate room that seemed more like a storage room. She saw a microscope off to one side. Karina's hesitation seemed to have given the woman enough time to place a drop of blood onto two pieces of glass. Dr. Girshwin glanced over. "Ah, good." She dug into a drawer, pulling out a syringe from a pack that was firmly sealed.

Karina took a deep breath, taking a seat in the only other chair before extending her arm, nervous fluttering in her stomach was not helping her increasingly difficult breathing. The woman barely seemed to notice. Slowly, after making sure Karina was prepared, she slid the syringe into Karina's skin. Karina held back a wince, watching the blood, her blood, flow into the tube. In some ways, it was fascinating to watch. In others, it made her want to pull back. Within no time, the doctor was done and giving her a bandage while she swung around, already messing with the gadgets and microscopes. "This will take some time, so wait outside." She spoke firmly, eliciting no argument from Karina who hurried back out with a frown as she clutched her arm.

Maxwell walked over, hesitant before patting her shoulder. The little girl stayed in the corner, legs rocking back and forth as she watched quietly. "Come on, let's take a seat and wait. It's better than just standing here, right?"

Karina nodded and took a seat where she'd been earlier, next to Finnagen. He was still fast asleep, but she could tell he was recovering fast, just like Lex had. She didn't realize she was brushing his hair out of his face right away. When she did realize, she didn't stop.

"You like him."

She jerked and turned to Maxwell, catching his somber gaze. He gave her a faint smile.

"Well," she hesitated before shrugging, resuming her action. "Yeah, he's been a good friend. He helped me when..." she trailed off, hearing Maxwell sigh as he shifted in his seat.

"I don't know much about him, what's he like?"

Karina peered sidelong toward her sibling, who was staring at Finnagen with an indecipherable gaze. Karina gnawed on her lip for a moment before speaking. "He's nice, if a little awkward. He's always talking and sometimes just seems to act before he thinks. You know, we met when I ran into him at a mall in the gated community."

"Oh, right, Lex mentioned that, but..."

"Oh, right, I never told you."

She pulled away, turning her focus on Maxwell. Her sibling appeared outright confused and she couldn't help but smile. "Well, why don't we exchange stories? I bet she'll be a while."

Maxwell clenched his fingers into his clothes, his knuckles white as he dipped his head, deep in thought. Finally, he nodded.

"I guess I'll start." Karina leaned forward, ruffling his hair, causing him to squawk in indignation before she continued, grinning, "It started when I went out for a walk to clear my head right after we left the Resistance, or so I told myself. I guess I was a lot more out of it than I thought because..." She told her story, making sure to leave out the specifics of her injury and her thought process. After which Maxwell began to tell his side. She felt a pang of guilt and remorse as he spoke, his voice low. So, neither of them had a good time of it. She shook her head and went to respond when she heard a click and jerked. She turned, just as Dr. Girshwin stepped out of the doorway, her expression gleaming in interest and fascination.

Maxwell shot up and hurried over with Karina coming up behind, much slower. "So? She has it, right?" Maxwell asked.

Dr. Girswhin examined them both quietly before saying, "From what I could acquire and deduce from my limited examination, yes. She does."

Karina felt her knees go weak and she quickly grabbed Maxwell's arm, hearing him yelp in surprise. She knew she shouldn't have been surprised, she had been told it, but that didn't stop the giddy feeling of relief that welled up in her veins or the grin that found its way on her lips.

Maxwell just shook his head before turning back to Dr. Girshwin as she continued, "However, I cannot do anything with it here. Not only do I not have the equipment, I do not have the time, just like you." She glanced toward Finnagen, a strange mix of emotions flashing over her face before she focused on them once more.

"We'll leave in an hour. Your friend already left, correct?"

The nods she received must have been proof enough because she turned, facing one of the walls. "Let's not put what he's doing to waste. I'll drive so you all can sleep." She grinned. "After all, the Canadian border is a long way away from here. At least, the area just south of it is, isn't it?"

Her grin widened at their shocked expressions.

The Canadian border? Karina slowly turned her head toward Maxwell, catching his just as flabbergasted expression. A moment later, the grin he was wearing she knew reflected on her own lips.

They were so close, almost to their goal. They had Dr. Girshwin on their side, she knew she was the cure just like Maxwell and they had a new destination in mind. While a lot of things were still a mess, she was at least grateful she was once again with her twin. Lex's decision weighed on her mind, but she knew it was for the best. Lex helped them immensely, as much as she wished she could help him, she knew she couldn't, but she wasn't worried. She knew she would see him again, once this whole mess was over and done with.

Finnagen's stirring caught her attention and she darted over as he mumbled out some incoherent words before catching her gaze. "Hey, Finn." She spoke up, unintentionally shortening his name, but deciding she didn't mind. He didn't seem to either if the delight she saw was any indication.

"Is it my birthday?"

She let out a snort before pulling back. "No, actually, we're going to be leaving soon, are you alright with tha—?"

"Leaving?" He scanned the room before shrugging. "As long as I'm with you, I don't care." He chuckled as Karina felt her face warm at his words. She heard Maxwell choke in surprise in the background, but ignored it as she helped Finnagen sit up. "So, where are we going?"

"Just south of the Canadian border."

Finnagen's gaze flickered to Dr. Girshwin and he stiffened. He opened and closed his mouth as Dr. Girshwin, seeming to read something in his expression that Karina couldn't, twisted her lips up in a smirk. "You seem to recognize me. Most fortuitous."

She turned to Maxwell and Karina. "I'll go gather what supplies we need." With that, she left and Karina wondered.

Who was Dr. Girshwin?

Her gaze moved to meet Finnagen's shocked one and she shook her head. "What about your parents?"

Finnagen seemed to snap out of it, glancing toward her before pausing. Debating for a moment, he let out a breath. "I'll talk to them tomorrow and explain what's going on. I figured it would be a while before I returned home anyway. I'm just going slightly farther than I originally planned."

"Are you sure?"

Finnagen peered at her with a quiet contemplation before he smiled warmly. "Yes. They will understand. You saved my life after I did something so reckless so, well, I want to." He shrugged. "Plus, I know they are alright. I want to make sure you are as well."

Karina found herself looking away. Maxwell watched quietly, a hint of surprise on his face.

"Alright." Karina smiled. "Glad you could join us."

"Well, of course." Finnagen chuckled before wincing. "Though, we are going to go slow, right? I'm still kind of tired."

"Don't worry. We aren't going to go too fast," Dr. Girshwin spoke up, leading Yvette up to the small group. "After all, we have a long way to go."

Karina agreed. Either way, they had help. Finnagen was cured. Maxwell was safe, and they finally made it out west. Her mother wasn't exactly safe, but she was with Madeline, so she would take what she could get. She wouldn't be surprised if there was still more to do, but...

She pulled Finnagen into a hug, causing the boy to yelp before reaching over, catching Maxwell, and pulling him close as well. "Thanks," she muttered, causing them both to relax in her grip.

She pulled back, mentally laughing at Finnagen's blissful expression and bright red cheeks as Maxwell examined her, searching her gaze for a moment before a warm smile fell over his lips.

Dr. Girshwin held a slightly cocked grin as she stood to one side with Yvette watching, a hint of awe on her face.

There was so much she still needed to do, still needed to say.

However, in that moment, she was just happy to know everyone she loved was still alive and that their journey, all of their journeys were almost done.

They would be safe if she held out, just a little longer.

Once they reached the border, once they created the cure, then both of them, both she and her brother, would be free.

She couldn't wait.

Also by Julie Boglisch
at
Rogue Phoenix Press

Epidemic
The Elifer Chronicles Book One

Chapter One

The soft chime of a clock resonated through the two-story house at a steady rhythm. A moment of silence ensued, only to be broken by the sharp clack of running footsteps as they pounded down the stairwell. Veronica Elifer tilted her head up just in time to see her son dart past the kitchen doorway. Her eyes caught brunet hair and a lithe frame as he moved toward the front door.

"Maxwell," she called after her son.

"Sorry, Ma, but I'm going to be late!" her son replied as he threw on a pair of sneakers without even untying the laces.

Veronica crossed her hands over her chest. "Be home by dinner, all right?" she demanded which got a sharp nod from her son, along with a cheeky grin. She rolled her eyes at her son's antics.

"Of course," he replied before he darted out the door.

The door swung shut.

"That boy."

She glanced at a single picture set near the sink. The glass frame glistened as she picked it up. She gripped the picture tightly.

"Felix," she whispered.

The picture showed two people who stood side by side in obvious joy. A tall man with sea-green eyes and a small goatee stood with one arm around a young woman. The woman held one hand to her bulging stomach as she leaned against the man. Both smiled broadly toward the camera.

"You know...he's growing up to be just like you," she said, as she gazed solemnly at the picture. "I can't believe they're already fourteen, almost fifteen. Time does fly, doesn't it?" She paused before she continued, a little softer.

"Has it really been four years since then? Since that incident? You saved them then, but..." She tried to rid herself of unwanted thoughts before she looked out the kitchen window. "I just hope neither of them has to go through the same things you did."

She stopped before she gazed up toward the crystal-clear sky. She felt her expression shift to one of determination and fierce defiance as she stared up, as if in a prayer to the heavens. "I can't let it happen again."

Never again.

She heard a soft knock and jerked up. She turned warily toward the doorway, gently placing the photo down. She walked over and slowly opened the door.

There was no one there. She looked around then peered toward the ground. A white letter lay on the pavement. She squatted down and picked it up. She flipped over the paper and froze as her free hand moved up to her mouth. Her eyes widened as her fingers trembled.

"Felix!"

~ * ~

Maxwell gritted his teeth in annoyance as he ran down the street. He couldn't believe he was actually going to be late for school. He was usually never late! He frowned as he berated himself for his screw-up. Oh, his twin was going to have such a riot when she saw this. He skimmed over cracked pavement and brown sidewalks. He could see pristine hedges on either side of the long street, hiding brilliant white but squat houses. Windows were flung open to the fresh autumn morning air as people milled about, watering plants, lounging outside on plastic chairs or lying on the bright and fluffy green grass. Flowers swayed in the early morning breeze.

Maxwell took in the quaint village landscape. *It's such a beautiful day out,* he thought.

Long bangs draped into his eyes on either side of his face. In slight annoyance, he brushed them behind his ear as he moved his pace to a walk. He got his breath back as he looked at the clothes he had hastily thrown on in his panic, a gray sweatshirt with blue jeans. He had a black bag draped over his shoulder which he knew from memory had his name sewn into the smallest flap.

"Maxwell."

He peered up at the sudden shout. To his right, heading toward him, was a middle-aged woman. She wore a summer dress and had a bright smile on her face.

"Hello, Maxwell, running late to school? I saw your sister a while ago. I was surprised to see you weren't with her."

"Yeah, guess she didn't want to wake me. So, what's going on?" he asked as he finally took notice of a line of people behind her.

The woman glanced back and chuckled, a sheepish expression on her face. "I'm taking a quick break. I need it, considering how busy it's been, what with winter coming in a few months and the harvest festival a little before that, everyone's doing last minute preparations, just the usual."

"Ah, I see...must be pretty hard," he replied.

"You're right, it is a real strain sometimes, but at the same time, it's quite nice. That reminds me, are you available this week? I need some help with the store and it seems like everyone else just wants to enjoy the last bits of summer," she stated with a frown.

Maxwell, hesitating for only the briefest of moments, nodded.

She beamed. "Great. I know with school having only started a few weeks ago you're still getting in the swing of things, but I'm glad you're willing to help." She glanced at the watch on her wrist. "Oh boy, I have to get back, my break is almost over. Actually, shouldn't you already be..."

Maxwell blinked in confusion before he squinted at the watch the woman held out to him. He stared uncomprehendingly, before he yelped. *Crap!* he thought as he felt his eyes widen. "I'm sorry! Thank you for reminding me. I'll see you later. I'm going to be late," he exclaimed and with a quick wave, dashed down the road.

He noticed the woman return to her post outside her home to take care of the crowd gathered there.

The town had a population of around three thousand people and most residents had their own shop right outside their home, just like that woman. Each specialized in specific things, such as carpentry, clothing or food.

It isn't really odd though, Maxwell thought, as he ran down another street. He skimmed around a corner, just in time to avoid an elderly woman heading rather briskly in the other direction.

"Sorry," he shouted toward the woman, who only held a look of bemusement.

He let his thoughts continue where they left off. Considering the town was completely surrounded by trees, trees and more trees, each tree, according to scientific calculation, was easily over ninety feet tall. They cast long shadows over the houses and roads, even in the morning sun. Many people thought it was peaceful and quaint.

Of course, there were always exceptions.

He thought of his sister right off the bat.

Maxwell passed more houses and heard people call out enthusiastically from stands and windows alike. He waved before he continued on. His breath came in shorter and shorter gasps. Unfortunately, he couldn't take another break, considering how late it was getting. He gripped his backpack tightly so it wouldn't fall off, annoyed that his home was so far away from where he needed to go.

It was only a few minutes later that he reached the heart of town. A cobblestone plaza lay in the middle, surrounded by pavement. Right in the center of the plaza was a fountain with an eagle spreading its wings wide. Water spouted out of its beak, which was pointed upward toward the sky. On one side of the plaza was a church. Its steeple soared over the plaza. Granite steps led up to double doors made of oak.

The bell rang. It chimed over the town in a sweet melody. He peered at the steeple as he waited for the final chime. The final note rang out beautifully for a moment, before silence took over. Maxwell stared solemnly toward the bell tower before he let out a resigned groan. He turned to examine the rest of the plaza. On the other side, parallel with the church, was a school. It was a small one-story-tall building that filled up half the square by itself. He could just barely see people dart in the doors. Next to it was the convenience store. It was the go-to for anything that couldn't be made by hand.

Maxwell took in the crowded streets before he spotted a familiar figure. He hurried over to the figure.

Standing by the school was a girl about the same height as Maxwell. She leaned her back against the brick wall of the school in a nonchalant, and slightly annoyed posture. Her raven-black hair curved around her face, and fell just a little past her chin on either side. The rest of her hair was pulled back sharply and tied up in a high ponytail.

She wore a blue halter top with short tan shorts. Her arms and fingers were clad in black fingerless gloves that reached comfortably to her elbows. Worn but well-used hiking boots covered her feet. Long black socks surged up to just below her knees, finishing the ensemble. She also had a backpack draped off one shoulder.

Her face expressed boredom as Maxwell stepped in front of her. His sister seemed to sense his presence. Sky blue eyes opened to acknowledge him as he leaned against the wall beside her to catch his breath.

"Took you long enough," she stated.

He felt her gaze on him before a grin crossed her face.

"I was starting to wonder whether you were going to skip. Of course, personally, I would be happy to do that."

Maxwell huffed in annoyance before he pushed off the wall. "You could have at least woken me up, Karina," he stated with a shake of his head. "School only just started and we're going to be late for the second time."

Karina raised her eyebrow.

"Don't say the first time wasn't your fault. You thought it would be funny to steal my alarm clock and replace it with a freaking spider! Who does that?"

Karina pushed off the wall. "It was only plastic."

Maxwell's shoulders drooped. "Anyway, let's get inside."

"Yeah, because you are oh so excited for math, right?"

Maxwell groaned. He never was going to live that one down, was he? "Oh, shut up," he muttered as they walked quickly down the wooden hallway to reach the first door on the right.

Of course, he didn't have to worry too much. Math, thankfully, wasn't till the end of the day, but still. They knocked and stepped in, just as Karina's name was called.

Karina waved. "Here," she shouted as she took her seat.

Maxwell groaned audibly at his sister's antics.

The room was a normal classroom with blackboards and rows of desks set up neatly in aisles. The teacher, a balding man in his thirties, glanced up with an unsurprised look. "Maxwell Elifer? Can you try to make sure you and your sister actually get here on time?"

Maxwell took his seat, but didn't comment. *I'm just lucky that we both even get to class,* he thought in annoyance as the teacher finished his roll call. *If it wasn't for the stupid alarm clock, I would have gotten here on time, along with Kari...* He mentally sighed once more and slumped in his seat.

Only to perk up as the teacher said, "Okay, class, pop quiz time."

Maxwell glanced around as a groan vibrated around the room, filled with about twenty students around his age. He dug into his bag and pulled out a pencil. He tapped it onto the desk as he waited. He could see Karina. Her eyes were closed and she was leaned back against the chair. An unenthused look sat on her face.

"Kari," Maxwell hissed under his breath, soft enough for only her to hear.

Why couldn't his sister at least try to look like she was paying attention?

Karina opened her eyes before she sent him a glare and let the chair fall back into place.

It was then that he received his quiz.

He quickly wrote down the answers and passed it forward. After another five to ten minutes, the teacher collected all the quizzes.

"All right, let's see how you did. Question one, what was the second name of The Great War and what followed?"

A kid near Karina raised his hand and spoke. "After the conclusion of the Great War, they renamed it World War I and shortly after came

World War II, promptly followed by the Eternal War Era."

"Good. Now, question two, what caused the name changes to occur?"

This time, another kid spoke up. "The name of the Great War was originally changed because it was easier to distinguish, after the second 'great war' started, which was which. The name of the time following World War II was changed because they noticed a connection between each successive war after the fact regarding certain superpowers, including the United States."

"That's correct, because of U.S. involvement in most wars post World War II, they deemed to call the entire period between that war and the Vietnam War the Eternal War Era, in order to more easily group them together. Now, final question, what was the consequence of that time?"

Maxwell raised his hand. "There was a depletion of goods, and as a result, they wanted to find more efficient ways to preserve society. As such, they created this place, so that people could learn about nature and grow in it. After the movement, the U.S. closed all borders officially and turned in on itself. It focused on recovering its own problems and, as a result, ended up booming in private businesses..." he trailed off as the teacher gestured to him proudly.

"That is correct. As a result, they didn't need this town, so now we just learn and live in peace."

Karina tched. Maxwell smirked toward his sister who had her arms crossed over her chest. He could see one leg jitter against the table.

"I hope everyone did well. Now, turn to page two hundred and fifty-four of our textbook and we'll get started on the Industrial Revolution..."

~ * ~

Maxwell sighed as he stepped out the door of the school. He saw Karina beam with joy as she ran down the steps in the direction of the forest right past the convenience store. "Come on, Max, I want to show you something. We can go home after, 'kay?"

Maxwell's eyes narrowed as he walked down the steps as well. The afternoon sun shone down over them as the school doors opened to the rush of students leaving classes. "Kari, I'm tired. Why don't we just go home and you can show me this weekend?"

"Max, come on, it won't take that long." She frowned as she faced Maxwell with sharp blue eyes, as if to dare him to argue.

His sister could be...interesting at times, but she did mean well. "Fine, what is it?" he asked as he hefted his backpack more comfortably on his shoulder.

"You'll see," she said, sounding relieved, as she went to walk away.

"Kari...it better not be something stupid, like trying to find wild animals, or racing through the trees again...didn't you almost break your ankle last time you decided to try to swing between the trees?"

Karina shrugged. A nervous grin sat on her face, which betrayed her nonchalant posture.

"Come on, Maxwell, it won't be THAT bad...please?" she begged.

Maxwell had to mentally reiterate to himself that his sister did mean well, even if she was a bit on the hyperactive side.

Karina started to usher Maxwell forward.

Great. I don't even know HOW she finds half the things she does. I always end up caught up in them...and usually not for the best. He let his thoughts trail off with a shiver. He remembered one too many times running for dear life while his sister would grin widely, even as she muttered apologies.

He could see Karina smirk and stick her tongue out playfully before she spun away. She seemed to pause before reaching an arm backward. She grabbed Maxwell's wrist and darted toward the surrounding forest. Maxwell yelped as he followed after the energetic girl. Karina was fast, much to Maxwell's consternation, as she ran down the road without a care, plunging right into the tree line. Maxwell stumbled behind her and yelped in frustration as he tripped over another root.

"Hey!" he shouted as his backpack slammed into his back.

Karina ignored him as they darted into the trees.

"Kari. Will you slow down?" Maxwell gasped out between wheezes, as he struggled to keep up with Karina's harsh pace. *Where the heck does she get all this energy?* he thought in exasperation.

"Heck no, come on, little brother, you should be able to do this much," she called back as she swerved around another tree. Maxwell barely managed to avoid it as he let a curse slip through his lips and under his breath the whole time.

"Karina, this is ridiculous! You're running way too fast. How do you have so much energy after a full day of school?" He yelped as he managed to scramble over a fallen tree limb that his sister practically jumped over. It didn't help that she gave him no warning she was jumping anyway which made him stumble over it.

He saw Karina frown as she tilted her head to look back at him. He felt her glare even as she faced toward the deep woods. "Stupid little brothers," she muttered under her breath as she leaped over another small fallen sapling.

"You're only about two minutes older than me," Maxwell replied curtly as he followed up her leap. This one he could actually make, even as his breath caught in his throat.

The two ran through the forest with rapid speed. Occasionally, they slowed to give Maxwell a break before Karina dragged him off again. The afternoon sun shone down brilliantly, as branches shifted in a light breeze. Fallen leaves coated the ground and crunched under their feet. Maxwell followed, somewhat unwillingly.

Finally, Karina slowed her pace down to a walk. Maxwell felt his lungs gasp for air as he forced himself not to lean forward and rest his hands on his knees like he wanted to. Why did his sister have to be so athletic compared to himself?

He heard wind whisper through the trees as he felt his sister's gaze on him. He tilted his head up enough from its drooped state to see her sheepish expression.

Sorry, she mouthed as he glared at her. Really? His sister was too hyperactive for her own good.

"So...um...how was your day?" she asked tentatively after he caught his breath and they moved on, thankfully much more slowly.

Maxwell put a hand to his face before he dropped it and spoke. "Just...great...I really just need a break," he muttered as his sister dropped her pace enough to walk beside him instead of in front of him. Her gaze was even, if a little confused.

"Break? From school? From the run?" she asked.

"Well, yes, that too..." he trailed off as he suddenly remembered why he woke up so late. To be more precise, why he hadn't gotten enough sleep to actually hear his alarm properly.

He noticed Karina's eyes on him and once more looked toward his sister. It only took a moment for understanding to flit across her face. "Dad..."

"It was four years ago today after all," Maxwell responded vaguely.

He felt Karina bump into his shoulder. "Come on. If we go at this pace, it'll take all day," she said, as she gently grabbed his hand once more. Maxwell nodded, grateful for the distraction as he followed after her at a faster pace that was still much slower than before.

It was only a couple minutes later, however, when he once more thought of it.

Maxwell's lips tightened into a thin line before he forced himself to relax. He looked to see his sister and cringed. The smile on her face was weak. He instantly recognized it as a fake, one only used when she didn't want to worry others.

Sorry, Kari, he thought as he noticed the grip on his wrist tighten. *You're still trying to forget as well.*

A long low sigh slipped through his lips before he found himself jerked to a halt.

He peered up to see a rocky cliff edge surrounded by trees. the rock wall seemed a lot more intimidating up close. Maxwell saw it from a distance through the trees for a while, but since his mind was preoccupied, he hadn't really thought about it. Not until it was in his face. He tilted his head up to take in the fact that a tree lay against the rock face precariously, looking ready to fall to the ground at any moment.

He saw his sister's smile widen as she let go of his wrist. He rubbed his wrist gingerly. "So, was there a reason why you dragged me out here? This is a nice rock wall and all, but that's about it."

"Geez. THIS isn't the spot. It's just on the way. Now come on. I can't wait to show Mom as well, if I can ever convince her to come with us."

Maxwell noticed his sister's eyes glimmer as she stared up at the rock face, her expression shining with the prospect. He peered down at the ground and felt his bangs fall into his face once more. He brushed his bangs back, looked up and said, "You do realize she wouldn't have the time, right? She's the only doctor and scientist in town. This morning was one of the few times she actually had off."

He saw his sister's expression falter for a moment before she seemed to steady herself. A glimmer like determination flashed through her eyes as she looked at Maxwell.

"It's worth a shot. She's been working hard ever since..." She paused before she sighed and continued, "I think it would be a good chance for her to take a break so that we can be like a family again. As you said, she rarely has time lately, so it would be nice."

Maxwell eyed his sister. He breathed in and slowly exhaled before he looked up at the rock face with a glare. He really wasn't looking forward to this. "I hope you don't expect me to climb that, because, you know, there's no way I'm going up that thing," he said.

He saw Karina shake her head as he continued to stare at the rock face. A cloud slid over the sky to dapple it in steely grey. "One day you'll be glad to have a chance. Anyway..." He finally pulled his eyes away from the treacherous, in his opinion, rock face to look at her. He noticed her eyes gleaming with an unidentifiable emotion. She flung her hands out to either side as she exclaimed toward Maxwell enthusiastically. "Don't you want to see what's beyond these trees? Beyond this place? In the past fourteen years, we have never been away from home, ever. Mom has, and so did Dad, when he was around. Don't you want to go into that world outside and see what else is out there?"

"No," Maxwell replied with a deadpan look. "I'm quite content with staying home. This town has everything we need. I don't see the point. Plus, what about Ma? We can't just leave her."

Karina closed her eyes and seemed to debate with herself for a moment before she opened them, and said, "We'll all just go together, I think that would be more fun anyway."

Maxwell stayed silent as Karina turned to face the rock face. She reached both arms forward to give them a good stretch. "We get to the top of our rock and you won't even have to worry about it anymore. Come on, it's easy."

Maxwell gave her a deadpan look as he felt his eye twitch. Karina noticed his expression and huffed. "Fine, I'll show you," she stated.

Maxwell scrutinized her. He tilted his head up as he noticed that everything seemed a shade darker. What was once a beautifully clear late-afternoon sky was now gradually being filled with dark, foreboding clouds. He frowned as an uneasy feeling settled in his gut. His sister seemed to sense it as well. Karina looked around once before she shook her head, as if to rid it of thoughts, and stepped toward the rock face. She pushed herself up with quick and efficient movements as her hands flew up the rocks with ease.

She reached the top and dangled her legs over it to look down. "You coming?"

"No way," he called as he tried desperately to hide the nervousness that seemed to want to slip into his voice. Heights...why heights? He blinked and glanced up once more as a low rumble sounded in the distance. "Um...how about we go back home? Ma is probably waiting for us." Maxwell said.

Karina tilted her head up to the sky. He heard a small, noncommittal noise from her before she frowned. "It does look like it's going to rain, doesn't it?"

Maxwell nodded. Karina slid over the edge and began to climb down. She took slow steps even as Maxwell felt something fall onto his cheek. He jumped as a yelp came from the rock face. He turned just in time to see Karina skid down the side. His eyes widened as he stumbled forward. Karina stopped only a foot or two below where she lost her footing.

His sister leaned against the rock face, still having a way to go. Her expression was a mix between stunned and slightly scared. Her clothes were ruffled. Her knees, elbows and hands were scratched up from trying to stay close to the rock face. A light stream of blood slipped from her fingers as a tremble racked up her spine. His sister let out a shaky breath as she took stock of any injuries. Both teens stayed in silence before Maxwell cautiously called up to her.

"You okay?"

"What do you think," Karina snapped back, her voice harsh.

Maxwell cringed as Karina stared at the wall face. Was she nervous?

Maxwell saw her grip the stone more tightly before she finished her descent, jumped to the ground and brushed herself off.

Maxwell muttered a quiet, "Show off," even as he let himself smile, relieved.

She gave him an annoyed look before she coldly walked past him. "Hurry up, slowpoke. We're going to be late."

Maxwell raised an eyebrow as he followed after her. *Wasn't that my line?* he thought in bemusement.

Karina ignored him as she walked determinedly onward.

Maxwell pursed his lips. Shadows fell over the tree canopies, as the sun's rays struggled to shine through the now completely darkened sky. "It looks like a big storm," he muttered as he eyed the horizon, feeling the apprehension well up more as he watched the fast-moving clouds.

The two continued back in an awkward silence. They kept their slow pace through the trees even as Maxwell tried to bring up a conversation. Sometimes, he made comments on the impending storm silently urging her to go a little faster, other times, he talked about how lazy the math teacher was, which was making learning the subject even harder, since it was also the last class of the day. Yet other times, he would bring up their mom.

He could see his sister glance at him, conflicted between her want to stay moody, and her wish to chat with her brother.

Moodiness won out even as a low rumble sounded once more in the distance.

"Well, this is more peaceful than I thought," Maxwell said as they slipped around another tree. *The times I don't want to talk, she annoys me to no end, the times I want to talk, she's as silent as the freaking trees...* He put a hand to his face as he quietly chuckled.

He never could understand the way his sister acted most of the time, even though they were practically inseparable since birth.

The clouds steadily grew darker as they walked. In the distance, they could hear the chime of the church bell, which signaled that it was around six, even though the dark clouds made it look like it was closer to midnight.

"Well... It looks like we're going to be late again," Maxwell muttered under his breath as he glanced at his sister's back. Karina gazed ahead steadily as she kept up with a firm pace.

They made it into the village center about five minutes later. Maxwell's legs shook from exhaustion as he stumbled tiredly after Karina. His stomach growled and his throat felt dry.

He noted how dark everything was. He could see windows that were previously wide open to the sun, shut tight, only a hint of light seeping through the panes. Plastic coverings sat over some of the plants and most of the stands, prepared for the storm. The streets were empty, to the point of it being almost eerie for both teens.

With each step, they picked up their pace as they passed house after house with barely any light peeking through. Occasionally they caught a flicker, the flutter of a curtain or the gleam of a back-porch light. Shadows weaved through the dwindling sunlight and cast tables, sheds and buildings in ominous textures. Trees and branches began to sway back and forth in the wind that started to pick up around the town. A low whistle could be heard as it swept through the houses, trees and vegetation. A groaning rumble sounded a distance away. With each moment and sound, the twins' steps grew faster until they ran, full speed, down the street. There was another low rumble in the distance that grew longer and louder. Street lamps flickered disconcertingly on either side of the road.

Soft pants could be heard over the incoming storm. An uneasy pressure filled the air as the smell of salt and water wafted toward their noses. A low rumbling boom sounded once more, suddenly a lot closer, which startled them.

Karina's eyes were narrowed in concentration as they sped around the final corner. Their house stood ahead, three down on the left. Its windows were opened with not a single light seen.

"Something's not right," Karina said as she slowed down to a cautious walk.

"You don't say," Maxwell replied, as he slowed himself down, his own thoughts in turmoil as he scrutinized the empty streets.

The storm's pressure seemed to grow, as if it begged to be let loose and break over their heads as another, longer, rumbling sound vibrated around the town. Wind blew stronger. It pulled at their hair and clothes. Maxwell breathed out. He hadn't even realized he held his breath to begin with.

Karina ignored him. She put a finger to her lips as she walked up the front steps. Her eyes seemed to zero in on the front door as she moved.

Maxwell eyed her in a mixture of annoyance and confusion as Karina purposefully held up a hand toward him before she stepped to the doorway alone. She hesitated before she thrust the door out of the way with a jarring bang.

Also by the Author
At Rogue Phoenix Press

Retrieval
The Elifer Chronicles Book Two

Maxwell and Karina, twins who are the cure to a disease which is ravaging the country, find themselves journeying to the distant locale of Collern City in search of their missing mother. Meeting strange allies and dealing with dangerous enemies, they must learn to navigate the treacherous streets and discover more about what is going on behind the scenes in both the gated community and outside of it. Meanwhile, their guardian and friend, Lex, struggles to deal with his family's desires. He finds himself caught between his own wish to flee his home, never to return. and the wish of his brother, Caym, who desperately wants him to stay.

Demon's Song
Requiem of Stone Book One

Alex always wished to see the Overlands, a place of sunshine and freedom. However, as a slave in the far corners of the Underlands, it was all but a dream. That is, until he's framed for murder and is forced to flee during a demon attack.

Searching for the answers to why he was framed and seeking a chance at the fleeting freedom he's always dreamed about, he journeys to the capital, meeting friend and foe along the way. But the Underlands are both beautiful and dangerous. Having a demon hunter on his tail and a witch whose sole desire is to become the high Seer around him, he's in for quite the journey.

Demon's Call
Requiem of Stone Book Two

Having escaped the city of Raynout, Alex, Rita and Milos find themselves journeying in search of Alex's mother and the answers she can provide. Their search leads them to the dangerous and unknown region of the north, where legend tells tales of its perilous waters. Along the way, they learn not only more about the Underlands, but about themselves as well as they struggle to come to term with who they are and where they belong. Meeting interesting new allies and a dangerous new enemy, the three of them must learn how to fully rely on each other... before the waters of the north tear them apart.

Ghost of a Memory

Kieran has seen strange white figures for the last year and a half, but to him it makes no sense, after all, how can they be ghosts if death doesn't exist anymore? Kieran, Felix and Mira live a peaceful life within their small town, a place with no crime, no death and, to most, no fear. However, that changes when Felix starts researching Kieran's strange symptoms, his ability to see figures others call ghosts. Soon, the figures become more active, but not just the figures, strange happenings begin to occur and now Kieran must race to figure out the truth... before he faces the same fate.

www.ingramcontent.com/pod-product-compliance
Lightning Source LLC
Chambersburg PA
CBHW051057030726
47504CB00006B/1668